ANNIE
LYONS

The
Choir
on
Hope Street

Available from Annie Lyons

Not Quite Perfect
The Secrets Between Sisters
Life or Something Like It

ANNIE LYONS

The Choir on Hope Street

ONE PLACE. MANY STORIES

HQ
An imprint of HarperCollins *Publishers*
1 London Bridge Street
London SE1 9GF

This paperback edition 2017
1

First published in Great Britain by
HQ an imprint of HarperCollins *Publishers* 2017

A catalogue record for this book is
available from the British Library

ISBN: 9780008196073

Set by CPI Group (UK) Ltd
Printed and bound by CPI Group (UK) Ltd, Croydon, CR0 4YY

Annie Lyons

Having worked in the worlds of book selling and publishing, Annie Lyons decided to have a go at book writing. Following a creative writing course, lots of reading and an extraordinary amount of coffee, she produced *Not Quite Perfect*, which went on to become a number one bestseller. Her second book *The Secrets Between Sisters* was nominated in the best eBook category at the 2014 Festival of Romance and *Life or Something Like It* was a top ten bestseller.

Her latest book, *The Choir on Hope Street*, is a story of power ballads, community, cake and hope. She tries to write stories which make people laugh and cry, although hopefully not at the same time. Annie lives in a shambolic money-pit of a house with her husband and two children plus a cat, who she pretends not to like. She enjoys channelling her inner Adele as part of her own beloved community choir and trying to grow cauliflower.

For The Churchfields Community Choir
– I can think of no finer people with whom to bless the rains.

CHAPTER ONE

NATALIE

'I don't love you any more.'

That was it. Six words delivered so simply, as if he were reading the news.

'Good evening and here is the news. The marriage of Natalie and Daniel Garfield, which lasted for fifteen years, is over. In a statement today, Mr Garfield said, "I don't love you any more." Mrs Garfield responded by punching him in the face and trashing the house.'

At least that's what I wished I'd done later but at the time an odd sensation of calm descended. It was as if this wasn't really happening to me. It was at best some kind of joke and at worst something that could be sorted.

This wasn't in the plan. This kind of thing was never going to happen to us. Other people split up, their marriages disintegrating like a swiftly disappearing desert island, but that was never going to happen to us. We were rock-solid – a steady ship; Nat and Dan, Dan and Nat. It had the ring of one of those American teen shows that Woody loved to watch on Nick Jr.; all jazz hands and sparkly teeth.

We were a great couple. Everyone said so. We were the kind of couple that others looked at with awe and secret envy. Everybody loved Dan. He's just one of those men who people like – old ladies, babies, men, women, children have all told me over the course of our marriage, what a really great guy he is.

I would go on nights out with my female friends as they ripped apart their partners and husbands, picking over their faults like vultures feasting on carrion. I would nod with sympathy but never really had anything to add. They would often turn their sleepy, drunken gaze to me, pat me on the shoulder and slur, 'Course you're lucky, Nat. You've got Dan. He's such a lovely guy.'

And he was. Possibly still is.

Dan was my husband, my soul mate. Of course he had his faults. The underpants on the floor and the toilet seat in the perpetual 'up' position were an irritation, but not exactly a major crime against domesticity. He was, *is* a good man – a good husband and father. He was my happy-ever-after.

Naturally, we had disagreements and wobbles. Who doesn't? We didn't spend as much time together on our own as we would like but that's to be expected. We're busy with work, Woody and life. Obviously it would be lovely to go on the odd date-night or even have sex but frankly, we were usually too knackered. I'd always thought that the shared bottle of wine on Friday night with a movie was good enough. Clearly I have been labouring under a major misapprehension.

Initially, I went into full-on denial mode when he dropped the bombshell. I wondered later if my body had actually gone into shock in a bid to protect myself from the truth. Certainly at the time, my brain sent me a quick succession of messages to counter his statement: *he didn't mean it* (he did), *he'd been drinking* (he hadn't), *he was tired* (true) *and angry* (not true). It wasn't until I'd picked over the remnants of that evening with various friends (my turn to be the vulture now) that I'd fully taken in the order of events.

It was a Tuesday evening. I hate Tuesdays. They make me feel restless and impatient. Monday is supposed to be the worst day but for me, it has always been Tuesday. I can deal with the post-weekend slump and Monday is usually my most productive day but by Tuesday, I am longing for the week to move 'over the hump' towards the downhill joy of Thursday. I often long for a glass of wine on Tuesday evenings but on this particular day I was disappointingly sober because I was having a so called healthy week. At least I was before he said it.

It was around 8.30 and we had just finished dinner. Woody was reading in his room before lights-out and I had been about to go and tuck him in. I normally love this part of the day: the feeling that another episode of motherhood is successfully complete; no-one died. Everyone is safe.

If I had been paying attention, I would have noticed that Dan was particularly uncommunicative during dinner. Again, it wasn't until later that I recalled the details: his downward gaze and hands fidgeting with the cutlery, his water glass, the pepper mill.

I had been telling him about a problem with my latest book. I am a children's picture-book writer and have enjoyed some success with my series of books about 'Ned Bobbin – the small boy with the big imagination', as my publisher tags it. There have been six books so far and my editor wants another three but I was struggling with ideas and wondering whether to take him down the super-hero route.

When I recalled the conversation later, I realised that I had done all the talking; posing and answering my own questions with just the odd 'mhmm' or nod from Dan. That was the problem with being a writer – you spent too much time at home on your own with no-one to talk to.

I talk to myself all the time when I'm working. I read back what I've just written, talk to the radio or hold imaginary conversations with all manner of people, including Ned. I read somewhere that adults have a certain number of words they need to say in a day and that the word quota for a woman is higher than a man's. I believe this. It isn't unusual, therefore, for me to unpack my day to Dan when he gets home. I thought he liked it. Maybe I was wrong about that too.

I had finished my dinner: an unimaginative stir-fry containing any vegetable-like items I'd found in the fridge on opening it at 7.30. Woody had eaten earlier. He was eight years old and always starving when he returned home from school so I tended to feed him straight away and then either Dan or I cooked our dinner later.

I stood up to clear the plates, reaching out for Dan's. He looked up at me and only then did I notice how pale he looked – his face, slightly pinched with age, but still handsome. He stared at me, unsmiling and I realised he was nervous.

'What?' I asked with an encouraging smile.

He swallowed and bit his lip. Then he said it.

At first I assumed he was joking.

'Yeah right, and I'm having an affair with James McAvoy.' I shook my head and made for the door.

'Nat.'

I paused, turning to look back at him. He was crying and that was when I knew it wasn't a joke. It was the first rumble of a threatening storm. Still, my brain told me to keep going, carry the plates out, kiss Woody goodnight, come down and sort this out. It was just another thing to be sorted, like pairing the socks in a basket of washing.

I could hear my heart beating in my ears as I padded upstairs, pausing outside my son's bedroom door. I focused for a moment on the wooden letters stuck to the upper panel, spelling 'WOODY'. Each letter was represented by an animal with the same corresponding first letter and I reached out a hand to stroke the wombat's cheery face. *I will sort this out. I'm good at sorting. All will be well.*

I pushed the door open, blinking into the half-light, feeling immediately reassured by the sight of my son. He was sitting up in bed, reading by the light of the twisty snake-lamp we had given him last birthday, propped up by the patchwork cushion my mum had made him when he was born. His chin was resting on his chest, that customary frown creasing his perfect face. He flicked his gaze in my direction and then back down at his book.

'How's Mr Fox doing?' I asked, as if nothing had happened, as if my world was still intact.

Woody sighed. 'Not good. Boggis, Bunce and Bean shot him.'

'Ooh, that's *not* good.'

Woody shook his head in agreement but kept reading, his eyes darting left and right. I looked around his room at the dog-eared football posters, the framed prints of scenes from my Ned Bobbin stories, the Lego models and the shelves stacked with books. Woody was a bookworm. He had learnt to read at the age of three and not really stopped since. He had probably read *Fantastic Mr Fox* at least fifty times. I felt a sense of calm descend. It would have been the easiest thing in the world to nestle down at the end of Woody's bed, to pretend Dan hadn't said what he had just said and hope that it all went away. I felt safe there.

'Time for lights-out, fella,' said Dan's voice from the doorway. I jumped, jolted back to reality. I couldn't see his face properly but his voice was throaty from crying.

Woody glanced at him and then me. 'Can I just finish this chapter, please?' His expression was wide-eyed and impossible to resist.

Dan stepped forwards and ruffled his hair. 'Okay, but then straight to sleep.'

''Kay,' replied Woody. 'Night, Mum.'

I leant down and kissed him. 'Night, darling boy. Love you. Sleep well.'

'Love you. Sleep well,' repeated Woody like a robot. 'Night, Dad.'

'Night,' said Dan. He turned towards the door and paused, looking back over his shoulder at me. 'Coming?'

I stared down at my son as if he might offer a solution. He sensed my hesitation and looked up. '*Night*, Mum,' he said again with a trace of impatience.

'Night,' I answered, turning and following Dan out of the room and down the stairs. We didn't speak again until we reached the dining room.

'I'm going to get a glass of wine,' I said. 'Want one?'

'No,' sighed Dan. 'Thanks. We do need to talk, Nat.'

'And that's why I need a glass of wine,' I said, making my way to the kitchen. I poured a polite helping and then doubled it. Taking a large gulp, I refilled it and carried the glass into the dining room. Dan was sitting at the table, his hands in prayer position.

I slid into the chair opposite. 'So,' I began, trying to stay calm and matter-of-fact. 'What's this all about?'

Dan ran a hand through his neatly parted hair and stared up at the ceiling. 'I'm leaving.'

I was surprised to learn that two gulps of wine could inflame immediate righteous anger. 'Because you don't love me any more?' I almost spat the words.

'I think so.'

'You think so?' I snapped. 'Because that's a fucking big statement if you're not sure. Do you love me or not? Simple question.' My voice was increasing in volume and it unnerved me. My childhood had been punctuated by anger between my father and mother. As an adult I had made a monumental effort to keep mine under control but all bets were off now. Red was the new black.

Dan stared at his hands, unable to look me in the eye. 'No, I don't and I'm sorry.'

The sarcasm devil took control of my brain. 'Well that's all right then. If you're sorry then I forgive you. That makes it all just fine.' I folded my arms and stared at him.

I couldn't get a grip on my brain somehow, couldn't work out what I was supposed to say or how I was supposed to feel. I had no point of reference for this moment. It felt like somebody else's life.

Dan tried to be reasonable. That was one of his greatest strengths. He was eternally reasonable and always took other people's opinions seriously. We rarely argued and this was largely down to Dan. He was able to defuse a situation like the most practised of bomb-disposal experts. 'I understand that you're angry, Nat, and you have every right to be, but if you'll let me, I'll try to explain.'

I took another deep gulp of wine before holding up my glass as if proposing a toast and saying, 'Please. Be my fucking guest.'

Dan swallowed. 'It's nothing you've done or said. You have always been the perfect wife.'

'If you're about to use the words, *it's not you, it's me,* I will get violent,' I retorted.

Dan looked at me, tears brimming in his eyes. 'I have tried to stay in love with you but I just don't have those feelings for you any more. I love you but I'm not in love with you.'

My head was spinning from a combination of wine and fury. I stood up. 'So you're planning to leave?'

Dan nodded. 'I want to speak to Woody first.'

'Very decent of you, but you'll have to come back to do that another time because I want you gone.'

'Nat.'

People talk about a red mist and others talk about an out-of-body experience but for me it was neither. I thought nothing and felt nothing but pure white-hot fury as I smashed the wine glass to the floor and screamed, 'GO! NOW! I WANT YOU FUCKING GONE!'

Whether out of self-preservation or respect for my feelings, Dan left the room. Moments later he reappeared with a bag, which I realised he must have been hiding in the back of his wardrobe for goodness knows how long. Waiting for the right moment. He had clearly been waiting for the right moment for a while.

He didn't try to speak to me again before he left and I was oddly grateful to him for this. I heard the front door close like a full stop to my life so far. I looked around the room, numb with anger, unable to cry. I looked at the shards of broken glass and swore.

The annoying thing about a burst of righteous anger is that you have to clear up afterwards. I went to fetch the dustpan and another glass of wine.

CHAPTER TWO

CAROLINE

I actually thought that I was going to kill her. It was as if she had some kind of death wish. She just stepped into the road without even looking just as I was turning the corner. It was incredible. If I hadn't stood up on the brake, I would have hit her much harder. Luckily, I was able to swerve so that I merely touched her and she sort of sat backwards onto the kerb. Of course, it had to be right outside the school, immediately after drop-off. Typical. I had to park on the hazard lines right outside the school, which obviously isn't allowed until 9.30 a.m. The headmaster was standing at the gate and he glanced my way as I leapt from the driver's seat.

'Apologies, Phil!' I cried, giving him a cheery wave. I noticed a gaggle of school mums who I knew from the PTA and tried to give them a reassuring nod as I hurried round to check up on her. I hoped they would just disperse but they had seen what happened and one of them was already on her way over. I recognised her as an annoying woman called Nula, who had been particularly disparaging about my idea to sell 'Loom Bands' at the summer fair.

'They're an absolute nightmare,' she had moaned. 'My cleaner is forever getting them stuck in the Dyson. And Alexis nearly took her little brother's eye out with one last week.'

She was one of those mothers who attends every PTA meeting, criticising each idea and failing to offer any of her own. She also insisted on running the Pimm's stall every year and drinking most of the profits. Her daughter had spat at Matilda when they were in Reception and I had obviously been on her hate list ever since I'd complained to their teacher. I didn't care though – you have to learn to rise above these things when you're the Chairwoman of the PTA. She was simply jealous that I had been elected to the post for a third consecutive year.

It took all my powers of control not to poke her in the eye as she rushed over, ignored my presence except for a haughty flick of her hair and sat down next to the woman, putting an arm around her shoulder.

'Are you all right, Natalie?' she asked in soothing tones. 'I saw the whole thing and can act as a witness if you need me to?' She flicked her gaze in my direction, her nostrils slightly flared. 'What were you thinking, Caroline?'

Trouble-making viper. Luckily, Phil had arrived on the scene. 'Are you all right, Mrs Garfield? Mrs Taylor. Would you like to come inside?'

'I think she's in shock,' said Nula. 'We should probably call an ambulance. And the police.' A shadow of smug satisfaction passed over her face as she uttered this last sentence. *That's it,* I thought, *no Pimm's stall for you this year. Three hours of Splat the Rat, you interfering shrew.*

The woman had been staring at the ground all the while but now she seemed to come to her senses. She looked up at us all, her face wide-eyed and fearful. I noticed with distaste that she was wearing pyjama bottoms and a hoody with trainers. To the untrained eye, the trousers could have just about passed as a pair of those awful floral things that everyone insists on wearing these days but she didn't fool me. I can spot M&S nightwear a mile off. Her eyes were heavy with dark shadows and her hair was scraped up into a loose bun. Many people think you can achieve this hairstyle in a matter of seconds but many people are wrong. The wispy-haired look takes practice and effort. This woman hadn't applied either.

I don't mean to sound judgemental but I despair of playground mothers sometimes. Where is their self-respect? We're all pushed for time in the mornings – the least we can do is apply a little eyeliner and make ourselves presentable. We're supposed to be role models for the next generation, after all.

I realised that I needed this problem to go away and fast. I knelt down in front of the woman and took her hands. I also remembered that you should never apologise in an accident situation. It makes you culpable. I leant forwards and smiled. 'It's Natalie, isn't it? How are you? Is there anything I can do?' I felt Nula's grip tighten around her shoulder but I pressed on. 'Are you hurt at all?'

Natalie stared at me. I gave her a reassuring smile, which she seemed to accept as she squeezed my hands. 'I'm okay,' she murmured. 'I just want to get home.'

'I can take you!' I cried.

Nula pursed her lips in irritation. 'Are you sure that's wise? Shouldn't we get you checked over, Natalie?'

Natalie shook her head. 'No, really, I'm okay. It was my fault. I wasn't looking where I was going, but if you could take me home, I'd be grateful,' she replied, looking up at me.

Nula dropped her arm from Natalie's shoulder, barely able to mask her disappointment.

'Of course!' I said, helping her to her feet. 'No problem at all. Thanks, Phil. Thanks, Nula,' I said, flashing a particularly saintly smile at the latter.

Phil nodded. 'Take care, ladies,' he said, before disappearing back through the school gate.

Natalie walked towards my car and opened the door. 'Let me know if you need anything, hon,' called Nula, squeezing Natalie's arm as she walked past. 'Bye, Caroline.'

I acknowledged her with a nod before jumping into the driver's seat. Natalie climbed in alongside me and slammed the door shut. 'Ooh, mind the paintwork!' I cried, trying to keep my voice light.

'Sorry,' she muttered, reaching over for her seatbelt.

'So, where to?' I asked.

'Hope Street, please, number thirty.'

'Oh, I live on that road,' I said. 'Number 232.'

'Ahh.' Natalie nodded. 'The posh end.'

Some people might have taken this as a criticism but I didn't. That house was my pride and joy. It had been a shell when Oliver and I had bought it in pre-Matilda days. We had worked hard to restore and rejuvenate it and it was a labour of love, particularly for me. We'd converted the loft, restored the brickwork, opened up the kitchen and made it into the perfect family home. I made no apology for the money spent or the effort made. We worked hard and we deserved it. Jealousy was a cheap and easy emotion.

However, I could tell that Natalie was only teasing as she made the comment with an almost-smile. I rewarded it with a breezy laugh. 'What a start to the day!' I remarked as we made the short journey back to her house.

She didn't answer so I looked over and noticed that her shoulders were shaking. At first I thought she was laughing until I noticed her tear-stained face. It was like something from a soap opera. She was nearing hysterics. Two thoughts entered my head; how am I going to stop her doing that and how can I deposit her back home as quickly as possible?

I scanned the numbers and pulled up outside her house. It was a pleasant enough terraced Edwardian. Oliver and

I had looked at a couple of these during our property search but had found them too poky, at least that was what I felt. Oliver was happy to go along with me. He's good like that. I remember when we first viewed our house, it had been dark and shabby, the overwhelming stench of old person lingering like rotting stew.

The estate agent, an upright impeccably dressed woman in her late fifties, who had reminded me of my wonderful headmistress, Mrs Biggs, had chosen her words carefully.

'This was a treasured family home but it needs to be updated, of course.'

'You can say that again,' said Oliver, taking in the peeling wallpaper, damp stains and alarming orange-swirl carpet. 'It could do with being condemned and re-built, if you ask me.'

The estate agent had shot him a look not unlike one Mrs Biggs might have given one of the cheekier girls at our school – amused but firm. 'It just needs a little TLC. Mrs Brown hadn't been able to undertake any home improvements in recent times.'

I had adopted my best Kirstie Allsop persona and walked from room to room, trying to avoid deep breaths because of the smell, opening my mind as one word emerged from the back of my brain.

Potential.

'I think it has great potential,' I observed, keeping my expression neutral. That's one thing my father had always taught me. 'Keep a poker-face, Caroline. Never give anything away.'

Oliver was watching me now. Unlike the estate agent, he could read me like a book. 'I saw your eyes light up like a child's on Christmas morning,' he observed later. 'I knew we'd found the one – resistance was futile.' He kissed me on the nose as he said this. 'My girl must have exactly what she wants.'

He was always so sweet like that back then. It was different when we were both working at the bank. We worked hard and partied even harder. They were very happy times, working all week, doing up the house at the weekends. We had builders in to start with but we finished it all ourselves. I can remember Saturdays, listening to cheesy music on the radio while we decorated. I feel as if I know every inch of that house.

I smiled at the memory but my thoughts were interrupted by a loud, gasping sob. I stared at Natalie. I'd almost forgotten she was there. She looked truly awful, her face red and blotchy. I watched with disgust as she used a sleeve to wipe one eye. I reached into the glove compartment and retrieved a tissue as I might do for Matilda. I held it out for her and she seemed so touched by this tiny act of kindness that it brought on a fresh round of tears.

'Thank you. Sorry,' she mumbled. 'You must think I'm a nightmare.'

Of course I did but I'm never rude. 'Not at all,' I lied. 'We all have off days,' although of course I rarely did.

'Would you like to come in for a coffee?' she asked, dabbing at her nose with the tissue.

'That would be lovely but I'm afraid I have an appointment.' This was only a half-lie as my cleaner was coming at ten and I always liked to be home to make sure she did her allotted two hours. I'd caught her leaving ten minutes early once.

Natalie nodded and smiled. There was an awkward pause as if she was waiting for me to say something, possibly ask her what was wrong, but I wasn't going to do this. I barely knew her and I had a policy never to get involved with strangers' problems. People loved to be so dramatic these days, longing for others to notice them, to affirm their existence with a 'poor you' or a Like on

Facebook. It was all very needy. I don't want to sound harsh but I can't bear needy people.

Happily, there was a tap on the car window. It was our postman and he was smiling in at Natalie. He was one of those men who insist on wearing shorts whatever the weather and he always seemed to be tanned and relentlessly cheerful. I couldn't recall his name until Natalie opened the passenger door and greeted him.

'Hey Jim. How are you?'

'Fine, thanks Nat. You look a bit down. What's up?'

I took this as my signal to escape. 'I'll let you get on then, Natalie,' I said.

She turned her head towards me. 'Okay then. Thanks for the lift, Caroline,' she replied, climbing out of the car. She shut the door with a slam. Again. 'Sorry,' she winced, holding up a hand in apology.

I smiled and shook my head, pretending it didn't matter before driving off. I glanced at Natalie and Jim in the rear-view mirror. They were already deep in conversation as he handed over a pile of letters, his face creased with concern. Natalie was obviously unloading that day's drama. I couldn't believe that she would be telling her troubles to the postman. The world had gone mad.

As I reached home and opened the front door, I exhaled with relief – another crisis averted. I noticed a plug of fluff hanging from the bottom of the radiator. I made a mental note to ask Rosie to give them a good clean and check the skirting boards while she was at it. I always took pride in keeping a clean and tidy house. Appearances are everything, after all.

CHAPTER THREE

NATALIE

'So are you sure there isn't someone else involved?' asked Ed.

'I'm as sure as I can be,' I replied.

'Has he actually said that though?'

'Woody asked him.' Ed looked surprised. I sighed. 'I know. He came round so that we could tell Woody what was happening and it was only when he said it, that I realised I'd forgotten to ask.'

'You forgot to ask?'

'Don't judge. I was really busy being very, very angry.'

Ed shrugged. 'Fair point. So what did he say?'

'He did the reasonable Dan thing, denied it vehemently, told Woody how much he loves him, that it's not his fault, that he'll be there for him whenever he needs him and that he'll be staying at his mum's for now. Blah, blah, textbook reassuring estranged father stuff.'

'How did Woody take it?'

'He asked for a biscuit.'

Ed surveyed the almost-empty tub of brownies. 'Takes after his mother. Has Woody talked to you about it since?'

I shrugged. 'Not really. I don't think eight-year-old boys do heart-to-hearts and, to be honest, he probably doesn't know what to think. I know I don't. I keep wondering what

I did wrong, searching my brain for the moment when it all went belly-up.' I reached for another brownie.

'You won't find the answer in the bottom of a carton of cakes.'

'Hmm, what about a tub of salted caramel ice cream?'

'Na-ah.'

'Jar of peanut butter?'

'Food of the devil – definitely not!'

'Shame, because that has basically been my diet since Dan left.'

'Well, I have to say, you're more together than I thought you would be.'

'I did cry in between dropping Woody at school and you arriving.'

'But you're not crying now.'

'I could start at any minute.'

'Don't worry, I'll slap you if you do.'

I laughed. 'What would I do without you?'

'Don't start – you'll set me off.'

'No, seriously, Ed. I needed a dose of your straight-talking no-nonsense today. Thank you.'

He grinned. 'Any time, sweet-cheeks. So what are you going to do?'

'I'm sort of waiting for Dan to tell me what he wants.' Ed grimaced. 'What?'

He shrugged. 'Just that I'm a bit surprised, that's all. I thought you'd be firing up the sass machine, fighting for yo man, getting a little fierce, sister!' He clicked his fingers and fixed me with a head-swivelling look.

I raised an eyebrow. 'Once more in English, please?'

'You know what I'm saying, Nat. You've got to stand up and fight for your man!'

'Who am I fighting? According to Dan, there's no-one else involved.'

'Which makes it so much easier! Think about it. You've been married for like a hundred years, haven't had sex for six months.'

'More like nine,' I muttered.

'Jeepers, it's worse than I thought. You've lost that lovin' feelin', darlin'.'

'If you're about to break into song, I'm leaving.'

'I'm serious, Nat. You've just become incredibly boring.'

'Wow. I'm so glad we had this chat.'

He grabbed my arm. 'I think you just need some proper time together, sweet-pea. Get dressed up, go out on a date, reacquaint yourselves a little.'

'Do you think that's all it is?'

'Of course! You know I'll have Woody any time – he is my godson, after all.'

'Thank you. I just don't know if a couple of dates is going to solve it though.' I remembered the look on Dan's face when he told me he didn't love me any more. He didn't look like a man whose problems would be solved by sharing a Wing Roulette with his wife at Nando's. He looked like a man who wanted to get away. Fast.

Ed seemed to read my mind. 'I know what Dan said but everyone says things they don't mean sometimes. He may have thought it at the time but I'm sure it won't last. I mean, there was a time when he didn't love you at all and then he fell in love with you, so there's no reason why he can't just do that all again, is there?'

'I guess,' I frowned, doubting his reasoning but grateful for his attempts to reassure me.

'It's got to be worth a try, hasn't it? I know how much you still love him.' I could feel tears mist my eyes. 'Don't cry, sweetheart. He's not going to fall back in love with a puffy-eyed snot monster.' I laughed. 'And you do look hot when you get dolled up on our nights out, so you should make the effort for Dan, don't you think?'

I gave him a weak smile. He put an arm around my shoulder and kissed the top of my head. 'Can't I just marry you?' I asked.

He laughed. 'That would be fine in terms of the no-sex thing but trust me, I'm a bitch in the morning. You deserve better, my gorgeous girl.'

I smiled. Maybe Ed was right about Dan and me. Maybe I'd been neglecting my own husband, forgetting that we needed to go out and have some fun. Plenty of couples hit these kinds of bumps in the road, so maybe I just needed to up my game a little. I started to think about where we could go – somewhere special with history. Perhaps we could go to the pub where we'd first met.

It had been just down the road from my college in town, a dark cavernous place with a huge bar on one side and uncomfortable tables and chairs on the other. I'd gone for a drink after lectures with a boy I fancied but who spent most of the time looking either at my breasts or over my shoulder for someone more interesting to talk to. In a desperate attempt to get his attention, I'd put 'Truly Madly Deeply' by Savage Garden on the jukebox with the intention of singing it to him. Yeah, I know. I'm one classy chick but desperate times and all that.

Just as the intro began, he'd downed his lager and declared, 'Need a slash,' before disappearing to the toilets. I took a large gulp of the cider I was drinking, even though I hated it and tried desperately not to look like Norma No-Mates.

Suddenly I was aware of a guy next to me at the bar. He was singing along to the track and much to my surprise, was looking straight at me as he did. I wasn't used to this kind of attention from men so I looked away, pretending that it wasn't happening, at which point, he grabbed my hand and continued with his full-on serenade. His singing was terrible but I was impressed that he knew all the words. Plus, he looked a bit like the guy from Savage Garden and he grinned at me with such dark-eyed intensity that I felt an unexpected urge to snog his face off. It was one of those moments when you find yourself thinking, *I'm starring in the movie of my life here.* When he finished singing, he kissed my hand and offered to buy me another drink. I accepted, ordering a glass of dry white wine because I detected that my life was about to change and I needed to assume a more grown-up persona. Fortunately, the other boy had found someone more interesting to talk to at the back of the pub and never returned. I woke up the following morning with Dan next to me and a hangover of epic proportions. I never usually slept with boys after a first date, much less a first meeting, but it just seemed to happen as if it was meant to. We'd barely had a night apart since. Until now.

So maybe that was the answer. We had to re-engage with our past, to remind ourselves of the feelings that had brought us together, to recapture some of our wasted youth.

'Thank you, Ed. I appreciate your advice and support. You're a good bestie,' I told him, planting a kiss on his cheek.

'Always here for you, angel.' He smiled.

I sighed. 'What a loss you are to the heterosexual female population.'

Ed grinned. 'If I had a pound for every time someone has told me that.'

I raised my eyebrows. 'You'd have a pound?'

'Har-de-fuckity-har. Now are we going to do any work today or what?'

I popped another brownie into my mouth. 'Ab-fer-lutely,' I said through a mouthful of chocolate deliciousness. 'Fo me wha yoo got.'

Ed shook his head. 'If only the fans of Natalie Garfield could see her at this moment.'

'I fink you'll find vey'd be very understanding – 'specially ver muvvas,' I sputtered.

Ed shot me a disapproving look. 'Are your fingers clean?' he asked, picking up his large black art case.

'Courth,' I answered, wiping them hastily on my trousers.

'Go and wash them,' he ordered, unzipping the case.

''Kay, Dad.' I carried our mugs into the kitchen. 'Want another cuppa while I'm out here?'

'No thanks, I'm all caffeined out.'

'I'm just going to have one more,' I said, flicking the kettle into life. I stared out of the window. It was early May and the garden was just beginning to bloom its way into colour. The apple tree looked particularly beautiful as it emerged into blossom.

I could remember the day we'd bought that tree. Woody had been three years old and Dan had decided that supermarket fruit and veg were poisoning his son. One Saturday morning, he had suggested a trip to the garden centre so that we could start to plant our own. It had been a beautiful spring day and I could remember Woody toddling happily between the rows of plants, pausing to point or shout, 'Dat!' at anything that interested him. It was one of those rare family outings where everything had gone to plan. Woody had napped in the car so that he was smiling and laughing throughout the visit, we had enjoyed carrot cake and coffee in the café (always a necessary pit stop for me) and Dan had been excited about the possibility of becoming the next Monty Don. He had filled our trolley with all manner of plants – courgettes, peas, sweetcorn, peppers, tomatoes and aubergines – before heaving three large bags of compost onto the space underneath. He had put his arm around me and kissed me and I remember feeling the sun on my face, hearing the gentle hiss of a sprinkler and the sound of Woody giggling with delight at a porcelain garden frog. It was a tiny moment and then Dan had disappeared with a wink.

'Just got to get one more thing.' He returned five minutes later, grinning and struggling with the tree in his arms. 'I've always wanted an apple tree,' he explained.

'How are we going to fit it in the car?' I laughed.

We drove home, singing along to 'I Gotta Feeling' on the radio, with our new tree poking out of the boot of our tiny VW Polo. I felt my heart sink at the memory as I gazed out at the tree, now festooned in cloud-like blossom.

'You're not moping are you?' called Ed from the dining room. 'You've gone very quiet.'

Damn him and his insightful perception. I had known Ed for over ten years and he knew me almost as well as Dan did. My publisher had paired us as a writer-and-illustrator team for the very first Ned Bobbin book and we had worked together ever since. He was a bit like a favourite brother, collaborator and best friend all rolled into one. He was the first person I'd called after Dan left too. Admittedly, I didn't call him until the next morning. I hadn't wanted to speak to anyone before that. The 'almost getting myself killed' aspect to that morning had made me realise that I needed someone to talk to and, as was often the case when life got tricky or sad, it was Ed that I called.

'I'm not moping. I was waiting for the kettle to boil.'

'Very well,' answered Ed. 'Anyway, come and look at Ned in his super-hero outfit. I think he looks rather dashing.'

'On my way,' I replied, pouring boiling water into my mug. There was a knock at the door. I could tell almost immediately that the person on the other side was impatient. You can tell a lot about a person by the way they knock at a door. We have one of those very loud metal door-knockers that always makes me jump. I would have liked a doorbell really but we'd never got round to installing one and at least the knocker got my attention. Whoever it was tapped it loudly and rapidly so that I slopped my tea at the sound.

'Damn, blast and bollocks!' I cried.

'Shall I get it?' offered Ed.

'Would you mind? Thanks.' I reached for a cloth. I heard Ed talking to someone whose voice I didn't recognise. They were speaking very loudly as people often do when they meet for the first time and are trying to size each other up. I heard Ed say:

'She's just in the kitchen, come through.' I hastily wiped the tea splodges from my top before turning to be confronted with Tilly's mum, Caroline, holding out a bunch of scarlet peonies.

'Oh, hi, Caroline,' I said. I was surprised to see her. We hadn't spoken since the incident with the car, even though I'd seen her in the playground. Woody and Tilly were in the same class and I'd heard him mention her from time to time but I don't think Caroline realised this. I got the feeling that I wasn't her sort of person. She had been the Chair of the PTA for years and to be honest, women like that terrify me.

I had baked some cakes for a sale once and something had gone wrong with the buttercream icing so that they sort of slumped overnight. Added to this, I had topped each bun with a Malteser. My friend Mel had sidled over and snorted with amusement, 'They look like boobs, Nat!' just at the moment I was handing them over to Caroline.

She had stared at the nipular cakes and then back at me before accepting the Tupperware box with obvious disdain and muttering, 'Thank you but please make sure you bake something more appropriate next time.' Obviously there hadn't been a next time.

She was beaming at me now as if we were old friends. 'Hi, Natalie. These are for you,' she said, handing over the flowers.

'Thank you. They're lovely.'

'My pleasure. I just wanted to check that you were okay after our little bump the other day?'

She said it like it was a fun thing – a mutually shared treat. 'I'm fine, thanks, and you didn't need to buy me flowers.'

'Well, I was in Waitrose and I saw them so I thought I would, plus Matilda told me that your son is in her class and that you write the Ned Bobbin books. I had no idea, so I thought I would pop in on my way home, say, "Hi," and just check that you're all right. You seemed very upset the other day.' She creased her face into a grimace of sympathy.

I realised then that she had only called in because of who I was. I get this from time to time. People are often very interested when they find out you're a writer.

'Wow! That must be fascinating!' they say. It isn't really. It's a job like any other and it involves staring at a blank piece of paper, desperately trying to think of some words, so it can be quite stressful too.

Or they'll smile at me with obvious envy. 'You're so lucky. That's my dream job.' *Really? Because my dream job is to be Mary Berry's official cake taster. You should aim higher, my friend.*

'You must earn millions,' is another one I hear occasionally. Hmmm, not especially. Although I am waiting for the Hollywood version of Ned's life to propel me towards retirement. It's turning out to be quite a long wait.

I did love my job but it was as frustrating as any other and often quite lonely. Dear old Ned had become quite popular amongst pre-schoolers and contributed towards the mortgage but man, he could be demanding.

So it was clear that Caroline had just discovered a new fact and decided that she wanted a writer as a friend. Still, there are worse crimes and I am pretty fantastic, despite now being a single mother with a worrying brownie addiction. 'It's very kind of you to pop by,' I said.

She smiled and nodded at me, glancing over at Ed and then back to me, waiting for an introduction. 'Sorry.' I said. 'This is Ed Jarvis.'

'Oh, my God! You're *the* Ed Jarvis. You illustrate the Ned Bobbin books. We love those books. They were basically the only thing that would get Matilda to sleep,' chimed Caroline. She shook hands with Ed. He gave her his best modest but charming smile. Caroline looked from Ed to me and back to Ed. 'This is so exciting! I can't believe I'm standing here with Natalie Garfield and Ed Jarvis – it's amazing!'

Ed and I exchanged glances. 'It is overwhelming,' he joked. 'To be honest, Nat and I rarely get any work done due to the overpowering nature of our awesomeness.'

I rolled my eyes whilst Caroline snorted with delight as if this was the funniest thing she'd ever heard. 'Soo, are you working on something at the moment?' she asked, eyes fixed firmly on Ed.

I shot him a look, which I hoped would say, 'No.'

'Actually, I was about to show Nat my roughs for the new Ned book. Would you like to see?'

'Oh, my God, I would love that!' gushed Caroline, pressing her hands to her heart as if he'd just offered her a date with Ryan Gosling.

I shook my head in disbelief. The problem with Ed was his ego. He loved to show off and he loved to get approval for his work. I know this is a normal human thing but he was basically a three-year-old when it came to his artwork and I was his mum. Today, Caroline was the auntie who only visits on occasion and Ed knew he had a captive audience. 'Follow me,' he said, grinning, leading Caroline into the dining room.

'Oh, wow!' breathed Caroline, taking in the sketches. 'These are gorgeous.' Ed stood back, basking in the glory.

Actually, they were pretty magnificent. He had given Ned a super-hero make-over, complete with mask, cape and dinky boots.

'You are so talented,' declared Caroline.

'Well, Nat?' asked Ed, looking at me. *Bless,* I thought. *He still needs approval from his mum.*

'They're wonderful,' I smiled. Ed beamed. I almost wished I had a gold sticker to give him. 'Just one thing, do you think he should have his pants over his costume like that? Maybe he should have a belt with the NB logo instead?'

Ed's face wrinkled into a frown as he took in the illustrations again. 'I thought the pants thing made it more fun,' he said.

'I think it's perfect,' declared Caroline.

'See? Caroline thinks it's perfect and she's an actual, real-life reader,' said Ed in a know-it-all voice.

I knew he was teasing but I was irritated by Caroline's interference. What did she know about books and writing? This was my world. She should stick to PTA cake sales and Farrow and Ball paint charts. I kept my voice calm. 'Let's see what the art director thinks, shall we?'

Ed glanced at me. He could tell I was riled. 'Whatever you think, angel-cake.'

I smiled with gratitude. 'Anyway, Caroline, thanks for dropping by and for the flowers.'

She looked at me in surprise. If she thought she was staying for a cuppa, she was mistaken. 'Oh yes, no problem at all. It was great to see you and lovely to meet you, Ed,' she cried with a sycophantic smile. I followed her to the front door. She paused, turning back to face me. She was one of those women who knew how to make the best of her features. She wasn't necessarily beautiful but she wore the right make-up, clothes and hairstyle to make herself effortlessly attractive and therefore rather intimidating to me. 'Actually, Natalie, there was something I wanted to ask you.'

Oh gawd, here it comes. She's got a brilliant book idea that she wants me to look at or she's going to enlist me to write all the copy for the PTA. And I'm too weak to say no. Damn you, Dan – this is all your fault.

'Did you know that they're planning to demolish Hope Street Community Hall?'

I was shocked. I had fond memories of the place. It was a fairly dilapidated building but it was much loved and used by the busy, chaotic toddler group, which provided a haven for new mothers on Monday, Wednesday and Friday mornings. I had found this a godsend when Woody was a baby. It was run by a group of retired ladies, who were basically like clucky, kindly hens, always willing to make you an industrial-strength coffee whilst they rocked and cuddled your fractious baby. On more than one occasion, during the intense early years, I had arrived looking like a character from *A Nightmare On Elm Street*, but returned home feeling almost human and reassured by their kindness and insistence that I keep up my strength by devouring at least twenty-five chocolate bourbons.

'Oh, that's really sad,' I said, feeling my eyes mist at the memory and then hating myself for being so bloody emotional at the moment.

'I'm glad you feel like that,' said Caroline, thrusting a flyer into my hand. 'Save Hope Street Community Hall' was printed on it in large red letters with details of a forthcoming meeting, which I noted with increasing dread was due to be held at Caroline's house later that week. I avoided her gaze by staring down at the flyer. 'So you'll come? I'm going to leaflet this street and the surrounding ones today. I think we'll get a huge response.'

I swallowed, ready to make my excuses. Single parenthood wasn't a status I wanted but it was a trump card today. 'Oh, I don't think I can make it. There's no-one to look after Woody,' I explained.

'Won't your husband be home?' she asked.

'Not any more,' remarked Ed, appearing behind us.

I glared at him. To his credit, he recoiled in horror, mouthing 'Sorry' to me.

Caroline's eyebrows were raised and I realised that I would need to explain before she cranked up the rumour-mill in the school playground. I sighed. 'My husband and I are having a few problems,' I said, feeling annoyed that despite my writer's credentials, this was the best I could come up with.

'Oh. Oh dear,' she said in a way that sounded to my ears like, *You've clearly failed. I'm pretending not to judge you, whilst judging you.* 'Well, I do hope you manage to sort it out and persuade him to come home. I don't know what I'd do if Oliver ever left. Not that he would, of course.'

'You can never be too sure,' I retorted.

'I know my husband,' said Caroline with a thin smile.

'I thought I knew mine too,' I replied with narrowed eyes.

'Anyway, ladies!' cried Ed, detecting the start of a bitch-fight. 'I love the sound of your campaign, Caroline, so I'm more than happy to baby-sit for you, Nat.'

'Thank you,' I said through clenched teeth.

'Thank you,' repeated Caroline, beaming at Ed in adoration. 'See you on Thursday then, Natalie. 7.30 sharp. Lovely to meet you, Ed.'

'You too.' Ed said, nodding with a grin.

Caroline gave us both a neat little wave as she skipped down the steps into her stupidly large, gas-guzzling car. 'Byeee,' she trilled before driving off in a haze of planet-destroying fumes.

'Judgemental cow!' I cried as I slammed the door behind me.

'I thought she was nice,' teased Ed.

'Shut up,' I said, jabbing him in the chest. 'You like anyone who admires your pictures. You're basically a three-year-old in a man's body.'

'Guilty as charged,' he laughed, holding up his hands. 'Where are you going?' he asked, as I pulled on my coat and grabbed my bag from the kitchen.

I fixed him with a look. 'I'm not having that prissy tiger mother judging me. And you're right. I need to be more proactive if I want to save my marriage.'

'So-o?'

'I'm going to surprise Dan at work and take him out for lunch, get the campaign rolling.'

'Good for you, honey,' he smiled. 'Good for you.'

An hour later, I was standing outside Dan's offices, checking my appearance in the window of the glass-fronted building. Ed had encouraged me to slow down, change into something 'casual but sexy', as he called it. My options had been limited but the blouse and jacket looked pretty good. 'And brush your hair,' he instructed. I had even put on lipstick. Usually, I just applied foundation and a dab of blusher so as not to frighten the Reception children in the school playground but actually, it felt good to make more of an effort. I did my best to stride with confidence into the building. This is always tricky where revolving doors are concerned but I managed to make it to the reception desk without having to go round a second time or falling over.

The woman behind the desk was immaculate with perfect hair, nails and teeth. A fleeting concern that Dan was having an affair with her leapt into my mind. I could feel my heart thundering as I approached the desk and said, 'Please could you call Dan Garfield for me. It's his wife.' I watched her face carefully at these words. No flicker of recognition, guilt or jealousy. *Calm that imagination, Nat, you crazy fool.*

'Just a moment, please.' She smiled, putting through a call. 'Dan Garfield? I have your wife here for you.' She listened to the reply. 'Er, okay, well she's standing right here. Do you want to speak to her?'

I frowned with confusion as she held out the receiver. 'Hello, Nat?' said a voice. 'This is Dan's colleague, Penny.' I could vaguely remember meeting her on a trip to the office with Woody once. She was pretty but I recall Dan saying that she was a bit annoying. Maybe that was a red herring, maybe she was in fact his dream woman and was about to confess to me.

'Hello?' I said, keeping my voice guarded. 'Is Dan not available?'

'He's left for the day,' she explained.

'Oh. Right.'

'Yes, sorry. He had another hospital appointment.'

'Pardon?' The world seemed to blur in and out of focus.

'Another hospital appointment?' said Penny but with less certainty this time. 'Sorry, Nat, I assumed you knew and had just forgotten.'

'Erm, yeah, of course, the hospital appointment,' I stuttered, not wanting to seem like more of a fool than I already felt.

'It's at St Peter's and he only left about ten minutes ago so you can probably catch him up. I'm sure he'll be glad of the company. He said how boring it was waiting last time.'

'Yes. Great. Thanks, Penny.' I handed the receiver back to the receptionist. 'Thanks. Thank you very much,' I said, needing to fill the air with words as a rising tide of panic swept over me.

I wasn't sure who was making my body walk out of the building, onto the street and along the road. All I knew was that I had to get to Dan. I had to be with him because suddenly I realised why he had left me. He was ill and he was going to die and in his ever-reasonable, ever kind and gentle way, he was trying to spare my feelings by facing it on his own. But I wasn't going to let that happen. I was going to go to him, comfort him and offer him all the support he needed. He wouldn't have to face it on his own. I would be there with him, right until the end.

CHAPTER FOUR

CAROLINE

'Okay, everyone, thank you for coming. Let's make a start, shall we?' I gave the group seated in my kitchen a warm encouraging smile. I remembered running meetings from my years at the bank and I'd always loved that dynamic buzz of people coming together, sharing their ideas and making things happen. Admittedly this was small beer compared to the deals I'd been involved with at Sheridan's but still, it was important.

Life was very different since I'd given up work but I told myself that it was a good different. Oliver went out to work, I stayed home and worked for Matilda – a demanding but nonetheless rewarding employer. Since she'd started school, I'd had time to take on worthwhile projects within the community, whether it be the PTA or this campaign to save Hope Street hall.

I had always thrown myself into life, done my best and aimed for excellence. I know some people feel intimidated by me. I can't blame them. I try to live up to my old school motto, *Ad summa nitamur* – 'Let us strive for perfection'. I know this isn't for everyone. Perfection is such a final word, but I believe you have to try. Anything else is just giving up.

Besides, I know people value me because I get things done. I'm on first-name terms with Julie in the school office and Mr Metcalfe, the Head, publicly thanked me after the summer fair last year. That's the thing, you're either a doer or a moaner. I never moan, I learnt that from my dad. He grabbed life by the throat and got on with it, even when he was ill.

'I'll go down fighting, Caroline,' he'd told me right at the end when he was in that awful place. I've never forgiven my mother for letting him die in there, surrounded by strangers. I insisted on staying by his side. I even slept on the floor one night whilst my mother went home to her comfortable bed. Dad had told me not to judge her, that it was hard for her, but I didn't see it.

My mother and I never talked about it, not even after he died. In fact, we hardly saw each other for a while. It was better that way. My grief was very different to her grief. Sometimes, I wonder if she felt anything at all – I certainly never saw her cry. It might have been different if I'd had a sibling to talk to but it was just her and me. We didn't have anything to say. I did try on a couple of occasions but she would always change the subject. It was as if Dad hadn't existed somehow, as if he were gone and that was that.

I took out a folder and handed copies of the agenda I had typed earlier to Phil, Head of Matilda's school, who was sitting to my left. 'Please take one and pass them on,' I beamed. I was pleased with the turn-out. There were six of us and I had received several e-mails offering additional support too. 'So, shall we go round the group and introduce ourselves?' There were nervous murmurs of agreement so I decided to take the initiative. 'I'm Caroline Taylor. I'm chair of the PTA at Felmingham Primary.' I shot a smile at Phil, who nodded in reply. 'And I've started this campaign because I think we all feel that Hope Street hall is an important part of our community.'

'Yeah, and we don't want the bloody Tories selling it off to some property developers to build posh houses that no-one can afford!' cried a large bald man, who I recognised as our postman. I shot him a look. I noticed that he was still wearing shorts. 'Sorry, Caroline,' he added. 'Didn't mean to jump in.'

'No, it's fine. We were going to go round the room one at a time but I'm glad you feel so strongly. Please, go on.'

He smiled at the group. He reminded me of a bear – he had a huge chest and a broad smiling face. 'I'm Jim the postie – you all know me. I live on the next street over in my parents' old house. I've lived here all my life and I can remember us celebrating the Silver Jubilee in that hall. My old mum used to tell me about the dances they had there during the war to keep up morale.'

I nodded my encouragement, already thinking about the flyers I could ask him to deliver on his rounds. 'So the hall has history. Phil, do you want to go next?'

Phil had been sitting back in his chair but he sat bolt upright as I spoke. He had swapped his sharp headmaster's suit for a casual-smart jumper and jeans. I appreciated Phil's style. He was well dressed and always professional. I think that's why we got on so well. 'Hi, I'm Phil, Head of Felmingham Primary. I agree with Caroline that the hall is an important part of our community. We've always had links to St David's Church, which I believe has used the hall in the past. I had a word with Father George, but sadly they only rent it from the council and they don't have the money to take it on.'

'Is that what it's all about?' asked a woman who I didn't know. 'I'm Pamela Trott, by the way. I run the Brownies and help with the toddler group. It strikes me that all these councils care about these days is money. What about the people? What about the kiddies and the mums and the old folk? Where's the sense of community?'

There were murmurs of agreement. 'Well, I see the community coming into my store every day,' said a school mother, who I recognised from the shop at the end of the road. 'I'm Doly and I run the shop with my husband Dev. We know most people on these streets and we know they don't want the hall to close.'

'But what can we do?' asked Pamela, looking worried.

'Shall we finish introducing ourselves and then have a look at the agenda?' I said, keen to get us back on track. 'Natalie?' I noticed her jump as I said her name. I also noticed that she was already on her second glass of wine and had nearly finished working her way through a bowl of root-vegetable crisps. Apart from Doly, she was the only school parent present. I had hoped that my school-mother friends, Zoe and Amanda, might appear but they had sent me texts about half an hour earlier with their excuses. It was fine, I knew I could count on their support when it was needed. I gave Natalie a smile of encouragement. 'So, Natalie is the children's book author, Natalie Garfield,' I said. She looked embarrassed. 'It's a shame Ned can't come and save us from this,' I joked. Natalie gave a feeble smile. I wasn't quite sure why she'd come if she wasn't ready to take part. I ploughed on. 'So do you have any ideas for the campaign?'

'Er, fundraising?' offered Natalie vaguely. I could tell that she wasn't taking this seriously.

'Well, yes, that might help but I think we need to be more focussed. If we could turn to the agenda, I have drawn up what I think needs to happen. I've done some research and the council are asking for offers in the region of half a million for the land. They say that there's room for three properties. I am proposing that we raise the money to buy it ourselves and run it as a local community project.'

'We're going to need to have lot of bake sales to raise that kind of cash,' observed Natalie, who had topped up her glass and was starting to slur her words a little. I noticed Doly raise her eyebrows in agreement.

'There used to be a choir,' said Jim, his eyes sparkling at the memory. 'They were pretty good, as I remember. My dad used to sing tenor.'

There were murmurs of approval. 'I remember that,' smiled Pamela. 'They won prizes, didn't they?' Jim nodded. 'I do love a sing-song,' she added. 'And the hall would be a lovely place to hold it.'

'The Hope Street Community Choir,' I offered. 'I love the sound of that.'

'Sorry, Caroline,' interjected Natalie. 'But how is that going to save the hall?'

I could see that Natalie was going to be a challenge. She was clearly one of those people who wore the issues from their personal life like a badge. She might as well have been wearing a T-shirt with the slogan, 'My husband has left me and this is now your problem.' I couldn't comprehend this kind of attitude. Everybody has problems. You can't foist them on all and sundry. That was plain selfish. Put up, shut up and get on with it. That was the only way.

I gave her a business-like smile. 'Choirs are the big thing at the moment, particularly community choirs. It will give our campaign a focal point. We can hold concerts, get the local media involved, really show the council that the hall is needed. What do we think?'

'Who's going to run it?' asked Doly. 'We need a choirmaster.'

'I think I know just the man for the job. Excuse me for a second,' said Phil, taking out his phone and leaving the room.

I was excited at the thought, as if we'd hit upon a really strong idea. 'So, can I count on everyone to join?' I asked.

Pamela, Doly and Jim nodded, with smiling enthusiasm.

'I've got nothing else to do,' sighed Natalie with a 'woe is me' look. She took another large gulp of wine. I made a mental note to only hand out the cheap stuff next time.

I heard my phone buzz from the counter with a call. I picked it up and glanced at the ID, feeling irritated as I recognised the number. They were always phoning me and to be honest, it was getting a bit much. I paid them enough, I didn't see why I should have to solve whatever problem they were having. They were the professionals and should get on with the job I'd employed them to do. I would be calling them in the morning to tell them exactly that.

I cast the handset to one side and turned back to the room, noticing with annoyance that Matilda was out of her bed and standing in the middle of the kitchen, grinning at everyone.

'Ahhh, bless her, what a poppet,' gushed Pamela, reaching out to pet Matilda's cheek.

Matilda was in her element. 'I just saw Mr Metcalfe,' she observed proudly, 'and you're our postman and you're Sadia's mum,' she said to Doly, 'and you're Woody's mum,' she added to Natalie.

'Matilda, what are you doing out of bed?' I asked, adopting a stern tone.

Matilda frowned at me. 'Couldn't sleep. You're too noisy,' she declared. Everyone laughed and she joined in. She loved an audience. 'When's Daddy coming home?'

This was a good question. I had called him earlier in the hope that he might make it home for bedtime so that I would get a moment to prepare for the meeting. I could tell he was in a bar. I heard someone order a large Sauvignon Blanc.

'Sorry, darling, just had some figures to finish,' he said.

'I know you're in the pub,' I replied. 'I'm not an idiot, Oliver.'

He had tried to sweet-talk me then, he could tell I was cross. 'I just popped in for one, my love. And anyway, I knew you had your thing so I thought it might be best if I stayed out of the way. I'll be home soon. Love you.'

I had hung up, swallowing down my fury. My *thing*? What was my thing these days? Running the PTA, ferrying Matilda to whichever social event was lined up and now this community hall campaign. I used to run a department of over one hundred people, delivering profits in excess of twelve million pounds and now, I was trying to persuade lazy mothers to bake cakes whilst negotiating with my cleaner about the removal of limescale from the shower screen. If I thought about it for too long, I would probably explode so I tried not to think about it. I got on with my life.

'Daddy's working late,' I replied, more for the benefit of the assembled company than Matilda. 'And you need to go back to bed, otherwise you'll be tired in the morning.'

Matilda scowled and folded her arms. 'Don't want to. I want to see Daddy first.'

I folded my own arms in reply. She stared back at me in defiance. I get this with Matilda. She's always been her father's princess and milks it for all it's worth. I can't blame her. I used to do the same with my dad.

I could remember snuggling on his lap, watching television while my mother was in another room. I can't ever remember hugging my mother. I must have done but she always seemed so remote and forbidding.

I do recall one time when a child had been unkind to me at school. I can't remember exactly what had happened but I remember being very upset. My mother was standing in the playground waiting for me. I approached her in tears but instead of reaching out her arms and pulling me to her as I would do with Matilda now, she had waited until I was by her side and then turned away and walked towards the gate. I had been incensed by her lack of feeling and my crying grew louder. At that moment she had grabbed my arm, ushering me out of the gate, hissing under her breath, 'Caroline! You're making a scene. Stop it at once!' I had stopped out of shock but it had started again when we got home, whereupon my mother had sent me to my room until dinner time. I was still upset by the time my father came home. He had appeared at the door and my tears began afresh.

'Hey, hey, what's all this then?' he asked. I told him everything including how my mother had sent me to my room.

He tried to make excuses for her. 'Your mother has a lot on her plate at the moment. I'm sure she just didn't understand.' He comforted and consoled me and we went downstairs to eat dinner in silence, my mother's face fixed and severe. Later that evening, I heard them arguing. I crept out of my bedroom and sat at the top of the stairs, trying to pull my nightie around my freezing legs and feet. They were in the dining room with the door closed but I could hear my father's voice.

'She's just a child! All she wanted was some sympathy.'

There was a pause before my mother replied. 'That's all anyone wants, Charles.' Then she opened the dining-room door, picked up her coat and bag and left the house. I sat a little longer, my heart beating in my ears, and then I heard my father crying. I'd never heard a grown-up cry before so it was unsettling. Part of me wanted to go downstairs and comfort him but part of me felt appalled. Parents weren't supposed to cry. However, I was more furious with my mother. She had made my father cry and left him alone. I crept back to bed and lay awake for hours until I heard my mother return and my parents go up to bed.

I am very aware of my relationship with Matilda when I think of my own mother and I have tried my hardest to ensure that I'm always available for her. We get along well enough, bake together, read together, all the things a parent is supposed to do with their child, but when her father comes home, it's as if I fade from her line of vision. I tell myself that it's because I'm the one who's here the whole time doing the boring stuff – school runs, homework, cooking and of course dishing out discipline but still, I would like her to look at me as she looks at Oliver sometimes.

I suppose I should just be happy that she loves her father so much. Fathers are the keepers of their daughter's hearts and I know mine fractured when my dad died. If I'm honest, it's never healed.

'How about I tuck you in, poppet?' asked Pamela, holding out a hand to Matilda. 'I remember when my daughter was little and she couldn't sleep, I'd sing her a lullaby. Would you like me to do that?'

Matilda looked up at her and nodded shyly. 'Thank you,' I said. 'If you're sure, but no more nonsense, young lady.'

Matilda pursed her lips. 'Why don't you give Mummy a kiss before you go up?' suggested Pamela.

I held my breath and felt my heart sink as Matilda turned on her heels and headed for the stairs. 'I've already kissed her goodnight,' she replied without looking back.

I glanced at the other mothers in the room. 'Children, eh?' I cried, laughing off my hurt and embarrassment. My phone rang again. It was the same number as before. I seized the handset and turned it off just as I heard the doorbell ring. 'Please, help yourself to more nibbles and wine,' I said to everyone before heading down the hall.

I opened the door and was surprised to find a man of around thirty, clean-shaven and smartly dressed, smiling at me. He seemed familiar somehow.

'Hello,' he said, 'I hear you're in need of a choirmaster. I'm Guy Henderson. I'm the new music teacher at Felmingham Primary. Phil just called me.'

'Goodness!' I exclaimed. 'That was quick. Come in' I led him down the hall to the kitchen. He nodded to the group and smiled at Phil as he entered the room.

'Everyone,' I said. 'This is Guy Henderson and he's the new choirmaster of Hope Street Community Choir.' There was a small cheer.

I noticed Natalie nudge Doly and whisper, 'I'm definitely going to choir now.'

'Lovely to meet you all. I've only just moved back to the area but I'd be delighted to help your cause. I've always wanted to set up a community choir,' said Guy, smiling.

'Excellent,' I said. 'That's wonderful – thank you. Why don't we hold our first rehearsal next Thursday – Pamela, would you be able to book the hall please? It seems like a fitting venue.'

Pamela nodded. 'Course, ducks – can't wait to get singing!'

'Fantastic – thanks so much. May I suggest that we all try to get as many people as possible to sign up?' Everyone murmured agreement. I reached for my glass. 'I would like to propose a toast. To the Hope Street Community Choir!'

'The Hope Street Community Choir!' we chorused.

'I'll drink to that!' cried Natalie, raising her glass with some gusto and almost falling onto Guy. 'Oops, sorry,' she said, giggling. 'Maybe I should have a glass of water.'

Or maybe you should lay off the free booze, I thought as I followed her over to the sink. 'Let me get that for you,' I insisted, fetching one of Matilda's plastic beakers from the cupboard and filling it with water. I was not about to risk my Dartington Highballs. They were a wedding present.

Natalie accepted the cup with a lop-sided grin. 'I bet you think I'm a complete mess, don't you?'

Not far off. I pursed my lips into a thin smile, thinking it might be best if I didn't answer.

'Well, you would be right, Caroline,' she slurred, gesturing towards me with her cup and slopping water onto the floor in the process. 'Whoops. Sorreee,' she cried.

Unbelievable. It was like having another child in the house. 'It's fine. I'll get it,' I said, reaching for the kitchen towel.

'No, no, no, let me,' she offered, lurching forwards and wresting it from my grasp. 'My mess. I'll clear it up.' She knelt down and made a half-hearted attempt to wipe up the spillage. She remained kneeling on the floor for a moment, gazing up at me like a child hoping for a biscuit. 'So anyway, guess what I did last week. Go on, have a guess.'

'Erm, you wrote another book?' I offered, glancing around the room in embarrassment, willing her to stand up.

'Haha! Very good. No. Last week, I thought my estranged husband was dying.'

I stared down at her. 'Oh, my goodness. How terrible.'

Natalie gave a drunken nod. 'Yes. Very terrible. And so I followed him to hospital, to offer my support and be there 'til death us do part and all that.'

'Well, that was very good of you.' I could see Phil looking over, a frown of concern on his face. I gave him a reassuring smile.

'I know,' slurred Natalie, staring down at the balled-up paper towel in her hand. 'I am basically a saint. So I turn up at the hospital ready to do my weeping wifey bit and guess what he was there for?'

'I have no idea.'

Natalie held my gaze as she delivered the punchline. 'A hernia.'

'A hernia?'

She nodded gravely before her face dissolved into hysterical laughter. 'A bloody hernia! I thought he was dying and he's just got a hernia.' She hugged herself, rocking back and forth as she laughed. Pamela and Jim smiled over at us, wanting to share the joke. I felt a rising sense of panic. *I have to get this crumbling wreck of a woman on her feet and out of my house. Fast.*

'How about you drink some more of that water before you head home?' I suggested with a breezy smile, trying to help Natalie to her feet. She was surprisingly heavy.

She staggered to a standing position and patted me on the chest. 'Thank you, Caroline. You're a pal,' she declared, patting my shoulder, her breath ripe with booze.

I took a step back. I wanted to extricate myself as quickly as possible. Fortunately, Guy had made his way over and was smiling at us both. 'Caroline, I'm going to shoot off but I just wanted to say that I'll see you next week and here's my number,' he said, handing me a card.

Natalie raised her water glass drunkenly at him. 'Looking forward to it, Gareth Malone,' she giggled. He grinned.

'I'll show you to the door,' I said with relief, hoping that Natalie would take the hint and follow Guy's lead soon. 'So, you used to live round here?' I asked as I led him down the hall.

'Yes, I grew up a few miles away.'

'We might know some of the same people. My maiden name was Winter – Caroline Winter.'

Guy froze as if he'd remembered something before turning to me and shaking his head. 'No, sorry. I don't think we've met before.'

'Funny,' I said. 'You look so familiar.'

'Yes, I get that sometimes – people are always saying that I remind them of someone. I have an everyman kind of face. Anyway, I must go. Good to meet you, Caroline. See you next week.'

'Thanks Guy. Bye!'

When Oliver came home later that evening, I was buzzing with excitement. He had bought me an enormous bouquet of creamy white roses and was slightly drunk but full of smiles and apologies for being late.

I kissed him on the lips. I was too euphoric to be cross any more. 'That's a lovely welcome home,' he said. 'I'm not sure I deserve it though,' he murmured as he started to kiss my neck and run his hands over my body. 'How was the meeting?'

'It was great,' I replied, moaning with delight at his kisses and wandering hands.

'That's good, that's really good,' he replied, as I reached my hand down the front of his trousers and felt him stiffen at my touch. I still had the power, you see. We still desired one another and that meant the world to me. For all his working late and my stay-at-home status, we still had the connection from when we were young and carefree. We still found each other attractive, we still wanted each other but it was more than just desire.

We remembered what it was like when we both worked; how we would meet after work for drinks or dinner, return home to our flat in Dulwich, make love and then fall asleep facing one another, connected by all the things we wanted in life. This connection remained. Whatever else has happened since, Matilda and all the joy and heartbreak we'd shared, that connection was still there. We wanted the same things and it was a pretty simple wish list – a happy child, a beautiful home, nice holidays, a good bottle of wine. We loved our life and we loved each other. It was as simple as that. People over-complicate things but I know what's important.

So as he parted my legs and nudged his way inside me, as we moved together as one, I felt that connection again. All was well in that moment. Everything was perfect.

CHAPTER FIVE

NATALIE

I nearly didn't go to choir. Ed had promised to babysit again but had phoned earlier that day full of sheepish apology. Some guy he'd been lusting after for months had asked him on a date. Could I get another babysitter and he promised that he'd do the next one? I brushed it off.

I wasn't that bothered about going. I'm not sure why I'd agreed. Actually, I am. I'd knocked back one too many glasses of Caroline's delicious wine. I saw the label and knew it had come from Waitrose. Anyway, I'd got a warm feeling from the wine and the assembled company. I like Jim. He's been the local postman forever and he is a kind man. Dan used to joke that he fancied me but he's fifty if he's a day and I've never seen him look at me in that way. He's like the street's uncle. I also remember Pamela from toddler group. She's got a good heart and I've always liked Doly from the shop. Woody and her daughter Sadia are good friends too and we sometimes help each other out with school pick-ups. The whole group had a lovely feel and when Guy turned up and Caroline proposed a toast, I got carried along by it. Plus, I thought it would be a new hobby, something to make me more interesting in my bid to save my marriage. Singing was sexy – people love singers. Look at Taylor Swift and Rihanna – they had more men interested in them than I'd had jaffa cakes and I've eaten a lot of jaffa cakes.

However, one week later, in the sober light of day and with a viable 'get-out' clause, I felt complete relief. To be honest, I hadn't felt like going anywhere much since Dan left. I felt vulnerable, as if everyone could see through my skin to the raw pain just below the surface. I knew that Caroline already had me down as a complete fruit-loop and I wasn't ready for another dose of 'my life's so much better than yours'. Plus, I'd really gone off brushing my hair and making an effort. I figured I could get away with it. Writers are supposed to be pasty-faced weirdos with an aversion to socialising. They're too busy creating to bother with other people or deodorant.

So it was something of a shock when I opened the door just after seven to find Dan standing on the doorstep, a lop-sided smile on his lips. I glanced down at my bobbled bunny pyjama-bottoms, tracing my gaze up to my oh-so-baggy but oh-so-comfortable hot-pink hoodie. No-one could pull this look off and call it style, not even Kate Moss.

'This is a surprise,' I ventured, offering the understatement of the year. I realised at that moment that a fortnight had passed since Dan's departure. This time two weeks ago, we had been happily married. Everything had been fine. What a difference a bombshell makes.

I felt a sudden surge of panic that he was coming round 'to talk'. I didn't want to be dressed like this when we talked. I wanted to be wearing something smart and sexy – those jeans he'd always liked with that top he said made my breasts look magnificent. I wanted to look magnificent as he told me why he wanted our marriage to end. I wanted him to be sure because I felt certain that if I reminded him of what he would be missing, he would change his mind. It would be like cooking bacon for a conflicted vegetarian and watching them drool. I definitely didn't want to have this conversation with unwashed hair whilst dressed like a sloven.

'Ed called me,' he explained. 'Said you needed a babysitter?'

This made me cross, firstly because Ed had called Dan without asking me and secondly because Dan had described himself as a 'babysitter'. I'm pretty sure it's impossible to babysit your own son. I think it's just called 'being a parent'.

We were still standing on the doorstep and Dan was peering past me, inching forwards. I was on the brink of telling him that he was mistaken and shutting the door when I heard Woody say, 'Hey, Dad.'

I stood back, defeated, and allowed Dan to pass. I looked down at the floor as he did so. I didn't want the awkwardness of that moment when we were supposed to look each other in the eye and kiss. I couldn't bear it.

'Hey, fella,' said Dan, approaching his son and drawing him into a hug.

'What are you doing here?' The question was simple but heart-breaking at the same time. It had only been a fortnight and yet Woody seemed used to the fact that Dan was now a visitor to our house.

Dan glanced at me. He heard it too. 'Well,' he replied. 'Your mum is going out so I thought I would come by and hang out with you for a bit, if that's okay?'

Woody shrugged. 'Okay. Do you want to see my new Match Attax cards? I swapped Diego Costa Hundred Club for Daniel Sturridge Star Player.'

'Cool,' said Dan, ruffling his son's hair. He transferred his gaze to me. It was a look that said, *You're good to go.*

I was thinking, *Don't make me go. I don't want to go. Let me stay. Please. I'll be no bother. I want to sit with you both, to just hang out and be. I want to keep hold of my family, to keep us together somehow.*

But they had disappeared into the living room, already lost in their chat about over-paid footballers, and I was left in the hall doing my best not to cry.

No-one was more surprised than me when I found myself standing in the draughty community hall, forty minutes later, with twenty or so mostly female would-be singers. It had been the call from Ed which had finally persuaded me to come. I snatched up my phone as soon as I saw his ID.

'I hate you,' I answered.

'Well, I love you,' he replied. 'And I'm not sorry. You need to get out of that house, and you can always talk to Dan when you get home. You can have a calm chat, instead of a hysterical, *please don't die, oh you've only got a hernia,* type conversation.'

'Ha bloody ha. You basically made me do that.'

'How so?'

'You told me to go get my man.'

'Yeah, "Go get your man." Not, "Blatantly misunderstand the situation."'

'Whevs. Did I mention that I hate you?'

'Except you don't. Now I'm off to flirt outrageously with the beautiful Mark. Go, sing your heart out and I'll call you tomorrow for a de-brief, 'kay?'

'O-kay.' I hung up feeling a little cheered. He was right. Annoying, but right.

There was an air of anticipation but also excitement, matching my own, as I walked into the hall. The chairs had been arranged in rows and people stood with their friends, eyeing Guy with interest and chatting nervously.

I already knew a few faces. Caroline gave me a nod of acknowledgement with a smile that didn't reach her eyes. She was there with her school playground clique. Pamela gave me a cheery wave and Doly looked up and smiled too. Jim the postman wandered over to greet me.

'Hello, Jim, I didn't have you down as a choir man,' I said, grateful to see a friendly face.

'Actually, I used to be in a band in the nineties,' he replied with pride.

'Oh, wow, anyone I've heard of?'

'So you know Take That?'

'Yes, of course,' I replied, ready to be impressed.

'Well, I was Robbie Williams in a tribute band called A Million Love Songs.'

'Oh. Wow. That's pretty impressive.'

Jim looked sheepish. 'Yeah well, it was until, you know, Robbie left the real Take That. So I had to go too.'

'That's a shame.'

Jim shook his head. 'Nah, Gary was a dickhead so I didn't mind really. We had creative differences.'

'Art imitating life,' I added, swallowing down a giggle.

'Exactly,' nodded Jim earnestly.

'Right everybody, shall we make a start?' The voice was direct and no-nonsense. We turned as one. 'My name is Guy Henderson. Thank you for coming along tonight to the first rehearsal of the Hope Street Community Choir.'

There was a small cheer. Caroline and her entourage gave a cheerleader 'Yay!' of approval.

Guy's mouth twitched into a smile. 'Caroline, would you like to say anything before we begin?'

Caroline rose to her feet and turned to face us. She placed her hand on her heart. 'I just wanted to say thank you so much for coming. It means a great deal to me and I know it will mean a great deal to our community.' It was starting to sound like an Oscar speech. 'I am sure that with Guy's help, we can make this choir into something vital for us all and that with the money we raise, we'll be able to save Hope Street hall!' Her clique whooped and cheered whilst everyone else clapped politely. 'Over to you, Guy.' Caroline bowed like a news reporter handing back a live-link.

I thought I noticed a raised eyebrow of amusement on Guy's face but it was fleeting. He gave Caroline a gallant nod of thanks before turning back to the assembled company. 'So, I want this to be fun and something we can be proud of but it's going to be hard work too. For tonight, we're going to do some warm-up exercises and get to know our voices. I've got a couple of songs to try and next week we start in earnest. Pamela here –' Pamela waved her hand like the queen and we all laughed '– is going to collect subs and organise a tea and coffee rota because apparently that sort of thing is very important.' He gave a wry smile. 'And I shall do my best to teach you the songs. Okay, find yourself a seat – those who like to sing "*high*",' he sing-songed this word with an impressive falsetto, 'please sit to my left, and those who prefer to sing "low",' he added in a trembling tenor, 'place yourselves to my right.'

I found a seat next to Doly, who rewarded me with a nervous smile. 'Can you sing?' I asked.

She gave a little side-to-side nod. 'So so,' she replied. 'My husband says I can but my children tell me to stop!' I laughed, feeling a fraction more relaxed.

'Right,' began Guy, taking his place behind the keyboard. 'Let's warm up our voices, shall we? Standing with your feet apart, relax, drop your shoulders. Don't look so worried – I'm not going to make anyone sing a solo. Yet.' His humour had the desired effect and as we laughed, we relaxed a little more. 'That's better,' he grinned. 'So, we'll

begin by humming up and down an arpeggio, like this.'
He played a chord and echoed the sound with four notes.
'La-la-la-la, la-la-laaaah,' he sang in a beautiful, clear
voice. 'And now it's your turn.' Several people cleared
their throats nervously. Guy played the same chord and we
joined in.

It felt strange at first to be singing in public, even though
we were just going, 'La, la, la.' Apart from belting out
tunes in the car and shower, I'd never sang and certainly
never in public. I got the feeling that I wasn't alone.
I glanced around the room. Pamela was frowning with
concentration, whilst Jim was singing with an impressive
tenor voice.

Guy played the next chord up. 'Now try this one.'
We did as we were told. 'Good! And now hum this one,' he
instructed, playing the next chord.

'Hmm, hmm, hmm, hmm, hmm, hmm, hmmmmm.'

'Excellent! Let's see how high we can go. And!'

We hummed and la-ed our way through each new set
of notes. I could hear Caroline's voice getting louder with
each arpeggio. We laughed as the notes became too high
for us and one by one we stopped singing. Soon, only
Caroline and Doly were still going. Guy fixed his gaze on
them and grinned with encouragement. 'Last chord,' he
declared. 'You sing first, Caroline, and then would you like
to try—'

'Doly,' whispered Doly, her neck flushed red with
embarrassment. 'Okay.'

Guy played the chord and Caroline sang the notes with
pitch-perfect trembliness as if giving an opening-night
performance at the Royal Opera House. Guy smiled as
Caroline's friends clapped noisily. He turned to Doly. She
gave a small nod and he played it again. Her voice was
completely different to Caroline's. Soft and gentle and

completely sublime. There was a pause after she finished. Guy stared at her for a moment as if he'd forgotten where he was before clapping his hands. 'Thank you, ladies. That was very revealing. So, it's clear that we can all sing the notes. Now let's see if we can sing the songs.'

I squeezed Doly's elbow. 'Your voice is amazing,' I whispered. She gave me a shy smile.

I watched Guy as he handed out sheets of song lyrics. He couldn't have been more than thirty and yet he was completely confident in his abilities. He was tall and neatly dressed; a man who obviously took care of his appearance. I wouldn't exactly call him handsome but there was something about the way he carried himself – assured and in charge – that was disarming. I noticed Pamela gazing up at him, wide-eyed and trusting, obviously already smitten. He had the room in the palm of his hand.

'So let's try "California Dreamin'", shall we?' suggested Guy. 'A relatively straightforward one to get us started.' He pressed Play on the backing track, raised his hands and we were off. I could remember singing this song as a teenager and loved its sixties folk feel. I felt my body lift as we began to sing. There were a few bum notes but actually, it sounded pretty good.

'Not bad for a first go,' said Guy. 'Now, let's up the ante and try it again with the lows taking the opening line and the highs replying, shall we?' He re-started the backing track.

'Well done,' smiled Guy when we finished. 'I see a bright future ahead of us. And as we're on something of a roll, let's try the next song. It's a bit trickier but I think we can do it.'

My heart sank as I turned to the next song-sheet. 'Something Inside So Strong' had always been a favourite of mine and Dan's. Whenever this song came on the radio, we would duet in a hammy, fist-pulling rendition, which often left us helpless with laughter.

'Oh, I love this song,' murmured Caroline from the row behind. 'So powerful.'

'Okay,' said Guy. 'Let's give this a go, shall we? A straight sing-through and we'll worry about harmonies later.' He pressed Play. As the intro filtered through the speakers and we joined in with Labi Siffre's unmistakeable voice, I could feel my body start to tremble.

Get a grip, Natalie, it's just a song. But I couldn't help it. I tried to brush away the tears and power-ballad my way through but it was no use. There was something inside but it wasn't very strong and seemed to consist mostly of tears and mucus. I turned away so that Doly wouldn't notice and spotted Caroline behind me. She was lost in the song, her eyes closed, possibly performing to one hundred thousand people at Wembley. I decided to cling on to my last shred of dignity and take my sobbing outside.

It was starting to get dark, the sky glowing pink and orange. I tried to feel cheered by its beauty but it only made me more depressed. I wanted rain, thunder and if possible a little snow to mirror my own cold misery. I fished into my pocket for a tissue and pulled out an old shopping list. It included items for a Thai curry, which I had made for Dan as a Friday-night treat a few weeks back. Inevitably, this brought fresh tears and irritation at the shambolic woman I had become. I considered making a run for it. No-one would miss me and I could make my excuses another time. I started to head towards the street.

'Natalie!' called a voice, which I immediately recognised as Caroline's. *Bugger. Maybe I could pretend I hadn't heard and keep going.*

'Natalie!' she repeated with increased volume. *That'll be a no then.*

I turned to face her, hoping that my eyes weren't as red and puffy as they felt. 'Oh, hi, Caroline,' I said, pretending that I'd only just noticed her.

'You're not going are you? We're only halfway through.' Either she'd been too caught up in powering through the song to notice my outburst or she had chosen to ignore it. Or possibly a little of both.

'I just—' I began. *I just what? I just need to run home to a man who doesn't love me any more and won't tell me why?* I took a deep breath. 'I'm just not sure if it's for me.'

'Is it the choice of songs?' she asked, moving closer. 'Because if it is, I know exactly how you feel. I used to sing in choir at university – it was all classical – Verdi, Brahms – wonderful,' she smiled, dewy-eyed at the memory.

'No, it's not that—'

'Oh, but you must stay. You're going to be such a valuable addition to the team with your profile and assets.' *Praise indeed. I sound like a Page Three model.* 'And I know how much you care about the hall, what it meant to you.' She stared at me. *Damn her. She knew which buttons to press. I am a nostalgia queen at the best of times but at this moment, I was clinging onto anything that reminded me of my happier past life.*

Caroline's phone buzzed with a call. She fished it from her bag and frowned as she saw the caller ID, pressing a button to silence it. 'Please stay,' she implored. Her phone rang again.

'Someone is keen to talk to you,' I observed. *That's it. Distract the bossy lady and then make your escape!*

She sighed. 'And someone needs to just get on with their job and stop bothering me,' she said, switching off her phone. 'So is the lovely Ed looking after your son this evening?'

'Er, no, actually. Dan is with him.'

'Oh, well, that's good news, isn't it?'

I guess our definitions of 'good' differ somewhat, I thought as I scuffed one shoe across the ground. 'I'm glad he's spending time with Woody,' I replied.

Caroline regarded me for a second. 'May I speak frankly, Natalie?'

I'd really rather you didn't but I fear you're going to, whatever I say. We all know that offering to speak frankly comes second only to 'Don't take this the wrong way' and 'With the greatest respect'. It is merely code for 'I am about to insult you and validate that insult by asking your permission first'.

Still, I was at a low ebb and starting to get desperate. 'Go ahead,' I replied, bracing myself.

She looked me in the eye. 'You seem like a good person and an attractive woman too.' *Wait for it. Wait for it.* 'But from what I've seen, you've let things slide.' *A killer glance at my hair.* 'It's important for a woman to keep her husband's interest.' I winced with feminist indignation. 'I mean, take Oliver and me, for instance.' *Oh, please, I wish someone would.* 'I know how to keep him engaged in our relationship and it's not just to do with sex, although of course that's important.' *Yeah, just a warning, Caroline. If you start giving me details of your week-long tantric love-making sessions, I will vomit.* 'Whenever I feel that we've lost track of our relationship, I'll make a grand gesture, do something special, just to keep things fresh and interesting.' She made it sound like a trip to the supermarket. 'For instance, last year I booked a sky-dive because it's something we've always wanted to do together.'

'Well, I'm afraid of heights so that's not really going to work,' I joked.

She narrowed her eyes. 'No, but you have to find something that does because it's so easy for things to change after you have children – to lose sight of you as a couple.' *Bloody know-it-all – bloody know-it-all with a point.* 'I'm more than happy to give you some suggestions if you would like?'

Visions of Caroline making Dan and me do a tightrope walk across the Thames popped into my head. 'Thank you, Caroline. I'll give it some thought.' She was a preachy cow but she meant well.

She nodded with satisfaction. Our conversation was interrupted as Guy appeared in the doorway. He smiled at us both. 'Hello, ladies. Are you enjoying it?' he asked.

'Oh very much, Guy, thank you so much for everything you're doing,' gushed Caroline.

He nodded and turned to me. 'And how about you? Sorry, we met briefly at Caroline's house but I don't know your name.'

'Natalie, Natalie Garfield.' Although who knew if this would be my name for much longer. 'Yes, it's been very emotional.' I'm not sure why I said this. I think it came from a movie but it was an honest answer.

He fixed me with a look. 'Music is a powerful weapon.'

Yeah, one which can knock you sideways if you let it, I thought.

'So, Guy, you didn't tell me where you grew up. I'll bet we know some of the same people,' interjected Caroline. 'Where did you go to school?'

'Kelsey Wood School,' he murmured. He seemed cowed by Caroline's interrogations. *Join the club, Guy.*

'Oh, my goodness! That's where my father taught.'

'Oh, really?' he replied without any real interest.

'Yes. Mr Winter? He was the Headmaster.'

Guy shook his head. 'I don't remember him.'

Caroline narrowed her eyes. 'No, you might be too young.' She was about to ask another question but Guy cut her off. 'Sorry, Caroline. If you'll excuse me,' he said. 'I really need to fetch something from the car for the next half of the rehearsal.'

'Of course.' Caroline beamed. 'I can grill you another time.' Guy looked scared. Poor man. I wondered if he knew what he was letting himself in for. 'He's marvellous, isn't he?' she remarked after he'd gone.

I shrugged. 'He seems nice.'

One of Caroline's friends appeared in the doorway. 'Caroline, do you want a cup of tea?' she asked.

'Thanks, darling,' replied Caroline. 'By the way, Zoe, this is Natalie Garfield, remember I told you about her – the children's book writer?'

'Oh, wow,' cried Zoe. 'We love Ned Bobbin in our house,' she said, showing me an impressive set of chalk-white teeth.

'Thank you,' I said.

'Are you coming?' asked Caroline, turning to me.

I nodded with a feeble smile. 'Yep, I am,' I replied, following her back into the hall. I was coming to realise that you couldn't run away from Caroline Taylor.

As I walked home after the rehearsal, I had to admit, albeit grudgingly, that I'd enjoyed myself. Despite my outburst, it was friendly and fun and even Caroline wasn't as bad as I'd feared. As I reached the front door, I felt my heart rise and dip with the thought of a) seeing Dan and b) having to talk to Dan.

'How was it?' he asked as I appeared in the lounge doorway.

'A bit emotional,' I replied, watching his face. 'We sang "Something Inside So Strong".'

He nodded. *Is that it? I cry my eyes out over a song and a shopping list for kaffir lime leaves and lemongrass. And you nod.*

'Do you remember when I nearly got the words from that tattooed on my arm at my stag do? I thought it was the perfect wedding present for you' He laughed. *So you do remember.*

'I forgot about that,' I smiled, the seed of an idea forming in my mind. I stared at him. *I miss you, Dan. I miss you so much.* 'Woody misses you,' I said. Actually, Woody hadn't said this but I was sure it was true.

'I miss him too,' he replied. *But do you miss me? Even just a little? Actually, I don't want to know. It's probably better if I don't.* 'Why don't I come round every week while you're at choir? That way, I'll get to see him while you go and do something for yourself.'

'My new hobby?' I suggested. I brightened at the idea. At least it would mean that I saw him regularly and we might have a chance to sort this mess out.

'Exactly. Did you enjoy it?'

'I did. I think it was good for me. I spend too much time at home with my own thoughts, you know?'

He reached out a hand and touched my hair. 'You deserve to be happy, Nat.'

I smiled at him, at the man I'd married, the man I loved. *Yes, I do deserve to be happy. Happy with you. That's what I signed up to when we got married. Please don't go. Please stay. Please pretend none of this has happened and let's try again.*

'I better make a move,' he said.

'How's your hernia?' I asked. *Wow, Nat, great conversation starter.*

He smiled. 'It's fine. I'm just waiting on the date for my op.'

I nodded. 'Sorry for my outburst last week, by the way. My brain went into overdrive.'

He shook his head. 'No, I'm sorry. I should have told you but what with everything …' His voice trailed off.

'Listen, I know we need to talk and I promise we will soon. We'll sort everything out.'

I nodded. 'We usually do.'

He put his arms around me and kissed the top of my head before he left. I stood for a moment in the hall watching the shape of him disappear, listening to his car drive off and then my hand felt where he'd left the kiss and I hugged myself. I stayed like that for a moment as if movement would disturb the feeling. Dan was still in my life and I could tell he still cared about me. All I had to do was to prove that this was a mere bump in the road, that I was the one – the all-new, all-singing, sexy, interesting wife, who he'd lost sight of. I was going to get Dan's attention again and I knew exactly how to do it.

CHAPTER SIX

CAROLINE

As I drove to the nursing home on a bright spring morning, I sang along to the Adele song on the radio. I wouldn't normally sing in the car but last night's rehearsal had rekindled my love of singing, leaving me feeling refreshed and ready to face the inevitable adversity of today's visit. Goodness only knows that I needed a little positive energy for what lay ahead. I was fully expecting an argument but I was ready too.

I couldn't have been happier with our first choir rehearsal. It would be a challenge to transform us into a proper choir but all in all, it had gone much better than I'd expected. The standard of singing was reasonably high and I could see that Guy was the perfect man to run it. I had even found talking to Natalie a surprising pleasure. She was something of an emotional train-wreck and I was happy that I'd been able to help her with a little marriage guidance.

When I got home from choir, I had flicked my phone into life to see that I'd had three missed calls and a voicemail message from the home. I recognised Peter Jarvis' humourless tone immediately.

'Mrs Taylor, we believe you're coming in to see your mother tomorrow. We need to have an urgent meeting to discuss her care options.'

Care options? It sounded so innocuous. I knew what they were going to say.

'Your mother's behaviour is increasingly challenging, we're no longer able to cope with her frequent outbursts. We may need to re-think.'

Re-think all you want. You knew the deal when you took her in and I pay you an extortionate amount to care for her. Take the money and get on with it.

The sun was shining as I pulled into the drive and one of the gardeners was planting some geraniums, begonias and snapdragons ready for the summer. All looked calm and lovely. I made my way through the door into the bright entrance hall. St Bartholomew's corridors bore the sharp tangy smell of old age underpinned by the cabbagey whiff of whatever meal had just been consumed. I loathed everything about the place but especially the smell. I always breathed through my mouth when I visited but could still detect the stench on my clothes when I got home.

The home itself was a pleasant enough chalet-style building with wide corridors and lots of windows looking out towards a lovely garden. Apart from being a nice enough place to live, I had chosen it because they had a specialist team who could deal with people with dementia. At least that's what they'd told me. However, given the number of calls I had to field because my mother was being difficult, I was starting to wonder.

I visited once a month because to be honest, that's all I could take. Quite apart from the shifting sands of my relationship with my mother, I couldn't bear to spend any more time than necessary in this place. It made me consider things I didn't want to think about – Zimmer frames, wrinkles and the pervasive stench of urine. This wasn't my world. I was young and fit and didn't want to be reminded of the inevitability of old age. Call me shallow, call me unfeeling but spend an hour in the company of my mother and you would feel the same.

The receptionist looked up at me from behind black-framed glasses that didn't suit her. She acknowledged me with a brief smile of recognition. There was judgement behind that smile.

'Good morning, Mrs Taylor. If you could just sign in, I'll let Peter know you're here.'

'Thank you,' I replied, taking the pen from its holder. I wrote my name before taking a step back into the waiting area, doing my best to ignore the neat piles of Saga magazines.

'Mrs Taylor,' said a voice behind me. I turned to see Peter Jarvis, manager of the home. He didn't even try to smile. 'Shall we go into my office?'

I followed him along the corridor. When I first came here to look round, they had offered me tea and cake. I could remember rooms full of snowy-white-haired old ladies and well-turned-out gentlemen doing stimulating activities, smiling and happy. This time, there was no offer of tea and all I could smell was that day's lunch, which reminded me of cat food. My stomach flipped.

Peter ushered me into his office and heaved his large backside onto the chair behind his desk. I took my place opposite him, noticing the certificates rewarding 'excellence in care' on the wall and a framed photograph on the desk of his similarly fat wife and two chubby children.

He pressed his fingers together and looked at me. 'Mrs Taylor, I have to tell you that we have a problem. Did you get my call last night?'

I was irritated by his accusatory tone. *How dare he talk to me in this way?* I decided that attack was the best form of defence. 'We most certainly do have a problem,' I replied. 'I pay a great deal of money for my mother's care and I do not expect to be called in the evenings because your staff are unable to do their job.'

He blinked at me in surprise before regaining his composure. 'Your mother tried to stab one of our staff with a pair of nail scissors.'

It was my turn to be surprised now. My mother had certainly been trying in the past but it was mostly verbal abuse. She had never tried anything physical. 'I see.' I wasn't sure what else to say.

'So you can understand that we have a problem. I appreciate that your mother requires specialist care but I cannot have my staff placed in danger.'

'Where is she now?' I asked. I had visions of her locked in a padded cell.

'In her room. We had to call out a doctor to sedate her. It took two nurses to restrain her. She's very strong.'

I felt an odd sense of pride at this, even though I knew it was wholly inappropriate. 'I take it she didn't actually hurt anyone?'

He shook his head. 'Our staff are well trained and fortunately the nurse in question saw what was happening and reacted quickly. She managed to get the scissors from her but your mother kept trying to fight them, which is why we had to call the doctor, unfortunately.'

'Can I see her?' I asked.

'She may be a little sleepy but I can get a nurse to take you to her, of course.'

'I meant the nurse,' I replied. 'I want to apologise on behalf of my mother.'

Peter looked confused. 'There's really no need.'

'All the same, I'd like to.'

'Okay, and then we can take you to your mother.'

'Well if she's sleepy, there's probably no point.' I knew I was trying to wriggle out of it. Peter Jarvis knew this too. He gave me a grave look.

'Mrs Taylor, I really think you need to see your mother. Forgive me if I speak out of turn but I think she needs to see you. The nurses tell me that she calls your name at night sometimes.'

Anger and guilt washed over me. 'You are speaking out of turn, but seeing as we are laying our cards on the table, I will try to reason with her if you can promise to continue with my mother's care as you see fit. Confiscate anything dangerous, sedate her if necessary but please, don't cast her into the street.' I stared him down, noticing how he shifted with discomfort in his seat. *See? I can layer on the guilt and drama too.*

He pursed his lips and smoothed his tie. 'We will continue to care for your mother but please take this as a first and final warning. If anything like this happens again, we may need to exclude her.'

My cheeks burnt red with humiliation but I took it. I had to. St Bartholomew's was my only hope. 'Thank you,' I said. 'I appreciate your honesty and commitment to her care.'

He nodded, raising his hefty bulk from the chair. I followed him back along the corridor. Two nurses were walking towards us. 'Oh, Laurie,' said Peter to one of them. A woman of about my age with an open, friendly face stopped and smiled at us. 'This is Mrs Winter's daughter.'

I watched her face and saw no flicker of reaction to the incident. In fact, she held out her hand to me. It was small and cool to the touch. 'Pleased to meet you,' she said. 'Shall I take you down to see your mum?'

'I'll leave you to it,' said Peter, turning away. 'I'll be in touch, Mrs Taylor. Thank you for your time.'

Laurie nodded to her colleague before ushering me along the corridor. As we reached the door to my mother's room, I stopped and turned to her. 'I just want to say sorry—'

Laurie held up her hand. 'There's really no need,' she smiled. 'Your mum would never hurt me. It's a stage of her disease, although I am concerned that something has upset her lately. She seems more het up than I've seen her before.'

'Oh. I see.'

'I've only been working here for about three months but she seemed a lot calmer back then. Have you noticed anything?'

I stared at her, unable to think what to say. I only saw her once a month so honestly had no real way of knowing. 'Perhaps.'

'I'm very fond of your mother. She thinks the world of you.' She smiled again.

'Does she?' I asked with genuine surprise. *Unlikely, given our history.*

Laurie nodded. 'She says your name all the time. I think she's lost in memories from the past but you're always in them.'

I felt my chest grow tight as she opened the door and I saw my mother lying in her bed. She looked tiny, like a child. Her face was grey, her hair matted and thin. I thought she was asleep at first but she turned her head towards me, a confused frown creasing her expression.

'Hello,' I said in a croaky voice.

Her face flickered with recognition but she didn't speak. She just gazed at me as if searching for the answer to a question.

'How are you, Mrs Winter?' asked Laurie. 'Are you feeling better today?'

My mother's gaze transferred from me to Laurie. She raised her eyebrows and then smiled in reply.

'That's good,' said Laurie. 'And lovely to have your daughter visiting too.' My mother glanced at me and then back to Laurie, like a spectator at a tennis match. 'I'll let you have some time together,' she said, giving me an encouraging smile before she left.

I stood by the side of the bed and took in my surroundings. I didn't usually come in here. My mother was normally sitting in the lounge area, staring into the middle distance, whilst activities such as bingo or singing went on around her. She reminded me of a lonely person at a party and I felt sad that she couldn't seem to take part in her own life any more. Then I would remember how she had barely participated when she'd had her marbles and dismissed the thought.

The room was very pleasant, with two windows looking out over the garden and apart from the adjustable bed, it felt much like a miniature version of her old home. There were fresh flowers on the table by the window and a bowl of fruit as well. She had brought one of her chairs, her bookcase and quite a few of her knick-knacks. She had liked to collect miniature Wade figures and these were all arranged on a little wall-shelf in one corner.

I could remember loving these as a child but never being allowed to touch them for fear of breakages. One day, I had crept into the dining room where they were kept and picked up a tiny porcelain hedgehog that I liked the look of. I made him jump from surface to surface but had accidentally chipped his perfect black nose. My mother appeared at that moment, turning white with anger when she saw what I had done. She sent me to my room but I had been happy to hide there until my father got home, whereupon he had done his best to quell her anger.

I stared at the figures now, noticing the replacement hedgehog my father had bought, resisting a childish urge to knock it off the shelf. I turned away.

My mother was looking at me again now, so I pulled up a chair and sat next to her bed. I wanted to get this

over with. 'Do you remember what happened last night?'
I asked. She seemed to shrink into the bed even more.
I should have felt sympathy but I was still heavy with
childhood anger. 'I've had to beg Mr Jarvis to let you stay
here.' My mother mumbled something. I frowned and leant
in closer. 'What did you say?'

'Sorry,' she whispered.

I was taken aback. Perhaps the sedation was still having
an effect. My anger started to dissolve. 'Okay, well, I'm glad
you're sorry.' She stared up at me with huge eyes made all
the more pathetic by her shrinking frame. I transferred my
gaze to the garden and was surprised to see Guy Henderson
wheeling an elderly lady in a wheelchair. My mother's eyes
rested on them too. There was a moment's silence before she
started to pound her fists on the bed, her face enraged.

I leapt up from the chair. 'What's the matter?' I cried.
She lashed out a fist in my direction but missed and
slumped down onto the bed, before looking up at me. She
seemed twice the size all of a sudden, her eyes narrow and
angry. *I recognise you now,* I thought.

'Fuck off,' she hissed.

'I beg your pardon?' I cried. I had never heard my
mother swear before.

'Fuck off,' she repeated. 'Fuck off, fuck off, fuck off.'

I pulled the emergency cord and within seconds Laurie
and a colleague were there. 'All right Mrs Winter, let's try
to breathe and calm down, shall we? Jem, call the doctor,'
said Laurie, taking my mother by the shoulders in an
attempt to soothe her.

'I have to go,' I said, heading for the door, not looking
back. 'I'm sorry,' I added, but I'm not sure to whom.
I hurried along the corridor, signed out and fled back to my car.

Once inside, I realised that I was shaking. I could
hear my heart beating, a sense of panic coursing

through my body. I could not believe what I had just witnessed and my urge to flee had taken over. I contemplated going back, to check if my mother was all right but I realised that I didn't want to. I simply didn't want to know. This woman was a stranger to me. She'd always been a stranger in that she never seemed like the mothers of picture books or films. There was no softness or gentle kindness in our relationship, no lap in which to snuggle or shoulder on which to cry.

Why should I care about her now if she had never cared about me? Why should I pick up the pieces of her shattered life? What was the point? She barely knew me.

The people at the home claimed that she asked for me but they could be making it up. There were flickers of recognition but it was fleeting. She was trapped in her own world, like she had trapped me in my room for every minor indiscretion as a child.

She hadn't wanted anything to do with me back then so why should I bother now? I didn't need her. I had carved out a life away from this ageing and decay. I didn't need it in my life. I could simply drive away and not come back.

And yet, there I remained. Silently cursing my indecision. *Why couldn't I just leave? Go back to the order and harmony of my real life?* There was a tap on the glass and I jumped in surprise at the sight of Laurie's concerned face. I wound down the window.

'Sorry,' I said. 'I just couldn't take seeing her like that.' It sounded as if I cared and I felt immediate guilt for being disingenuous.

Laurie gave me a reassuring smile. 'Of course. It's very hard sometimes. Do you have any idea what brought it on?'

I shook my head. 'We were just sitting, looking out into the garden. I saw someone I knew – Guy Henderson with an elderly lady in a wheelchair.'

Laurie nodded. 'Mrs Henderson has only recently arrived at the home. Sometimes, people with dementia react badly to change, a new face or someone who reminds them of something from their past.'

'I only met Guy this week, so there's no connection between my mother and his.'

Laurie smiled. 'Well, your mother is much calmer now, so we'll monitor the situation and keep in touch, okay?'

'Thank you,' I said. 'Thank you so much.' I gave her a final wave before starting the car and driving off, feeling relieved that my mother was someone else's problem for the time being, tucked away where I didn't have to think about her, her illness or the pain of the past.

Run away, Caroline. Run back to your place of safety and don't look back.

I switched on the radio. They were playing 'Weather With You' – a Crowded House song that Oliver and I used to sing along to while we were decorating the house at weekends. I turned up the volume and sang at the top of my voice, drowning my worries with happier memories.

CHAPTER SEVEN

NATALIE

'Mum! Pizza's ready!' yelled Woody.

'Okay,' I replied. 'Just finishing up.' I glanced back at the blinking cursor. I'd always thought that would be a good name for my writing memoir – *The Blinking Cursor* by Natalie Garfield. I smiled. I was in a good mood tonight. I was about to officially embark on the campaign to get Dan to fall in love with me all over again and I was excited.

I practically skipped down the stairs. I felt like a natural woman, every woman and a woman in love. Choir had obviously had a positive effect on me. We had a rehearsal tonight and I was in two minds as to whether I would go. The next hour would decide that for me, depending on Dan's reaction to my surprise.

I had contemplated telling Doly about it when I popped into the shop earlier but she wasn't on her own so I decided to keep it to myself for now.

'Are you going to choir tonight?' she asked with a smile.

'I'm planning to,' I replied. 'Have you been practising?'

'Only all the time. Never stops singing, this one,' said a man who was carrying a box from the back of the shop. 'She has the voice of an angel,' he added, his eyes glittering with pride.

Doly beamed at me. 'This is my husband, Dev.'

'Pleased to meet you,' smiled the man.

'Oh, is this your singing thing?' asked another, younger man, who was re-stocking the fridge. I could see a family resemblance to Dev. His dark-brown eyes twinkled with amusement. 'I bet it's all Abba and Spice Girls – a zigazig ahh! Am I right, brother?' he added, glancing at Dev.

Dev laughed but then noticed his wife glaring at him and adopted a serious face. 'I'm sure they sound wonderful,' he replied diplomatically.

Doly rolled her eyes at me. 'Pay no heed to my fool of a brother-in-law,' she declared.

'I'm Hasan,' said the young man, wiping his hand on his jeans before offering it to me.

I grinned. 'Good to meet you,' I said, accepting it.

'And you,' he replied, smiling, holding my gaze for a few seconds.

'Right, stop harassing my customers,' said Doly, shooing him away before turning back to me. 'Sorry about him. He likes to flirt with all the pretty ladies,' she added.

I felt a bit giddy as I walked home. I had been called pretty, received attention from a handsome young man, all without brushing my hair.

I've still got it and it's only a matter of time before Dan realises this too.

I walked down the hall into the kitchen, humming the tune to 'Everybody's Changing'. Guy had sent us a list of songs he wanted to try along with the music files so that we could practise. I loved this song. It reminded me of when Dan and I were first married, before we had Woody – simpler times. Not happier necessarily. Just simpler and more carefree.

Dan was just fishing some garlic bread out of the oven. Two pizzas already sat on the side. 'Someone's in a good mood tonight,' he said, smiling.

'Mum's always singing these days,' groaned Woody, appearing in the kitchen, helping himself to a glass of juice.

'I like singing,' I beamed, leaning past Dan to steal a piece of the bread. 'And I am in a good mood.'

'Well, I think you sound great,' said Dan, flashing me a grin. *That grin. The one that used to make my body ache with longing.*

'All your songs are old and boring,' declared Woody. 'You should sing something by Ed Sheeran.'

'Maybe we will,' I said, ruffling his hair. 'Anyway, it looks as if dinner's nearly ready. Could you lay the table, please?'

''Kay,' he replied, fetching knives and forks and carrying them into the dining room.

I watched as Dan cut the pizzas with a pair of kitchen scissors. *Maybe I should tell him now? He would be surprised and we would laugh, have a glass of wine and the scales would fall from his eyes.*

'What?' he grinned, flicking the oven gloves at me. 'What are you looking at, eh?'

'Dunno, the label's dropped off,' I teased. 'Anyway, didn't you used to poo-poo my pizza-cutting techniques?' I added, gesturing at the scissors.

'That's before I realised how brilliant they were, darling.'

Darling. He just called me darling. You didn't use that word casually. You just didn't. 'Do you fancy a glass of wine?' I asked, opening the fridge and taking out the bottle. There was always an open bottle in the fridge-door these days.

'Aren't you going to choir?'

'Er yeah, but one glass won't hurt. In fact, it actually makes your voice higher,' I said, pouring two glasses.

'Is that a fact?' he grinned.

I nodded, feeling my body lift with joy at our easy banter. *You must miss this as much as I do, Dan.* 'I'll take these in, shall I?' I asked, gesturing at the plates and garlic bread.

'That'd be great. Ta.'

He followed me into the dining room, where Woody was already sitting in his place. He looked up and smiled. *My lovely boy.*

Dan put the pizzas on the table and sat opposite him. I took my place to his left, just as I always had. I sat back and watched as Dan dished up the pizza to Woody and then to me. This was the main reason for my good mood. We were all together again. Just as we'd always been. I could almost pretend that the thing hadn't been said, that Dan was still living here, that he wasn't just having dinner with us before I went to choir, that he would be staying the night. Oh yes, I'm the great pretender.

'Salad?' he asked, gesturing towards the bowl.

'Thanks,' I replied. 'So, Woody, how was school?'

He shrugged. 'Good.'

'What did you get up to?'

'Maths, literacy, art.' He reeled it off like the world's most boring shopping list.

I persevered. 'What are you doing in art?'

He frowned. 'Can't remember.'

'Wow,' I teased. 'I'm so glad we had this conversation.'

He rolled his eyes. 'It's school. School is boring. End of.'

'He's not wrong,' said Dan, raising his eyebrows at me. 'Life doesn't really get interesting until you discover love.'

'Are you going to get a divorce?' Woody stared at us both, his face serious.

Dan and I looked at one another. It was a fair question. He sighed. 'Not at the moment, mate. Your mum and I need to work things out.'

'What things?' *Oh, Woody, I could hug you for your tenacity.*

'Grown-up things,' replied Dan. He reached out a hand to his son. 'Look, I know this is confusing for you but to be honest, it's confusing for us too. The thing that you have to remember is that your mum and I love you very much.' I nodded in agreement. 'And I want to see you as much as I can while we sort everything out, okay?'

Woody bit his lip. 'Okay.'

'And you can ask us anything or tell us what's bothering you any time, all right?' I offered.

'All right,' repeated Woody, but he didn't seem very sure.

'So how did the meeting go yesterday?' asked Dan, turning to me, obviously eager to move the conversation along.

'It was really good actually. Ed was on form as usual and the art director loves "Super-Hero" Ned. We're also thinking of doing a spin-off for his side-kick, Cat.'

'That's brilliant, Nat. We're proud of you, aren't we Woody?' said Dan, nudging my shoulder.

Woody nodded, wolfing down his pizza and wiping his mouth on his sleeve. 'Can I go and watch TV now please?'

I had been waiting for this moment. I loved my son dearly but I wanted to talk to Dan alone. 'Of course,' I replied. 'Half an hour, then pyjamas and teeth, okay?'

''Kay.'

Dan started to pile up the plates in readiness to take them to the kitchen. 'Wait,' I said. He looked at me, an expectant smile on his face.

For a moment it was as if nothing had changed. Here we sat, finishing dinner, nursing a glass of wine, about to take out the plates to the dishwasher – normal stuff that normal people do. 'I've got a surprise,' I said.

'Okay,' he replied, looking intrigued. 'I've got something to tell you too but let's hear your surprise. As you know, I'm one of the few people in the world who actually like a surprise.' This was true. I had thrown him a surprise party for his thirtieth birthday. He had always declared it to be the best thing anyone had ever done for him.

I hesitated for a second. *Shouldn't I let him go first? Maybe he wanted to tell me that he was having second thoughts.* 'It can wait if you have something you need to say,' I said, almost pleading. *Please tell me that it was all a mistake, that you miss me, that we can work it out.*

He smiled, ever the gentleman. 'Ladies first,' he encouraged. 'So what's this big surprise?'

I walked over to the stereo and pressed Play. The opening strains of 'Truly Madly Deeply' by Savage Garden began to drift through the speakers. I turned to him and smiled.

'Remember this?'

I had hoped that he would laugh and burst into song as he'd done all those years ago. I had hoped that this would be the moment when he would remember and see me as I'd been – the girl he'd fallen in love with. What had Ed said? If you've done it once you can do it again?

He seemed to be frozen to the spot. He didn't speak or move. I seized the moment. I rolled up one sleeve and held out my wrist for him to see. He stared at my arm. His mouth fell open and he gawped at me.

'You had a tattoo!' he cried, sounding less impressed and more appalled.

'Yes, but look what it says,' I urged. '"Truly Madly Deeply", Dan. It's our song.'

'Oh, Nat,' he said.

Those two words could be said in so many different ways: *Oh, Nat, how romantic. What a wonderful loving gesture.*

Oh, Nat, I hate to say it but I think you're a bit too old for a tattoo.

Oh, Nat, what have you done? Did you actually think that you could save our marriage by inking some words onto your skin?

I think it's safe to say that Dan's intonation implied a mixture of options two and three. 'I just wanted to remind you how we used to be, before life got a bit samey,' I said quietly, turning off the music.

'Oh, Nat,' he repeated, walking towards me and taking hold of my arms. This time I could tell that he just felt sorry for me.

I wanted the world to swallow me whole. 'You think I'm an idiot, don't you?'

'No, of course not. It looks cool.'

'Don't lie.'

'You had a tattoo!' came a voice from the doorway. Woody stood there looking horrified.

'Just a small one,' I admitted.

'Let me see,' he demanded. I held out my wrist. 'Truly Madly Deeply,' he read with a frown. 'What does that even mean?'

'It's a song that your dad and I used to really like.'

He scowled. 'That's so embarrassing.'

I pulled down my sleeve, feeling like an even bigger fool. It was one thing to evoke the sympathy of your estranged husband but quite a different matter to be judged by your eight-year-old. 'I'm late for choir,' I said, hurrying out to the kitchen.

'Nat,' called Dan, in that calm and measured tone. He followed me out.

'It's fine,' I said. It wasn't of course but I had to pretend, if only for my own sake. 'Anyway, you had something you wanted to tell me too?'

'I'm not sure this is the right time,' he grimaced.

'No, go on,' I said. 'Out with it.'

He ran a hand through his hair. 'I think we should try counselling.'

I stared up at him and nodded. *It could have been worse. He could have asked for a divorce there and then on the grounds that his wife was starting to go crazy.* 'You don't want to get a matching tattoo then?' I joked.

He laughed before putting his arms around me. 'What are we going to do with you, Natalie Garfield?'

I buried my face in his shoulder, enjoying the feel of his embrace for a moment, the smell of him. *I miss you, I love you, please don't give up on me.* I pulled away first, patting his chest. 'I better go,' I said.

'You did what?' exclaimed Doly as we took our places in the second row at choir that evening. 'Show me.'

I rolled up my sleeve. The word 'Madly' suddenly seemed gigantic, looming out at me like a signpost to my faltering grip on rational behaviour. *Yep, I was truly, madly losing it.*

'Oh, good heavens above, Natalie. What have you done to yourself?' cried Caroline, making me jump. I hadn't heard her creep up on us.

I held out my arm ready for the inevitable judgement. *Come on Caroline. Let's have it. It can't be any worse than my son's damning pronouncement.* 'It's a little bit common, Natalie.' *Or maybe it can.*

'Well it's partly your fault,' I told her.

'I'm sorry?'

'You were the one going on about grand gestures.'

'I meant nice dinners at Michelin-starred restaurants, not permanently marking your body in a declaration of love.'

'Well, it's done now,' I said pulling down my sleeve.

'I really don't think it looks that bad,' remarked Doly. 'And I think it's sweet that you wanted to show your husband how much you care.'

'Thank you, Doly,' I said, giving Caroline a pointed look.

'Could we get back to the business of the choir?' asked Caroline. 'I wanted to invite you both to a meeting next week. I think we'll make a great team so I would like you both to be on my choir committee.' She made it sound as if she were bestowing a great honour, rather than asking a favour. Doly and I exchanged glances.

'I'm not sure I'll be free,' I replied, ready to make excuses. I am a woman who would happily abseil down The Shard in order to avoid joining a committee.

'Oh, it's fine, I can work it around you both. We could do it after school whilst the children play together,' said Caroline breezily.

I was about to open my mouth in protest but Caroline was already on her feet, making a beeline for Pamela. I stared at Doly. 'What just happened?'

'I suppose we should take it as a compliment,' she smiled. I got the feeling that she was a woman who saw the best in everything. I gave a resigned nod as Guy clapped his hands together to get our attention. Our number had increased to around thirty and there were a couple more men as well as a few other school mums. I got the feeling that news of our fresh-faced choirmaster had travelled fast.

Guy seemed delighted by the turn-out. 'Welcome everyone, especially the newbies. It's great to see you all. Let's warm up as per last week. Everyone stand up, drop those shoulders, plant those feet, breathe from the diaphragm. And!' This time Guy moved from high to low with the chords and it was Jim's turn to shine as the arpeggios got lower and lower. We all laughed and cheered at his impressive baritone voice. 'Well done, Jim!' declared

7 (p. 58 - tenor)

Guy. 'So, have you had a chance to practise the songs I sent round?' There were positive murmurs. 'Excellent. I want to run through last week's songs, along with "Chasing Cars", "Everybody's Changing" and "Halo". And the good news is that Pamela has baked a lemon drizzle cake, so the rewards will be bountiful.' Everyone laughed and Pamela blushed.

I looked up to the ceiling and felt my body relax as we worked through the songs. The roof of the building was a wooden beam structure and the sound reverberated around it wonderfully. I started to forget my earlier embarrassment and feel a little more positive.

Counselling could be a good thing. Counselling could lead to problem-solving and working through issues to find a resolution. I just wish I'd thought of it before forking out a hundred quid on body art. It had bloody hurt too.

'You're all sounding great,' nodded Guy after we'd run through all the songs once. 'The only problem is that you look bloody miserable and you don't move. You look like a bloody miserable bunch of statues actually.' We glanced at one another, giggling with embarrassment. 'So I'm going to put on a piece of music and I want you give in to it. It's the funkiest piece of music ever written and it's actually impossible not to dance as soon as it starts.'

I felt my body tighten with nerves.

Please, sir, can I be let off dancing? I only dance when I'm drunk.

Guy smiled at us all, reading our thoughts. 'Don't be embarrassed. Don't be shy. Just let the music lead your body and ignore everyone else in the room. And enjoy it! No more miserable statues.'

He pressed Play. A pulsing bassline followed by a funky piano tune filled the room. We all stared at each other for a moment before Jim started to move in time to the music.

'Come on everyone!' he cried. 'I'm no dancer but this is Stevie Wonder!' We laughed, buoyed by his bravery. Pamela embarked on a very impressive shimmy. Doly smiled at me and we began to dance, me in my customary 'hips and legs' style and she with Bollywood-esque gentility. It felt a little awkward at first but became easier because we were all giving it a try together. I looked round for Caroline and spotted her disappearing out of the door. *Coward.*

As the song finished, Guy gave us a round of applause. 'Well done, everyone. That was not easy and you rose to the challenge admirably. Remember, we're all boogie men and women and we need to try to channel that into our performance. Sing, dance, smile and enjoy. That should be our mantra. And now, time for some well-earned tea.'

The room was buzzing at tea-break and I noticed that Caroline still hadn't reappeared. I also noticed that she was without her school-mum entourage this evening. I fetched two cups of tea and accepted two slices of cake from Pamela.

I made my way through the door and stood back for a moment, noticing that she was on her phone. 'Okay, thank you, Peter,' I heard her say. 'Yes, I know you're doing all you can for her and I appreciate it. I understand that she's difficult but really, you're our only hope. Yes, all right. Thank you. I'll speak to you again tomorrow.'

I waited until she had hung up before coughing to make my presence known. She looked round in surprise. I took a step forwards. 'I thought you might like a tea and a slice of Pamela's lemon drizzle cake.' I smiled, holding it out to her. She stared at me as if no-one had ever offered her cake before. 'Please don't make me eat two slices,' I added.

'Thank you,' she said, accepting the cake and tea. 'I don't usually drink caffeine after 3 p.m.'

I thought she was joking but her face was deadly serious. 'I am basically three parts caffeine to one part gin,' I observed. She gave me a blank look. *Fair enough. It wasn't that funny.* We stood in silence for a moment. I'm not great with silence. I tend to fill it with banal chit-chat. Silence makes me nervous.

I noticed that she was still taking mouse-like nibbles of her cake, whilst I had finished mine a good two minutes before. She was staring into the middle distance and she looked … actually she looked a bit sad. 'Is everything okay, Caroline?' I asked. I noticed her shift a little, uncomfortable at the question. 'You can tell me to mind my own business but it seemed as if that phone call upset you.'

She seemed surprised at the question, as if it had been a while since someone had asked how she was. She opened her mouth and then shut it and took a sip of tea. She eyed me and it was a look that was questioning if she could trust me.

'You don't have to talk about it,' I said. 'But sometimes a problem shared and all that.'

'It's my mother,' she said quietly. 'She's not well.'

'Sorry to hear that,' I offered. 'Is she on her own?'

'My father …' she hesitated, struggling at the mention of his name. 'He died,' she said, biting her lip.

'I'm sorry,' I repeated. 'My father died a few years back too.'

She nodded, her face softening at the shared confidence. 'My father died five years ago and I still miss him every day. It's hard, isn't it?'

It wasn't that hard for me. I didn't miss my father, to tell the truth, but I wouldn't admit it. 'Yes, I said. It is hard. At least we've still got out mothers, eh?'

Caroline gave a hollow laugh. 'My mother is a challenging woman, always has been, even before her illness.'

'What's wrong with her, if you don't mind me asking?'

She looked at me. I could tell she rarely talked about this. 'Dementia,' she said.

'That's a very cruel disease,' I remarked. 'My grandma had it and it was like watching an old clock wind down. I take it she's in a home?'

Caroline nodded. 'She's been going through some very aggressive episodes. They're struggling to contain her really.'

'Poor thing. That must be very frightening for her,' I said.

Caroline stared at me as if she'd never considered this before. 'Yes, yes, I suppose it must be,' she said, staring off into the distance. 'Anyway, how did Dan react to your tattoo? I know Oliver would have been horrified!'

Back to earth with a bump then. 'Actually, he's suggested that we go for counselling.'

'Sounds as if he's serious about saving your marriage,' she observed.

I brightened at the thought. If Caroline the perfectionist gave it a thumbs-up, it had to be a positive step. 'Yes, I suppose it does,' I smiled.

Doly appeared in the doorway. 'We're starting again,' she said.

As we made our way back inside, Caroline turned to me. 'So, could you come to a meeting next week? I'd really appreciate your input.'

Say no! Say no! You've got enough on your plate. Don't look her in the eye! She looks really sad and you're a sucker for sad, imploring types. 'Okay, but only if there's cake.' *Yes, I know I'm a sucker but I may have negotiated cake as part of the deal. Don't judge me.*

She looked unsure so I added, 'That was a joke, although cake is always welcome. And if we're going to work together, you're going to have to get used to my borderline sarcastic sense of humour.'

'I'll try,' she said. 'And thank you,' she added as we returned inside and deposited our empty cups.

'For what?'

'For listening.'

I smiled. 'Writers are good listeners but don't upset us, otherwise you might end up in a book, usually as a character who comes to a sticky end.'

She laughed. 'That's funny.'

Yes, I thought as I took my place next to Doly. *Funny but also true. Dan had better watch out.*

CHAPTER EIGHT

CAROLINE

I hadn't had a particularly good start to the day. In fact it had been bloody awful. Matilda had been the madam from hell as soon as she woke up, refusing to eat her breakfast and taking an age to get ready. She's never like this for Oliver. She's always a perfect angel at the weekends when he's taking her to swimming lessons. She bats her long eyelashes at him and does exactly what he asks. It's a different matter with me before school. It's as if she's trying to test me, to get a reaction. I do my best to stay calm but I'll admit I had to scream into a cushion whilst I was waiting for her at the bottom of the stairs. It's a tactic I've learnt when life gets too much. I rarely raise my voice. I believe that I would be letting myself down if I resorted to such screaming matches. I've seen enough school mothers bellowing at their offspring at the playground gates to know that I would never shout at Matilda.

I was also aware that Natalie and Doly were bringing their children round that evening after school and I needed to keep Matilda in a good mood so that she didn't throw the whole meeting into chaos. I knew that she was looking forward to having them round too. As she sloped down the stairs, frowning and cross, I gave her a warning.

'Best behaviour, Matilda or I shall have to tell Woody and Sadia's mothers not to come after school.'

She scowled at me as she put on her shoes but I could tell she'd got the message. I managed to get her to school after that without further incident but as I returned home, I received a text from my cleaner Rosie telling me that her son was ill and she wouldn't be round today. This was a disaster. The house was a tip. I couldn't have people seeing it in that state. I hurried home, knowing that I would have to do it. Don't get me wrong, I'm not a princess. I can clean my own home but if you can afford a cleaner, why wouldn't you have a cleaner?

I also had things to prepare for the Hope Street Hall campaign. I needed to come up with a plan for the website, work on a strategy for our social media activities and think about T-shirts. I did not need to be cleaning the toilet or, as I discovered when I got home, removing fox excrement from the driveway.

I had just finished hoovering the lounge when my phone rang. It was the home. Again. Apparently, my mother was showing repeated displays of aggression and they had been forced to confine her to her room.

'It's not a long-term solution, Mrs Taylor,' said Peter Jarvis.

'I appreciate that,' I replied. 'And I appreciate what Laurie is doing for her.'

Peter sighed. 'To be honest, you're lucky to have her, Mrs Taylor. She's your biggest ally in here. If it were down to me, I would have excluded your mother by now.'

I bet you would, you overweight chump. I swallowed my anger. 'I understand,' I said. 'And I am grateful. To you and especially Laurie.' I wrote myself a reminder to buy her an expensive bouquet and deliver it on my next visit.

'Very well,' he replied. 'We'll keep things on review for now.'

'Thank you.' I put down the phone and made myself a strong coffee before tackling the kitchen. It was nearly lunchtime by the time I'd finished and I'll admit to a new-found grudging respect for Rosie. I knew she didn't really like me. I could tell that I wasn't her type of person and to be honest, she wasn't mine either, but she always did a good job. She was quick, efficient and the house looked immaculate after she'd finished. My efforts were pretty good. I took more care over the cushions than she did but it had taken a lot longer.

I was just sitting down to plan that evening's choir committee meeting before school pick-up when the doorbell rang. I opened the door to find Zoe standing in front of me. She looked me up and down and I realised that I was still wearing the hoody top and leggings I'd changed into to clean. Admittedly they were Super Dry but they were also covered in fluff.

'Babes, are you okay?' she asked, looking concerned.

'I'm fine, darling,' I replied, running a hand through my hair. 'My cleaner let me down so I had to do it myself.'

'Oh God, how awful for you,' purred Zoe with sympathy. 'So-o, I was just passing and thought I would pop in for a quick cuppa, if you've got time? Feels like ages,' she added, walking past me without waiting for a response. 'Oops, missed a bit.' She smiled, pointing a perfectly manicured finger-nail at a cobweb in the corner.

I followed her down the hall to the kitchen and flicked on the kettle. 'How are you?' she asked, looking round at my scattered papers.

'I'm good, thanks,' I replied. 'Busy but good.'

'Oh, yeah, you've got this community hall thing on the go, haven't you? You're so good, Caroline. I wouldn't bother if it were me but you're really – what's the word?' She studied me for a moment. 'You're so noble,' she decided. 'Taking a stand and sticking up for what you believe. I think it's great.'

'Thank you,' I said, filling two mugs with hot water.

'Personally, I think they should have knocked it down a long time ago. I mean, what's wrong with building new houses? There's a real crisis in London at the moment.'

I shrugged. 'It's important to the community. People want it to stay.'

'But do they actually use it?'

'Well yes, there's the toddler group—'

'Oh, heavens, is that still going? I remember taking Rufus once but never again. It was like a zoo and the place was filthy. It should be condemned.'

'So I take it I can't count on your support?'

She squeezed my hand. 'Oh, darling, of course I'll support you. You know that, but I just think you have to be realistic.'

'I'll bear it in mind.'

Zoe pouted at me. 'Aww, sorry babes, don't get huffy. I'll lend my support whenever I can. I'm just pretty biz at the mo, you know. I haven't got time to sing in a choir. Did I tell you that we're extending the kitchen and knocking through to the dining room?' I shook my head. 'It's a bloody nightmare, Caroline, I can tell you. Dust everywhere and absolute chaos and it all falls to me. Paul just isn't interested. Plus, Fired Earth delivered the wrong bloody tiles and I've just found out that John Lewis are out of stock of the Miele oven and we won't get delivery for twelve weeks. Twelve weeks!'

'Awful,' I commented.

'It really is,' nodded Zoe. 'Anyway, Amanda and I were only saying the other day that we should get together for drinkies soon. What do you say?'

'Sounds lovely.'

She beamed at me. 'Thanks for the tea,' she said, placing an almost full mug in the sink and kissing me on each cheek. 'Got to dash. I need to get to Fired Earth before pick-up – read them the riot act,' she laughed.

I glanced at my watch after she'd gone. There was just half an hour before pick-up and no time for me to prepare anything. I sighed as I arranged the chairs ready for the meeting. My phone buzzed with a call. I spotted Natalie's ID and answered feeling heavy with disappointment. No doubt she was going to cancel.

'Hi, Caroline? Just wondered if you wanted me to bring Matilda home? No point in us both going to the school.'

I was astonished. 'That would be very kind,' I replied. 'Thank you.'

'No worries. Could you just call the school to let them know?'

By the time Natalie, Doly and the kids arrived forty-five minutes later, I'd had time to scope out a website plan for Pamela's son and blue-sky some social media ideas for the campaign.

'Thank you so much, Natalie,' I said as I opened the door and let them in. 'That was really very kind of you to bring Matilda home.'

She laughed. 'It's no biggie, Caroline. Doly and I do it for each other all the time. Just holler if you ever need me to do it again. Or maybe you, Amanda and Zoe already help each other out?'

We didn't actually. Matilda had been round to play with Zoe's son Rufus once and declared him to be 'a very mean boy'. Amanda had a nanny so playdates never seemed to be an option. 'Sometimes,' I replied vaguely.

'Who else is coming apart from us?' she asked.

'Pamela. She offered to make a cake and I accepted, as I remembered what you said.'

Natalie gave me a smiling nod of approval. 'Very good.'

'Phil can't make it but Guy is coming later and I'm hoping that our local councillor, John Hawley, is able to come. He said he'd try.'

'Is he on our side?'

I nodded. 'He says he can't promise miracles but he'll support our bid to buy the hall.'

'He is a good man,' said Doly. 'He came to our aid when our shop was attacked by those hateful men.'

'What happened?' I asked.

'It was just after the London bombings. They tried to attack my husband with a baseball bat, called him bin Laden and said that our kind wasn't welcome here.'

'How terrible,' I declared.

Doly shrugged. 'It happens. It is just ignorance but it is frightening, particularly for the children.'

There was a knock at the door. 'I'll get it,' said Natalie.

'Thank you,' I said. 'I'll make some drinks and sort snacks for the children.'

'I'll help you,' offered Doly.

Natalie returned moments later followed by Pamela and John Hawley. 'You made it, John,' I said. 'It's good to see you.'

He was a short, dishevelled man of around fifty with uncombed white hair and an air of crumpled chaos. 'I wasn't allowed to miss it,' he said. 'This lady wouldn't let me,' he added, gesturing towards Pamela.

'Oh, get on with you,' said Pamela, batting him away. 'John and I go way back,' she explained. 'Been trying to fight for our community for years, haven't we, John?'

He nodded. 'As I said to you on the phone, Mrs Taylor, I am on your side but my political opponents at the council hold all the cards, sadly.'

'I know and I really appreciate your time,' I said. 'I just need to take these in to the children and then we can get started.' I carried a tray of drinks and biscuits into the living room. Woody was sitting on the sofa surrounded by Doly's three daughters and Matilda.

'Hello, I've brought you some snacks,' I said, putting down the tray.

'Oh yay!' cried Matilda, showing off. 'Come on, guys.'

She and the girls fell upon the biscuits whilst Woody sat back, glancing up with huge eyes. I felt a little sorry for him in amongst a largely female contingent. 'Would you like something, Woody?' I asked.

He shook his head. 'No thank you.'

'Woody is sad,' reported Matilda.

'Oh, I'm sorry to hear that,' I said, smiling at him. 'Can I help?'

'His mum and dad are splitting up,' reported Sadia, who was in Matilda and Woody's class at school.

'Well then, you must be very kind to him,' I told the girls.

'We're going to cheer him up with a make-over,' said Matilda.

'Are you sure that's what Woody wants?'

Woody shrugged, resigned to his fate. 'I don't mind.'

'See?' said Matilda triumphantly. 'Sadia, you and I can do his hair and Julia and Liza can do his make-up.'

'Can I do his nails?' squeaked one of the smaller girls.

'No, Liza, you're too little,' bossed Sadia.

'Be gentle,' I said. 'We're just in the kitchen if you need us.'

'Okay, Mummy,' beamed Matilda. *My model daughter. For now anyway.*

I returned to the kitchen. Doly and Natalie were laughing and joking as they made tea for the others.

Was I envious of the ease with which Natalie socialised? Everyone seemed to like her, despite her chaotic, flaky

*nature. Did I long to be liked as she was? Here comes
Natalie – she's great because she never takes anything
seriously and we all love a clown. Not a jot.* Humour is all
well and good until there's something serious to deal with.
That's where I come in. I've always been able to put aside
personal feelings when necessary. Some people may think
me stand-offish but I think it's one of my greatest strengths.

'Shall we start?' I said, ushering people towards the chairs.

I tried to stay positive during the meeting. It's something
I'm good at but John had obviously experienced these
things before and it was starting to become apparent that
our bid to buy the hall wasn't a straightforward one. 'Even
if you raise the money you need, there is no guarantee. You
have to prove that this community really needs the hall,
that it is vital for the area and to be honest, that people will
vote against my political opponents if they try to close it
down.'

'Money and power,' murmured Natalie.

John nodded. 'It may just seem like a community hall
to you but if it becomes a political hot potato, you're more
likely to win.'

'So what do we need? Petitions, Twitter campaigns,
local news?'

'And the rest. You need something national,' he said,
folding his arms.

'What, like a calendar where we all pose nude along
with strategically placed song-sheets and music stands?'
quipped Natalie. Everyone laughed.

'That's been done before,' I said, keeping my face
straight, irritated by Natalie's levity. 'We'll think of
something.'

'If you'll excuse me, I need to get to another meeting,'
said John. 'The council is threatening to close a women's
refuge and I've promised to lend my support.'

'Fighting battles on all fronts, eh John?' I observed.

'You have no idea,' he replied, rising wearily to his feet.

I followed him down the hall. 'Thank you for coming.'

He turned to face me. 'I have to be honest with you, Mrs Taylor. I think yours is a worthy cause but I can't honestly see you winning.'

My heart sank. 'I appreciate your honesty,' I nodded.

'It's the part of my job I hate the most,' he sighed.

I opened the front door to find Guy standing there, his finger hovered over the bell. He had the look of an excited teenager about him. 'Good timing as ever, Caroline,' he grinned.

'John, this is our choirmaster, Guy Henderson.'

'Pleased to meet you,' said John. 'I'll be in touch, Mrs Taylor. Goodbye.'

'Bye,' I said, feeling heavy with disappointment.

'Bye,' echoed Guy, before turning to me. 'Caroline, I've had a brilliant idea,' he said, pulling a flyer from his pocket. 'Is everyone still here?' he asked, looking towards the kitchen.

'Go through,' I answered, standing aside to let him pass.

I followed him to the kitchen. Everyone smiled as he entered. He had that affect. There was a great energy and positivity about Guy Henderson. I liked that about him. 'Good evening, ladies,' he smiled. 'I have in my hand a piece of paper –' he held up the flyer for us all to see '– which I believe could be the solution to our problem.'

'Is it a cheque for a million pounds?' asked Natalie. *She really couldn't help herself.*

'What is it?' asked Pamela.

'This, my cake-baking genius,' said Guy, 'is a flyer for the Community Choir Championships!'

'The what?' frowned Natalie.

Guy grinned. 'It's a competition to find the best community choir, with the final to be hosted by that choir guy, Andrew Munday, at the Royal Albert Hall!'

'Wow!' I said. 'I don't suppose there's a prize of half a million pounds up for grabs, is there?'

Guy pulled a face. 'Now that would be too good to be true. Sadly not, but it would put our campaign on the map.'

'True. How do we enter?' Visions of vast concert halls packed with cheering crowds filled my mind.

Guy studied the flyer. 'There are two heats – one for regional London in Croydon, one for London as a whole at St Martin-in-the-Fields. Four London choirs go through, and the final is on July the twentieth.'

'Yay! A choir trip to Croydon!' cried Natalie. More laughter. *Stop laughing. It only encourages her.* 'Listen, I don't want to be a party pooper,' she said. 'But do we honestly think we've got a snowball in hell's chance of winning this?'

Ignore the naysayers and keep going, Caroline. Just like Dad used to tell you. 'Positive belief,' I said. 'All we need is to believe.'

'And rehearse like mad,' said Guy.

'And pray,' added Doly.

'And bribe the judges,' said Natalie. I stared at her, outraged. 'I'm kidding,' she laughed, patting me on the arm. 'I warned you about my sense of humour, Caroline.' *Yes, you did, I just didn't realise that you would make absolutely everything into a joke.*

'Are we up for it then?' asked Guy.

'What have we got to lose?' said Pamela. 'It's got to be worth a try and even if we don't win, we might save the hall, which is why we're here, after all.'

'I know that we can make it,' said Natalie.

'Really?' I asked in surprise.

'Yeah, because we've got—' She started to click her fingers and dance, singing the chorus to 'Something Inside So Strong'. The assembled company, including Guy, laughed and sang along. *Honestly, did this woman take anything seriously? Was her whole life just a huge joke with endless opportunity for punchlines?*

'Oh, come on, Caroline.' Natalie grinned, noticing that I wasn't joining in. 'We need all the rehearsals we can get.'

I sighed before turning to Guy. 'We'll need to sort a strict rota and ramp up the media campaign. Doly, are you happy to phone all the media contacts?' She nodded. 'Pamela, you're sure your son can sort the website?'

'Of course,' grinned Pamela. 'He'll do whatever his mum asks.'

'That's great. Thanks, everyone. Guy, shall we sort the rehearsals now, along with a list of songs, and then I can e-mail them round later?'

'Sounds like a good plan,' agreed Guy.

At that moment, Woody appeared in the kitchen doorway, surrounded by his posse of girls. He looked an absolute fright, his hair sticking up from his head in a punk style, his face covered in bright-pink blusher, electric-blue eyeshadow and shocking red lipstick. His nails were an alarming shade of blue.

Natalie squawked with hysterical laughter. 'Woody, you look fantastic – like a young David Bowie!' she cried. I must say she was much calmer about it than I would have been.

He rolled his eyes but laughed along. 'I think he looks bootiful,' said Liza, the smallest of Doly's daughters. She planted a kiss on his arm.

'Come on, heart-throb,' laughed Natalie. 'Let's get you home.'

I followed Natalie and Woody to the door. Woody skipped down the garden path. 'Natalie?' She turned and smiled at me. 'I just wanted to say that if you ever need me to have Woody, just ask. He and Matilda get on so well, it would be no problem at all.'

She looked pleasantly surprised. 'Thank you, Caroline. That's very kind.'

I nodded, feeling pleased for having offered. 'Are things, er, okay?' I asked. *Please don't give me details – I'm merely being polite.*

She glanced back at Woody before answering. 'We're starting the counselling tomorrow,' she replied, giving a thumbs-up before backing down the garden. 'Wish me luck!'

'Er, good luck,' I said as I waved her off.

After Pamela, Doly and the girls had left, Guy and I sat at my kitchen table drinking yet more tea as we discussed rehearsals and songs. 'I meant to tell you, I saw you the other day,' I said.

'Oh yes?' he replied, his eyes fixed on the plan.

'At St Bartholomew's. That was your mother, wasn't it?'

He hesitated for a moment, his pencil poised over the page. 'It was,' he said after a pause. 'So how do you think this looks?' he added, pushing the paper towards me. He seemed to want to change the subject so I didn't pry further. I understood this. I didn't like others knowing my business either.

'It looks great,' I said. 'Do you honestly think we've got a chance?'

'I don't know but it's got to be worth a try, hasn't it?'

'So why are you doing this?' I asked him.

He looked at me and I saw a sincerity in his eyes that I recognised. 'Probably for much the same reasons as you. I grew up round here and I don't like the way communities are being plundered for the sake of saving a few grand.' I smiled. I understood and admired this. He glanced at his watch. 'Yikes, I'm late. Sorry, Caroline, but I need to go. I'll see you for the next rehearsal and I was also thinking we should organise a gig, just something small scale in a pub so that we get used to singing in public. The first round is in a month.'

'I'll get onto it in the morning,' I smiled.

He nodded before gathering his things and hurrying down the hall. 'No need to show me out. I'll see you later,' he called over his shoulder.

After he'd gone, I poured myself a glass of wine, feeling excited about our plans. Matilda appeared in the kitchen doorway. 'I'm hungry,' she complained.

'Oh, heavens!' I cried. 'You haven't had any supper!' *What was happening to me? I always cooked from scratch.*

'Is that wine?' she asked, glaring at the glass.

'Just a small glass, darling. Now how about fish fingers?' *Plan B. There's always a plan B, although it's rarely required in my world.*

She looked confused. 'I thought we only had those when friends come round for tea as a treat.'

'Well, how about a Tuesday-night treat?'

'O-kay,' she said with some reluctance. 'We usually have pasta on a Tuesday. I like pasta.'

'Oh, for God's sake, Matilda, do you want the bloody fish fingers or not?' I cried. *Heavens! Where did that come from?*

She stared at me for a second before her face crumpled. 'You shouted at me! And you swore! When's Daddy coming home?'

'I'm sorry, Matilda,' I said, panicking at my sudden loss of control. 'That was very wrong of Mummy. I'll cook you pasta if you like,' I added, holding out my arms and trying to fold her into an embrace. She shrugged me off.

'Can I have chips?' she sniffed.

'What's the magic word?' *Calm, Caroline. You can get control of this situation. Just stay calm.*

She rolled her eyes. 'Please.'

'Okay.' *That's better. Order is restored.*

'And can I watch TV with tea as a Tuesday-night treat?'

How could I refuse? Matilda knew which buttons to press and most of them were labelled, 'guilty mother'. 'Yes, all right, but just for tonight.'

I turned on the oven and shook fish fingers and chips onto a baking tray. I looked at the glass of wine sitting on the side and in one quick move, I poured the rest of it down the sink, feeling instant relief. Natalie might need a glass or two of wine to drown her sorrows every night but I was made of sterner stuff.

CHAPTER NINE

NATALIE

I arrived early for once, before Dan in fact. The counselling centre was one of those modern, comfortable buildings with lots of light, airy rooms and spongy, uncomfortable chairs. As I sat in the waiting room, my stomach skipped with anxiety. I had felt positive in the run-up to today but now I was a frenzy of nerves. I kept telling myself that all would be well, that admitting the problem was halfway to solving it. The trouble was that I hadn't actually identified the problem. I didn't have a problem. We did because Dan had decided we did. Thoughts whizzed and pinged around my brain like balls on a pinball machine, never quite hitting their target, leaving me dazed.

Get a grip, Natalie. All you have to do is be honest, let Dan work through his issues, finish the course, pick up the certificate and go back to a life of – a life of what? Domestic bliss? No such thing. Domestic average, more like.

A life of muddling through, being tired but being content. Life wasn't perfect and accepting that meant you could enjoy a sort of happy. That had to be good enough. That was what I wanted, anyway.

Dan arrived five minutes before the session was due to start. He seemed surprised that I was already there. I was known for my lateness, whereas he was always on time.

He leant down to kiss me on the cheek. His face felt chilly and I caught the whiff of his scent. He didn't wear after-shave. It was the smell of him and it made my heart ache.

'You're on time,' he teased.

'Of course,' I replied, 'this is important.' He glanced at me and I gave him a small smile. I was determined to do this properly. I was a woman who would joke her way through anything but this didn't feel funny somehow. This was where it got serious.

'Mr and Mrs Garfield?' said a female voice. I felt my spirits drop as I turned to face an attractive young girl, who was probably in her mid twenties. As wrong as it may sound, I wished that she were a balding man in his fifties with life experience and less-impressive breasts. I rose to my feet as she held out her hand for me to shake. It felt tiny, like a child's. She ushered us towards the door with a smile. 'We're in room thirteen just down the hall.'

'I hope that's not a portent of doom,' I joked. *Shut up, Natalie, we're taking this seriously, remember?*

As we entered the room and took our seats in front of her, I started to feel sick. How had my life reached this point? How could this be happening? *Positive thoughts, Nat. Go to your happy place.* I looked towards Dan. He saw my fear and reached out to squeeze my hand. I noticed the woman glance at this gesture. He moved it away as soon as he saw her looking.

'My name is Abigail Waters. I'll be your counsellor over the course of all our meetings. Today is about me trying to understand what you need, to assess your expectations and see what it is you hope to get out of this. Then we can discuss a programme of sessions. Is that okay?' I glanced at Dan, who was nodding, so I joined in. 'Great, so maybe we could talk about what brings you here today. Who would like to start?'

Dan and I exchanged glances. I could see that he was unsure of what to say and it irritated me. He was the one who had suggested this, for crying out loud. Did I have to do everything? I turned to Abigail. 'He told me that he doesn't love me any more.' It sounded ridiculous – the kind of thing a child would say to their mother because another kid was being mean to them.

'I see. And have you had any discussions about the reasons for this?' she asked.

I turned my gaze to Dan. For a moment he looked unrecognisable – shrunken, dejected, ashamed. I felt a rising sense of panic as I looked back at Abigail. 'The thing is, we still get on just as we always did. We talk about our days, share time with our son. Nothing has changed except Dan's not living with us at the moment and for some reason, he can't tell me what's wrong.'

Abigail nodded but didn't comment on what I'd said. Somehow this annoyed me. Instead she turned to Dan. 'Do you have anything you'd like to add?'

He stared at his feet and nodded. He couldn't look at me. 'Everything that Nat says is true,' he confirmed.

Abigail nodded again. She was so calm and measured.

I wasn't. 'Is that all you can say?' I cried. 'Are you just going to sit there barely speaking? Are you going to continue to ignore my feelings with your pathetic silence?' I spat the words.

'I'm sorry,' he whispered.

'Natalie, I can see how angry you are. Could you tell me what you would like to get out of these sessions?' asked Little Miss Reasonable.

Mrs Unreasonable glared at her. 'I want my life back!' I raged. 'I want to know what the fuck this is all about and I want to get my life back. For the sake of my son and me.'

She nodded. 'I understand and I will do all I can to help you. What I am seeing is a communication problem.'

'No shit, Sherlock,' I hissed. 'Sorry,' I said with immediate regret.

'It's fine,' she replied. 'I am going to suggest a series of individual and pair sessions so that we can get both parties communicating properly. Do you think that will work for you both?'

Dan glanced up and nodded. I shrugged. 'I guess so.'

'Good,' she said. 'So I am going to give you a couple of questionnaires to fill in confidentially and return to me. Then I'll set up the necessary appointments, okay?'

'Thank you,' replied Dan.

'Fine,' I said.

As I read the questions in the waiting room, it occurred to me that my marriage was now being determined by the kind of quizzes I used to pore over with my friends as a teenager.

Q6: The most important thing to keep a relationship fresh is?

I looked over at Dan, who was staring down at the questions and making the occasional mark on the paper. In a time before this, I would have nudged him and quipped, 'Oi, is the answer to Question 6 "clean pants"?' We would have chuckled and all would have been well. However, there was nothing amusing about this situation and by the time I had filled out both questionnaires, my boiling anger had been reduced to a simmer and I felt exhausted. I handed my paper in to the receptionist, who promised that Abigail would be in touch. I nodded and headed towards the exit without looking back.

I heard Dan hurrying after me but kept walking. 'Nat, wait!' he called.

I walked out of the front door, onto the street. He caught up with me, grabbing my arm. 'Please, Nat.'

I turned on him. 'That was humiliating!' I hissed. 'YOU wanted to come for counselling, Dan. YOU. Not me. And so we go, but you don't speak. Do you have any idea how that made me feel?'

'I'm sorry,' he implored. 'I'm so sorry. I know I'm not being fair but I'm just struggling at the moment. Nat, please.'

I looked into his eyes and realised that he was crying. I wanted to stay angry, really I did, but he was still my husband and I still loved him. I put my arms around him and held him, like a child. I wondered at the pair of us, standing on the street like this, a weeping man and a confused woman. 'Why can't you just talk to me, Dan? Why can't you tell me how you feel?'

'Honestly?' he replied, pulling back from our embrace.

'Honestly,' I said.

'Because the truth is, I don't know how I feel at the moment.'

I patted his shoulders. 'Okay. Okay then. Talk to that woman-child in there,' I said, gesturing behind us. 'See if she can't inject some youthful wisdom into our lives.'

He nodded weakly. 'Thank you. I think it will really help.'

'I hope so.'

He glanced at his watch. 'Listen, I would suggest a coffee but I've got to go and meet someone, so—'

I nodded. 'You go. Are you still okay for Thursday?'

'Absolutely. I look forward to Thursdays.'

Me too, I thought, but not for the same reasons. I watched him head off along the street, worrying that what I thought was a bump in the road of my marriage had turned into a bloody big pot-hole. I felt my phone buzz in my pocket with a call and pulled it from my pocket. That was a mistake.

'Natalie! Where are you?' barked Caroline.

I glanced back towards the centre. 'I've just left the counselling session and I'm off home to work.'

'How quickly can you get to Croydon?' she asked, ignoring everything I had just said.

'Er, why?'

'Because, Radio Croydon want to interview us at noon about the community hall campaign.'

'Us?'

'Yes! They want to talk to me because I'm campaign manager and you because you're Natalie Garfield. So I'll see you there at 11.45, okay? I'll text you the address.'

And with that she was gone and apparently I had just over an hour to get to Croydon. On reflection, I should have phoned her back and told her that I couldn't go. In fact, I should have said 'no' to Caroline right at the start of this whole community hall debacle. I had too much going on, too many balls juggling above my head and I was starting to lose my grip on a few of them. Actually, I was starting to lose my grip full stop. Unfortunately, 'no' wasn't a word that Caroline understood, which is why I found myself hurrying along the street towards the Tube.

I spied a coffee shop on a corner by the station and decided that I needed a shot or six of caffeine to get me through the next few hours. And that was when I saw them. Dan had his back to me but I could see the woman. She was beautiful with wild, curly hair and huge eyes. She must have been in her late twenties and she was staring into my husband's eyes as he held her hand. I froze. This was the moment when I was supposed to react, when I was supposed to storm in there and confront them. I was meant to stand in front of them, furious and magnificent, demanding to know what the fuck they thought they were playing at.

I, Natalie Garfield, was the wronged party and I would seek my revenge. It's strange because that's what I always

thought I would do. In the film of my life, I am tough –
I am Wonder Woman, smart, kick-ass and in charge.
In reality, I am really quite tired, usually in need of caffeine
and keen to let someone else take charge. Which is why
I turned and ran away. I sat on the Tube, feeling numb and
bruised, my mind racing again. This was obviously what
Dan was trying to work out – it was a clear 'her' or 'me'
kind of situation.

Of course, at this stage I really should have gone straight
home. I should have asked Doly to collect Woody, shut the
front door, watched a weepy movie, eaten my body-weight
in chocolate digestives and given in to a fit of hysterical
crying. So it was strange when I found myself getting on
the train to Croydon. Apparently, my heart wanted to give
in but my head had decided that even spending an hour
or two in the company of Caroline 'less empathy than my
fingernail' Taylor was better than letting me wallow in self-
pity. Bloody brain.

As we left the radio station two hours later, I could see
Caroline watching me. I knew what she was thinking.

*Is Natalie okay or should I phone a mental health
professional?*

I was wondering the same thing myself.

'I need a drink,' I said, crossing the road, not waiting
to see if she followed me. She did follow me and
moments later we found ourselves in one of the more
unprepossessing pubs on earth. The carpet was brown, the
walls were brown, the bar was brown and sticky. 'What do
you want?' I asked as I approached the bar.

'I don't usually drink at lunchtime,' she replied.

'Suit yourself,' I said. 'A large gin and tonic please, not
too much tonic.'

The barman, whose neck was the same width as two of
my calves put together, glared at Caroline in a way that

could only be described as hostile. 'Just a diet tonic for me, please,' she offered.

He fetched our drinks and placed them on the bar without a word or a smile. I looked up at him. 'Three eighty,' he growled.

'Please,' corrected Caroline. I almost laughed at her gumption but she held the man's gaze as he scowled back at her.

'Please,' he added.

'Manners maketh man,' she murmured, as I led us to the least filthy table I could find, ignored the crumbs underneath it and sat on a chair facing the rest of the pub. It was a huge place with half a dozen screens showing sports news that no-one was watching. An elderly couple sat by the window eating what looked like fish and chips. There was a scattering of unhappy-looking lone drinkers, mostly men, nursing pints and crosswords. It was a depressing scene. I took a large swig of my drink and welcomed the anaesthetising sensation of alcohol.

'So,' began Caroline, watching my face, 'how do you think that went?'

I shrugged. 'Okay, I guess.' *'Okay' may have been a tad inaccurate. 'Car crash' or 'bloody disaster' were probably more appropriate, but then the world always looks brighter after a sip of gin.*

She nodded. 'I mean, I appreciate why you decided to break into song. It illustrated our point very well, but you were a little pitchy.'

Everyone's a critic. I took another gulp of my drink and looked her in the eye. 'Well, I'm sorry. I was nervous and the DJ put me on the spot by asking us what we like to sing.' In truth, I was very wound up and hadn't even meant to sing – it had sort of come out, like a nervous reflex. I was just relieved that no-one I knew was likely to hear it.

'Okay, so it wouldn't get me a place on *The X Factor* but it was entertaining. The DJ loved it.'

'I suppose,' she observed. 'However, I do think it would have been better if you hadn't sworn.'

'I only said "bollocks".'

'On live radio.'

'No-one listens to Radio Croydon. And anyway, you didn't tell me that MP was going to be there. He was bloody patronising.'

'I know, but you probably shouldn't have called him a supercilious twit.'

'I don't agree with his politics and I hate the way his government insists on selling off everything that makes life better, like refuges, libraries and community halls. He annoyed me,' I added, folding my arms.

'I think we all heard how much he annoyed you, Natalie,' said Caroline, her face serious. 'It's just that you need to keep calm in situations like these. Otherwise we lose popular support.'

All right, Alistair Campbell. It was Radio sodding Croydon, not Question Time. *Enough of the spin-doctor act.* I glared at her. 'If you don't like what I say then don't ask me to come. In fact, just don't ask me at all. I've got too much shit to deal with at the moment. I haven't got time for this.'

She stared at me in surprise. She'd touched a nerve and for once she seemed to realise it. 'Did the counselling not go as you hoped then?'

It was my turn to be surprised. *Do I detect a note of actual concern in her voice? Surely not.* I sighed. I needed to talk to someone about this and in the absence of Oprah, Caroline Taylor would have to do. 'The counselling was okay but on my way over here I saw Dan with another woman.'

Caroline didn't seem surprised. 'And who was she?'

'I have no idea.'

'What do you mean? Surely you confronted them?'

I did confront them but only in my mind. Does that count? 'Er no, not exactly.'

'Natalie! Why didn't you go right in there and demand to know what was happening?'

'I don't know, okay? I just don't know! I'm scared or stupid or weak. Or probably a combination of all three.'

Caroline fixed me with a look. 'Shall I tell you what I'm going to do?'

– Contradict my damning assessment of myself?

– Beat up Dan and his floozie for me?

'What?' I asked, feeling a little scared.

'I'm going to come home with you, help you pick out an outfit – you know, the one that makes you feel powerful?'

'Oh, sorry, Caroline, my Wonder Woman outfit is at the dry cleaner's.'

She fixed me with a stern look. 'Natalie, if you want to save your marriage, you need to start taking life seriously.'

I shrugged my shoulders in reply.

She seemed satisfied as she continued. 'I will collect Woody from school and look after him while you go and meet Dan. Don't give him a get-out. Just tell him when and where you're meeting and then stride in there and demand to know what's going on.'

'Are you sure that's a good idea?' *Because I think going home and hiding under the duvet until everything's sorted is a better option.*

'Do you want to save your marriage or not?'

Well, when you put it like that. 'Of course.'

'Then this is what needs to happen. You have to know where you stand before you can solve it. Trust me. This will work.'

We were interrupted by my phone ringing. 'Oh, crap,' I said as I noticed the caller ID. It was my agent. 'Hi, Barbara,' I answered, wincing, ready for a telling-off.

'Dear heart!' she boomed. 'I have good news.'

'Really?'

'Really. You're an internet sensation, my cherub. Calling that MP a fascist chump could be the best thing you've ever done. You're a heroine of the people.'

'Oh. Right.' This was an unexpected turn of events.

'So you're probably going to be quite interesting to the media. I shall do my best to police but you can expect to feature in *Metro*, *Mail Online* and quite a few others either this evening or tomorrow. Congratulations. I'll give them your number, okay. And Natalie?'

'Mhmm?'

'Next time you plan to take a political stand, do me a favour and give me a bit of effing notice, will you? I don't like surprises.'

'Of course. Sorry.' I hung up.

'What was that about?' asked Caroline.

'Apparently my interview has hit the media – must be a quiet news day.'

'Oh, but this is wonderful,' cried Caroline, leaping up and almost knocking over our drinks. 'Well done!'

'Thank you,' I said, feeling anything other than jubilant.

'Right, onwards and upwards! We need to get you spruced up before you go and meet Dan.'

'Are you sure this is the right thing to do?' I asked, staring at her imploringly. *Please say, 'No, going home and eating an entire tub of Cookie Dough ice cream is far more sensible.'*

'Of course. You have to keep fighting, Natalie. You can't give up.'

Can't I? Why do I have to keep on fighting?

Hearing that your husband doesn't love you any more is heart-breaking but realising that he loves someone else instead of you, that you have been effectively evicted from that place in his heart and replaced, is devastating. Who wants to rake through that steaming pile of dirt, to receive formal confirmation that your love is no longer required?

You are no longer the one and only. You're just alone and lonely.

'Come on, chop, chop,' breezed Caroline as we made our way to the tram stop. I could see that she wasn't going to let me get out of this. 'Face the fear and do it anyway,' she said.

Facing the fear was just about right, as well as dreading what I would find out along the way.

CHAPTER TEN

CAROLINE

The pub was quite busy as I arrived with Zoe and Amanda. I was grateful for their support. I had known them both since Matilda was small and we shared a similar sense of what was important. Plus, they both had impeccable taste in clothes and furnishings. Amanda was an interior designer by trade and always happy to give advice on the latest styles. We approached the bar. Tony the landlord smiled as he recognised me.

'Hi, Caroline. Can I get you ladies a drink?' We ordered Prosecco. Tony eyed me as he poured three glasses. 'Great turn-out this evening. It's usually pretty empty on a Thursday night but you've attracted quite a following.'

I smiled. 'We've got a very successful media campaign.'

He laughed. 'Yes, I heard about the radio show – about time someone stood up for the community.' He pushed the glasses towards us. 'This one's on the house.'

'That's very kind – thank you,' I said. 'Are the others here already?'

He nodded. 'They're setting up through that doorway in the next room. If tonight goes well, I'll be booking you every week,' he joked.

'Shall we go through?' I said to the girls.

'You go, babes,' said Zoe. 'Mands and I will sit in here for now, 'kay?'

I nodded and walked through to the other room. Until relatively recently, The Goldfinch Tavern had been one of those London pubs that I had always been too terrified to enter, rather like the pub Natalie and I had the misfortune to go into yesterday. However, about a year ago, it had been bought by a chain, who had renovated it to look like a trendy local with exposed brick, painted wood floors and expensive artisan beers. It was just what the area needed.

'Evening, Caroline,' smiled Guy as I entered the room. 'This is great, isn't it?'

I nodded. Pamela bustled over. 'Ooh, Caroline, I heard you and Nat on the radio. You were wonderful, really wonderful.'

'Thank you. Is Natalie here yet?

'I think she popped to the loo,' she said.

'I'll just go and check she's okay.'

I followed the sign to the toilets. Natalie was standing at the mirror, putting on lipstick. I was pleased to see that she was making an effort. She glanced up as I entered. 'Come to check up on me?' *Oh dear. She'd already had a couple of drinks. That didn't bode well.*

'I was wondering how you were after yesterday?' I said. 'It was difficult to talk with the children there.' This was an understatement. It had been chaos and Natalie had seemed in a hurry when she picked up Woody. She had told me that it was all fine. I wasn't sure if I believed her.

She sighed. 'Apparently, the girl is a daughter of one of Dan's old college friends. He's known her since she was small and ironically he was counselling her. She'd fallen out with her parents and it was Uncle Dan to the rescue!'

'Do you believe him?' I asked. *Because I'm not sure that I do.*

'I've decided that if I think about any of it too much, I will go insane.' She puckered her lips and blotted them together.

'So you do believe him?'

She fixed me with a look. 'I don't think I have a choice.'

Doly appeared at the door. 'Curtain call!' she cried.

'Are you sure you're okay?' I asked Natalie on the way out.

'I'm fine, Caroline. Really. The show must go on!' she said with a bitter smile.

We gathered in one corner of the pub. I looked into the audience to see if Amanda and Zoe had come through but they were nowhere to be seen.

It was fine. At least they'd turned up. It didn't matter where they sat. Besides, it was time to focus on the job at hand.

I was surprised to realise that I was feeling a little nervous. This was very unlike me.

'There's a photographer from the local paper here tonight,' whispered Doly.

'Oh, I wish I'd known. I'd have washed my hair,' grinned Jim, stroking his bald head. Everyone laughed.

'Okay, shall we begin with a gentle warm-up? How about "S.O.S."? Nice and easy to get us started?' said Guy. We nodded in agreement. I found myself standing between Natalie and Doly. 'So, it's going to be different to rehearsals because of the background noise but don't let that put you off. Breathe and sing from down here,' he said, gesturing towards his diaphragm.

He started the backing track and we were off. People looked up from their tables as we began to sing. I noticed them smiling and nodding along to the music. I did my best to channel my nerves into positive energy.

'Great,' said Guy, when we'd finished. 'You just need to up the volume a tad and remember to smile but otherwise great. So, order of songs will be "California Dreamin'", "Chasing Cars", "Something Inside So Strong", "Everybody's Changing" and "Halo".'

It wasn't an absolutely perfect performance. The harmonies were a little off during 'Chasing Cars', we were out of time with the backing track for 'Halo' and it was clear that we had quite a bit to do on 'Something Inside So Strong' in time for the south-east London choir heats, but I have to confess that I enjoyed every second.

I hadn't expected to feel quite so uplifted. It made me realise how rare it was to feel like that nowadays, as if I'd forgotten how to enjoy myself. Usually, I was too busy worrying about my mother or Matilda to relax. What were people in my situation called? 'The sandwich generation.' Too caught up with raising our children and fretting about our parents to enjoy our lives any more. Stuck in the middle, anxious, tired and never having any fun. But this was fun. This was wonderful fun – singing, entertaining, being part of something joyous and special. I loved it.

I noticed Natalie wipe away a tear at the end of 'Something Inside So Strong'. I was about to reach out a hand to touch her arm but I thought better of it. It would have probably made things worse.

'That was brilliant,' murmured Doly as we finished. The crowd were cheering and calling for an encore. Jim was waving and bowing. Guy turned to address the crowd.

'Thank you very much,' he said. 'It's just a short set tonight as we haven't been together long, but we would welcome any new attendees and please, if you haven't signed the petition to save Hope Street Community Hall, do so tonight. Tell your friends, tell your local councillor, your MP and your mum that we want the hall to stay.'

There was a cheer of agreement. Guy continued, 'We'll be competing in the Community Choir Championships in a couple of months' time and we really need your support to convince the council to keep the hall open for local people. Thank you.' Everyone applauded and Guy turned back to us. 'I think we deserve a drink, don't you?'

I followed Natalie and Doly into the bar area. I noticed that Amanda and Zoe were sitting at a table in the far corner. I was a little hurt that they hadn't bothered to come in to listen but brushed it aside as they waved for me to join them.

Amanda topped up my glass. 'Sounded sublime, darling,' she said. 'And your choirmaster is a real dish, isn't he?'

I laughed. 'You're terrible, Mands. He's just started as the music teacher at school.'

'Wow, I must get up to the playground a bit more often,' she purred.

Zoe and I exchanged amused glances. 'Is that the woman you nearly ran over one day then?' asked Zoe, gesturing towards Natalie.

I nodded. 'She was in a bit of a state. She's got problems with her marriage. She saw her estranged husband with another woman yesterday but apparently he claimed that she was, "just a friend",' I said, making inverted commas with my fingers. *Why did I say that? That was low.* I immediately wished I'd kept quiet as Amanda and Zoe leant in like hyenas going for a kill, feasting on gossip.

'Ooh,' winced Amanda. 'Who would honestly believe a line like that? Mind you, she's a bit all over the place, isn't she?'

I looked over to the bar. It was clear that Natalie had over-indulged on the Prosecco. She was laughing and swaying drunkenly as she talked to Doly and Guy.

At one stage she had to grab his arm to steady herself. He was very chivalrous but it was rather an outrageous display.

'Still, I'm not surprised after hearing her on that radio interview – it was a little OTT. Are you sure you know what you're getting into, darling?' asked Zoe.

I took a sip of my drink. 'She's managed to get the campaign noticed so it's all to the good, I suppose.'

'No such thing as bad publicity, eh darl?' said Amanda.

As if on cue, Natalie appeared at our table. 'Hellooo!' she cried, lunging forwards and wrapping her arms around me. I stiffened at her touch. 'Ooh sorry, I forgot you don't do physical contact,' she giggled, taking a step back.

I noticed Amanda staring with a look of horror on her face. She'd never been one to conceal her inner feelings. Natalie noticed it too. 'Oh, hello, Amanda, isn't it? Are you okay? You look as if you've just smelt a turd.' She sniggered and took another sip of her drink. Amanda raised her eyebrows at me.

'You're not very friendly, are you?' she slurred before turning to Zoe. 'What about you? Are you friendly?'

'Natalie,' I said. 'You're embarrassing yourself.' *And me.*

Natalie stared at me. 'Oh sorry, Caroline – are you not talking to me because you're with your little school-mum clique? Don't I fit in? Will you only talk to me when you need something?'

'Look, we were having a private chat and you've interrupted, which is very rude. Your husband may be having an affair but that's no excuse,' said Amanda, folding her arms.

Thanks, Amanda. You've dropped me in it now.

Natalie froze. She stared at me, hurt and disappointment etched all over her face 'How dare you? I told you that in confidence, Caroline.' I felt my stomach dip with guilt.

Guy appeared by our table and touched her gently on the arm. 'Nat? Why don't I walk you home?'

'Natalie…' I began.

She held up one hand. 'Don't, Caroline. Just don't.' She turned to Guy. 'Right, I need to go and have some fun. Are you coming?' She headed for the door. Guy stared at me for a second before turning and following her. I noticed Doly and Pamela looking over and tried to give them a reassuring smile before turning back to Amanda and Zoe.

'Dear me,' said Amanda, refilling our glasses and taking a sip from hers. 'Some people are so touchy. Mind you, she seemed to have your choirmaster in the palm of her hand so I'm sure she'll be fine.' Zoe laughed. I pretended to join in with a weak smile but really I was feeling guilty – horribly, horribly guilty.

Another bottle of Prosecco between the three of us helped to numb some of my worries but my guilt still niggled. I said goodbye to Amanda and Zoe on the corner before heading off towards home.

As Amanda kissed me on both cheeks, she said, 'Good luck with the crazy bitch.' Zoe laughed.

For a moment I was transported back to secondary school and a girl called Mary who I used to like. She had been a quiet, studious sort but with a biting sense of humour. We were pretty inseparable for the first three years of secondary school until a girl called Danielle joined. She already had an impressive bust and claimed to have given blow-jobs to at least three boys. There was something about her that seemed so mysterious and dangerous and I started to form a friendship of sorts with her. One day, Mary and I were sitting at lunch when Danielle appeared at our side.

'Mind if I join you?' she said, sitting down without waiting for an answer, stretching her long legs out under the table and flicking her hair.

I noticed Mary flinch but I said as casually as I could, 'Course not.'

She took out a foil-wrapped package. Inside was a tortilla wrap filled with what looked like chicken. It seemed so much more exotic than my boring curled-bread cheese sandwiches. At that moment, I wanted to be her friend so badly, for her to like me and to unlock the secrets of her exciting world. 'So-o,' she began, picking out a piece of chicken and popping it into her mouth. 'How many boys have you given hand-jobs to?'

I noticed Mary flick her gaze nervously in my direction. We had no frame of reference for this kind of chat. We were only fourteen and our knowledge of sex didn't extend beyond Mrs Cooper-Rowe's embarrassed teachings of what her lisp forced her to pronounce as 'thexual intercourth'. Yes, we read *Cosmopolitan*, our eyes and brains boggling with the complexity of G-spots and masturbation but we didn't understand it. We rarely came into contact with boys and when our school organised discos with the local boys' grammar, we were always far to terrified to talk to them, whilst they were far too immature to do anything apart from skid across the floor on their knees.

But whilst poor Mary wanted the ground to swallow her up at this moment, I wanted to know everything. It was time. I needed this.

'Oh, just a couple,' I said vaguely. Mary frowned at my lie but I couldn't stop now. 'How about you?'

'Seventeen,' replied Danielle. 'Although one of them was my older cousin, which I know is a bit gross but actually, it's not illegal.'

'Probably should be,' observed Mary. I held my breath as I noticed her clap a hand over her mouth. Danielle fixed her with a narrow-eyed stare. It was the stare of big cats when they've locked onto their prey.

'So, Mary, Mary, quite contrary, how many boys have you blown?'

Mary flushed scarlet from her neck to her forehead. 'That's none of your business,' she said, trying to keep her cool. She glanced at me, the desperation plain for all to see. *Help me,* said the look, *you're supposed to be my friend.*

We have to face choices throughout our lives, some big, some small. So when I flicked a smile at Danielle and then turned back to Mary and said, 'It's only a joke,' I had made a choice. I had chosen Danielle over Mary – the lion over the gazelle. Unsurprisingly, Mary never spoke to me again and was haunted by the rhyme which the mean girls chanted as she passed.

'*Mary, Mary, quite contrary, how many boys have you blown?*'

I never joined in but I was always with them, which is basically the same thing.

I think that's why, when Amanda dismissed Natalie as a 'crazy bitch', I didn't laugh. I just smiled goodbye and headed off up the road.

It was a mild night and I felt the promise of summer evenings ahead as I noticed nodding crowds of tulips in the gardens along Hope Street.

I let myself in through the front door and stood in the kitchen for a second drinking a glass of water. I took out my phone, my mind set on texting Natalie. My fingers hovered over the buttons. What should I say? I wasn't one for apologising without good reason but I knew when I'd over-stepped the mark. I typed,

Dear Natalie, apologies if you took offence,

before replacing it with,

apologies for any offence caused.

I stared at the words for a second before deleting the lot. These things were best dealt with face to face and not when you were a little drunk. I refilled my water glass and climbed the stairs.

Matilda was just coming out of the bathroom. 'You're very late, Mummy, it's the middle of the night,' she observed, scandalised. I laughed, reached forwards and kissed the top of her head. It was warm and comforting. 'Ooh, you stink of booze,' she said.

'Where did you learn that word?' I asked.

She shrugged. 'Daddy.'

'Do you want me to tuck you in?'

'No thanks,' she said before turning on her heels back towards her bedroom. My heart gave a leap of longing. *Please let me tuck you in, let me smooth your hair and kiss you goodnight.* She shut the door behind her and that was that.

I opened the door to our bedroom. 'Hey,' I said as I noticed Oliver propped up in bed, staring at his iPad.

'Hey you,' he replied. I sat next to him on the bed. He continued to stare at the iPad so I wheedled my way in front of it. He laughed. 'Oh, you want some attention, do you?'

'Yes, please,' I said, snuggling closer.

'Are you drunk?'

'A little,' I said, wrapping my arms around his chest. He kissed the top of my head before continuing to swipe at the screen. I waited for a second before beginning to kiss his neck and work my hands over his body. 'But I'm not too drunk for this,' I added, kissing his chin and mouth.

He stiffened but not in the way I was hoping. 'Sorry, Caroline, I'm not really in the mood tonight,' he said.

'Oh,' I said, trying and failing not to feel hurt. I couldn't remember the last time he had rejected my advances, in fact I wasn't sure that it had ever happened.

He knew what I was thinking and pulled me to him, kissing me gently. 'I've just got a lot on my plate.'

'Is everything okay?' I asked, shifting to one side, studying his face for information. He sighed and was about to open his mouth to speak when his phone rang. He glanced at it. 'Sorry. I have to take this,' he said, climbing out of bed and heading downstairs as he answered. 'Jamie, what's going on?'

He didn't return within five minutes so I got ready for bed. By the time I'd cleansed, moisturised and brushed my teeth, he'd returned. 'What's going on?' I asked.

He ran a hand through his hair. 'There's a merger going to be announced tomorrow.'

'Oh. Right. What does that mean?'

He furrowed his brow. 'It means upheaval, change and redundancies.'

'But you'll be okay? You're vital to their operations, aren't you? They can't manage without you?'

He pulled me close and kissed me. 'If only you were in charge, darling.' He smiled but I noticed worry in his eyes. 'I don't know, Caroline. I just don't know. Look, I need to do some work, make sure I'm on it when the Americans arrive tomorrow. You go to bed, okay?'

'Okay,' I said, feeling uncertain. 'I love you,' I added, kissing his cheek.

He smiled. 'I love you too. And don't worry, everything will be fine.'

I climbed into bed feeling a growing sense of unease. These were the words my father had used before he'd got his final diagnosis. I turned out the light and closed my eyes, hoping that alcohol would lull me into easy sleep. I was just beginning to drop off when my phone buzzed. I thought it was a text but then it buzzed again, signalling a phone call. I rolled over and glanced at the screen. It was

the nursing home. I answered, ready to give them a piece
of my mind.

'Do you have any idea what time it is?' I replied.

'I do actually, Mrs Taylor.' I recognised Laurie's voice.
'But I'm afraid it's urgent. Your mother has managed to get
out of the home and we don't know where she is.'

CHAPTER ELEVEN

NATALIE

There are at least half a dozen facts that, despite my age and experience, I have failed to grasp since becoming an adult. These include the fact that you should never buy clothes which require you to slim down before wearing them (it would be easier to travel through time) or the fact that there is literally nothing you can do with quinoa to make it edible.

However, one of the biggest facts is that drinking in order to banish your woes is folly. Firstly, it leads to a hangover and secondly, far from banishing your woes, you magnify them to elephantine proportions but dint of the fact that you now have a hangover. It's a cyclical and very wearying problem.

In my heady pre-motherhood days, hangovers were do-able. I could pull the duvet back over my head and wait for the bilious, head-hammering sensations to pass. Sometimes it would take all day but often I had all day.

Today, however, I had to do the school run and this involved movement and clothes and words. I also had to make Woody's packed lunch and encourage him to get ready too. It felt like hell on earth.

He was already sitting at the dining-room table, reading the back of the cereal packet whilst spooning Shreddies into his mouth.

'Mormin,' I managed, trying to avert my gaze from his congealing breakfast.

'You look terrible, Mum,' he observed. Clever boy. 'Are you okay?'

No, I am on the brink of falling to bits. Please could you hurry up and become a grown-up so that you can sort it all out for me?

'Am fine,' I lied. 'Just need tea and shower.' By some miracle, I managed the shower but not the tea and I also managed to cobble together a packed lunch without throwing up. *Be proud, Nat. You're a shambles but you did it,* I thought as we stepped out into the bright spring morning on time, my sunglasses offering the scarcest comfort to my pounding head.

Woody and I walked side by side in the sunshine. I felt him take hold of my hand. My throat thickened. *Don't cry, you moron.* It was tricky though. He didn't often hold my hand these days and any mother will tell you that there's nothing more reassuring than the feeling of your child's hand in yours. The fact that Woody took my hand unprompted made it worse. It was as if he sensed that I needed some TLC. Plus, I get ridiculously emotional when I'm hung over – I think it's the guilt and regret. As we reached the school gate, he let go.

'Bye Mum,' he said. I leant down to kiss him, watching his bobbing form disappear into the classroom. *Come back! Don't leave me!* I turned away partly to stop myself from running after him and partly because I had just clocked Caroline at the far end of the playground, looking in my direction. I was still furious with her after last night and certainly didn't have the strength for her perfect-mother routine today. As I turned out of the gate, I walked straight into Guy.

'Morning,' he smiled, taking a step back. 'How are we feeling?'

There was a knowing look about him as if we were sharing a joke. I took a deep breath. 'A little fragile but I'll be fine,' I said, glancing over my shoulder towards Caroline. She was heading in our direction. 'Sorry, Guy, I've got to dash,' I added as casually as possible.

'Me too,' he smiled. 'But I'll see you at the hall later?' I gave him a confused look. 'For the meeting with the people from the council?'

'Is that today?' I asked with a rising sense of dread.

He nodded. 'Twelve-thirty. I finish here at twelve so should be in good time. By the way, I really enjoyed last night. I know you were a bit worse for wear but I had fun.' There was that smile again, a look of something shared. I wished for the life of me I could remember what it was.

'Yes, it was fun. I'll see you later then,' I said, heading off towards home. My brain raced as I walked back along Hope Street.

Stupid bloody brain. Why do you always do this to me when I get drunk? I ran through last night in my mind.

Arriving at the pub? Tick.

Enduring Caroline's interrogation in the loo? Tick.

Singing at the gig? Tick.

An eventful conversation with Caroline and her bitchy friends? Half a tick as it starts to get a bit hazy there.

Going home and drinking lots of water before falling asleep at a respectable hour? Yeah, actually I don't think that happened.

Then it hit me. Like a bullet through my skull.

Leaving the pub with Guy and insisting that we go somewhere else because I needed to 'have fun'?

Tickety tickety tick.

Fuckety fuckety fuck.

Oh, brain of mine. Why do you do this? Yes, I was at a low ebb and, yes, things are rocky with Dan, but that doesn't mean that you can let me drink too much and then go dancing with another man.

Oh shit. There was dancing. I went dancing. With another man. While the first man was at home looking after my son. That's bad. That's very bad.

I let myself in through the front door and collapsed in a sorry heap onto the sofa as the fog in my mind started to lift.

Things go wrong when I dance. I'm actually a very good dancer. Well, I think I am. But I tend to get a bit flirty when I dance. This hasn't been a problem during the past twenty years because I've only ever had Dan or Ed to dance with and it's fine to dance flirtatiously with your husband or your gay best friend. Nothing bad ever happens. But dancing flirtatiously with the eligible choirmaster, who declares it to have been 'fun', is bad. That's just a fact.

Calm down, Natalie, this is just your overactive imagination coupled with a feverish hangover. Guy Henderson is an honourable man. It was very likely just, 'eating ice cream' or 'jumping on a trampoline' type fun, not 'kissing the good-looking choirmaster' type fun.

Oh crap. Did you kiss the good-looking choirmaster in a moment of madness? Think, stupid brain, think!

I almost leapt off the sofa in fright as my phone rang. I fished it out of my pocket and winced as I saw it was Dan.

Dan my husband. The man who was minding Woody while I went out dancing with another man last night. The man who had seen me come back from a night out dancing with another man. Way to go on saving your marriage, Nat.

'Hello?' I croaked on answering.

'Nat? I just wanted to check that you were okay. You seemed pretty far gone last night.'

I tried to read his tone. He didn't sound angry. Mind you, Dan rarely got angry. 'Yeah, sorry about that. I think I got a bit over-excited with the Prosecco.'

He laughed. 'No worries. Good job your friend was there to help you home.'

'Mmm. What did you think of Guy?' I asked, as casually as I could.

'He was surprised when I opened the door. I had to explain who I was, but he just wanted to make sure you got home okay. He seems like a good bloke. I'm glad you've got people looking out for you.'

Why? So you don't have to? For some reason, this annoyed me. 'So anyway, you know this girl I saw you with?'

I heard Dan sigh. *Don't you dare, mister.* 'You mean Robin's daughter, Fleur?'

Fleur? Who calls their daughter 'Fleur'?

'Her mother's French, before you start getting judgey about her name,' said Dan, knowing me all too well.

'I didn't say a word. I just wondered how long it had been going on?'

'Nat, nothing is going on.' *Stop digging, Natalie. Digging is ill advised at the best of times and a very bad idea when you have a hangover. Your mind makes things up. Like the possibility that you kissed another man or that your husband is lying about an affair.*

'By going on, I meant how many times have you seen her?'

'Actually, I'm seeing her tonight.'

'I'm sorry?' I was outraged, my head pounding with fury and the effects of last night's booze.

'Calm down, Nat. I'm going to see her boyfriend's band in Camden. She asked if I would go along and give them some advice about the act.'

*'Calm down' is such an odd little phrase and rather
than encouraging me to relax, it invariably incites a level
of Incredible Hulk fury.* 'You want me to calm down?'
I snapped. 'You're going to a gig with a twenty-something
strumpet, casually stomping all over my feelings with your
size tens, and you think I should calm down! Bloody hell,
Dan. What's happened to us?'

*I knew what had happened to me. By using words like
'strumpet', I was starting to sound dangerously like my
mother.* Dan heard it too.

'Strumpet?' he teased. 'You'll be calling me a flibbertigibbet
next and making me watch repeats of *Midsomer Murders*.'

Normally, this would have made me laugh. We'd always
joked about my mum's funny little habits or exchanged
glances when she'd said something vaguely politically
incorrect, but not today.

*You've crossed the line, fella, and I, Natalie Hulky
Garfield, am going to smash you back across it.*

'Don't you dare use my mum to joke your way out of this!
She's had enough shit to deal with since Dad died, in fact
she had quite a lot when he was alive, and maybe she
leads a quieter life and likes her routines, but actually,
Midsomer Murders is a very good drama and –' *Okay, Nat,
you're starting to lose it now. You'll be declaring undying
love for John Nettles next.* '– And, she doesn't deserve your
contempt.'

'Woah, Nat, I was only joking, like we always do.
I'm sorry.'

'Yes, well, things have changed, haven't they? I'm not
sure that joking our way through this is going to help.'
*Wow, Natalie. That actually sounded rather considered and
mature. Not bad for a woman with an evil hangover.*

'Fair enough,' he said. 'And as for your concerns about
the gig, Fleur is just a friend who has asked me for a

favour, and that's the truth. I am helping her as I would help any friend. I don't know what else to say. You just have to believe me, Nat.'

Do I? I'm not really sure what to believe. My burst of anger had worn me out. I didn't want to talk about it any more. 'Fine. Whatever,' I said. 'I'll speak to you over the weekend.'

'Okay,' he replied before hanging up.

I flopped back onto the sofa feeling weary and hollow. It was as if I was losing control of everything I'd held to be true. You could never accuse me of being a control freak but despite my chaotic appearance, there has always been a semblance of order in my life. I have always had a rough idea where my husband was, trusted him implicitly and known that my emotional plates were still spinning on their sticks. At the moment, I had no idea what Dan was doing, or whether I trusted him, whilst the plates started to slide to the floor. I also knew that I was on rocky ground being indignant with Dan as far as Fleur was concerned when I couldn't quite recall what had happened with Guy last night. My life was, put simply, omnishambolic.

I heard Jim making his way up the garden path, belting out 'Chasing Cars'. He tapped on the knocker. I hauled myself up from the sofa and opened the door. He looked a little shocked by my appearance but barely missed a beat as he said,

'Morning, lovely. Wasn't last night brilliant? And it's a beautiful day. Here you go,' he handed me a pile of mostly bills. 'Oh and I dug out that CD I promised you.' He reached into his pocket and handed over a copy of *Ella Fitzgerald sings the Cole Porter Songbook.* 'My mum used to play this whenever she needed a lift. Said it was like bathing in milk and honey.'

I thought I might cry. I was so touched by the gesture. 'Thank you, Jim,' I said. 'That's really kind.'

He gave me a broad grin. 'My pleasure, lovely. I'm going to lend one to Caroline too. Everyone needs a bit of Ella in their life. Well, I best get on. Mind how you go.'

I closed the door behind him and carried the CD to the stereo. The Savage Garden disc was still in there. I took it out, replaced it with Jim's CD and pressed Play. I sank into the nearest chair, leaned back and listened. Jim's mother was right. Ella's voice made you feel as if someone had crawled into your ear and started to massage your brain. It was soothing, beautiful and exactly what I needed this morning. I loved the humour of 'Miss Otis Regrets' and wiped away a tear during 'Every Time We Say Goodbye'. Never mind Abigail and her counselling, this was therapy for the soul. Ella Fitzgerald should be available on prescription for the heartbroken and hung over. By the time the CD had finished, I knew what I had to do.

I arrived back at the school just before twelve. Guy appeared moments later. He smiled with surprise.

'Did Caroline send you to fetch me?' he joked.

'Not exactly,' I replied. 'I wanted to talk about last night.'

He grinned. 'You're having selective amnesia, aren't you?' he teased.

'A little,' I winced. 'When you said we had fun, we didn't kiss, did we?'

He stared at me for a moment, his clear-blue eyes amused by the question. 'We did not,' he replied.

'Oh, thank goodness. That's such a relief,' I said.

He laughed. 'Wow, don't feel you need to let me down gently, Nat. Give it to me straight.'

'Sorry,' I implored. 'It's just that I'm married – well, separated – well, not quite separated – my husband – you met him last night – we're going through a tricky patch and—'

Guy waved away my concerns. 'Nat, it's fine, honestly. You don't need to explain. I just told you that I had a good time because it was the truth. If you were single, I'd ask you out, but you're not, so I won't. It's no biggie.'

'Right, yes, that's great. Good. Thank you,' I gabbled.

He smiled at me. 'I'm happy to be friends if you are?'

I gazed up at him, deciding that it would actually be good to have a friend like Guy. 'Yes please.'

'Okay,' he said. 'Now, shall we go? I don't think Caroline likes late-comers.'

Pamela and Caroline were already there when we arrived along with two men, who had their backs to us. Caroline was doing all the talking and I could hear phrases like, 'vision for the future' and 'multi-functional community space' being bandied about. I looked around the hall with fresh eyes. It certainly needed some work. There were patches of damp in various corners and it looked as if the ceiling needed to be replaced. It had that wooden floor and musty old school-hall smell too, which I rather liked. The entrance hall was lined with little coat pegs labelled with the names of the children who came to the toddler group and the walls of the hall were decorated with colourful artwork: boggle-eyed smiling faces of the children with wool for hair, silver cardboard stars and a month-by-month chart listing each child's birthday. It had such a friendly, lived-in air, I felt quite nostalgic for the days when I would bring Woody here, chatting to the other mothers whilst he hurtled round on a little trike or made clumsy but beautiful hand paintings, which had always taken pride of place on our fridge.

This was a happy place and it deserved to stay, so that more children and their parents could make memories, older people could get wildly competitive over a game of bingo and our choir could grow into something special. Suddenly, this seemed really important and I realised that I needed to make it happen. I needed to park my annoyance with Caroline and save this place. It may sound ridiculous but I almost felt that if I could save the hall, then I could save my marriage too, as if one might drive the other. Maybe it was a long shot but it had to be worth a try.

We strode over to where they were standing. Pamela grinned up at us both. Caroline was still deep in conversation. I cleared my throat. The men turned. One of them was John Hawley, our biggest supporter for the campaign. My heart sank when I recognised the other man as the MP who had been my sparring partner on Radio Croydon. Excellent. My throat went dry.

The man seemed amused as he held out his hand. 'I don't think we've been properly introduced. I'm Tim Chambers. Also known as the supercilious twit,' he grinned.

I took his hand and gave a nervous laugh. 'Natalie Garfield. It's, er good to meet you properly.'

His handshake was firm and confident. 'I've taken a personal interest in your campaign since we last met, Ms Garfield. Despite what the press say, my party isn't about taking vital services away from communities. We will listen when the plea is as passionate as yours.' He delivered these words with a look of intensity, which surprised me. He was sharp-suited with an easy charm about him that I could imagine had won him many women voters. He must have been roughly the same age as me with prematurely greying hair which suited him, although he obviously knew it. I think I'd been too angry to notice anything other than his patronising demeanour when we met before.

'Yes, we're very lucky that our local parliamentary member has climbed down from his ivory tower to be with us today,' observed John Hawley with a wry smile. He cut a very different figure to Tim Chambers. His hair was a mess, his suit ill-fitting and rather lumpy.

Tim smiled. 'Despite coming from different hues of the political spectrum, Mr Hawley and I both care about our communities. Unfortunately, as his political party spent all the money last time round, our party has had to make some very difficult decisions during our term in government. Obviously we'd love to support every initiative but there simply isn't the money.'

'Well thank you both for coming,' said Caroline, obviously keen to move the conversation on. 'We appreciate you taking the time.'

'So, tell us about this wonderful hall,' said Tim, looking round at the peeling paint and cracked plaster. 'Why is it so important?'

'Let me show you round,' gushed Pamela, clearly taken in by Tim's charms.

'Lead on, dear lady,' smiled Tim with a reverent bow. Pamela giggled and I noticed John roll his eyes as he followed with the rest of us in tow.

'I've been helping to run the toddler group for years,' explained Pamela. 'It's very popular and lots of mums and dads would be lost without it. Natalie here used to bring her boy, Woody.' Tim nodded as she talked. 'We hold bingo nights for the older people, there's a Brownie pack and now we have the choir.'

'But the point is,' interrupted Caroline, 'we could make it so much more, which is why it needs to stay so that it can become a real hub.'

'I absolutely see where you're coming from,' said Tim.

'Wait for the "but",' warned John.

Tim ignored him. 'We merely need to be as rigorous as possible with our spending. We have a duty to the taxpayer, you see.'

'But people want this,' cried Pamela. 'We've got a lot of support for the campaign to keep it open. We've got two thousand followers on Twitter, we've already raised five thousand pounds and we've got a Lottery grant application pending. People care about this place!'

Tim took hold of her hand. I feared that Pamela might faint as she stared up into his eyes. 'I can see, Mrs—'

'Trott. Pamela Trott.'

'Mrs Trott,' he repeated. 'I can see that you are an absolute lynchpin of this community and I promise that I will do all I can to help you.'

'Thank you,' breathed Pamela.

Guy and I exchanged glances. 'I believe,' went on Tim, 'that the property developer has submitted plans and that the council will take a decision regarding all of this on – when is it, John?'

John sighed. 'The twentieth of July.'

'That's the day of the Community Choir Championships,' said Guy.

'Talk about the day of judgement,' I muttered.

'Well …' Tim smiled. 'Thank you so much for showing us round. It's been an absolute pleasure. John is your man vis a vis council matters and I will do my best to represent you in my parliamentary capacity. I am of course at the end of the phone if you need anything.' He reached into his inside pocket and handed us each a business card. When he passed one to me, he fixed me with a half-smile. 'It was good to see you again, Ms Garfield. I'll confess I enjoyed our radio show banter.'

'Yes, er, sorry about the fascist thing,' I mumbled.

He grinned. 'I've been called a lot worse. I hope our paths cross again,' he added, reaching out to shake my hand. 'Good luck, everyone, and goodbye.'

John nodded his goodbyes before shambling off behind him. 'We'll speak soon,' he said.

'Well,' I remarked as we stepped outside. 'That was interesting.'

'It certainly was,' said Guy. 'I think you've got a fan,' he added, nudging me.

'Who? Tim Chambers? Do me a favour!' I laughed, although I had a disconcerting feeling that he might be right.

'So, the twentieth of July it is,' said Caroline.

'Come on, this calls for a group hug,' insisted Pamela, gathering us all together into an awkward embrace.

I noticed Caroline eyeing me. 'Could I have a word, please, Natalie?' I nodded. Pamela and Guy waved their goodbyes and I walked with Caroline into the sunshine. 'I want to apologise on behalf of Amanda.'

I folded my arms. *Oh no, Caroline. You don't get to pass the blame on this one*. 'Just Amanda?'

'And Zoe.'

I raised an eyebrow. *This isn't easy for you, is it? Well tough luck, love. You owe me.*

She pursed her lips. 'And me too, of course. I'm very sorry, Natalie. You told me those things in confidence and I had no right to tittle-tattle.'

My mouth twitched with amusement at the phrase, 'tittle-tattle'. I bowed my head. 'I accept your apology.'

She exhaled with relief. 'Thank you. I appreciate that. I've got so many other things to worry about, with my mother at the moment.'

'Why, what's happened?'

She sighed. 'She's been thrown out of the nursing home, so it looks as if she's coming to live with us!'

'Oh, wow.' *That's going to throw your perfect life off kilter for a bit,* I thought with just a hint of schadenfreude.

'Wow indeed.'

'Well, maybe it will be an opportunity to sort things out.'

Caroline frowned at me. 'I very much doubt it. This is definitely just a temporary measure until I find another home that can take her.'

'If you say so.'

'I do,' she declared. 'And now if you'll excuse me, I need to go home to make the arrangements before I pick up Matilda. See you later.' She hurried off in the direction of her house.

I shook my head and headed for home. What a day. I felt exhausted. On the plus side, I was still married, my head was clearing, I hadn't kissed Guy and Caroline Taylor had apologised to me.

Yay. Go me.

I glanced at my watch as I practically fell through the front door. Perfect. I had just enough time to make a mug of tea, eat too many biscuits and collapse on the sofa in front of *Escape to the Country* before I had to pick up Woody. I needed to keep going but for the time being, I was going to lie down in a darkened room and rest my fevered brain.

CHAPTER TWELVE

CAROLINE

Well, they do say that if you need something done, ask a busy person. I mean, I know I'm good at managing campaigns, problem-solving and crisis-handling, it's just that they don't usually all come at the same time. I was pretty much running the entire Hope Street Community Hall Campaign, whilst worrying about Oliver's job and now contending with my mother. Normally, I thrive on stress but this was pushing me to the limit. I'd even had to delegate my PTA responsibilities vis-à-vis the summer fair to the ghastly Nula. Phil was very understanding but I could tell he was disappointed that I wouldn't be running the show. I'd had ambitions of donkey-rides this year.

I collected my mother on the Saturday after our first choir gig. As I entered the home, Laurie was in the reception area waiting for me. Her usually calm and smiling demeanour had disappeared. She looked serious and rather distraught.

'I'm sorry it's come to this,' she said as we walked along the corridor. 'I tried to plead your mother's case to Peter, but he was adamant.'

I bet he was, I thought. 'It's all right,' I said. 'And thank you. Really. For everything.'

She gave me a sad smile. 'I've printed off some documents for you about caring for people with dementia.'

'That's very kind.'

'And I'll give you my mobile number. Call me. Any time.'

'I don't want to put you to any trouble—'

'I wouldn't offer if I didn't mean it,' she said firmly. I nodded my gratitude.

My mother was sitting by the window staring into the garden as I entered. The room was bare, her possessions boxed up, the small items of furniture she owned stacked in the corner.

'I'll try to fit as much into the car as possible but my husband or I will have to come back for the rest,' I told Laurie.

'It's fine,' she said. I noticed that there were tears forming in her eyes. 'Would you like me to wheel your mother to the car?' she asked.

No, I'd like you to keep her here so that I don't have deal with this.

'If you wouldn't mind,' I replied, feeling unexpected envy at her obvious fondness for my mother. What could she see that I couldn't?

'Of course not,' she said. 'The porter will fetch your mother's possessions.'

'Thank you,' I said. 'Shall we go then?'

She moved towards my mother, touching her gently on the arm. 'Patricia? Caroline is here. Remember I told you that you're going to stay with her for a little while?'

My mother looked round to gaze at me. Her face was expressionless but seemed to soften into something approaching satisfaction as she murmured, 'Caroline.' I gave a brief smile and nodded before turning back towards the corridor. Laurie followed, pushing my mother in silence.

With a certain amount of difficulty, we managed to manoeuvre her into the car by the time the porter had loaded up as many of her possessions as he could fit in the boot.

Laurie grasped my mother's hand, tears brimming her eyes. 'Goodbye, Patricia. Take good care,' she said, leaning across to kiss her cheek. She handed me a sheaf of papers before I climbed into the car. 'This is the advice I was telling you about and I've written my number on the top. Please don't hesitate to call if there's anything I can do. Your mother needs you, she really does.'

Does she? I find that hard to believe.

'Thank you,' I nodded before climbing into the driver's seat. 'Right,' I said, feeling the panic grip as I started the engine. 'Let's go.' My mother remained looking forwards, her face impassive and impossible to read. Laurie waved as we drove off but my mother didn't look back for a second. We travelled home in silence, and my heart grew heavy as I thought about Laurie and her obvious affection for my mother, whilst realising that I had very little. She was my mother but only in name. I wondered at Laurie, at this relative stranger in my mother's life and realised that actually, I was the stranger. Your mother was the person you were supposed to know inside out but the truth was, I didn't know her at all.

'Reminiscence – talking about past experiences with the dementia sufferer can have a very positive effect on their outlook. Make a memory box including photos from earlier in their life.'

I put the document to one side and flicked on the kettle. The thought of talking about the past may be helpful for my mother's condition but I was pretty sure it wasn't going to have much of a positive effect on me. I didn't relish the idea of chatting about all the times she flew into a rage at my slightest misdemeanour. Or how she would shout at me, her face up close to mine so that all I could see was her snarling teeth, her stale coffee breath making me want to gag.

As I had led her into the house on our return from the home, I couldn't quite translate this tottering, shrunken woman into the same one that used to instil fear and loathing in me.

Oliver had been typically charming, opening the front door and helping her inside. Matilda came bouncing down the stairs, her face bright with excitement. She had wanted to come and collect my mother but I had said no. She seemed so joyful at the prospect of having her grandmother here. I wondered at how opposed this was to my own feelings.

'Nanny!' she cried, leaping from the third step and flinging her arms around my mother's waist.

Nanny. Such a friendly and jolly title for a person. A person so unlike my mother.

I didn't have the heart to suppress Matilda's enthusiasm though. I detected that I was going to need all the help I could get with this particular situation. 'I'm so happy to see you! Do you want to come and see my bedroom?'

My mother stood in the hall, looking around her in utter astonishment, clearly wondering where she was and who on earth these people were.

'Why don't you let Nanny settle in first?' suggested Oliver.

That was that then. My mother was now a nanny.

'Would you like a cup of tea, Patricia?' he asked, helping her with her coat. She stared at him as if he'd just asked her to explain the secrets of the universe. He mimed a cup and saucer. 'Tea?' he repeated. When she didn't answer he glanced at me with a shrug.

'She probably doesn't want one,' I observed.

Oliver pulled me to one side. 'I don't think you should talk about your mother as if she isn't here,' he said.

I rolled my eyes. 'Sorry, but if she won't answer, it's difficult to know what to do.'

My mother looked at me. 'Caroline,' she said.

'Yes, I'm Caroline, this is Oliver, my husband, and this is Matilda,' I replied, pointing to each of us in turn.

'Why are you shouting?' Matilda frowned. 'Is Nanny deaf?'

'No, she's not deaf,' I replied, feeling my hackles rise. 'She just doesn't always understand what's going on.'

At that moment I became aware of a dripping sound and turned to see my mother urinating onto the floor. She stared at me with what I detected was a note of defiance.

'Oh, my God!' I cried in horror. 'What are you doing?'

'Aw, poor Nanny,' said Matilda. 'She needed a wee.'

'But the toilet's just there!' I cried, opening the door to the downstairs bathroom.

'Caroline, it's fine,' said Oliver. He turned to my mother and patted her arm. 'It's all right, Patricia. We'll get this cleared up in no time. Caroline, why don't you take your mum to the toilet and I'll clean this up. Matilda, could you fetch some wipes, please?'

'Of course, Daddy,' beamed Matilda.

Why is everyone taking this so calmly? I thought as I led my mother to the downstairs cloakroom and helped her remove her sodden tights and underwear. *This cannot be my life.*

As I binned the offending articles, I wondered how I had allowed this to happen. How could I be saddled with this helpless woman, who had made my childhood so miserable? How could it be that my beloved father had died and left me with her? This wasn't me. I didn't deal in old age and decay. I left her on the toilet and rummaged in her bag for clean clothes. I helped her on with these, trying to forget about what I was doing. It was like looking after an oversized baby really. Once she was sorted, I led her to the living room and, putting a towel onto the leather sofa, I sat her down. She didn't comment on anything that had just happened. I went to the kitchen and took out my iPad, ready to start the search for a new care home straight away.

I was surprised to find how much of a relief it was to have Matilda there whilst dealing with my mother. Often her noise and chatter would irritate me but now they were a welcome interruption to the morose air which had descended on the house since my mother arrived. It wasn't really anything she said or did because in truth, she said very little. It was more her presence; a silent, brooding presence locked in a body which had no way to express itself any more. I found being in the same room as her depressing; a reminder of the loss of faculty and the cruelty of the ageing process.

I'm not proud to admit that I basically left Matilda and her to it in the living room, because in actual fact, I couldn't face being with her. For Matilda, having my mother here was like having a new pet, albeit a slightly old and unresponsive one. Later that afternoon, I paused on my way upstairs with a basket of laundry to watch them together. It struck me at that moment how well matched old and young people are. They have a lot more spare time on their hands, for a start, and they also have an ability to chat without needing a response. It was a match made in heaven.

'So shall we play a game or I could show you my teddies or we could watch TV?' suggested Matilda, smiling up at her new friend.

My mother stared at her with a soft expression. 'Caroline,' she said.

'No, Matilda or Tilly or some of my friends call me Tills,' explained Matilda patiently. 'That's Caroline,' she added, pointing at me. 'She's my mum and my dad is in the kitchen. He's called Oliver.'

'Caroline,' repeated my mother, looking up at me with the same gentle expression.

I looked away. *I don't want to talk to you. It's too late.* 'Matilda, could you fetch yourself a drink and a biscuit please?'

'Can I eat it in here with Nanny?'

'As long as you don't make crumbs.'

''Kay,' she said, dashing towards the kitchen.

I felt my mother's eyes on me. 'Would you like a cup of tea?' I asked, glancing down at her and doing my best to keep my voice at a reasonable volume.

She reached out, her skin-and-bone arm floating in the air, seeking contact. My body stiffened. 'Caroline,' she said again. 'My Caroline.'

I'm not your Caroline. I gave a polite smile. 'I'll just take these upstairs and then make you some tea,' I said before making a hasty retreat.

As I made the drinks, Oliver appeared behind me and put his arms around my shoulder. 'Hey, darling, how are you doing?'

I sighed. 'I'll be better once I've found a solution for my mother.'

'You make it sound as if she's a problem.'

I turned to face him. 'Oliver, she needs full-time care. We can't give her that.'

'Are you sure that's all it is?' He kissed me on the cheek to show that he wasn't criticising.

We had talked about my mother over the years. He knew the history but it wasn't something I dwelt on. That wasn't me. The past was the past and that was that.

'It's too late to go over it now. You can see how she is. We're not going to resolve the issues in our relationship at this stage.' *And besides, I don't want to and I don't want to think about why either.*

He smiled. 'She does seem different these days though – more mellow somehow.'

'That's her condition. She doesn't have a clue what's going on.'

'She dotes on you,' he observed.

'She thought Matilda was me five minutes ago,' I replied, brushing him off.

He hugged me tight and then kissed me again. 'You must do whatever you think best, my darling.'

Yes, I must and for now, that involves getting my mother out of my house as soon as possible.

I finished making the tea and carried a mug into the living room for my mother. Matilda was sitting next to her and they were looking at one of the photograph albums I had been showing her recently. 'Look, that's you and Grandpa with Mum. You look very smart, Nanny. Do you know where that was taken?'

My mother's face had changed. She looked animated and wide-eyed as if her brain was firing into life.

'It looks lovely, wherever it is,' said Matilda. 'Somewhere by the sea, I think. Mum looks funny in her little outfit and sunhat.' She glanced up at me before whispering to her grandmother. 'She actually looks a bit podgy,' she giggled.

'Clacton,' said my mother in a husky voice, glancing up at me. 'Clacton.'

'Ooh, it looks nice. Maybe we could all go there one day, Mum?' enthused Matilda.

'Maybe,' I said. *Such a useful word – 'maybe'. It embraces possibility without ever committing.* 'I've made your tea,' I added, placing the mug on a coaster in front of my mother. She gave me a fleeting smile of thanks. I turned, ready to escape.

'Let's look at some more,' said Matilda. 'Mum, do you want to look too?' Both she and my mother were staring up at me with pleading eyes.

I didn't. It was one thing to look at photographs with Matilda, to fill the blanks in the family tree of her mind with pictures; but I couldn't – wouldn't – look at them with my mother. I wouldn't pretend that we shared treasured memories. There was no game of Happy Families to be played here.

Still, I hated disappointing Matilda. I swallowed down a raw feeling of guilt. 'I'm afraid I need to get on with dinner,' I lied, turning swiftly on my heels. Once in the kitchen I put on the radio, letting music drown out my thoughts. I sang along and thought about the three care homes I had lined up to visit the next day.

Problem solved. Crisis averted.

However, the search for a new nursing home proved to be more challenging than I thought. Clearly, that irritating jobsworth, Peter Jarvis, had felt it was his duty to inform any prospective new home about my mother's issues.

'We don't feel that we could offer your mother the care she requires,' said the manager of one place I phoned.

What with the campaign and the day-to-day care of my mother, I'd had little time to leave the house, let alone take the matter further. It was therefore with an unexpected amount of relief that I found myself leaving Oliver, Matilda and my mother at home and heading to Croydon for the south-east London regional choir heats on Sunday. Yes, even Croydon town centre seemed a more enticing prospect.

I had offered to pick up Natalie and immediately wished that I hadn't, as she was predictably late. I thought she would appear at the door as soon as I pulled up. I had said nine o'clock sharp but I noticed that all the curtains were still drawn. I sighed and got out of the car, realising that I would need to ring the bell.

A man, whom I guessed to be Woody's father, opened the door. He wasn't my type – too much facial hair – but I could see that he was attractive, with dark hair and smiling brown eyes.

'Hi, I'm Dan. You must be Caroline. You've probably realised by now that Nat is always late, so why don't you come in for a sec?' he said, standing back to let me pass.

I glanced at my watch. 'Okay, thanks,' I replied, stepping into the hall.

Natalie's face appeared at the top of the stairs. 'Oh hi, Caroline. Sorry, I thought you said nine-fifteen. I just need to dry my hair and I'll be with you.'

No, I said nine o'clock. And I texted to remind you last night because I knew you would do this.

I did my best to mask my impatience. 'It's fine. I wanted to get there early but we've got plenty of time,' I said, smiling casually at Dan. I heard the sound of a hairdryer upstairs.

Dan grinned at me. 'Would you like a coffee while you're waiting?' he asked.

'No, I've just had one, thanks,' I replied. I spied the kitchen from where I stood in the hall.

Did people really enjoy this kind of chaos? There were empty pizza boxes, beer bottles and the remains of that day's breakfast strewn over every surface.

Dan noticed me looking. 'Excuse the mess,' he said. 'Haven't had a chance to clear up yet.'

'I understand,' I smiled. *Except that I don't. I never leave the washing-up overnight. I can't bear an untidy kitchen.*

Woody appeared in the doorway. 'Oh hey, Tilly's mum,' he said.

'Hello, Woody,' I answered. 'How are you?'

'Good, thanks,' he replied. 'Is Tilly with you?'

'No, *Matilda* is at home with her father,' I said, correcting him.

'Oh, isn't she going to see the choir?' he asked, sounding disappointed.

'No, she isn't. Why? Are you?'

He nodded. 'Definitely. Dad's taking me,' he said, looking round at his father.

Dan smiled. 'Got to support your mum, haven't we?'

I felt a pang of sadness. Here was a man estranged from his wife, who was supporting her in every way and yet my own husband wouldn't be there to support me.

Woody seemed to pick up on this. 'We'll cheer for you too, if you like,' he said.

I felt a tug of affection for this little boy. 'Thank you, Woody.'

'You're welcome, Tilly's mum.'

I was about to correct him again but thought better of it.

'Sorry, Caroline,' said Natalie, hurrying down the stairs, doing up her blouse as she went.

'Aww, Mum!' cried Woody, uttering enough embarrassment for both of us.

'Sorreee,' sang Natalie, reaching forwards to kiss him on the forehead. 'Mwah! Love you. See you later. Okay?' She looked towards Dan, who gave a smiling thumbs-up.

Dan and Woody were still there waving us off as I started the engine. I'll confess to feeling a little envious at Natalie's easy affection with her son and the way Dan was supporting her, despite their situation.

'So,' I said. 'That's Dan.'

Natalie stared out of the window. 'Yup, that's Dan. He stayed over last night – we had a bit of a family evening.'

Why did people feel the need to share information that no-one had asked for?

'U-huh,' I replied, trying and failing to mask my disapproval.

She glanced at me. 'What does "U-huh" mean?'

'Nothing, nothing at all. It's none of my business.' *And that's the way I intend to keep it.*

She folded her arms. 'Come on, out with it.'

'What?'

'You obviously have an opinion about this, so out with it.'

'Only if you want to hear it.' *And I doubt you will.*

'Caroline. Just tell me. Otherwise I will be forced to change all your pre-set radio stations to Kerrang,' she threatened, hovering a finger over the buttons.

I shivered at the prospect. 'Okay. I just wonder if it's a good idea for you to let Dan dip so freely in and out of your life. I'm not sure I'd allow Oliver to do that.'

'Well I don't have a lot of choice, do I? He's Woody's dad.'

'And you're Woody's mother. You have a say too, you know. Plus, it must be confusing for Woody not to have boundaries regarding when his father's around. Children need boundaries.'

She went quiet for a moment. 'I'm doing my best, Caroline.'

I could tell she was hurt and I felt a little guilty. 'I'm sure you are. I'm just telling you how I see it. Of course Woody has to see his father, but maybe just at set times.'

'Maybe,' she murmured.

'You have to protect yourself sometimes, Natalie,' I said more gently. 'Otherwise he'll walk all over you.'

'Dan wouldn't do that.'

'I'm sure, but then you never thought he'd do this, did you?'

Oh dear. Maybe that was a little too candid. Natalie went quiet and stared out of the window. I'd obviously struck a nerve. 'How about some music?' I suggested, turning on the radio. 'Everybody's Changing' was playing and I began to sing along. I glanced at Natalie with smiling encouragement. She rolled her eyes before joining in, picking up the harmony. Actually it sounded pretty good and the tension was broken.

'How are things with your mother?' she asked after the song had finished.

I would have told most people that things were just fine but I knew this wouldn't wash with Natalie. She was such an open person. I'd have to give her some details, just not all of them.

I sighed. 'It's a bloody nightmare, if you must know. I can't bear being in the same room as her, whereas Matilda adores her. I'm having no luck finding a new home that will take her at the moment, so we seem to be lumbered!'

'Have you tried talking to her?'

'What's the point? She can barely speak and I don't have anything *to* say.'

'Are you sure?'

'Natalie, I know you're going through counselling at the moment but I would appreciate it if you didn't psycho-analyse me.'

'Methinks the lady doth protest too much.'

'The lady will drop you off and make you walk if you carry on in that vein,' I retorted.

'Just telling you how I see it,' she said with a wry grin.

'Touché,' I smiled.

It was still early when we arrived at the Fairfield Halls – a large modernish concert hall and something of a haven in the cultural wasteland of Croydon. There were a lot of nervous-looking people milling about, mostly women with the odd man thrown in for good measure. We had arranged to meet at the far end close to the coffee bar and I noticed Pamela and Guy already there with a few others. Pamela looked very red in the face.

'Good morning!' I smiled as we joined them.

'Morning,' grinned Guy. 'How are we feeling? Raring to go? Are the words to "Something Inside So Strong" etched into your subconscious?'

'Labi Siffre haunts my dreams,' joked Natalie.

'Is it me or is it very hot in here?' asked Pamela, fanning herself with the programme.

'It's not that warm,' I observed.

''Scuse me then, I'm having a moment,' she said, hurrying off to the bathroom, muttering, 'bloody menopause.'

'We'll see you in there,' I called after her. 'Let's go up,' I said to the others.

We made our way up the stairs to a registration table. It was very crowded so I volunteered to register us.

'The Hope Street Community Choir,' I announced, smiling broadly at a woman with a list.

'Hope Street, Hope Street … ah, here you are,' she said. 'You're on in the second half and you're last. The ushers will show you where to sit,' she added, handing me a card. 'Good luck.'

'Thank you,' I replied, feeling a sudden rush of nerves.

'Last on is either a really good thing or a really bad thing,' observed Guy when I told them.

'I think it's a really good thing,' I said. 'It gives us time to eye up the competition.'

'Let's go with that,' smiled Guy.

'I'd rather go first,' said Natalie. 'Get it over with.'

'We'll be fine,' I told her. 'Deep breaths, everyone. Come on, let's go in.'

The concert hall was grander than I'd remembered – a mixture of ambient lighting and an open modern design gave it a soft and rather intimate feel. We took our places in the seats behind the stage and everyone started to relax a little.

'I think this might be fun,' murmured Doly, taking in her surroundings.

'I intend to enjoy myself,' agreed Jim, who I noticed was wearing a jaunty red waistcoat over his white shirt. It gave him the appearance of an usher and I wasn't surprised when one lady asked him where the toilets were. 'Up there on the left, darlin',' he replied with a friendly smile.

'Where's Pamela?' asked Natalie, looking worried.

'I'm sure she'll be back soon,' I said. Sure enough, Pamela appeared moments later. She still looked very flushed but I was relieved to note that she'd stopped sweating.

She sat down with a sigh. 'Oh, my stars, getting old is no fun at all,' she declared, fanning herself.

'Are you okay?' asked Doly.

'Yes, thank you, dear. It's just the change, you know? It all went a bit pear-shaped after my hysterectomy.' I winced. Doly smiled and nodded politely. I noticed Guy and Natalie exchange glances. Pamela took a swig of water from a bottle in her bag. 'I'll be all right in a sec,' she added, closing her eyes. 'Just need to get my breath back.'

I looked around at the other competitors. Most were wearing the choir-performance uniform of black skirt or trousers and white top, but I noticed one small group of women who were all attired in smart matching dark-blue trouser suits with sequin detail on the cuffs and pockets. They looked very professional. One of their number turned and caught sight of me looking. There was a moment's recognition before she started to wave.

'Caroline! Oh my God, is it really you?' she cried.

'Danielle!' I replied. 'Wait there, I'll come to you.' As I made my way over, I noticed the other women in her group shift and stare at me, unsmiling and suspicious.

Danielle seemed pleased to see me, though. She looked almost exactly as she'd done at school – huge blue eyes and a glowing peachy complexion, although I did note with a certain satisfaction that her lips were a little plumper than I'd remembered and I could see virtually no wrinkles. She'd definitely had work. She held me at arm's length. 'How long has it been? No, don't answer that. It will make us feel old. You look fabulous,' she declared.

We laughed. 'How are you?' I asked. I hadn't seen her for at least ten years. We used to meet up every now and then for drinks but then she'd gone to live in Australia for a while and the communication had filtered out.

She twisted a strand of hair around her finger as I remembered she used to do when we were at school. 'I'm wonderful,' she replied. 'Living in a ridiculously huge townhouse in Dulwich, married to Owen, who's in property.'

'Lovely,' I said, swallowing my jealousy. 'Any children?'

'Two boys – my pride and joy. They're away at boarding school, having the time of their lives.'

I nodded. 'So you're taking part in the competition?' I asked.

She glanced at her group and then back at me in surprise. 'We're the Dulwich Darlings,' she purred. I looked blank. 'We were on that show with Andrew Munday – you must have seen it? Everyone said it was a travesty that we didn't win.'

'Oh, right. How marvellous.'

'I know, isn't it just? So we're doing this today as a formality to give it a bit of prestige. The organisers asked us and we couldn't say no,' she said with a smug smile. 'We'll fly through this and the next round but there'll be some pretty stiff competition when we reach the final.'

'Well, good luck,' I offered.

'Thank you, darling. And you,' she glanced over to where my fellow singers were standing. 'Is that your group?' she added, wrinkling her nose condescendingly.

'Yes, we're the Hope Street Community Choir.'

'Oh, I heard about them. You're trying to save that little community hall, aren't you?'

I bristled at her use of the word 'little'. 'We've got a lot of support.'

'I'm sure,' she smiled. 'And let me know if you want any help from the Dulwich Darlings – we'd be only too happy to use our celebrity status to help you. Here's my number,' she added, thrusting a card into my hand. It said, 'Danielle Sheldon, Musical Director, Dulwich Darlings.'

'Thank you,' I replied, forcing a smile. 'I best get back to the others.'

'Of course. Lovely to see you,' she said, turning swiftly away.

I walked back to my seat, an unexpected surge of fury coursing through my veins.

'Who was that?' asked Natalie as I sat down next to her. 'Bit OTT, aren't they?'

'They're the Dulwich Darlings,' whispered Doly. 'They're amazing.'

'Oh. Right.'

They're also our arch-rivals, I decided as the lights went down, signalling the start of the heats. *And I have every intention of bringing them down.*

For seasoned competitors, being last on the bill may be an advantage but for us, it proved to be something of a disaster. For a start, it meant that we heard every other performance and this made us more nervous. I kept noticing details of what people were wearing and how they were standing.

We had to sit through the Dulwich Darlings' performance of 'True Colors', too. It was over the top but they were very good. 'They're the ones to beat,' whispered Guy. *Yes, preferably over the head with a club,* I thought, surprised at how agitated I was.

When it was our turn, I felt jittery and truth be told, a little foolish.

What were we thinking? We were never going to win this. We had no place here.

We took our places and I noticed Natalie look out to the audience, where Woody and Dan sat smiling and waving. I felt an unhelpful stab of jealousy, wishing that Oliver and Matilda were there too. I did my best to channel my nerves into confidence as Guy stood before us.

Then as we began to sing, something remarkable happened. I could still feel my nerves dancing in the pit of my stomach but they were numbed as the music washed over me and carried me along. For a small moment the worries about my mother, all the stresses and strains of my life, disappeared. I was lost in the music, caught up in the words of the song. I did feel strong, I did feel powerful. My body tingled with goose-bumps. Unlikely as it may sound for a woman, standing on a stage in Croydon singing in our mishmash of a choir, I felt wonderfully alive.

Guy was nodding at us with delight. We sounded good. Better than good. We sounded fantastic. It was different to the pub. The audience were captive in front of us and from the grins on their faces, I knew they were enjoying it too. True, our movements could have been more relaxed and polished. Jim danced like a puppet, all jerky arms and gangly legs, and Pamela often moved in the opposite direction to everyone else, but we were starting to feel like a choir. A proper choir who took part in competitions and, who knows, maybe even won them!

We were just reaching the end of the song and I remember feeling regret that it would be over too soon, when there was a loud thump. We turned and gasped as one at the sight of Pamela crashing to the floor in a messy heap.

Her barrel-shaped husband, Barry, rushed along the aisle, shouting, 'Pammy!', whilst we all gathered around and the audience whispered their concerns to one another.

'Give her some space,' ordered the St John Ambulance man who charged on from the side of the stage, clearly overjoyed to have an actual incident to deal with. He knelt by her side just as Barry arrived.

'Can you hear me, Mrs—'

'Trott. Pamela Trott,' I answered. I glanced up and could see Danielle and her group looking on, shaking their heads with disdain rather than sympathy. I would bring them down all right.

'Oh, Pammy,' cried Barry. 'Can you hear us?'

Pamela gave a little sigh and opened her eyes. Barry and the St John Ambulance man helped her to a sitting position. 'I'm all right,' she said. 'It's just these bloody hot flushes. Made me go all dizzy. Sorry, my ducks. Did I ruin it?'

We all smiled at one another. 'Not at all,' said Guy. 'You were the star of the show.'

Jim turned to the audience. 'She's all right!' he cried. 'Mrs Trott is all right!'

I'm not sure how it happened but all of a sudden the audience was on its feet, whooping and cheering with delight. Pamela managed to take a bow and we stood together basking in the applause, laughing with surprise.

'A standing ovation on our first performance,' laughed Guy. 'Well done, Pamela!'

CHAPTER THIRTEEN

NATALIE

'Mum! Can you stop singing that song – it's annoying!' cried my scowling son.

'I have to practise, grumpy-pants. We've got the London Finals coming up soon.' I grinned, turning off the shower and wrapping myself in a towel. 'Anyway, "God Only Knows" is a good song. Brian Wilson is a genius.'

'Justin Bieber is a genius,' he declared, folding his arms.

'That's not the word I would choose but everyone's entitled to their opinion.'

Woody sloped off, returning moments later. 'It's eight twenty-one. We're going to be late. Again.'

'We're not going to be late, Woody,' I said, rushing into the bedroom and pulling on miscellaneous items of clothing. 'We're going to be right on time.' *Or possibly five minutes late.*

Moments later I emerged dressed, with slightly damp hair. 'Come on, Mum!' called Woody from the bottom of the stairs with rolling-eyed impatience.

'Yep, sorry. Just coming. Right, got my rucksack, got my packed lunch, got my wipes, tissues and water bottle. Got my money for the gift shop. Let's do this!'

'You don't need wipes – we're not babies and we're not allowed to go to the gift shop. Mr Henderson said.'

'Well, Mr Henderson is my friend so he might let me go,' I said in a three-year-old's voice. Woody frowned. 'Okay, okay, it was a joke. I'll leave my money at home.'

'Can we *please* go now?' sighed Woody, opening the front door.

'Okay, boss,' I quipped, following him down the path onto the street. I glanced at him as I walked along. Woody's face was fixed in a frown of concentration, staring straight ahead, his hair a riotous mess.

Oh, Woody, please don't ever change. Please always be exactly as you are right at this moment.

I reached out a hand to ruffle his hair. He ducked away. 'Mum! Don't be embarrassing.'

'What?' I laughed. 'I'm your mum and I love you. Deal with it.'

He shrugged. 'Just don't embarrass me today by calling me by my nickname or something.'

'What? Woody Woodpecker?'

'Mum! Stop it!'

'Sorry,' I giggled as we walked on in silence. I was looking forward to today. I hadn't been on one of Woody's school trips for ages and we were visiting the Horniman Museum, which I loved.

I also loved my son. Dearly. In the crumbling wreckage of my marriage, he was the small but strong fireman, lifting me above it all. And he didn't even realise it.

I elbowed him playfully. 'You're happy that I'm coming along, aren't you?'

'Ye-es,' said Woody, fixing me with a look, 'but stop being so needy, okay?'

'Okay,' I nodded. *Fair point.* On arrival at school, I dropped Woody in the playground before heading to reception, where the other parent helpers were gathering. Guy appeared moments later.

'Good morning all,' he smiled. 'Thanks for volunteering today. I think it's going to be a great trip. We're just sorting out the kids and then we'll be on our way.' He turned to me. 'So have you recovered after our triumph at the weekend?'

'I actually enjoyed it far more than I thought I would. Poor Pamela, though.'

'At least it was the end of the performance,' said Guy with a smile. 'I thought it gave us a rather dramatic finale. I think the judges liked it.'

'Stop it! That's so mean,' I giggled.

'Not at all. I've told her to do it for every round. It gets us sympathy points.'

I guffawed. 'You're terrible. I popped round to see her. She was mortified.'

'I'll make a big fuss of her at tonight's rehearsal. Are you coming?'

'Yes, provided Dan shows up.'

He nodded. 'And everything's okay?'

'I'm fine. Thank you.' And I was. To a point. My life now was hardly any different to my life of three months ago. I worked, I looked after Woody, I ate, I slept (less than I had but if I couldn't sleep, I worked), I watched crap TV. None of these things had changed.

It was just Dan. He had changed. He had re-framed my life. It was as if my world had been in focus and now it was blurred and indistinct. I was straining my eyes to see, trying desperately to work out what the picture was now. The problem was that the picture kept changing. Every time I thought I had an idea of what was going on, it morphed into something else.

I was grateful for Woody and the choir but if I stopped to think about my life beyond that, it felt as if I was standing on an increasingly rocky surface. The only thing I could cling to at the moment was the counselling process. Dan assured me that it was working for him but I couldn't honestly say it was helping me. I wasn't sure if it was the process or Abigail that I had an issue with. There was something about the way that she listened without comment that I found unnerving. I wasn't a big fan of silence at the best of times and part of me just wanted to be hugged and told how to solve this.

And despite everything that had happened, despite the rollercoaster of Dan and me over the past few months, the fact remained that I loved him and I couldn't get past that. I might not be able to decipher what was the truth and what was a lie, or indeed the real reason for him leaving. The only thing that remained for me was the love.

'I'm glad you're okay,' smiled Guy, before turning away. 'I just need to rally the troops and then we'll be on our way.'

I nodded. If only he knew.

The Horniman Museum is something of a hidden treasure, situated on the South Circular Road, which holds this corner of south-east London in a grubby embrace. Woody and I have spent many happy hours here, visiting the 'stuffed animals room', as he calls it, which contains the weird and wonderful results of many a Victorian taxidermy experiment (the badgers always held particular fascination for him), or watching the spooky moon jellyfish in the aquarium as they wafted like tiny ghosts across their neon-blue tank.

Today, Guy had arranged for the children to take part in a gamelan ensemble in the huge music room downstairs. They were buzzing as they arrived and snaked their way down to the venue. I followed my group, which contained Matilda, Woody and two other children. They were a lovely bunch – bright, full of questions and observations. I was enjoying listening to their chatter and occasionally joining in the fun. Before their session in the music room, they had time to look around the gallery, which contained the biggest collection of musical instruments in the country. Each one was catalogued too and you could sit at a desk and press buttons to hear recordings of them playing. My group were happily working their way through the aerophone, or 'blowy, vibraty' section according to Woody, whilst I stood back a little, reading a display about accordions. They had been merrily pressing and listening, making the occasional comment, when suddenly I overheard a snippet of chat.

'Are your mum and dad getting a divorce then, Woody?' asked Matilda.

I held my breath. 'Dunno,' he answered.

'Does your dad not live with you any more?' she continued.

'No. He was living with my nan but he's going to get a flat. I heard him tell her.'

I froze. This was news to me.

'So will you go and live with him?'

'Maybe at weekends,' Woody shrugged.

'Can I have a go on the button now?' asked one of the other boys in their group.

'Yes, in a minute, Harrison. Woody and me haven't finished,' bossed Matilda. *Like mother, like daughter.*

Panic rose up inside me. *I have to get out of here. I need some air. And a place without thirty school kids playing recordings of bagpipe music.* I spotted Guy. 'Is it okay if I nip to the loo?' I asked.

He laughed. 'Of course. I'll keep an eye on your group.'

'Thanks,' I said, darting from the room. Once in the atrium, I felt the world begin to spin as thoughts flooded my mind. *If Dan wasn't being honest about his living arrangements, what else was he lying about? I have to know.* I grabbed my phone, stabbing at the buttons. I held the phone to my ear. *What am I going to say? How will he respond this time?*

'Nat?'

'When were you going to tell me that you were moving into a flat?' I demanded. He didn't reply. In the formula of love, hesitation equals lying. 'Well?' I barked.

'I didn't say that.'

'So our son is a liar?'

'No, I'm not saying that either. He just misunderstood.'

'Enlighten me then.'

'I think the conversation took place before the counselling started and we were talking about what might happen if our separation became permanent. I mean, Mum's place is very small and as you and I have always said, you really shouldn't live with your parents once you're over the age of twenty. Mum gets antsy if I don't leave the dishcloth in a certain way.'

Oh, he was good. He was trying to wriggle his way out with easy humour. Not today, Dan. Not today. 'You're lying.'

'Nat, can we talk about this some other time?'

'No, we bloody can't!' I shouted. 'You don't get to defer my feelings because it's not effing convenient. Until you can be straight with me and my son, you don't get to drop in any time you feel like it. In fact, I want you to stay away.'

'Nat, don't do this.'

'Too late. You make your bed, you bloody lie in it.' I ended the call, my body shaking with fury. I turned round to see Guy and a group of a dozen schoolchildren, including my son, staring at me in shock.

Brilliant. That was the award for most embarrassing mother of the year in the bag, then.

Woody was barely speaking to me by the time we got home. I phoned Ed in tears. He arrived within the hour carrying a *Match of the Day Magazine* and a tray of Krispy Kreme doughnuts. He folded me into his arms and let me sob.

'Come on, sweetheart. It's going to be okay,' he soothed.

'I've fucked it all up, Ed. Woody hates me. Dan hates me. I hate me.'

He held me at arm's length and looked into my eyes. '*I* love you. And it's not just because I love a drama. If I decided on a whim to go into the vagina business, you'd be top of my list.'

'Above Angelina Jolie?' I joked.

'Yes,' he replied with a whimsical nod. 'Above Angelina.'

'I feel a bit better now.'

'Good,' he said, reaching for the tray of doughnuts. 'Now shove one of these down your gob while I go and talk to your boy.'

'Thank you,' I said weakly.

He returned ten minutes later. 'Sorted,' he told me. 'He was embarrassed but he doesn't hate you. I think he just needs a hug.'

'Okay,' I said. 'Hugs I can do. Maybe I shouldn't go to choir though?'

Ed gave me a stern look. 'You are going to choir because Woody and I have a date with Liverpool versus Fenerbahçe, and no-one comes between me and Daniel Sturridge.'

I laughed. 'Fair enough. I'll just go and check Woody's okay then.'

'Good girl,' smiled Ed. 'You will sort this, you know.'

I climbed the stairs and knocked on Woody's door. 'Yeah?'

I opened it and peered round. He was sitting on his bed, reading the magazine Ed had bought him. He looked up, his face guarded and serious.

Please smile at me. You don't know this but at the moment, I pretty much live for your smile.

'I just wanted to say that I'm sorry for embarrassing you.'

'It's okay,' he said, staring up at me with big eyes.

It wasn't okay but I appreciated him saying it. 'Can I have a hug?' I asked. He gave a small nod. I sat down on the side of his bed and wrapped my arms around him. I felt him pat my back, gentle and consoling. After a while, I pulled away. 'Is there anything you want to ask me?' He shook his head. 'Are you sure?'

'It's fine, Mum. Honest. You go to choir.'

I stared into his eyes.

My beautiful boy. The only perfect thing in my life and the best thing I've ever done and here you are, telling me what you think I want to hear.

I could have dug deeper, tried to make him express some buried feeling or worry, but he'd been through enough emotional upheaval lately. We both had. All we could do was keep going. I hugged him again and kissed the top of his head. 'See you later, lovely boy. Enjoy the football.'

'See you later, Mum.'

'I love you,' I said in a voice full of hope.

'I love you too,' he replied in a matter-of-fact tone.

That would do for now.

Doly gave me a friendly wave as I arrived at the rehearsal. I decided that she was exactly the right person to sit next to this evening. I needed a Doly-sized dose of calm.

Guy clapped his hands together. 'Good evening, singing friends,' he cried. 'Firstly, well done again for Sunday. I never doubted us for a second and a big thanks to Pamela for creating such a dramatic ending to the performance.' Pamela giggled with embarrassment as everyone laughed. 'But seriously, you had us worried, so we got you a little something to say we're glad you're okay – we couldn't cope without your weekly bakes,' added Guy, producing a bunch of tulips from behind his back.

'Oh, lovey, you shouldn't have,' gushed Pamela, moving forwards to accept them and crushing Guy in a tight embrace, leaving a lipstick mark on his cheek as she kissed him.

'That's made my evening!' He laughed, wiping his cheek. 'And now, this is where it gets serious. The London Finals are looming so we really need to crack "God Only Knows" tonight. Let's warm up and then go for it, okay?'

I looked around the room. There was no sign of Caroline. I glanced at my phone. No text either. This was very unlike her. I nudged Doly. 'Where's Caroline?' She shrugged.

We began to sing. For some reason, we were distinctly off-key. I noticed Guy wince with alarm as we strangled 'God Only Knows' into submission.

'Okay,' said Guy, looking a little concerned. 'It's time to up the ante. Everyone on their feet, standing in two rows facing one another.' We did as we were told. I found myself staring up into Jim's broad beaming face.

'All right, Nat?' he grinned.

'Depends what old Gareth Malone over there's got planned.'

'Okay,' said Guy. 'We are going to practise making eye contact.' There was a collective groan. He held up his hands. 'I know, I know, but if we want to take this choir from being bloody good to bloody marvellous, we need to feed off one another. So, we will use the genius of Brian Wilson to help us. We are going to look into one another's eyes and sing alternating lines.'

I felt my mouth go dry. I was very fond of Jim but I had never held any longing to look into his eyes.

'Let's just try it, shall we? This side starts,' said Guy, pointing to my row. He pressed Play on the backing track.

I took a deep breath and looked up at Jim as I sang. It was toe, buttock and fist-clenchingly embarrassing. I wanted to look anywhere but into Jim's eyes but, as with the dancing, because we were all doing it, it became moderately less hideous as the song went on. We made a better sound too.

'Not bad,' said Guy when we finished. 'And a great improvement on our nightmare first attempt. I think it will help if we can acknowledge one another when we sing. It will bring us together as a group. I'm not suggesting holding hands but I think facing inwards and making eye contact will make for a better performance. And now, let's end this embarrassment and break for tea.'

There was a jovial cheer.

'How was that for you?' grinned Guy during the tea break. 'Did you and Jim form an unbreakable bond?'

'Of steel,' I retorted. 'Where's Caroline tonight? Did you give her a heads-up on the eye-contact thing? Is she hiding at home until you give her the all-clear?'

He looked at his phone. 'That's weird. She hasn't sent me a message. Do you think she's forgotten?'

'This is Caroline,' I said. 'She doesn't do forgetting.'

'True. I wonder if she's okay.'

'I'll nip up to her house now,' I said. 'Save me a piece of carrot cake if I'm not back.'

'What's it worth?' he grinned.

'You won't get punched if you do?'

He laughed. 'Fair enough. Violence in a woman is never pretty.'

I hurried along the street. There were lights on in Caroline's house but the curtains were drawn. I rang the doorbell. There was no movement from within. I waited a few seconds and tried again before taking a step back and staring up at the house. I couldn't imagine that Caroline would be out. I got the feeling that Tilly's bedtime routine was carved in stone. I spotted a figure staggering down the hall from the kitchen.

'Who is it?' demanded Caroline.

'Caroline, it's Natalie. Are you okay? We were at choir and wondered where you were.'

There was a pause. 'Sugar,' she said before opening the front door. I had never seen Caroline like this before and I suspect I wasn't alone. Her hair was bedraggled, her eyes were like those of a panda and she had clearly sunk quite a few glasses of wine. 'Come in,' she said, hiding behind the open front door so as not to show herself to the outside world.

I followed her down towards the kitchen. The television was on in the lounge and a frail elderly lady was staring at it. I paused in the doorway.

'Hello, you must be Caroline's mum. I'm Natalie,' I said. The woman glanced up at me and then stared back at the screen without answering.

'Oh, don't bother with her,' slurred Caroline, carrying on to the kitchen. 'She won't remember.'

'Er, nice to meet you,' I said before following Caroline. There was an empty wine bottle on the side and a new one on the go. 'Are you all right?' I asked as she slumped herself down at the kitchen table.

'Am fine,' she slurred, picking up her wine glass and taking another sip. 'Want one?'

Like you wouldn't believe. 'All right, but just a small one please.'

She fetched me a glass and poured it almost to the brim. 'Cheers!' she cried, tapping her glass against mine, slopping wine onto the table in the process.

She didn't even rush to clear it up. Things must be bad. 'Here's to shit days,' I said, taking a sip and sitting down opposite her. 'So what's happened to you?'

'Oh, nothing much, just the usual having to deal with my mother, another home having rejected her application and, oh yes, Oliver has lost his job.'

'Oh bugger. Sorry.'

'Bugger indeed,' she agreed. 'And now he's gone AWOL and has switched off his phone.'

'Double bugger.'

'Double bugger and bollocks,' she confirmed, waggling a drunken finger. 'What about you?'

I like this new drunken, sweary Caroline. She reminds me of me. 'I took your advice and told Dan to stay away.'

'Well cheers to that!'

'Not really. I phoned him while I was on the school trip and Woody overheard.'

She grimaced. 'Bugger.'

I nodded. 'So what are you going to do?'

'Get drunk.'

'I think you've already done that.'

Caroline gave a clumsy nod. 'Great. I always like to finish my to-do list. As you well know.'

This really is an all-new Caroline. She's even making jokes at her own expense.

I watched her for a moment. It was time for an intervention. 'Listen, Caroline, you don't have to take my advice but I'm a woman who has drowned her sorrows on more than one occasion and you just end up feeling like shit the next day, so would you let me make you a coffee to help you sober up?'

Caroline shrugged. 'If you like.'

I switched on the kettle and found a mug. 'I'm sure everything will be okay,' I offered, putting a glass of water in front of her.

'Are you?' I could tell she meant me rather than her.

'Well, no actually, but you've got to keep going, haven't you? Isn't that one of your mantras?'

She gave a weak smile. 'I suppose it is. Sorry. You must think I'm a nightmare.'

'Don't worry about it. We all have our off days and anyway, you can always shun Waitrose and come shopping at Aldi with me,' I joked, placing the coffee in front of her. Caroline frowned.

Whoops. Clearly not ready to joke about it yet.

'Look, do you want me to stick around and chat? I was going to go back to choir but I'm happy to stay if you want company?'

Caroline stared at me as if I'd just suggested an orgy. 'I'll be fine. Thank you. You go.'

Off you pop, Natalie. You are dismissed.

'All right. If you're sure. But I'm always around if you need someone to talk to.' I knew this wasn't really Caroline's way, but it was mine, so I felt compelled to offer.

'Thank you, Natalie. And thank you for checking up on me.'

'Bye then,' I said, standing up and heading towards the door.

'Bye,' she replied, without looking up.

I thought about warning against the perils of self-pity but decided against it. Lord knows, I'd indulged myself more than was probably healthy in recent times. I tiptoed out of the house, shutting the door behind me, and headed back to choir and cake.

CHAPTER FOURTEEN

CAROLINE

I have to confess that having Oliver at home was not turning out to be the unexpected pleasure I'd hoped it might be. For a start, he was very untidy. I was used to him leaving newspapers and dirty mugs all over the place but normally only in the evenings and at weekends – it was a contained messiness. However, now he was home all day, he left a trail of empty bowls, dirty plates and mugs. The kitchen was littered with filthy saucepans, used tea-bags and crumbs, whilst the toilet seat was always in the 'up' position and there was never any milk.

He has also told me that he intends to use this time as a 'sabbatical'. His firm have been pretty generous with his severance package and he seems to think that this means he can take all the time in the world to decide what to do next.

'I want to do something worthwhile, Caroline,' he smiled, running a hand over his five-day stubble. 'Something different. Make a change, you know?'

How about changing out of the jogging bottoms you've been wearing for the past three days? That would be a start.

I didn't say this, of course. I didn't want to suppress his enthusiasm. I tried a different tack. 'Have you called your old contacts to see if they have any leads on jobs?'

He shook his head vigorously. 'I don't think that's right for me. I think this is an opportunity to do something new and exciting.' He pulled me into his arms and kissed me. I considered telling him that he really needed to brush his teeth but kept my counsel. 'Meanwhile, I'm going to enjoy some precious time at home with my beautiful wife and darling daughter. How about I take Tilly to school?'

'Yay, Daddy's taking me to school!' cried Matilda, jumping up and down. 'Will you pick me up too?'

'If you like, pumpkin,' grinned Oliver.

'This is the best day ever,' declared Matilda, running off to find her shoes.

Thank you, Matilda. Please don't feel the need to spare my feelings. Daddy's home now, so Mummy can go and boil her head. Well I won't let it bother me.

'Fine. I'll take this opportunity to get to the gym early,' I said, reaching for my trainers.

'Yeah, actually. About that …' began Oliver.

'What about that?' I asked.

'We got the gym membership through work. So it's a bit of a no-go now,' he winced.

'Okay. I'll put it on the card.'

'Yeah, I'm just not sure we should be forking out on luxuries like gym membership,' he said. He spotted the look of horror on my face. 'Just for the time being. I'm sure we'll be able to re-join once we're back on our feet,' he added.

'Right. Okay,' I said. 'Anything else? Am I still allowed to shop at Waitrose, or is it the 99p store for us now?'

'I love the 99p store,' observed Matilda. I ignored her.

Oliver sensed my irritation and put one arm around my shoulder. 'We may need to make some cuts but it's fine for now,' he said, kissing the top of my head.

Fine for now? What does that even mean? That it won't be fine in the future? That I will actually have to comprehend shopping at Aldi with Natalie? I shivered with dread.

'Come on then, Daddy. We don't want to be late,' said Matilda, grabbing hold of his hand.

'Bye then,' I said, standing in the hallway, watching them go.

'Bye,' said Matilda without a backward glance.

I tend not to let life ruffle me. I am of the belief that you should get on with it and not allow yourself to become a victim of circumstance, but there was something about the casual way with which my daughter brushed me off that upset me a little.

It wasn't helped by the fact that she had formed such a strong and easy bond with my mother. They were constant companions. My mother's communication skills were limited now but Matilda seemed to have brought her out of herself somehow. It was as if a light had been switched on in the back of her brain again. They would often look at photographs together and one day, I had found some old cine-films in the loft. I was curious to see what was on them so I had them converted into DVDs. One Sunday afternoon, Oliver and I sat down with Matilda and my mother to watch them.

'These are funny,' laughed Matilda. 'Everyone looks as if they're walking really fast.'

It was true. There was no sharpness in the resolution or slickness in the production like the digital films of today, but there was a charm in the way that the people on screen had been told to walk towards the camera and try to look natural. There was one particular film of me at about the age of three or four. It looked as if we were in the middle of a big field, the blanket of green stretching all around us, the sky a pure blue; the perfect day really. My father had obviously been filming, instructing my mother and me to walk towards him from a distance. My mother looked so young and bright. I gazed in wonder as she caught hold of my hand and we skipped along, happy and giggling with delight. I couldn't remember laughing with my mother as a child. She always seemed so cross to me.

I glanced over at her. She was sitting very upright on the sofa, staring at the screen, her face expressionless as usual, but I noticed tears streaming down her face. I felt an unexpected ache in my chest and with it, a surge of panic.

This is a mistake. We shouldn't be watching this. It's too late for this.

'You look so happy!' declared Matilda, gazing up at her grandmother. 'Oh, Nanny, why are you crying?' she asked in alarm. She raised herself onto her knees and wrapped her arms around my mother, planting tiny kisses on her face. 'Don't cry, Nanny. Don't cry,' she soothed.

I felt Oliver reach for my hand but I gently pulled away. 'I think I'll make some tea,' I said before leaving the room. Once in the kitchen, I heard the sob I'd been suppressing escape from me. It sounded like the noise a distressed animal would make.

Don't put yourself through this, Caroline. You don't need to. Everything was fine as it was, the past was set as you remembered it. Where's the sense in dredging things up, things that can't be resolved? Don't upset the balance now.

I regained my composure. It was just an old film. It didn't mean a thing.

By the time Oliver reappeared twenty minutes later, I had made us both coffee and was sitting at the kitchen table checking the choir's Twitter feed. We had over three thousand followers now including, I noted with annoyance, Danielle and the Dulwich Darlings. She had even posted a response to the video of our south-east finals performance:

'You guys are ADORABLE – I want to adopt you all. #bless'

Whereas I had an immediate and over-powering urge to push her off a cliff.

'Everything all right at the school?' I asked as Oliver sat down next to me at the kitchen table.

'Fine,' he smiled. 'I saw your friend, Nat is it?'

'Natalie,' I replied. 'How about Zoe? Did she say, "Hi"?'

He furrowed his brow. 'I don't think I saw her. Mind you, I can't remember what she looks like, but Natalie made a point of speaking to me. She seems nice.' He picked up his coffee mug and took a sip. 'Ahhh, I could get used to this,' he grinned, leaning back in his chair.

'Don't get too used to it,' I warned. 'We don't want to end up on the breadline.'

'That won't happen. I've got enough money to keep us going for at least six months.'

'And pay for holidays?'

He took hold of my hand. 'If the lady wants a holiday, the lady shall have a holiday,' he said, kissing his way up my arm.

'I don't mean a camping holiday, by the way,' I said.

Oliver stared at me. 'Now actually, that's a really good idea. Tilly would LOVE to go camping, I'm sure. Just think of it – the great outdoors, cooking in the open, sleeping under the stars—'

'Freezing to death and holding onto the tent in a torrential storm,' I added.

He laughed. 'It would be fun. You would love it.'

'I love nice warm hotels with spas attached,' I said firmly.

He smiled, shuffled his chair closer to me and started to kiss my neck. 'And huge four-poster beds too?'

'Provided the sheets have a thread count of at least eight hundred,' I murmured.

He kissed me on the mouth and stared into my eyes. The sound of my mother shuffling into the kitchen made us both jump.

Oliver leapt from his chair. 'Patricia!' he cried. 'Would you like a cup of tea?' She stared at him before shuffling back out again. 'That'll be a no then,' he laughed. 'Right, I'm going for a shower,' he said, kissing me again and heading for the stairs.

Moments later the doorbell rang. 'I've got it,' I called.

I made my way down the hall, peering through the glass to see if I recognised who was there. I expected it to be Jim with a parcel but the person was much smaller. I opened the door to a woman, who I didn't recognise immediately, although I knew we'd met before. She was slight with short hair and elfin features and a veritable array of ear piercings. She smiled at me. She had a natural beauty and warmth, which said, 'I am a good person. You can trust me.'

'Mrs Taylor? Do you remember me? I'm Laurie. I was your mother's care worker.'

'Oh yes, of course,' I said, a little confused. 'Would you like to come in?'

'If it's not too much trouble. I hope you don't mind me dropping by. It's my day off and I just wondered how Patricia was?' she said. I was astonished. This woman had given up a day off to come and visit my mother.

'She's just in the lounge. Do go through. Can I get you a tea or coffee?'

'A tea would be great, thanks. Milk, no sugar.'

I watched her enter the room. 'Patricia! Do you remember me? Laurie?'

I glanced into the lounge and was amazed to see my mother reaching out her arms to embrace this woman. 'Laurie,' she said with a smile.

I busied myself in the kitchen, suppressing the envy I felt.

It's ridiculous, Caroline. You don't want a relationship with your mother. It's too late. Remember?

I stayed in the kitchen for a while. I thought I'd leave them to it. It was better that way. After a time, I heard Laurie helping my mother to the toilet before appearing in the doorway.

'So, how are you coping?' she asked.

'Fine,' I said. *If you can call the daily washing of soiled bedsheets and living with a stranger in your house 'fine'.*

I noticed Laurie take in her surroundings, smiling at the pictures and photographs on the fridge. 'Is this your daughter?' she asked.

'Yes. That's Matilda. She's eight,' I replied.

'I bet your mother loves her,' she observed.

I knew that Matilda adored my mother but I hadn't really considered how my mother felt. 'They have formed quite a close bond, yes,' I admitted.

'And what about you?'

'Pardon?'

'How is your bond?'

'Well, it's fine.' *There's that word again. I'm fine. She's fine. We're fine. Everything's fine. Now please stop prying.*

'Don't take this the wrong way, Caroline, but I know that you didn't visit your mother very often and I also know that she dotes on you.'

Dotes on you. Oliver had used the same phrase. I smiled at Laurie. She was kind but she didn't understand. 'Look, Laurie, I appreciate you coming and I'm sure my mother does too, but you don't know what happened in my family. It's private and I don't need anyone interfering.'

Laurie fixed me with a look. There was no judgement in her gaze – it was more as if she were trying to read my soul, to glean the truth because she knew I was hiding it. 'I'm not here to make you feel guilty or uncomfortable,' she said. 'I just know from experience that the pain and regret you feel after someone dies can become almost unbearable if you don't do your best for them while they're alive. I see something in your mother – a pain and distress, a hidden upset she needs to resolve. I'm sure that you have your reasons for not allowing her to do that but I would beg you to think again. For her sake and for yours.' She reached across the table and squeezed one of my hands, her smile understanding and encouraging.

'I'll think about it,' I said. *I won't but I have to say something to bring an end to this.*

She nodded and stood up. 'Thank you for the tea. I'll pop in to say goodbye to Patricia and see myself out.' I heard the front door close behind her and then the sound of Oliver coming down the stairs.

'Who was that?' he asked, standing in the kitchen doorway.

'No-one important,' I replied, rising to my feet and gathering up my bag. 'I'm just going out for a bit. Is it okay if I leave you here with my mother?'

'Of course, darling,' he said, kissing me on the way past. 'We'll be fine. I'm going to get online and suss out some new job opportunities.

'Great,' I smiled. 'Good luck.'

I drove into town and spent a couple of hours indulging in a little retail therapy. This was a rare treat for me but one which I felt I deserved today. The hall campaign could wait, the issues with my mother could wait, hopefully indefinitely. I made my way to my favourite boutique on the high street. The woman behind the counter knew me by sight and was always happy to recommend clothes or jewellery that she felt might suit me. I soon found a dress and a top I liked and carried them to the changing room to try on. I had just taken off my top when I heard two voices that

I recognised – Amanda and Zoe. I was about to get dressed again so that I could go out and greet them but something stopped me – to be honest, I was a little miffed that they were meeting up without me. Amanda was often visiting clients nearby and we would meet for lunch. I took out my phone to check our WhatsApp group but there was nothing. I stayed where I was and listened, my adrenaline starting to pump.

'How about this, Mands?' asked Zoe, holding up something for her inspection.

'That's pretty but a bit last year,' observed Amanda. They were right outside my changing room.

'Mmm, maybe. So anyway, I haven't had a chance to tell you – I saw Oliver today.'

I held my breath.

'Oh yes?' said Amanda, ready for gossip.

'Oh, my God, he looked terrible. It's like he's given up since he lost his job.'

'Terrible,' echoed Amanda. 'Poor Caroline. Have you seen her?'

'No. I think she might be keeping a low profile. Mind you, you can hardly blame her.'

'Totally. I mean, I thought about inviting her today but it's probably hard for her financially.'

'I thought the same. What about the drinks thing next week? Shall we ask her to that?'

Amanda sighed. 'Best not. That cocktail bar is pretty pricey, plus she'll probably just be moaning. You know how she can be.'

I felt my body go rigid as Zoe laughed. 'True, she does put a dampener on things sometimes. Let's just keep it the two of us then.'

'Perfect. Are you going to get that? I'm done here.'

'No, I'll leave it for now. Let's grab lunch.'

I heard the shop bell tinkle, indicating their departure. I stayed still for a moment, suddenly aware of the sound of my own heart. I felt crushed, as if I couldn't breathe. *I must not cry. I must not cry.* I looked at the clothes still on their hangers, before pulling my top back over my head and leaving the changing room.

'Any good?' smiled the lady behind the counter.

'No, not today, thank you,' I said, before hurrying from the shop. I practically ran to my car and sat in the driver's seat, wondering what to do next. I was rather surprised when I found myself sitting outside Natalie's house ten minutes later. I rang the doorbell, my face ready with a smile.

Natalie's face, on the other hand, was set in a frown, which relaxed a little when she saw me on the doorstep. 'Oh, Caroline, hi. Do you want to come in?' she asked.

'If you're not too busy,' I replied.

Natalie sighed. 'I've been farting about all day trying to finish the next Ned story, so a distraction would be welcome.'

'Thank you,' I said, following her to the kitchen.

'I'm just making a sandwich. Would you like one?' she asked.

'That would be lovely – thank you.'

She opened the fridge. 'Okay, we have cheese – or – er, cheese?' She grinned, holding up a parcel of cheddar.

'Cheese is fine, thanks,' I replied, shouldering off my coat.

'So-o, how are you? Is everything okay?' she asked, looking at me with genuine concern.

How to answer? I hate my mother and my friends have been mean to me? You sound like a six-year-old, Caroline. Besides, I don't hate my mother. I just don't know her, not really and I'm starting to wonder if I'm being a little unfair.

The truth was, I'd never tried to talk about these things before because I'd never felt the need, but now, I was hitting a low point. My ordered life was starting to look a little less than ordered and I was beginning to feel desperate. I didn't really have anyone else to talk to. Oliver had enough on his plate and Natalie had offered. Plus, I found her easy to talk to. She may have been chaotic but she was kind.

'I had a visit today from the woman who used to be my mother's carer,' I began.

'Oh, that was nice of her.'

I nodded. 'Yes, yes it was.' I thought for a moment. 'She believes there are issues which my mother is trying to resolve.'

'What kind of issues?'

I stared at the ceiling. This was hard. 'Issues relating to our relationship.'

'I see. But you don't feel as if you can talk to her?'

Actually, I don't want to talk to her. I'm scared of talking to her. I hesitated. 'I find it tricky.'

She nodded. 'It's not easy. I had a similar thing with my father when he was dying.'

'And what did you do?'

Natalie stared at me and puffed out her cheeks. 'You and I are very different. I'm not sure I'm the best person to advise you, Caroline.'

'Please,' I said.

Natalie heard the desperation in my voice. She took a deep breath. 'I talked to him, did my best to work through it,' she said. 'I had a very trying relationship with him but I always took Woody when I went and actually, they had a good relationship – better than my own with him. And now my father's dead, I'm glad I did it because I did my best. Life isn't about smooth edges and neat endings. It's about doing your best. At least, that's what I think.'

This was an alien concept to me but it was starting to make sense. 'Thank you,' I said.

'You're welcome. Now, do you want pickle in this sandwich?'

I laughed. 'I'll have whatever you're having.'

'Pickle it is then,' she said with a grin.

'How about you? Are you talking to Dan?'

Natalie sighed. 'Not really. He took Woody out for pizza the other day but I hid in my office when he rang the doorbell and he stayed in the car when he dropped Woody back.'

I couldn't imagine how that would feel. 'I'm sorry, Natalie. It must be hard for you.'

She shrugged. 'I have good days and bad days. Choir days are always good days though,' she said, handing me a sandwich.

'Very true,' I agreed.

'Well, there's one thing we have in common then,' she said with a wry smile. 'That and a love of cheese-and-pickle sandwiches.'

I laughed. 'A match made in heaven.'

Maybe sharing isn't such a bad thing after all, I thought as we sat and chatted. *Maybe sharing with the right people actually helps. Maybe it enables you to face things you'd never thought possible and resolve them once and for all. Maybe. Just maybe.*

CHAPTER FIFTEEN

NATALIE

'Jim, I think your bud-up-bahs might be a bit off,' said Guy, following our third run-through of 'God Only Knows'.

'My bud-up-bahs are always off,' giggled Doly, nudging me. 'Natalie? How are your bud-up-bahs?'

'What? Oh, sorry, yes, bud-up-bahs, all over the place,' I agreed.

'You seem a bit distracted tonight,' observed Doly. 'Are you okay?'

'I'm fine,' I lied. 'It's just been a long day.' This was true. It had been a long day and I felt as if I'd been hit repeatedly with a boxing glove filled with every conceivable emotion.

BAM! Searing fury.

POW! Extraordinary sadness.

WHAM! Unexpected attraction.

It was very confusing and to be honest, I felt exhausted. When Ed appeared half an hour before choir, I'd had an overwhelming urge to send him home and eat my own body-weight in cheese. Like I said, it had been a very confusing day.

Still, the London Choir Finals were looming and one of my more annoying traits is that I find it almost impossible to let people down. So when I'd seen Doly earlier that day during an emergency run for jammie dodgers (I would like to claim that these were for Woody but I'm fooling no-one) and she had asked if I was going that evening, I couldn't refuse. Besides, I enjoyed the singing. It enabled me to release tension in a wholly fulfilling way. Plus, it was cheaper and less knackering than kick-boxing and there was always cake. I'd wrestle a tiger for a decent slice of Battenberg.

I was glad to see Caroline back to her ebullient self. I heard her giving Pamela instructions about T-shirts during the break. Apparently, there had been an online vote to decide if we should go for a shade of teal or ecru and Pamela couldn't quite accept that teal was the majority choice.

'It's just that ecru doesn't suit everyone, Pamela,' explained Caroline. 'It washes people out and we do have our male singers to consider.'

'I preferred the brown,' observed Jim, rather ill-advisedly choosing this moment to join their conversation.

'See?' huffed Pamela. 'Jim prefers ecru.'

'Do I?' said Jim, looking confused.

Caroline held up her hands for calm. 'I'm sorry, both, but the majority have chosen teal. It's democracy in action. Don't you agree, Natalie?'

I was painfully aware that three sets of eyes were upon me, expectant and ready to narrow if I gave the wrong answer. I smiled. 'I'd be happy with either,' I said. 'Now what triumph have you baked for us this week, Pamela?' I added, putting an arm around her.

She gave me one of her indulgent grins. 'Triple-chocolate brownies,' she replied, holding up a gigantic tin, which was promptly fallen upon by an appreciative crowd.

'That was a neat deflection,' observed Guy, helping himself to a fat slab of chocolate heaven. 'You could work for the UN with those skills.'

I gave a little bow. 'Why thank you. I am actually thinking of going into international diplomacy if the writing career takes a nose-dive.'

He laughed. 'And what about other stuff?' He said 'stuff' in that wincing way men adopt when they feel uncomfortable talking about affairs of the heart.

'By "stuff", do you mean my imploding marriage?' He grimaced. I nudged him. 'It's okay, I'm being mean because you're a man and I basically blame you for all this.'

He put one hand on his heart. 'Fair enough. I take it on the chin and apologise for men everywhere. You should avoid us at all costs.'

I smiled. 'Well, you're one of the good ones so I'm not going to avoid you.'

He pretended to doff a cap. 'I shall do my best to restore your faith.'

I curtsied. 'Thank you, kind sir.' *This feels good. I miss indulging in a bit of silly banter with a man.* 'And how are things with you?'

'I'm fine. I've got my mother settled into her new home – she seems pretty happy.'

'Oh, that's where my mother was before they threw her out,' scoffed Caroline, appearing from nowhere. *How does she do that? It's as if she's got special powers.* 'How are you finding it? The home manager, Peter, is very officious, isn't he?'

I could see Guy shrink away at her questioning and to be honest, I was irritated by her interruption. *Jog on, Caroline. Can't you see that I'm enjoying a bit of harmless flirting here?*

'They've been pretty good with Mum, actually,' he admitted.

'Well they were a nightmare with my mother. They said that they could cope with her condition but basically they kept her confined to her room and then they lost her one night. It's a scandal! I would be very wary if I were you,' she warned Guy.

'Thanks,' said Guy uncertainly. 'Right, we better get started again.' He smiled at me before returning to the front of the room. 'Okay, my singing friends – I know I don't need to remind you that we're singing at the School Summer Fair on Saturday and then the London Finals are on Sunday, so we need to up our game. From my experience, the choir always gives the worst performance at the final rehearsal, so in that respect, we're doing great!' There were a few groans of concern. 'But don't worry. We just need to focus. I propose singing some of our old favourites and then one last run-through before we call it a night, okay? Let's clear away the chairs and stand as we'll be for the performance.'

'Any progress with the counselling?' Caroline asked as we stacked the chairs at the back of the room. I stared at her in disbelief as a few fellow choir members glanced our way.

Keep your voice down, I wanted to say. *What happened to the Caroline who sat in my kitchen eating a cheese sandwich, chatting like a normal person? I prefer her to this loud-mouthed know-it-all.*

Instead, I stared at the floor and murmured, 'A bit,' in a non-committal way. This was actually true. There had been progress, but the kind of progress where someone suggests the opposite of what you were hoping for. My baby-faced counsellor, Abigail 'I'm just being honest, Natalie' Walters, had suggested today that I consider the realistic possibility that not all broken marriages are salvageable.

It was progress – progress towards marital Armageddon.

I left the session feeling like a child who had just been told that both Father Christmas and the Tooth Fairy aren't real. My body was shaking and I felt as if I was about to either be sick or cry. Or both. It wasn't the best.

I had planned to go home and work but realised during the train journey, that my brain wasn't capable of writing funny happy stories today; dark psychological thrillers where marriage guidance counsellors meet grisly ends perhaps, but definitely not books aimed at anyone under five. I made a detour at the station, heading to the nearest coffee shop, where I ordered an ill-advised double-shot flat white and weirdly, no pain au chocolat. It is a sign that I'm approaching the abyss when I turn down food. That's the moment when I know I'm in big trouble.

I had sat at my table for a long time, watching the other customers with their normal happy lives. Actually, there was a good chance that they were dealing with all kinds of issues but at that moment, I was the only person with real problems. I observed the exhausted woman with the sleeping baby in a pushchair, enjoying a precious moment of peace, and hated her. I watched the young dude plugged into his Mac, frowning at the screen, and I felt utter loathing.

You people don't understand what it's like to be me. My misery reigns supreme.

'Natalie?' I looked up from my brooding stupor into the smiling face of Tim Chambers, local MP and, to my mind at that moment, utter cretin.

Really? I'm having a quiet coffee whilst indulging in a session of unadulterated self-pity and the world sends me this man. Thanks. Thanks a bunch.

'Oh, hi,' I replied in an off-hand way, hoping he would take the hint and leave. He didn't.

'This is nice surprise,' he remarked. 'May I join you?'

Quick, Nat! Make up an excuse. 'I have to get my overdue library books back before I run up a fine?' 'I have

*a contagious disease that only Tory MPs can catch?' What
can I tell you? I'm not good under pressure.*

'Okay,' I sighed.

'Can I get you another?' he asked, pointing at my
empty cup.

'Another flat white with an extra shot please,' I said.
Keep the caffeine coming.

He returned with our drinks, put down the tray and took
off his jacket, neatly folding it over the chair before he
sat down. 'So,' he said, passing me my drink. 'Pardon my
frankness but you seem a little down. Is everything all right?'

*What the hell. I'm never going to be bosom buddies with
this man. Besides, seeing as everyone else was being so
straight-talking today, I may as well join in.*

'I've just been for counselling,' I said. He raised his
eyebrows. 'Marriage guidance,' I added.

He nodded. 'I've done a little of that myself,' he said.
It was my turn to raise an eyebrow. 'How are you finding
it? I have to say I found the endless quizzes a bit much – as
if I were trying to save my marriage via the medium of a
gameshow.'

I gave an involuntary laugh. 'I know what you mean.
They're like those crappy magazine quizzes I used to do as
a kid.'

He grinned. 'Oh yes – *Cosmopolitan*'s were always the
best. I learnt everything I needed to know about girls from
those mags.' I stared at him. 'I had three sisters,' he added,
'in case you think I'm a weirdo.'

I smiled. 'And did they help? The quizzes I mean, rather
than your sisters.'

He put a hand on his heart. 'I'm recently divorced, so
possibly not. And as for my sisters, they like to tell me
everywhere I've gone wrong with women. I probably
deserve it,' he shrugged.

Heavens, a straight-talking politician – now that's unusual. 'So where have you gone wrong?'

He stared up at the ceiling for a moment before counting them off on his fingers. 'I'm vain, egotistical, arrogant, selfish and a liar.'

Very straight-talking. 'Wow, that's what your own sisters say? Harsh.'

'No, that's what my ex-wife says, but then she was the one who had the affair, so it's a little bit "pots and kettles".'

'And what do you think?' I asked.

He gazed at me. I hadn't noticed before but he had intensely green eyes, like a cat's. 'I think I have been all those things but I'm trying to be a better man.' There was something heartfelt about his words that struck me. Here I was, sitting with a man whose political convictions were a million miles away from my own, who I wouldn't have trusted for one second and yet, I felt an odd affinity with him. It was a bit of a worry, but then, life seemed to be taking quite a few unexpected turns of late.

'Well, you can't do any more than that,' I said.

He nodded. 'And what about you? Excuse me for speaking out of turn, but what kind of idiot would let you slip through his fingers?'

It was outrageous flirting – a completely blatant attempt to charm. Normally I was immune to this kind of nonsense. However, today was different. Today I was a woman who was losing hope and actually, this statement gave me goose-bumps. It was such a direct declaration. I took a sip of my coffee. 'An idiot I thought I knew,' I conceded.

'Sorry,' said Tim. 'I really should mind my own business. Why don't I do my compassionate MP bit and ask you about your community hall campaign?'

We talked for another hour or so about the campaign and the choir and I felt my attitude towards Tim alter dramatically. Far from being a smug politician, I felt that he was listening. As we put on our coats to leave, he turned to me.

'It was really good to see you, Natalie. Thank you for taking the time to talk to me. I can see how much the hall means to your choir and the community. Whilst I can't make any promises because this is technically a council matter, you have my word as your local MP that I will do my very best for you and your supporters.'

'Thank you,' I said. 'And thanks for the coffee.'

'And as for your situation,' he added, 'I wish you all the luck you need. I hope you resolve it to your satisfaction and remember, I'm just a phone call away if you want to chat to someone who's been through it. And I'm more than willing to do *Cosmopolitan* quizzes with you,' he joked.

I laughed. He held out his hand and as I took it, he pressed my hand to his lips. 'Sorry,' he smiled. 'Couldn't resist.'

I blushed. I actually blushed. *Blimey, Nat. You've lost it, love.*

The confusion continued to reign supreme as I left choir and returned home. I had thought that Ed might stick around or perhaps even stay over. I had chucked a bottle of Prosecco in the fridge before choir in the hope that we might have a heart-to-heart over the latest ups and downs of my day, but by the time I'd turned my key in the door, kicked off my shoes and pulled on my slippers, he was out of his seat and putting on his coat.

'Have you got a date? You smell like you've got a date,' I observed, sniffing his neck on the way past. 'That's your pulling after-shave.'

'It's not after-shave, you pleb. It's eau de parfum.'

I pulled a face. 'Whatevs. So you don't want to stay and get merry with your BFF then? I have had a very interesting day.'

He pouted in apology. 'Sorry, gorgeous. I've got an early start but let's make a date soon, 'kay?'

''Kay,' I replied.

He wrapped his arms around me and kissed the top of my head. 'Always here for you, my darling. You know that, don't you?'

I accepted the hug with gratitude. 'Yeah, I know. Was Woody okay?'

'He was a complete sweetheart, as ever. He beat me at *Fifa* about fifty times.'

I smiled. 'That's my boy. Thanks for tonight.'

'Any time, my love. Any time. So Dan's moving to a flat in Forest Hill then?'

I nodded. 'Apparently. After all his denials, it turns out that it *is* too cramped at his mum's and he wants to be nearer to Woody. He says it's temporary until things are sorted out. Who knows what to believe? I heard about it via text. We're not speaking at the moment.'

He hugged me again. 'I'm sorry, honey.'

I sighed. 'Thank you. Now bugger off. I want to eat ice cream in front of *Gogglebox* without you judging me.'

He laughed. 'I'll see you soon,' he said, kissing me again. I waved him off and then locked the front door before going to the kitchen to fetch something suitably sugary. It wasn't until I returned to the lounge with tea and a large tub of Maltesers that I realised that I hadn't actually told Ed about Dan's flat. I was going to tell him that evening.

I hadn't mentioned it to Woody yet either. So it made me wonder how he knew and then it made me realise that he must be in touch with Dan, which confused me further because he hadn't told me this. In fact, Ed, with his trademark penchant for injecting drama wherever possible, had been adamant that he wouldn't have anything to do with the 'shit-bag' until he had 'come to his effing senses' and told me 'what the bejeepers was going on'.

It was becoming steadily clearer to me that the list of people who I thought I could trust, who I believed would never lie to me or let me down, was getting smaller and smaller by the day.

CHAPTER SIXTEEN

CAROLINE

I was starting to wonder if this train journey was ever going to end, although everyone else including Oliver seemed to be having a whale of a time. The children loved the endless word games which Natalie suggested they play, and they were thrilled when she conducted them in a loud and energetic rendition of 'Good Vibrations'. Even Oliver had joined in whilst I sat staring out of the window, pretending that I wasn't with them.

'Come on, Caroline, we need to warm up our voices,' laughed Natalie.

Oh, heavens, her mania seems to be bordering on hysteria today. This is deeply concerning. I hope she can keep herself in check.

'Ooh, that's the London Eye, isn't it?' cried Matilda, jumping up and down as we crossed over the river. 'And there's Big Ben!'

'And the Houses of Parliament,' remarked Woody seriously. 'That's where that man works, isn't it, Mum?'

'Which man?' smiled Natalie, slinging one arm around her son's shoulders and peering out across the river.

'You know, the one who trips up old ladies and steals their money. George Whatshisface.'

'Osborne?' asked Oliver with a frown.

'That's the one,' nodded Woody.

'Natalie!' I cried. 'How can you mislead your son like that?'

She laughed. 'Technically it's only bending the truth. What can I say? I'm a writer. That's basically my job.'

'It seems a tad irresponsible to me,' I observed.

'Of course it does, Caroline,' teased Natalie, raising her eyebrows at Oliver, who laughed.

The cheek – sharing jibes about me with my husband!

'Right, here we are. Matilda, Woody, hold hands while we get off the train please,' I said, dismissing my irritation and focussing on the children.

'I'm not holding hands with a boy,' said Matilda. 'Even if it is Woody, who is actually my best friend.'

'You're very wise to be wary of boys,' declared Natalie. 'But you can trust this one,' she added, ruffling her son's hair.

'Mum!' complained Woody, ducking away from his mother.

'Oi, don't you start being mean to me. I've got enough problems with unreliable men at the moment. I thought I could count on you!'

Oh dear, here we go.

'Come on,' said Oliver, sensing the need to move us on. 'First one to see Nelson's Column!'

Woody and Matilda ran ahead as we made our way across the station concourse onto the Strand. It was a bright, sunny day and I was excited at the prospect of the London Choir Finals.

I was pleased that Oliver and Matilda had come along to support too. It had actually been Matilda's suggestion, although I think that she and Woody had been talking about it at school.

I had noticed a slight change in her attitude towards me since my mother had come to stay with us. It was quite subtle but every now and then she would ask me a question about my childhood and what 'Nanny' had been like. I still winced at the name 'Nanny' but Matilda had locked onto it and it seemed wrong to challenge her.

It was hard to give a positive spin on my relationship with my mother and often I found myself just talking about Dad instead. Still, she seemed to enjoy this too and only yesterday had come to me with a picture she had drawn. It was of seven figures, six of them standing on the ground with one hovering above on a cloud. She had given it the heading, 'My Family'.

'This is Daddy, me and you,' she explained, 'and this is Gran and Gramps, that's Nanny in a chair with some biscuits and this,' she added, pointing to the figure floating above the rest, 'is Grandpa. He's dead but he watches everything we do from heaven.'

I felt my throat tighten and my heart swell with love. *Dearest Matilda.* 'It's beautiful,' I said. 'Really. Would it be okay if I framed it?'

She seemed surprised but pleased. 'If you like.'

We crossed the road and made our way to St Martin-in-the-Fields, where the Final was due to take place. I had made sure we were early. I had even told Natalie a small white lie so that she arrived at our house half an hour before we needed to leave.

'There's an hour until it starts so I suppose we should go in and warm up,' I said to her.

'How about I take the kids for a drink and a cake somewhere and we'll come back later?' suggested Oliver.

'If you're sure that's okay,' said Natalie. 'Here, let me give you some money for drinks.'

Oliver waved her away. 'My treat,' he said. 'Okay, come on kids, wish your mums luck or tell them to break a leg or whatever,' he added, leaning forwards to kiss me.

'Break a leg? That's funny,' laughed Matilda. 'Break a leg, Mum,' she said, grinning at me.

'See you later,' I smiled.

'Oliver's lovely,' remarked Natalie. 'You're lucky.'

'Yes, I suppose I am,' I nodded. 'Although I'd feel a lot luckier if he found a job and I could get my mother into a new place.'

'Did you leave her at home on her own today?'

'Lord no. I've asked Laurie, who used to care for her at the home, to come over. I offered to pay her but she wouldn't take anything.'

'That was kind of her.'

'Yes it was. So how are things with Dan?' I wouldn't normally ask but it felt only polite.

Natalie sighed. 'I'm having a day off thinking about it today. I just want to enjoy the singing.'

I smiled. 'Fair enough. I'm having a day off thinking about my mother. Shall we go and find the others?'

We were the first from our choir to arrive and as we stepped into the church, we both exclaimed at its beauty. 'Wow,' breathed Natalie. 'This is stunning.'

She was right. I had been here a few times before but I'd forgotten how breathtaking the interior was with its white pillars, beautiful stucco ceiling and ornate chandeliers. It had the air of sacred beauty and I felt my heart beat a little faster at the thought of performing here.

'Caroline! How wonderful to see you again.' My moment's reflection was interrupted by Danielle, striding towards me from the altar end of the church. She and her fellow Dulwich Darlings were resplendent in sequin jackets, which I noticed, to my horror, were a shade of teal.

'Snap!' she cried, holding out the fabric of her jacket to my T-shirt as she reached us. She air-kissed me and nodded to Natalie. 'So! You had T-shirts printed. So adorable.

We thought about it but decided to go a little more upmarket, a little more Dulwich, you know?'

Oh, I know. I know exactly what you're saying, you judgemental harridan.

'Still, it may help you if the judges think we're linked in some way,' she added, barely able to conceal her bitchiness.

'Well, I wish you luck,' I replied, swallowing down my irritation.

She pursed her lips. 'We don't really need it but thank you,' she chimed. 'Now, you must excuse me, darling. I need to get back to the sound-check. They don't do it for every choir but as we're celebrities, they make an exception,' she added with a wink before strolling back to her fellow singers.

'What a cow,' observed Natalie.

I laughed. 'Thank God you said that. I thought it was just me.'

'Heavens no. What's with that "so adorable" and "we're celebrities" crap?' asked Natalie, parroting Danielle's voice. 'Actually, love, you're not a celebrity, you're a big fraud in a sparkly jacket,' she added. I guffawed. Natalie smiled. 'So tell me the truth, did we really need to be here this early?' she asked.

Oh dear. I've been found out. I gave her a guilty look. 'Strictly speaking no, but it did mean you got to see Danielle again,' I joked. 'I know how fond you are of her.'

She laughed. 'Careful. You're starting to sound like me. I guess it has got me all revved up and determined to beat the witch, though.'

'That's the spirit,' I smiled. I was relieved that Natalie seemed more relaxed and less hyper than she had been on the train.

'Good morning, lovely ladies,' said Guy, appearing alongside us with Doly, Jim, Pamela and others in tow.

'Did you get an earlier train? We just had an impromptu warm-up on the way.'

'Yes,' said Natalie. 'Caroline made us leave last night so that we'd be here on time.'

'Ha, ha,' I said, rolling my eyes.

'My T-shirt feels a bit tight,' said Jim, pulling off his jacket and raising his arms above his head, revealing an alarmingly hairy belly.

'Maybe just don't lift up your arms,' suggested Natalie with a giggle.

I smiled. The assembled group were in an excited albeit slightly nervous mood and it felt good to be part of this. We'd had a run-through the day before at the School Summer Fair. I had suggested this, partly to give us practice for singing in public and partly because I wanted to be involved. It was the first year since Matilda had started school that I hadn't been running the show. My PTA rival, Nula, had taken the reins and I wanted to make sure I was there just in case there was a crisis or Phil, the Headmaster, needed me. In the event it all ran pretty smoothly. There were issues with the windy conditions, causing one teacher to be nearly knocked out by a runaway gazebo, and we ran out of Pimm's halfway through the event, but apart from that, I had to concede that all was running as well as could be expected. Of course I didn't tell Nula this. I fully intended to be back in charge for Christmas and I didn't want her getting ideas above her station.

The choir sang an extended version of the set we performed in the pub. Everyone seemed to enjoy it and some of the parents who had spent too long at the Pimm's stall even joined in, but it was pretty good-natured. I spotted Zoe and Amanda watching together and noticed Amanda making comments whilst the pair of them cackled like magpies. Afterwards, they were all smiles and hugs towards me. I noticed that Natalie kept a distance.

'Darling! It was a triumph!' trilled Amanda.

'Wonderful, absolutely wonderful,' echoed Zoe. 'I'm just super-sorry I can't find the time to come along and join in.' Amanda nudged her and she giggled.

At that moment I realised how much Amanda reminded me of Danielle and every other bitchy so-called friend I'd had. These were people who don't like you for who you are but who are always trying to make themselves look better, usually by putting you down. It was a thunder-clap revelation when it dawned on me that I hadn't missed either of them at all.

'Shall we grab a Pimm's then?' cooed Amanda. 'Although that woman who stole your job doesn't seem to have ordered enough. Total disaster!'

'Disaster,' repeated Zoe.

I smiled. 'Actually, I need to go and find Oliver and Matilda, so if you would excuse me—'

'Oh,' said Amanda, looking surprised. 'See you around then. Are you coming, Zoe?'

'Absolutely,' said Zoe, flashing me a smile that didn't reach her eyes. 'See you around, Caroline.'

I turned away, feeling as if something I no longer needed had ended. It felt very good indeed.

My happy mood had continued into the next day. I felt so positive about the choir and everything we were doing. I actually couldn't remember the last time I'd felt this way about something. I decided that today was going to be a good day and win or lose, I intended to enjoy myself.

'Right, singing super-stars,' grinned Guy. 'Let's find out where we need to be, shall we?'

We were first in the running order and I felt a frisson of nerves as we assembled at the front of the church. I could see Danielle smiling in that indulgent, patronising way, which was something of a trademark for her. I felt my fists clench but then I spotted Matilda and Oliver sitting with Woody a few rows back. I noticed the way Matilda leant against her father, craning her neck to get a better look. We locked eyes and she gave me a carefree wave of glee. It made my heart soar and with it my confidence. Guy stood before us, his face bright with enthusiasm. He nodded, raised his hands and we began to sing.

There is something about singing in a church, regardless of whether you have faith or not, that taps into the soul. There is a deeply satisfying and spiritual quality to the sound that a group of human voices can make in a space like that. This space was particularly conducive, the acoustics lovingly thought out to make the most of the power of sound. I felt my spirits lift as we began to sing. Everything seemed to fall into place and the harmonies sounded beautiful. Our movements were better, less forced and more natural, and we smiled at one another as our music filled the air. It was a near-perfect performance and I felt that we deserved to go through. We'd worked hard, we'd created something special. We had arrived.

I glanced at Natalie and saw that the corners of her eyes were wet with tears. She caught sight of me and we smiled at one another. It was a smile that said, 'Isn't this wonderful?'

After we'd finished I held my breath. Some part of me wanted to slow down time, to savour this moment because there was truly nothing like it. The audience clapped and we bowed as one before leaving the stage to sit amongst our friends and family.

'Well done, darling, I'm proud of you,' said Oliver, kissing my cheek as I sat down next to him.

'It was lovely, Mum,' admitted Matilda.

'Thank you,' I smiled. 'Thank you for coming to support me.'

We settled down to listen to rest of the choirs. The standard was very high among the other groups and there were only four spaces up for grabs in the Final. Guy and I exchanged nervous glances. The Dulwich Darlings came on to sing last, giving a slightly over-the-top rendition of 'My Heart Will Go On'. Danielle's face wore a pained, closed-eyes expression throughout.

'She looks constipated,' whispered Natalie, nudging me. I laughed.

Whilst the judges were making their decisions, our choir gathered for a post-mortem.

'The standard is very high,' observed Doly.

'You were the best by a long shot,' said her husband Dev, putting an arm around his wife. She rewarded him with a smile.

'I think my bud-up-bahs were still a bit off,' remarked Jim. 'I blame the T-shirt.'

'You need to stop having double helpings of my cakes,' scolded Pamela, patting his stomach.

'They're coming back,' said Guy, pointing to the judges, who were emerging from the crypt. We took our places. I felt Oliver take hold of my hand.

'Ladies and gentlemen,' said the head judge, an older, debonair man, who reminded me a little of Len Goodman. 'Thank you to all our choirs for taking part today. My fellow judges and I have had a very difficult time choosing which four London choirs should go through to the Final. However, we have made our decision and I am pleased to announce that the four winning choirs are—'

I closed my eyes.

'The Dulwich Darlings.' There was a cheer. I suppose it was too much to hope for. He waited for the noise to die down. 'The Walthamstow Warblers.' Another cheer.

'The Clapham South Singers.' More jubilation. 'And last but by no means least …' My hands felt clammy and my mouth went dry.

Please, please, please.

'The North London Nightingales.'

I felt Oliver squeeze my hand as my shoulders dropped in disappointment. 'Bad luck, darling,' he whispered.

A sombre mood hung over our group as we trooped back to the train station.

'Ah well, lovies, we tried our hardest,' said Pamela. 'It just wasn't to be, but it doesn't mean we've lost the hall. The choir and campaign are still going strong.'

We murmured agreement but the disappointment weighed heavily as we waited for the train. I spotted Danielle and her fellow Darlings striding across the concourse towards us. 'Caroline! Sweetheart, I'm sooo sorry,' she said, kissing either side of my head and holding me at arm's length.

'It's fine,' I said, wishing the ground would swallow me up or actually, preferably her.

'It's just that the standard is so high,' she said, talking down to me as if I were a child. 'And you guys are fabulous, but not everyone is an actual singer.' She bestowed a supercilious smile on the assembled company. 'I mean you can all sing but you're not singers. That's all it is, but keep up the brilliant work and if you want us to back your hall campaign, just say the word. We'll be happy to do it for a reduced fee. Pas de problem.' She gave us an annoying little wave before leading her entourage to the train.

'The cheek,' declared Pamela. 'Who does she think she is? Mariah bloody Carey?'

There was no singing on the train journey back home. I could tell that we were all wondering if there was any point continuing with the choir. But I agreed with Pamela. The hall campaign was still running so we had to carry on. Plus, it felt as if we'd created something necessary and important with the choir. I know I needed it at the moment.

Natalie and Oliver were happily playing word games with the children so I decided to find Guy.

'Are you all right?' I asked, sitting down next to him.

He nodded. 'I thought we were in with a shot but the standard was very high.' His phone buzzed with a call. 'Excuse me for a sec,' he said. I looked out of the window, staring at the London landscape as we trundled home. 'Yes, this is Virginia Henderson's son. Right, okay. Well, I'm coming in later. Thanks for letting me know. Bye.'

'Everything okay?' I asked.

'That was my mother's home,' he answered. 'She's had a chest infection and they were just updating me on how she's doing. I'm going in to see her later.'

'I'm glad that she's getting better care than my mother did when she was there. Mind you, my mother is a very challenging woman.'

'How are you coping, having her living with you?'

I sighed. 'We're coping. Laurie, who knew her from the home, is with her today. She thinks there's something from her past that's troubling her, some unresolved issue which she wants to sort out.'

Guy stared at me for a moment. 'Do you have any idea what it is?'

I shook my head. 'Not a clue. And I don't think that we're going to find out now.' *And some truths are best left unsaid.*

'Caroline—' began Guy. His phone buzzed with another call. He looked torn for a second.

'You better get that,' I told him.

He swiped the screen. 'Hello?' He was frowning as he answered but his face was quickly transformed into a grin of disbelief as he listened to the person on the other end. 'And you're absolutely sure? That's incredible. Thank you. Thank you very much!' He ended the call and leapt to his feet. 'Listen up, singing friends. I have fantastic news!' Everyone turned to face him. 'That was the organiser of today's London finals. Apparently, the North London Nightingales have been a little naughty. One of their number is actually a professional singer.'

'No!' cried Pamela, scandalised.

'Yes, and what is more, they have been disqualified and, as a result, we are going to the Final!'

The cheer that echoed round the train carriage was deafening.

'In your face, Dulwich Darlings!' shouted Natalie, punching the air. Everyone laughed. We parted company at the station in a jubilant mood.

'Right, I'll e-mail round a new schedule of choir rehearsals,' said Guy. 'Brace yourselves, you're going to be eating, drinking and sleeping music from now on.'

I smiled as I walked back home in the sunshine, holding hands with Oliver, whilst Matilda skipped ahead. *My perfect family. Perfect until we walk back through the front door, that is.*

As predicted, my happiness quickly dissolved as we reached home and Laurie appeared in the hall, looking troubled.

'Is everything all right?' I asked with a rising sense of dread.

'Patricia's fine. I just need to have a word with you please, Caroline.' I followed her down to the kitchen. Laurie turned to face me. 'Your mother was muttering something in her sleep and I wondered if you knew anything about it? I think it might hold the key to what's troubling her.'

Why can't she leave well alone? I was grateful to Laurie for sitting with my mother and offering support but I didn't have the time or energy for this.

I swallowed down my impatience. 'I see.'

Laurie peered at me, as if trying to read my mind. 'I think it might help you both. She kept muttering about a "Virginia". She kept saying, "Virginia bitch, Virginia bitch," and, "That boy, that boy." She became so agitated that I woke her up in the end. She was very distressed.'

I spent most of my childhood feeling distressed because of her. Am I supposed to be sympathetic now?

'It was probably a bad dream,' I said dismissively.

Laurie pursed her lips. 'I think we both know that there's more to it than that.'

Maybe there is, but I'm not about to delve. Delving does no good. What on earth can I discover now that will be of use to me?

My father is dead and I miss him every day. I keep a tight lid on my grief but it's there nonetheless. Grief never goes away and anyone who says it does is a liar. To dig around in the past would be to defame his memory and I will never do that. He loved me whereas my mother seemed to resent me and to be honest, the feeling was mutual.

The world is basically full of heroes and villains, light and dark, good and bad. My father was the hero, my mother was the villain. That was that and that is how it will always be for me. I need it to be this way. I need this order of things.

I folded my arms. 'Well, thank you, Laurie. I'll keep an eye on her. Now please can I give you something for your time?' *And then please leave and stop digging around in my life.*

'I don't want any money, thank you Caroline. Just think about what I've said. Please?' She fixed me with that look.

I turned away. She knew I wasn't going to do anything and it saddened her. I couldn't bear that look. It made me feel guilty.

I gave a brief nod and followed her down the hall. She paused in the lounge, reaching down to kiss my mother. 'Bye, Patricia. Take good care,' she said, patting her shoulder. 'Look after Nanny. And Mummy,' she said to Matilda, who grinned at her.

At the front door, she turned back to me. 'Anger eats you alive if you allow it to,' she said. 'I let it do that for a while and it nearly destroyed me. I had to forgive. It was the only way.' I didn't answer. *Please leave. Please leave us alone now*. 'Goodbye, Caroline.'

'Bye,' I said, closing the door with relief. I made my way back to the kitchen without even looking into the living room. I could hear Matilda chatting happily to my mother and told myself that this was good enough. It had to be. Any mystery surrounding my mother would remain a mystery and that was all there was to it.

CHAPTER SEVENTEEN

NATALIE

'Natalie, dear heart, are you with me?'

'What? Oh, sorry. My mind was elsewhere. What was it you were saying?' I stammered.

Barbara Nicholls fixed me with a stare from over the top of her half-moon glasses, which when not in use hung around her neck on a gold chain. It was a look that made publishers cower and usually give in to her ever-exacting demands. To be honest, I was a little scared and I was her client.

'Natalie, I know you're going through a shitty time with Dan but you really need to focus. The book business has evolved. You have evolved. Gone are the days of lunches that flow effortlessly into dinner and writers sitting in their garrets waiting for their muse to strike.'

'Tricky to get wifi in garrets, so I've heard,' I joked. I immediately wished I hadn't as her eyes narrowed into slits. 'Sorry,' I added.

'Dear heart, I am endlessly fond of you. And Ed. You were my first and, as everyone knows, you never forget your first.' She snorted with amusement at her own joke. I wriggled with discomfort. 'No, but seriously, you're so much more than clients to me. You're like my children and actually, in lots of ways, I prefer you to my own children, ungrateful little shits that they are,' she reflected. 'So, as I was saying, publishing has changed. Writers need to see themselves as businesses and in your case, with dear Ned Bobbin, as a brand.' I nodded enthusiastically in a way that I hoped implied that I understood. 'This little guy,' she said, pointing to a framed cover of the first Ned book on the wall behind her, 'has enormous potential. I'm talking lunch boxes, water bottles, pyjamas – the opportunities are endless.'

'Lunch boxes,' I repeated, nodding.

'So we need to think differently, okay? And as for this next contract you're being offered, I think we should play hard ball.'

I grimaced. I had seen Barbara's hard ball in action. I seem to remember it resulted in a lot of weeping and gnashing of teeth and possibly the loss of some hair. 'I'm not sure, Barbara,' I began.

'Ed agrees with me,' she said airily.

'Does he?' I bristled at the mention of his name. He had sent me a couple of 'Hey Girl' Ryan Gosling pictures over the weekend, which I had pointedly ignored. I was tired of trying to second-guess what Dan was thinking, what Ed knew, what I knew, so I'd wimped out and stopped guessing.

She nodded. 'Obviously I need both of you to be on board but he and I are pretty much on the same page.'

Coward. I knew exactly what Ed was like. He was even more scared of Barbara than I was. 'It's just that I have a really good working relationship with my editor, Emily, and I would feel bad—' I began.

'Pfff! This isn't about being nice to people,' interrupted Barbara. 'You are a business, Natalie, and Emily works for a business. They don't care about you as a person. They care about how much money you make them. End of.'

'They sent me a lovely notebook for Christmas,' I said, shrinking in my seat.

Barbara's eyes looked as if they might pop out of her face. 'Notebooks! Come on, Natalie. You have to stop being so nice. This is business.'

'All right, I'll think about it,' I said. *Now stop shouting, scary lady, and go back to your usual job of ripping out editors' throats.* The whole thing made me want to go home, crawl under my duvet and stay there for a very long time. I had started writing because I liked words and books, and I had started writing books for children because I like children. I was not Donald Trump, who I was pretty sure didn't like any of these things.

Barbara looked at me, her eyes softening. She removed her glasses and walked round to perch on the desk next to me, taking one of my hands between her meaty, ring-covered paws. 'I don't mean to scare you, Natalie. I have your best interests at heart. That's what you pay me to do. Let's reconvene in a week or two when you've had a chance to consider things and maybe talk to Ed.'

I nodded. 'Okay. Thanks, Barbara.'

She squeezed me to her ample bosom before I left, half-crushing me in the process. Then she held me at arm's length and studied my face. 'And how are things with Dan?' she asked, adopting an uncharacteristically sympathetic tone.

'Yeah, not great,' I confessed with what was effectively the understatement of the decade.

'Aww, dear heart,' she said, squeezing my shoulders so that I thought she might break them. 'Men are shits and that's just a fact. I have been happily divorced for twenty years with just my cats for company. I can highly recommend it.'

Now I was scared. I hated cats. 'I'll bear it in mind,' I replied with a wincing smile.

The sky was thick with heavy grey cloud as I left Barbara's offices. They were situated in what had been an insalubrious part of town but which was latterly up and coming thanks to a plague of property developers bringing with them a raft of artisan bread-makers and coffee shops.

I glanced at my watch. I still had a few hours before I needed to get back for Woody. I made a sudden and surprising decision to fetch some coffees and doughnuts and head over to Ed's flat, which was a short hop away on the Tube. Maybe I'd been a bit unfair towards him. There was probably a perfectly logical explanation as to why he knew about Dan's new flat. Maybe he'd heard via someone else or on one of those social media sites I didn't bother with but which Dan and Ed both loved. Yes, that was probably it.

I strolled along in the sunshine, humming the tune to 'Fix You'. It was the song Guy had chosen for the Finals and I loved it. I felt a little more cheerful. I was looking forward to seeing my best friend. It was impossible to stay cross with Ed. He always knew what to say and how to sort things. He would reassure me and I would joke about the song and how he was my Chris Martin and always knew how to fix me.

I reached Ed's flat and buzzed the intercom. There was a brief pause before he answered and I saw the grainy image of his face appear on the screen.

'Nat!' he cried with a level of exaggerated shock that was extreme, even for Ed.

'Sur-pri-ise!' I sing-songed, holding up the bag of doughnuts. 'I've bought coffee and your favourites!'

'Wow!' he shouted at an alarming volume. 'That is a huuuuuge surprise. It's so good to see you. How are you doing?'

I frowned that he wasn't just buzzing me up. 'Starting to get a little chilly, to be honest. Can you let me in?'

'Hahaha! You're the funniest woman I know, Natalie Garfield.'

'Thank you and if you let me in, I can continue to amuse you, you know – *in the warm*,' I said with emphasis. Then the penny dropped. 'Oh, have you got company?' I asked, doing a nudge-nudge mime.

Ed looked horrified. 'Noo, of course not. Come on up!' he cried, buzzing the door open.

I shook my head as I made my way up the stairs. *Boys are so weird.* 'Hey yoooou,' he gushed as I met him in the doorway on the first floor. 'Come on into the kitchen, why don't you?'

I followed him along the corridor. There was a familiar smell in the air, one which I couldn't quite place. 'Sorry the flat is such a tip,' he said, hurriedly placing some cups into the dishwasher. I looked around. It was as immaculate as always, the slate-grey work surfaces polished and shiny, the sink sparkling in a way that mine never did.

'You should see my house. I'm thinking of leaving the cobwebs until Halloween – I reckon they'll have morphed into something truly terrifying by then,' I joked.

Ed laughed. 'So-o,' he said, turning to face me. 'How are you, sweetheart?'

'Bit shit actually,' I replied, sitting at one of the high-backed stools in front of the breakfast bar and helping myself to a doughnut before pushing the bag over to him. 'Dan and I are still communicating via text only.' I wanted to ask him how he knew about Dan's flat but I also wanted to enjoy just being with my bestie for a bit. I took a large bite of the doughnut. Custard oozed down my chin. 'Man, I forgot how good these are. Don't you want one?' I asked.

'I'm okay at the moment, thanks darling,' he said.

'You're not on one of your diets are you? Like the one where you had to eat liquidised kale and your poo came out looking like—'

'Liquidised kale,' he laughed. 'Yes, I should have just cut out the middle man and poured it down the bog in the first place.'

I giggled. 'Anyway, enough about me. What's going on with you? How is the delectable Mark?'

Ed took a sip of his coffee and grimaced. 'Alas, he is no more.'

'You killed him?' I joked.

He sniggered. 'No, apparently I was a bit too old for him.'

'Ouch,' I observed. 'What a bitch. His loss.'

Ed smiled. He stayed standing while we talked, seeming a bit reserved. I wondered if it was because we hadn't seen each other for a while. 'So how about we go and paint the town a nice shade of magenta one evening?' I suggested.

He nodded in a 'could do' sort of way.

I frowned. Something was definitely wrong. 'Ed, what's going on?'

'Nothing, nothing's going on,' he replied, feigning ignorance. He wasn't good at this. 'Actually, sorry, Nat, could you excuse me? I just need to nip to the loo,' he said.

'Fine. Don't mind me – I have coffee and doughnuts. Throw in James McAvoy and I'm pretty much set for life.'

He walked past me, pausing to kiss the top of my head. 'You're a treasure, Natalie Garfield,' he said.

Oh yes. I'm an absolute treasure. A nice person. A good woman. Someone who deserves to be happy. So why does it feel as if life is constantly punching me in the face all the time?

I took a sip of coffee. I heard Ed whispering in another room. Being a mother, I have the hearing of an elephant and can instantly recognise when someone is talking without wanting to be heard. I wondered if he was on the phone but then I heard another voice answer, soft and reasonable. It was a voice I knew very well.

I felt the world begin to spin around me as I jumped down from the stool and walked towards the sound. I reached for the door-handle of Ed's room and wrenched it open. Ed met me in the doorway.

'Natalie!' he began, trying to stand in front of me, but it was too late. I pushed past him and there, sitting on the bed, looking at me with utter shame, was my pathetic excuse of a husband.

I didn't even swear, which is unusual for me. There were no words. There were no sounds to describe the utter horror that I felt at that moment. I stood for a second, staring from Ed to Dan and back again. I had a sudden awful feeling that I might be sick. *Please, God, don't let me be sick.*

It was Ed who tried to take my arm. 'Nat—'

I pushed him away. 'Don't fucking touch me!' I said, my heart pumping fast as unspeakable anger flooded my veins.

'Nat, this isn't what you think it is,' said Dan, standing up and walking towards me.

Fight or flight? Punch him in the face or hurl yourself through the window? My brain was struggling with which to choose. I took a step back, fumbling towards the door. *Flight. Run away, Nat. Run away as quickly as you can.*

Dan followed me. 'Nat, let me explain. Please.'

I turned on him. *Fight. Yes, fight now, Nat. Tell the bastard what he needs to hear. It's about bloody time.*

Fury rose up and came spilling out as I spat the words. 'No!' I shouted. 'You don't get to call the fucking shots. So you're ready to talk now, are you? I mean, what the fuck is this? Did you get bored being married to me? So now you've decided to try being gay for a while and you're shacked up with my best friend? Well, whoop-de-fucking-doo. I hope you'll be very happy. You deserve each other.'

I turned and fled down the stairs. *And now we run away. Now we run and don't look back.*

'Nat!' cried Dan. 'Please.'

'Let her go, Dan,' said Ed.

Yes, let me go, you selfish bastard. Watch me run and not look back, running away from your lies and your betrayal and your utter, utter contempt for me, our marriage and everything we've shared for the past twenty years. You have broken my heart. I am done.

I ran to the Tube, trying to wipe away the flood of tears as they fell. I slumped into a seat and sobbed. I didn't care any more. Fortunately, this is London and people leave you alone. The other passengers looked alarmed but no-one was going to ask if I was okay. I was probably some nutter.

Actually, that wasn't far from the truth. I had certainly lost my grip on reality. I had no idea who Dan was and no idea where that left me. All I knew was that my world was in pieces, lots and lots of pieces, too numerous and complicated to repair.

A terrifying thought struck me. *How am I going to explain this to Woody?*

Oh hey, sorry, son, but your dad is actually gay. Yeah, it's really weird. We were together for the best part of twenty years and I had no idea. Oh, and he seems to have moved in with your Uncle Ed, but it's all good because now you'll have two dads, so double birthdays and Christmases – yay!

I know it happens. It's just that I never thought it would happen to me.

By the time I collected Woody from school I was feeling utterly empty but I had at least managed to stop crying.

One thing I've learnt about weeping is that you can't do it all day. You run out of tears eventually and it's very tiring.

I stood by the edge of the playground, desperately hoping that Woody would come out early and alone. Unfortunately he was arm-in-arm with Matilda, which meant that we now had to walk home with Caroline. Marvellous.

'Can we get an ice cream, pleeeease?' asked Woody as we passed the van parked outside the school gates.

'Pleeeeease, Mummy?' said Matilda, joining in.

'Fine by me,' I replied.

'Only on Fridays, Matilda. You know the rules,' said Caroline, giving me a superior look.

Oh, piss off, Caroline, you judgemental cow.

Woody frowned. 'We can have ice cream when we get home,' I whispered. He gave me a cheeky wink, which made my heart soar with love and nearly brought on fresh tears. *Keep it together, Nat. For everyone's sake.*

'So how was your day?' asked Caroline. I was considering how to answer this question when she leapt in. 'Mine has been absolutely manic! I've basically been on the phone to the choir competition people all day. Lord knows when I'm supposed to get anything else done.'

Yes, it must be a nightmare still being married to a man who isn't gay, living in a perfect house and having to basically make phone calls all day. What a drag.

She chattered on and on all the way along the road but actually it was a blessed relief not having to think or talk about the day's events. As we reached her house, she smiled. 'Right, well, I'm sorry. I can't stand about chatting all day. There's so much to do. See you later!'

Unbelievable. The woman was completely unbelievable.

Woody told me about his day as we walked the rest of the way home. He was in a good mood because he'd got a gold sticker for a class project. His excitement was a welcome distraction.

'How about that ice cream?' I suggested as we got home.

'Yes, please!' he cried. 'With sauce and sprinkles?'

'With sauce and sprinkles,' I confirmed.

'Yessss,' he declared with a fist-pump.

As I set about making it for him, I went to the fridge and spotted the bottle of wine I'd opened yesterday. I glanced at the clock.

Surely four o'clock could be considered wine o'clock in some cultures?

I poured myself a small glass and carried it into the lounge along with the ice cream.

A treat for Woody for his gold sticker and a treat for Mum for –

– having the worst day ever?

– finding out that her husband is a closet homosexual and having an affair with her best friend?

– do I need another reason?

We sat companionably chatting about everything and nothing. Pretty soon the ice cream and wine were all gone.

'Do you have any homework?' I asked.

Woody nodded. 'I need to "up-scale" some adverbial clauses.'

'Sounds painful,' I joked.

'It's not,' said Woody with an earnest frown. 'It's just changing some words.'

'Oh, well, would you like your writer-mum to help then?'

'Nah, I'm good,' he said, picking up his homework book and a pencil. 'Thanks for the ice cream,' he added before disappearing upstairs.

Don't go. Don't leave me alone with my thoughts and a temptingly open bottle of wine calling from the fridge.

I picked up a magazine and flicked idly through the pages before throwing it aside. *Who am I kidding?* I thought as I poured myself another large glass. *If there was ever a night when I needed to get drunk, this was it.*

I carried my glass into the dining room and sat, staring out towards the garden. It had started to rain and all of a sudden I felt completely alone. It was like a soap opera. *Betrayed wife sits alone at table drinking wine and staring out at the rain.* It would be comical if I had someone to share the joke with. *Someone like Dan. Or Ed.*

I felt a sob rising up and cursed myself. *I will not become an emotional wreck. I will not allow that to happen.*

I fetched my phone. I had put it on silent after the fifth call from Dan. Did he honestly think that I'd want to talk to him today? I considered who else to call and realised that there was literally no-one I'd want to talk to; no-one who would understand. And then a thought entered my mind. Before I'd had a chance to realise that it was a bad idea, I was dialling a number.

'Tim Chambers?' said the voice after just one ring.

'Tim. It's Natalie Garfield. Do you remember? From Hope Street?'

'Of course. How lovely to hear from you. How are you?' I was silent for a moment. 'Is something the matter, Natalie? Is there anything I can do to help?'

The question was so simple and it struck an immediate chord. I began to cry. Again. *Seriously, this has to stop.* 'I think my husband's having an affair with my best friend,' I blurted. 'My best *male* friend, and that's why he doesn't love me any more.' I closed my eyes at the horror of saying this out loud. It was like something from the front cover of one of those crappy mags I bought from time to time.

My husband ran off with an alien. My wife tried to sell one of the kids on eBay.

Like I said, I never thought this would happen to me.

'Oh, Natalie, how awful for you,' said Tim.

'I'm sorry,' I sobbed. 'I just don't really have anyone to call, and you said that if I ever needed to talk to someone who's been through a separation—'

'Of course. Are you at home? Would you like me to come over?'

I hesitated. *Nat, you're in a bit of a state. This isn't a good idea. Then again, it seems as if marrying Dan was a pretty rubbish idea, so what the heck?*

'Yes, please,' I said pathetically. 'If you're not busy.'

'I need to finish up here and then I'll come over at about seven, say? I'll bring a takeaway, shall I?'

'That would be lovely,' I said, crying fresh tears at his kindness. *Oh, my stars. Get a grip, woman.* 'I live at number thirty Hope Street.'

'Okay, see you in a bit.'

I hung up wondering what on earth I was playing at.

I have officially taken leave of my senses and what's worse, I don't give a damn. I need to get drunk and I need someone to talk to while I do that. Admittedly, a Tory MP wouldn't have been my first choice but nothing is really making sense at the moment. Plus, he's promised a takeaway. I'd sell my grandmother for a decent chicken chow mein.

Four hours later, Woody was tucked up in bed and I was really quite drunk and laughing. This was unexpected, considering earlier events, but it was very welcome too. Tim was telling me about all the things that had been thrown at him during his time as a politician.

'There's eggs, obviously, and flour is a popular one. The baked beans were unusual, particularly as they were still in the tin.'

'The perils of public office,' I slurred. He smiled and nodded. 'So you don't drink at all?' I added, topping up my glass and helping myself to a prawn cracker.

He shook his head. 'It's been five years, four months and twelve days,' he said.

'Really?'

He laughed. 'No, not really, but I am a recovering alcoholic. Let's just say I'm a nicer person without the booze.'

I nodded. *He is a nice person, nicer than I'd expected.* There was a knock at the door. I rolled my eyes. 'I don't want to talk to anyone, unless it's someone bringing cake. Then I'll talk to them.'

'Would you like me to go?' offered Tim.

'That would be really kind,' I smiled.

I heard him open the door and then I heard Dan's voice. I closed my eyes. I could hear that Dan was surprised by Tim's presence. I knew I had to face him. I made my way into the hall.

'Nat,' he said from the front doorstep.

'Dan, go away. I've got nothing to say to you today.'

'Please, Nat, I really need to talk to you.'

'She wants you to go,' said Tim firmly.

'This is none of your business,' replied Dan.

'I'm prepared to make it my business.'

'Just stop! Both of you,' I cried. 'Dan, go away. I don't want to talk to you today and Tim, thank you, but you don't need to fight my battles.'

Dan looked as if he wanted to speak but thought better of it. 'I'll go but I'll call you tomorrow, okay?'

'Whatever. I probably won't answer. Now get lost, will you?' Dan looked at me, his face loaded with sorrow, before turning away. I felt dizzy with anger and alcohol.

Tim closed the door and turned back to me. 'Are you okay?'

I wasn't okay at all but luckily I was too drunk to realise it. 'Yeah, I'm fine. And I need more wine because I would like to propose a toast.'

Tim followed me back into the living room. I scooped up my wine glass. 'I would like to propose a toast to discovering something new, and I'm not talking about my husband for once.' Tim was watching me. His face was soft and kind and actually, really very handsome in a posh-boy kind of way. 'To Tim Chambers – who is all right for a Tory.'

'Wow, Natalie,' he smiled. 'That's practically a declaration of love.' I gave a drunken bow and nearly fell over. 'Whoa there,' he laughed, catching hold of me.

'Thank you,' I said, patting his chest.

'For what?'

'For rescuing me.'

'Like a knight in shining armour?' His eyes twinkled with amusement. I noticed laughter-lines when he smiled. I'd always liked laughter lines on a man.

I giggled. 'Or a Tory on a donkey.'

'That as well,' he laughed, glancing at his watch. 'I should probably get going.'

I nodded, following him to the door. He paused on the front step. 'I meant what I said, Natalie.'

I looked up into his intensely green eyes. 'What's that?'

'That he's an idiot to let you go,' he replied.

I stared at him for a moment before I leaned forwards and kissed him on the lips. They were warm and welcoming. 'Sorry,' I said as we pulled apart. 'I just wanted to see what it felt like.'

It felt good and thanks to the alcohol, completely guilt-free.

He smiled and touched my cheek as he left. 'I'll see you soon,' he said, climbing into his car and driving off. After he left, a car which had been parked on the other side of the street revved into life and pulled out onto the road. It struck me as rather odd but I was too drunk to care. I went back inside and fell into bed.

CHAPTER EIGHTEEN

CAROLINE

'Natalie, you look terrible,' I said as I spied her walking home after drop-off that morning.

She stared at me from behind dark glasses. 'Thank you, Caroline. Remind me to come to you whenever I need a pick-me-up.'

Oh dear. Someone was a little tetchy this morning. 'Is everything all right?'

She sighed. 'Yes, I just have a tiny hangover.'

I raised my eyebrows. 'What did you tell me about alcohol not solving your problems?'

'Again. Thank you but if you could spare me the lecture today, that would be marvellous.'

'O-kay. I'm sorry,' I said without really meaning it. *There was no need to take out her bad mood on me.* 'So, will we be seeing you at choir later?'

She rolled her eyes. 'I dunno, Caroline. I'll have to see. Sorry, but I've got to dash. See you later.'

'Bye,' I said. *How irritating and how typical of Natalie and people like her. They had no staying power. The slightest whiff of trouble in their personal life and everything else was put on hold.*

I made my way back home and opened the front door, remembering with a sinking feeling that Oliver had gone to a meeting. He'd looked a lot like his old self as he headed out before breakfast, wearing one of his sharp-fitting business suits.

'Very handsome,' I told him as he kissed me goodbye. We lingered over our kiss for a moment.

'Euw!' complained Matilda, hiding behind a box of Shreddies on the breakfast table. My mother sat, chewing her toast, staring into the distance as usual. She seemed to chew everything about five hundred times.

'Good luck, darling,' I told him. 'You'll be amazing.'

'Thank you,' he replied. 'I'm excited about this. Hopefully, I'll have a big surprise for you soon. See you later, Tills. Bye, Patricia. Have a good day, girls!'

I uttered a silent prayer as he left. *Let it be a good job with a six-figure salary. Please let us be able to afford a fortnight in the Maldives and let me be able to find a new home for my mother before then. I really need some unbridled luxury back in my life,* I thought as I wiped up Matilda's spilt milk and glanced at the bedsheets from my mother's bed, which were waiting to go in the washing machine. It was a daily occurrence, a revolting daily occurrence.

The washing machine was on its final spin as I let myself in through the front door. I peered into the living room. My mother was staring at the television screen, not watching, just staring. It was on pretty much twenty-four/seven these days. I had always wondered why nursing homes just left their residents in front of blaring TV sets for hours at a time. I realised why it was now. It was to drown out the awful silence of people essentially waiting to die. I honestly felt that was what my mother was doing now; merely existing, her body locked in time, unable to function as it had done but unable to cease functioning too. It was such a depressing thought and I hated her for making me think it.

I didn't stop to speak to my mother, I just carried on down to the kitchen, keen to get on with my 'to do' list. I flicked on the kettle and feeling weighed down by the silence in the room, I decided to put on the Ella Fitzgerald CD that Jim had recently lent me. I remembered Natalie telling me that she had borrowed a different one and how wonderful she had found it.

I pressed Play and started to listen. I expected to be soothed and lifted by what I heard but for some reason, I felt deeply unhappy. It stirred up unexpected sadness and sorrow and I realised that I hadn't heard these songs since my father had been alive. I also remembered that these were songs that my mother and father had played and sung along to on day-trips we had shared.

I could almost smell the velour-seated interior of the old Maxi we used to have and see the chunky cassette player on the dashboard. The memory was so deeply buried that I nearly cried out as I recalled sitting in the back of the car with the scratchy brown-check picnic blanket, listening and laughing as my parents smiled and sang. It was like seeing the old cine-film and I couldn't bear it. Any happy scenes from my childhood had long since been replaced with the anger and bitterness of my mother, like an old canvas painted over with a new picture.

I was about to turn off the music when I heard singing; not Ella Fitzgerald's perfect harmony but a small, reedy voice joining in with 'Top Hat, White Tie and Tails'. I turned in surprise to see my mother standing in the middle of the kitchen, lost in the music, her face rapt as she sang along.

What on earth is she doing? Part of me wanted to snap her out of it. It looked so odd. But part of me wanted to see what would happen. She seemed so happy, so different all of a sudden. She didn't seem to see me but I believe she could see my father because at one point she reached out her arms.

'Oh, Charles,' she said. 'We love this one, don't we?'

And then I realised. She was there again, sitting next to my father in the car on a day-trip to Clacton, happy, beautiful and in love. She swayed in gentle time to the music. I watched the whole ghostly performance as she carried on singing and dancing, lost in time. When the piece finished, she drifted back out of the kitchen, towards the living room, as if nothing had happened. I felt shaken by what I'd witnessed. I was so used to seeing her motionless and often helpless.

It was as if I'd seen my mother as a completely different person, a younger version of herself trapped in an old person's body. She had been young once. She had been happy once.

What had happened to the Patricia Winter who had lived, loved and laughed with my father? How had she become replaced by such an angry and bitter woman, who made the childhood I recalled so unhappy and devoid of love?

I started to recall Laurie's words and wonder. Something had happened, something deeply troubling. I realised that I didn't want to hold onto my anger any more. I could now see what it had done to my mother, how she had lost her happiness and hope because of it. I didn't want the same to happen to me. I didn't want to continue to be angry after she was gone, forever wondering what had caused her anger.

I had to know.

I went into the living room. My mother was back in her chair, her face fixed on the screen. I walked over and switched off the television. Her eyes remained glued to the blank screen. I went to the bookcase and pulled out a photo album. I sat down next to my mother and flipped it open. I stared at a picture of me in a sun hat sitting in front of my mother on the beach at Clacton.

Where to begin? How do you start a conversation after so many years of not talking?

'I remember that sun hat,' I remarked. 'I never wanted to take it off.'

My mother's head dipped as if listening, but her eyes still stared forwards.

She can hear me. This is progress.

'I was thinking about our day-trips in the old Maxi, with you and Dad singing along to those Irving Berlin songs – "Top Hat, White Tie and Tails", "Putting on the Ritz".'

My mother turned to look at me, the corners of her mouth inching upwards.

Keep going, Caroline. Keep talking.

'You remember too, don't you?' She moved her head down slightly; the merest of nods. 'You were happy then, weren't you? And then something happened, didn't it?'

The corners of her mouth moved back down as the ghost of a frown spread across her brow.

Never mind the frown, keep asking the questions. You're onto something.

'What was it? What was it that happened?'

She started to shake her head very gently as the frown deepened.

Maybe I should have stopped but I wanted to know. Something drove me on to find out. 'Who was Virginia? Who was that boy?' I asked.

She stared at me in horror and suddenly her face looked more familiar, transformed to one of anger and hurt. 'Virginia bitch, Virginia bitch!' she growled.

I felt a pang of fear but kept pressing. *No going back now.* 'But who is she? Who is Virginia?'

'Virginia bitch, Virginia bitch,' she shouted, pounding her gnarly fists on her lap, harder and harder.

I was frightened by her anger. I'd pushed it too far. 'Stop it!' I cried. 'Stop it, mother! Stop this at once!'

'Virginia bitch, Virginia bitch!' she repeated, hitting her lap and chest with increasing ferocity.

'Stop it, mother! Please stop it!' I caught hold of her hands and held onto them. She was strong but I managed to make her stop. She was starting to weep now, worn out by her own efforts. She rested her head against my arm. I hesitated for a second, paralysed by the fear and anger of my own past before I found myself placing an arm around her shoulder and patting her gently. The roles of mother and daughter reversed.

There, there. We're all right now.

'It's okay,' I said. 'We don't have to talk about it. It's okay. Really. Stay here a second. I'll be right back.'

I hurried to the kitchen and fetched the Ella Fitzgerald CD. I put it on in the lounge. Soon my mother seemed happy and calm again – the other, younger Patricia Winter. After a time she closed her eyes and went to sleep. I watched her for a while, realising that I needed to know the truth. It was high time.

I returned to the kitchen and reached for my phone. Laurie answered after just two rings.

'Caroline?'

'You said to call if I ever needed anything.'

'Of course.'

'Please help me. I need to find out who Virginia is and what she did to upset my mother.'

'I was hoping you'd call. I think I actually might know but I need to make some phone calls first.'

'Thank you. Thank you so much.'

It was a little after five when the doorbell rang. Oliver was home, reassuring me that he'd had a very productive day, but he didn't want to say more until he'd had confirmation. Matilda was reading to my mother and I was starting to make dinner.

'I'll get it!' I called, heading down the hall. I had hoped that it might be Laurie with news, so I was surprised to see Guy standing on the doorstep. He looked pale and worried. 'Hi Guy, is everything okay?'

He swallowed, his face deadly serious. I realised he was nervous. 'Caroline, are you able to come somewhere with me? We'll need a couple of hours.'

I glanced behind me before turning back to him. 'What's this all about? What about choir?'

'I think we may need to cancel choir this evening. This is important, though. I'll wait for you in the car.'

He was starting to worry me now. 'Can't you tell me what this is about, Guy?'

He hesitated before he answered. 'I need to take you to see my mother. Her name is Virginia Henderson.'

I stared at him in amazement. 'Virginia.'

'Please, Caroline. Will you come?'

I ran back inside and quickly brought Oliver up to speed, then I grabbed my bag and ran out to the car. We drove to the care home in silence. Guy was clearly uncomfortable and to be honest, I was in shock.

Laurie met us in reception. 'Are you okay?' she asked.

'I think that depends on what I'm about to be told,' I replied.

She nodded kindly. 'It will come as a shock but you need to know.'

I felt my body stiffen. *I don't like surprises, shocks or anything that occurs without notice.* She led Guy and me along the corridor, past my mother's old room and around the corner to another wall of doors. She paused outside one and knocked.

'Come in,' called a frail female voice.

'After you,' said Laurie, opening the door and ushering me inside. Guy's mother sat at a table by the window, identical to the one in my mother's room. She was gazing up at us, a nervous expression on her face.

'Hello, Mum,' said Guy, leaning over to kiss her.

'I think you better sit down,' said Laurie to me. 'Mrs Henderson has something she wants to tell you.'

I sat down at the table and stared expectantly at Guy's mother. She was a tiny woman, as frail as a sparrow, and, I estimated, a little older than my own mother. She was looking at Guy and wouldn't meet my gaze.

Guy turned to her. 'Mum, you have to tell Caroline. It's not fair that she doesn't know the truth.'

The truth.

She kept staring at him. 'I can't,' she whispered.

Laurie knelt down beside her. 'Virginia, you have to tell Caroline what happened. She needs to know why her mother was behaving the way she was. I know you understand this.'

Mrs Henderson gave a small nod before transferring her gaze to me. She looked frightened. 'I'm sorry, dear,' she said.

'Why?' I asked. 'What could you possibly have to be sorry for?'

She looked down at the floor. 'Your father …' she began.

'My father?' I replied. 'Did you know him? How did you know him?' Panic rose up inside me.

The old lady looked as if she might cry. 'He's Guy's father,' she said with a sob.

The world started to blur around me. 'W-what?' I stammered. I looked at Guy. He was staring at me and suddenly I saw something in his eyes, something familiar I'd noticed the first time we'd met.

Blue eyes. Bright-blue eyes, just like my father's. My darling father. My hero.

'But this isn't possible. My father was married to my mother. They were together until he died,' I protested. *A pathetic, pointless protest.*

'He had two families,' said Guy. 'He lived with you most of the time but he came to stay with us some evenings and at the weekends.'

'Oh, my God,' I murmured. 'He lied to me.' Betrayal slammed my body like a wrecking ball. 'How on earth did he stop people finding out?'

'Your mother knew,' said Virginia, through her tears. 'She put up with it. We both did, really. I did it because I loved him. I was a fool and I'm sorry.'

I stood up, feeling hot and faint. 'I have to go,' I said. *It's too much. I can't listen to this. I don't want to be here.*

'Caroline, please don't go,' said Guy. 'Let's try and talk about it. We can make everything all right.'

I stared at him. *My half-brother. I had a half-brother.* 'You knew! All the time you knew and you didn't think to tell me! How could you run the choir, how could you socialise with me and not say anything? How could you do that?' Fury surged through my body. 'How dare you? How dare you?'

'It wasn't like that, Caroline. I didn't know who you were to start with. I wanted to talk to you but you seemed so closed to it.'

'Oh, so this is my fault, is it? This is all my fault? No! This isn't happening. This can't be happening. I have to get out of here.'

'Caroline—' Laurie began.

'No! I should never have listened to you! I didn't want this. I didn't want any of this!' I shouted as I fled the room and ran down the corridor. My body was shaking as

I reached reception and remembered that Guy had driven me here.

'Please, Caroline! At least let me drive you home,' cried Guy, running after me.

'You stay away from me! And my family! Do you hear? I don't want anything to do with you!'

I ran out of the door of the home and onto the main road. I rushed to the nearby railway station. Luckily, it had a mini-cab office. I fell into a cab and told the driver where I wanted to go, then I slumped back into the seat and stared out of the window, my brain whirring as revelation after revelation sped through it.

I have a half-brother. And a lying, cheating father; a father who hasn't even done me the decency of staying alive so that I can hate him. And my mother. My mother, once young and full of joy, transformed by anger, weary with bitterness at having to deal with my father's double life.

Everything I thought I knew was imploding, my world was being turned on its head and I realised that I had no idea how to handle it.

CHAPTER NINETEEN

NATALIE

Caroline had dumped me in it. Yet again and without even having the decency to ask. I just received a call from a BBC researcher to confirm a time for 'the interview we discussed with Mrs Taylor'. I'm not good when I'm put on the spot and particularly nervous around journalists.

I think it dates back to when I was running the school newspaper at secondary school. A boy called Jeremy sabotaged an entire edition by changing all the names featured to 'penis'. I had wanted to become a journalist until that moment and I still shudder today at the memory.

So receiving a phone call from a BBC journalist filled me with dread and awe. The BBC is the pinnacle for me. It was basically like getting a call from Sir David Attenborough. The researcher was kind and friendly. She told me that they would love to 'just pop round' and do a 'tiny' end-of-the-news piece about the campaign. 'It's really no big deal.'

I agreed with gushing enthusiasm. Then I ended the call and wanted to throw up.

No big deal? This is a very big deal. I don't want to be on television. I don't want to brush my hair and worry about whether my eyebrows are presentable and I definitely don't want to change out of my elasticated-waist trousers.

I was just back from the school run and had several hours of writing planned, after which I would collect Woody and bring him home to share biscuits and tales of our day. I was also wondering about phoning Tim to see if he wanted to pop round for a glass of wine. Well, he could drink water and I would have the wine anyway. It had been a week since I'd seen him and I'd enjoyed our evening. It had made me forget all the crap and stress of my other life for a bit. The kiss had been a mistake but only a minor one, to my mind.

It had also been a week since I discovered Dan at Ed's flat. I had been ignoring calls and texts from both of them. I even sent Dan a very childish 'Just fuck off!' text. I thought it might make me feel better but it just made me sad.

I knew I would need to sort things eventually, if only for Woody's sake. But for now, I wanted to deny everything and indulge in some harmless flirting with a Tory MP.

Yes, I know. I was officially crossing the bridge of sanity into crazyland. Hey ho. There had been a lot of unexpectedly events over the past few weeks. I was just going with the flow, albeit a flow with more twists and turns than a corkscrew.

I had fire in my belly and anger in my bones. Usually I kept it in check but I got the feeling that if pushed, I could do some real damage.

I was therefore pretty wound up when I called Caroline about the interview. Not only had she dropped this particular surprise in my lap at the last minute but she had also cancelled choir the evening before with barely any notice or apology. 'Unforeseen circumstances,' was the reason given in the very brief text. I probably would have been sympathetic if it weren't for the fact that she had been particularly annoying lately. Plus I was peeved because I had managed to find a babysitter for once.

'Caroline?'

Her voice sounded husky and flat. 'Natalie, this isn't a good time.'

Dismissive cow. How bloody dare she? 'Well, pardon me for not phoning at a good time. It wasn't a brilliant time for me to get a phone call from the BBC about the interview they're doing this afternoon.'

'Oh, that.'

'Yes, that! When were you planning to tell me?'

She sighed. She actually sighed as if I was boring her. 'Apologies. I've been rather busy.'

Apologies? That's the word used by people who never apologise or think that they're wrong. 'Yes, well, I'm rather busy too. I have writing to do and … stuff. Why does it need to be me?'

'Because,' she said, as if she were addressing an idiot, 'you're the closest thing our campaign has to a celebrity.' She managed to make it sound like an insult.

'I write children's books.'

'Yes, which is even better because everyone loves children's books and that makes you very appealing.'

'How flattering.'

She ignored my sarcasm. 'What time are they coming?'

'Two o'clock,' I replied with weary resignation.

'Fine. I'll see you then. And maybe wear something a little bit—'

Clean?

Fashionable?

Less frumpy?

'A little bit?' I demanded, barely containing my fury at her utter, bloody cheek.

'Smart,' she said finally. 'Anyway, I must go. See you later.'

She hung up. I glared at my phone before casting it onto the bed and doing the very mature thing of hopping from foot to foot whilst flicking V-signs at an imaginary Caroline. 'Fuck off, fuck off, fuck off!' I cried. This time I did feel a little better.

I spent the next hour in a blind panic, worrying about what to wear. I had a shower and washed my hair before going into the bedroom and throwing all the half-decent clothes I owned onto the bed in the hope that this might force two matching items together. I was just trying on an ancient wrap dress that made both my bosom and belly look enormous when there was a knock at the door. I cursed, flung on my dressing gown and jogged downstairs, hoping that it was just Jim with a parcel.

Of course, life is never kind at these moments. The last people you want to be confronted with when you are wearing a bulky dressing gown over an ill-fitting dress along with a hastily wrapped towel-turban, are your estranged husband and the best friend with whom you suspect him of having an affair.

Before my marriage had become a car-crash in which there were no survivors, the three of us would have laughed about this. Ed would have teased me for looking a state and Dan would have told me I'd look beautiful in a bin bag. That was then. This was now.

I stared at the pair of them standing on my doorstep, looking for all the world like a couple of naughty schoolboys. 'This isn't a good time.'

'Please, Nat. I need to talk to you,' said Dan. 'We both need to talk to you.' His eyes were pleading. *Those eyes. They had won my heart once. My poor fractured heart.*

The trouble was that my heart was now scorched by anger and blistered with hurt. There was a pounding fury where kindness and sympathy had once lurked. I was basically like the bionic woman but instead of replacing my body parts, all my emotions had been replaced. Mainly with negative ones – angry, sweary, negative ones.

'This isn't a good time,' I repeated. 'In fact, I'm not sure that there's ever going to be a good time to have this discussion.' I glared at the pair of them. 'Why don't you just piss off back to your love-nest?'

'Nat, there's nothing going on.' This was Ed's voice. 'You have to listen to Dan. Please.'

I turned on him. 'Do I? Do I really, Ed? And why is that? To make you feel better? To ease your troubled conscience? Fucking hell, you were my best bloody friend. I trusted you. I told you everything, and it turns out that you were laughing at me and shagging my husband. You couldn't make this shit up!'

'Please, Nat,' begged Ed. 'I would never do anything to hurt you, sweetness. You're my best friend and I miss you!' His eyes were misting with tears.

'Don't bloody cry,' I snapped. 'You don't get to turn this into one of your drama-queen moments. This isn't about you.'

He nodded. 'Sorry. I just can't bear the thought of losing you.'

'Whatever,' I said. 'And what about you? Can you bear the thought of losing me? Or Woody, for that matter?' A woman walking past with a small rat-like dog stared up at us in alarm. 'Keep going, madam,' I cried, 'there's nothing to see here. Just a couple of traitorous men and a fool.'

'Nat, please can we discuss this inside? Even if you don't care, think of Woody,' said Dan.

I nearly punched him when he said that. My hand balled into a fist as I jabbed my finger at his chest. 'Don't you fucking dare use our son to make me feel bad. You do not get to do that.' I did take a step back though. 'Come the fuck in or fuck the fuck off,' I said. *Wow, Nat, your Tourette's is getting worse.* I led them into the living room and folded my arms. 'I would offer you tea or coffee but I hate you so I'm not going to.'

They trooped in, sitting on one sofa each. I remained standing with my arms folded. I realised I was shaking.

Keep your arms folded, Nat, it's the only way you're going to hang onto the righteous anger and not dissolve into tears.

I stared at Dan. 'So, say your piece and then you can get lost.'

He ran a hand through his hair and looked up at me. 'I'm not sure where to begin.'

'Oh dear, shall we get Abigail on the phone so that she can tell you what to say?'

His gaze was so sorrowful. For a fleeting second he looked just like Woody.

Don't look at him, Nat. He'll melt your anger and then you'll have nothing left.

I turned away as he began to speak. 'I know I've caused you a lot of heartache over the past few months and for that I am truly sorry. That was never my intention. I had to work everything out in my own head before I could talk to you.'

'So talk to me then,' I dared him.

Dan hesitated. 'Talk to her,' said Ed.

He looked me in the eye. 'There's nothing going on between Ed and me. I'm not gay.'

'What?' I said, an involuntary laugh of surprise escaping from my mouth. 'So what were you doing at his flat?'

'Believe it or not, I went to Ed because he knows you better than anyone. I wanted him to help me work out the best way to talk to you. The counselling has helped me put my thoughts in order but I wasn't sure how best to approach you.'

'For fuck's sake, Dan. I'm your wife. You should be able to talk to me.'

'I know and I'm sorry. I understand why you're angry – you have every right to be but the truth is, I had to be sure.'

'Had to be sure of what?' As I asked the question, I knew the answer and it made me feel sick. Sick and scared.

He stared into my eyes. I wanted to look away but something stopped me. 'Nat, I still love you. I'm just not in love with you,' he said.

'Oh, and our sixteen-year-old therapist made you see this, did she?' I snapped.

He held my gaze. 'Actually, you did.'

'I beg your fucking pardon? How dare you try and level this at me! I didn't walk out and abandon my family.' I felt hot with fury. 'Do you know what? I don't want to hear this. Get out.' I pointed towards the door.

'Nat, I know you hate me and you have every right to, but you should hear what Dan has to say,' said Ed softly.

Bloody Ed. He knew me so well. He knew I could rant for England, and he knew how to stop me in my tracks too. I was furious with him but I knew he was right. I sighed and sat down, gesturing for Dan to continue.

Dan hadn't taken his eyes off me. He ran a hand over his mouth. 'So you remember when my dad died...' I nodded. '...and you told me at the time that I should go for counselling because you didn't think I was dealing with my grief.'

I rolled my eyes. 'And you told me to go back to my incense-burning and dismissed the whole thing.' I remembered it all too well.

Dan's father had died about two years ago and, having endured the demise of my own dad, I considered myself to be a world expert in dealing with grief. I remembered finding Dan's demeanour a little unusual. I never saw him cry once. I know some men don't cry but actually Dan wasn't one of them. He cried on our wedding day, when Woody was born, when Liverpool won a cup. All the usual stuff.

But when his dad, with whom he'd had a good relationship, died, he seemed to shut off somehow. In the early days leading up to the funeral, life had been busy. There wasn't time for emotional outbursts but at the funeral, when his mum, his relatives and even I were wailing like banshees, he stood dry-eyed, staring forwards at the coffin. He delivered the eulogy in his calm and reasonable way, offered comfort to his mother and anyone else who needed it. I had watched him carefully over the following weeks, waiting for him to fall apart, ready to comfort and console, but he never crumbled and as far as I was aware, never shed a single tear for his dad.

He turned to me. 'Well, you were right. I never dealt with that grief and it started to eat away at me.' He looked at the floor. 'It got pretty bad. I never told you because ...'

'Why? Why did you never tell me?' I pleaded.

He stared up at me with mournful eyes. 'I was ashamed.'

'Ashamed?' The word hung there, low-hanging fruit in the dying tree of our relationship. 'Ashamed of what?'

He hesitated.

'Say it,' I demanded. *Hold onto your anger, Nat. Make him tell you. You have to hear this. It's going to hurt, like pulling off a plaster, but you have to do it.*

'I was ashamed – that my feelings for you had changed.'

I folded my arms. 'So your dad dies and suddenly you don't love me any more.'

Dan shook his head. 'It wasn't like that.'

'Well, how was it then, Dan? How was it? Tell me.'

He ran a hand through his hair again. 'There wasn't one thing. It happened over time. After dad died, I didn't feel sad or angry or any of those things you're supposed to feel. I just felt empty. Completely hollowed out. It made me question everything about life, about what kind of man I was and what kind of life I was leading.'

I stared at him. 'You were leading a family life. With Woody and me.'

'I know. And I love you both so much, but I just didn't feel that I fitted in any more.'

'Fitted in any more? What the hell does that mean? We're a family. You married me. We had a son. It's the stuff of life. You get on with it.'

'But that's just the thing, Nat. I couldn't get on with it. And I saw the way you carried on, being a brilliant mother and wife, but I felt as if I couldn't be part of it any more, as if my whole life was a lie.'

'You're saying that your life with Woody and me was a lie?'

'No, I'm saying that I was lying to myself about being able to stay. And I did stay for a while, I tried to suppress my feelings and carry on.'

'Big of you,' I snorted.

He ignored my sarcasm. 'But I realised in the end that it was wrong. I wasn't being fair on you or Woody by staying.'

I stared at him. 'How could you think that? Why couldn't you talk to me? Am I really that bad?'

He shook his head. 'Quite the opposite. You're absolutely perfect, Nat.'

Oh yeah, I'm really perfect. The perfect bloody idiot. I gave a bitter laugh. 'Well I've never been called THAT in my life. I think you must want the next house down.'

'It's true. You deserve better than me.'

No, I don't. And I don't want it either. Couldn't you just try a little bit harder? I folded my arms. 'So you decided that just buggering off would be the best thing?'

'In the long term, yes.'

'And what about us? What about Woody? What about me? Don't we get a say in your life-changing moment?'

Dan stared into my eyes. 'You have to believe that I never wanted this to happen and I never ever set out to hurt you or Woody. I just can't ignore this any longer. I won't make you happy by staying. I honestly believe that now.'

'And what about you?' I snapped at Ed. 'What do you have to say about this?

Ed's eyes were pleading. 'Honestly, Nat, Dan only came to me for advice. He wanted me to help find a way to tell you without hurting you or Woody.'

'Well, you did a bloody crap job,' I snapped. Ed looked chastened.

'Look,' said Dan. 'I know this is a lot to take in. It's been a lot for me to take in too.'

'Well, boo flipping hoo,' I snapped. 'I hope you're not after my sympathy.'

'Of course not,' said Dan, so reasonable I could have slapped him. 'But I can't live a lie any more and we have to find a way through this.'

'Do we?' I snarled. 'Do we really? I didn't ask for any of this to happen. You have done this and all of a sudden, "we" need to find a way through it? No, Dan, this is your mess. You sort it. Now fuck off out of my house.' I stood up and folded my arms, waiting for them to leave.

Dan rose to his feet. 'I understand that you're angry. I know it's a lot to take in but please don't shut me out.'

'What part of "fuck off" do you not understand? And why do you have to be so bloody reasonable all the time?

Why am I the mad woman, ranting and raving, while you sit there and blithely announce that you don't love me any more? Why do you get to be so cool and calm while I fall apart?' I could feel tears pricking my eyes but my rage stopped them from falling.

Ed was staring at me. I could see that he was on my side. He knew that I needed to rant, get angry and would calm down later. In lots of ways he knew me better than Dan. In fact, at this moment, he probably knew us better than we knew each other. 'Come on, Dan. I think you should leave Nat now. She's upset and needs time.'

'Thank you, Professor Freud,' I snapped but I was grateful for his interjection.

Dan walked slowly from the room. 'Please call me when you're ready to talk. I want to make this right, Nat.'

I wouldn't look at him. How could he make this right? Only going back to how we were before would make this right, but that was impossible now.

Ed stood up and turned to me. 'I know you're too angry to talk but I just want to say that I'm sorry for letting you down and I will do anything to win back your friendship.'

I looked at him, my face set in a frown, but I gave a barely discernible nod of acknowledgement. He placed a hand on my arm and looked relieved when I didn't shrug him away. Then he turned and left. I stayed where I was until I heard the front door close. Then I sank onto the sofa and sobbed. My anger dissolved into sadness, like the witch melting at the end of *The Wizard of Oz,* as I realised that my marriage was over and I didn't have a clue where to go from here.

After half an hour of pure unbridled self-pity, I dragged myself off the sofa and went to find my phone. Caroline answered after two rings.

'Natalie? Is there a problem?' She asked this in a 'what now?' tone of voice.

'I'm going to have to cancel the interview,' I said.

'Natalie, this is the BBC. You don't cancel the BBC.'

'Well, I've got to.'

'Is Woody ill?'

'No.'

'Well then. What possible reason could there be?'

I hesitated. In my list of people I'd most like to confide in about the death of my marriage, Caroline Taylor didn't figure highly. I suspected that Katie Hopkins might offer more compassion. 'Natalie, we have fewer than two weeks until the Final. The BBC want to feature our campaign as their end-of-the-news story this evening. You can't bail out because of last-minute nerves. You'll let everyone down.'

Thanks for the guilt trip, Caroline. I really need that today. 'I just have a lot going on,' I retorted.

'We all have a lot going on,' she said without a shred of sympathy or interest. 'Sometimes you just have to buckle down and get on with it. I'll see you at two.' And she hung up. Again.

You've just told your husband to get lost but you can't deal with Caroline Taylor. Congratulations – you are officially the biggest loser on the planet.

I stomped around the house in a foul mood but managed to make myself look half decent in a pair of smart jeans and a blouse. I spent the two hours before the film crew arrived googling 'my husband isn't in love with me any more' like a woman possessed. Unsurprisingly, it offered no comfort and I felt miserable and nervous when Caroline and the film crew appeared. They set up in the dining room whilst Caroline fussed over them, wittering about 'the best light' and someone she once knew who was a cameraman. I was relieved. At least it stopped her from bothering me.

The woman conducting the interview put me at ease and I soon forgot the cameras as we started to chat.

'So, Natalie and Caroline, tell us what the Hope Street Community Hall Campaign is about.'

Caroline jumped straight in. 'Well, Anita,' she said with her best TV-presenter smile, speaking directly into the camera. 'It's about preserving something which is dear to our community's heart and maintaining it for generations to come.'

Anita nodded. 'And you've formed a choir as well?' she asked, looking at me.

Caroline leapt on this. 'Yes, Anita. It's the Hope Street Community Choir and we're going to be performing at the Community Choir Finals hosted by your very own Andrew Munday at the Royal Albert Hall on the twentieth of July – tickets available now!' For some reason, she thought this would be a good moment to break into song. Anita and I stared at her in amazement as she issued forth an awkward rendition of the chorus from 'Something Inside So Strong'.

'Thank you, Caroline,' said Anita with a wry smile. 'That was enlightening. And Natalie, if I could turn to you for a moment,' she said with meaning. 'What made the writer of the Ned Bobbin stories want to get involved?'

I hesitated. Really I wanted to answer, 'I didn't want to. Caroline made me,' because that was partly true. However, I realised that there was another reason. 'I used to take my son to the hall as a baby. It saved me in lots of ways,' I told her.

'How do you mean?' asked Anita, leaning forwards.

I swallowed. 'Well, when you become a mother, life is very intense and sometimes you feel a bit lost. The Hope

Street group offered a place to go, to be with other mothers, and in lots of ways it stopped me losing the plot.' I wiped away a tear, feeling my cheeks flush with embarrassment. 'Sorry,' I said. 'It's just that these places are vital to parents and older people – all sorts of people really. They need to be preserved as something at the heart of our community rather than viewed as an unaffordable resource. You can't put a price on what they give people, and that has to be worth saving.'

'Thank you,' said Anita, before turning back to the camera. 'As you can see, there's a huge strength of feeling and a great deal of support to save the Hope Street Hall. For more details, go to the BBC website. This is Anita Vangani reporting for BBC London News.'

The cameras stopped rolling and Caroline turned to me. 'That was a great idea to cry. I wish I'd thought of it,' she said, genuinely impressed.

I shook my head in disbelief. The camera crew packed up quickly before heading off. I walked to the door with Anita. 'Thank you for that,' she said. 'I can see you care a lot about this.'

'I do,' I nodded.

She stared at me for a second. 'Look, I probably shouldn't be telling you this but I received some information from a source about you.'

'Sounds a bit James Bond,' I said, feeling unnerved. 'What kind of information?'

She took out her phone and flicked it into life. 'I was sent these pictures,' she said, holding it up for me to see. The images were grainy but you could clearly see Tim Chambers and me standing on my doorstep kissing.

Oh, shit.

'Look,' she said kindly. 'You seem like a lovely person, who genuinely wants to do something good in their community and, God knows, we could do with a few more of those. My advice is to keep a low profile before you get dragged into some MP sex scandal. I'm just here to interview you for the end-of-the-news baby-panda slot but the Red Tops will run these pictures in a second and suddenly your campaign will be getting publicity for all the wrong reasons.'

I nodded. 'What can I do?'

She sighed. 'Not much. I know a few people so I'll try to play them down for you, but just be careful, okay?'

'Thank you,' I said. 'I appreciate it.'

'Good luck, Natalie,' she smiled, before heading out of the door.

Caroline appeared in the hall. 'What were you two talking about?' she asked. 'You seemed very chummy.'

I cleared my throat. 'Nothing of note,' I lied.

'I thought it went very well,' she said.

'Even the singing?' I teased.

'What was wrong with my singing?' she asked, looking hurt.

'Nothing, nothing at all. Why was choir cancelled last night, by the way?'

She pursed her lips as if considering how to answer. 'Guy had some personal affairs to attend to. Now I really must go. See you later.'

I shook my head as I watched her go, leaving without a single word of acknowledgement. I suppose I was a fool to expect it.

Thank you, Natalie, I really appreciate you giving up your time. Apologies for dumping that on your doorstep like a big turd, Natalie – I know how much stress you're under at the moment. You're a real pal, Natalie. I would be more likely to get a declaration of love from Tom Hiddleston than hear Caroline Taylor come out with any of these sentences.

I shook off my irritation. Frankly, I was exhausted after Ed and Dan's visit and all that it had brought. I also realised that at least Caroline's sheer bloody rudeness had taken my mind off the demise of my marriage and my unwelcome walk-on part in an MP's sex scandal. You had to count your blessings, after all, however small they may be.

CHAPTER TWENTY

CAROLINE

I honestly contemplated giving up. After finding out the truth about my father, the fact that I had a half-brother and most troublingly, that I had misjudged my mother so harshly for so long, the plight of some community hall seemed utterly trifling. Ridiculous really.

Part of me wanted to shut the door on the outside world, gather my husband, daughter and mother together in one room and keep them there, safe and insulated. I didn't want to face Guy or Natalie or sing in a choir. I wanted to hide away like a frightened animal, licking my wounds as I tried to come to terms with my father's utter betrayal of me.

Dear Daddy, how I loved you, how I worshipped your very being. How I hate you now.

I don't remember much about the journey back from the care home. It felt like a dream, one of those feverish ones you have as a child, where everything looms over you, large and frightening. Images of my father's smiling face morphing into something twisted and repulsive drifted through my mind.

'Here we go, love,' said the cab driver as we pulled up outside our house. I stared up at the windows. The lamp in the corner of the lounge was bathing the room with soft warm light. Oliver and Matilda came into view. He was spinning her round and round. Her head was tipped back and she was laughing. I could hear her shouting, 'Nanny! Save me!' I paid the driver and fled from the cab, running up the path, fumbling for my keys. I burst in through the door and into the living room. I had to get to them, to my family. Oliver looked up with surprise and joy. *My Oliver. My darling husband.*

'Mummeee, save meeee!' cried Matilda from her upside-down position. I laughed and scooped her up, covering her face with kisses. She giggled and we fell back onto the sofa next to my mother, who was smiling, glassy-eyed, but still smiling. She reached over a tentative hand, frail and purple with the marks of age, and wiggled her fingers gently under Matilda's chin.

'Tickle, tickle,' she smiled.

I felt sorrow catch in my throat. She loved Matilda and she had loved me, did love me, but she'd been betrayed and her love had been shoved aside by anger. I wished she had been honest with me. I wished she had told me the truth about my father.

Or did I? Would I tell Matilda if Oliver did the same to me? Or would I try to protect her, to protect that precious father–daughter relationship? I just didn't know but I also realised that I didn't want to be angry with her any more. I couldn't. She didn't deserve it and I didn't want to hold onto it as she had. I could see how it had torn her apart, leaving her empty and alone. I didn't want to end up like that. I wanted to break free of the past. I just wasn't sure how.

I waited until Matilda was in bed and my mother was watching television before I told Oliver. We sat in the kitchen sharing a bottle of wine. He listened, staring at me in shock as the story unravelled.

'It's incredible,' he said. 'Poor Patricia. Poor you.' He reached across the table and took my hand.

I gave him grateful smile. 'What should I do?'

'What do you want to do?'

'I don't know.'

'Guy seems like a good bloke.'

'But what will people think?'

He stared into my eyes. 'Who cares what people think? I love you, Matilda loves you, your mother loves you. That's all that matters. Everything else is just detail.'

'Maybe,' I said. I wasn't so sure.

'Caroline, you're allowed to have a less-than-perfect life, you know. In fact, it often saves a lot of trouble.'

I reached over and kissed him. 'Thank you.'

'For what?'

'For being one of the good guys.'

He grinned. 'I'll take that as a compliment from my beautiful wife with her high standards.'

'You should,' I smiled.

That night my sleep was filled with fitful dreams of my mother shouting at my father, of Virginia and Guy standing in the background, but Guy was younger, a small boy with his mother standing behind him, her hands on his shoulders. My mother was screaming at my father and he fled, running towards Guy and Virginia. I woke with a start, feeling clammy and agitated. After taking Matilda to school the next day, I made a deliberate bee-line for Guy.

'Are you free this afternoon? I think we should talk.'

'Yes, yes I am,' he replied. He look relieved.

'Good. How about Costa at two?'

'Great,' he smiled. 'See you later.'

I returned home to find Oliver getting ready to leave whilst my mother sat at the kitchen table eating a piece of toast.

'Hello, darling,' he said as I walked in. 'I'm just about to leave but can I pour you a coffee before I go?'

I smiled at him. *My wonderful husband. My constant. My rock.* 'Yes please.'

I sat down opposite my mother. She was staring into the middle distance, chewing on her toast, crumbs falling down her front. I felt something click inside me. 'Let me get that,' I said, brushing the toast remnants from her front and tucking a napkin into her jumper. She looked up at me, her face soft like a child's.

Oliver placed a mug of coffee in front of me and kissed the top of my head. 'I've got to dash but I hope to return with a big surprise,' he grinned before he disappeared down the hall. I heard the front door close behind him.

And then there were two. Sitting in silence. I watched my mother, still chewing, methodically, steadily. I realised that for all the time she'd been staying with us, I hadn't really looked at her face properly.

Her hair was wispy and I could see bare patches of scalp where it had become so thin. Her face was patterned with wrinkles, fault-lines on the map of a life. Here were the frown-lines caused by worry and regret, there were the faintest laughter-lines left behind by the happiness of youth and around her mouth, anger-lines from pursed lips and bitter disappointment. Her eyes looked out but didn't see, although I noticed how they glittered with joy when Matilda was around.

I sipped my coffee and wondered where to begin, indeed whether to begin at all. I didn't want to mention Virginia or Guy. I knew how much it upset her. I would have to take a different tack.

'I know about Dad,' I said, peering into her face. 'I know what he did.'

Her expression didn't change.

'I know that he had another family. That he betrayed you. Us.'

Nothing.

'I know about Charles. About what he did to you. How he let you down. I wish I'd known sooner. I wish you'd told me. I could have helped. We could have helped each other.'

'Charles?' My mother's voice was husky from lack of use. She looked up towards the ceiling. 'Charles?' she asked, as if he were about to appear.

I sighed. 'Charles isn't here. He's—'

'Dead. Charles is dead,' she said, looking at me.

'Yes.' I nodded encouragement.

Come on, we can do this. Let me help you. It's not too late.

I continued. 'And I know what he did. How he let you down. Why you were angry for all those years. I understand now.'

'Charles.' Her gaze transferred towards the ceiling again.

She can't hear you. This is useless.

I cast around the room for inspiration and a thought hit me. I walked across the kitchen and put on the Ella Fitzgerald CD again.

I turned and looked at my mother as 'Let's Face the Music and Dance' drifted out through the speakers. The words seemed so apt. There was very likely trouble ahead but if the choir had taught me anything, it was how music eased the pain and enabled you to face life, to face the unexpected.

I was astonished when my mother pushed herself up to a standing position and started to dance towards me. She held out her hands. I hesitated but she kept moving towards me and I had no choice but to take hold of them. She fixed her eyes on me and began to sing and to my surprise, I heard myself join in. It felt strange to begin with but her look was one of calm; the laughter-lines had returned. We moved around the kitchen, this tiny bird of a woman and me, in a strange swaying dance. I felt her hands in mine, the warmth of her touch and the essence of what this moment meant.

I love you and I'm sorry. From mother to daughter. From daughter to mother.

I wiped away a stray tear. I didn't want the song to end.

When it did finish, she stared at me for a second before the next track came on and we began again. By the end of the CD, we were laughing. We had barely spoken. The music had said it for us and what had begun as strange and a little awkward, became natural and wonderful.

It was a moment. A precious moment when we became mother and daughter again. I didn't know if my mother would remember it, if the memory would disappear when the music stopped, but I would. I would remember for both of us.

Oliver returned hours later looking elated. We were still in the kitchen, sitting at the table eating lunch.

'Good afternoon, ladies. How are we?'

I glanced at my mother who was staring into the distance, chewing methodically as if nothing had happened. It didn't matter. I knew what had happened. 'We're very well, actually,' I smiled.

'Wonderful! That's just wonderful!' he cried, leaping from foot to foot. He was as skittish as a puppy.

'So-o. How did it go? Do you have any news?'

'As a matter of fact, my beautiful wife,' said Oliver, leaning over to kiss me, 'I do have some rather exciting news.'

'Oh yes?' I smiled.

Hooray for exciting news, hopefully with the promise of a family holiday with my mother, somewhere warm that could cater for all our needs!

Oliver grinned. 'So-o. I've been talking to some of my old contacts …'

'Yes?'

Hooray for old contacts bringing Oliver another city job with the promise of a bonus. Maybe we could re-landscape the garden with a new patio, where my mother can sit and relax in the sunshine.

'And, they have been incredibly supportive.'

Wonderful. I love them all.

'So, I am going to re-train as an artisan bread-maker and start my own business.'

My stomach dropped to the floor. 'What?'

'An artisan bread-maker,' repeated Oliver with a grin. 'You know how I like to make bread and I've always wanted to learn properly. Plus, it's very on-trend. So, I'm hoping to take over one of those empty retail spaces on the approach to the High Street and I was thinking that we could go into business together,' he said, dancing over and folding me into his arms. 'I think we'd be the perfect business partners,' he added, kissing me.

This cannot be happening. 'Well,' I began. 'That's not what I was expecting.'

'I know! Isn't it wonderful?'

That's not exactly the word I'd choose.

'It's just the change we need, Caroline. A new start, a new beginning. A wonderful new opportunity!'

I don't want to change. I don't want a new beginning. I've just resolved things with my mother. I need everything else to go back to normal now.

But Oliver was too excited to notice and I didn't have the energy for an argument or the heart to tell him how I really felt. He spent the next half hour telling me all about his plans, about the course he was going to go on, the cost of set-up and innumerable other details that I can't recall. I felt numb with panic and clueless about how to deal with this. I glanced at the clock. I was meeting Guy in twenty minutes.

'I have to go,' I said, cutting off Oliver mid-sentence, rising to my feet. I felt as if I were wading through treacle.

'Oh okay, darling,' Oliver said, grinning. 'We can talk about all this later.'

I touched my mother briefly on the shoulder before I left. She turned her head and smiled up at me. I squeezed her shoulder in reply.

I felt as if I were in a dream as I drove into town and headed for the coffee shop. I ordered a cappuccino and found a seat at the back of the café facing the door. I wanted to be ready when Guy arrived and I needed a moment to gather my thoughts.

Why was everything in my life being turned upside down? My relationship with my father, my life with Oliver, my friendship with Guy. How strange that the most positive relationship in my life at the moment was the one with my mother.

I spotted Guy before he saw me. He looked nervous, casting around as he walked through the door. He noticed me and gave a small wave before making his way over to my table.

'I was worried you might change your mind,' he said.

'I thought about it but we do need to talk,' I told him.

He nodded. 'Would you like anything?' I shook my head and he went to place his order. He returned a few minutes later with coffee and a large slice of carrot cake. 'I never normally get time for lunch,' he smiled, sitting down opposite me and eating a mouthful.

'So,' I began. 'How long have you known?'

He fixed me with a look. I saw my father in his eyes and stared down at my coffee.

'Since I was eleven. My mum had always told me that my father worked away during the week and only came home at weekends. I went to secondary school and saw a photograph of him on the wall and wondered when my dad had found time to be Headmaster at my school if he was working in Scotland most of the week.'

'What did she tell you?'

He sighed. 'She cried. Then she told me that she had met him when she was working there and he was the Headmaster; that they had fallen in love and had me. She told me that he loved me very much but that he had another family and that it was a big secret and I couldn't tell anyone. Otherwise terrible things would happen.'

'What a twisted web we weave.'

He nodded. 'I didn't realise that your mother knew.'

'No, she kept it well hidden. It pretty much destroyed her. So how did you get on with him?'

'We had a decent relationship. I loved him. He was my father but I felt betrayed after I found out the truth. I was jealous of you because you got him all week, whereas I only saw him at weekends.'

'Yes, I got him all week along with my angry, bitter mother. It was like skipping through a meadow.' *Calm down, Caroline. This isn't Guy's fault.*

'I'm sorry, Caroline.'

'For what?'

'For not telling you sooner. To be honest, I wasn't sure if you'd want to know.'

You and me both. 'Some truths are best left unsaid?'

'Or lies.'

'Well you're right. I didn't want to know. My father was my biggest hero, the man who defined my life, but now—'

'Now?'

I sighed. 'He's gone and my mother is still alive and she needs me.'

'I need you,' said Guy. I stared at him in surprise. 'My family life was fractured and I would like to try and repair it. Personally, I think you'd make an excellent big sister.'

'Bossy, you mean?' I smiled.

'I never said that,' he laughed.

'I don't know, Guy. What will I tell Matilda?'

He shrugged. 'That I'm her long lost uncle? Kids love that kind of thing and they're far more accepting than adults.'

That was certainly true. 'I'll have to think about it,' I said.

'Fair enough,' he nodded, but I could tell he was desperate for me to agree. 'Can I get you another coffee?' he asked, pointing at my empty cup.

'I wouldn't mind a green tea please,' I smiled. I watched him walk away. He needed me. He wanted a sister.

Oh, Dad, look at all the hurt you caused, all the anguish and betrayal. Four lives devastated by your selfish ways.

'Caroline!' called a voice, interrupting my thoughts. My heart sank as I spotted Danielle in the queue in front of Guy. She accepted a takeaway cup from the barista and strode over to me. 'Enjoying a little me-time, are we? Gosh, I wish I could. It's just all go at the moment!' Guy arrived with our drinks. She stared up at him and then back towards me. 'Now then, what's all this? A little tête-à-tête with the choirmaster, eh? How scandalous!'

My imagination conjured up the thought of what would happen if I tipped her coffee over her head. My brain stopped me carrying out the thought. Just.

'We're having a meeting about the Choir Final, actually,' I lied.

'Oh, I'm relieved that's all it is, because your choir really doesn't need another scandal,' she leered.

I stared at her. 'Another scandal?'

She was almost exploding with delight as she told me. 'Oh, heavens, have I spoken out of turn? It's all over the internet so I presumed you'd know. Your friend Natalie and Tim Chambers the MP? There are pictures of them kissing and allegations of an affair. His party are trying to play it down but it's a huge embarrassment and it's not exactly going to help your little campaign, given that he's taken a personal interest. I know someone at the council and apparently it could be the nail in the coffin for Hope Street Hall – I mean they couldn't exactly decide to keep it open after this, could they? It would seem as if an interested party had influenced them and that would never do. Bless her, she probably thought she was helping your cause by jumping into bed with him, but I daresay it'll be full steam ahead with the property developers now. Such a shame. I know how hard you worked.' She glanced at her watch. 'Sorry, darling, got to dash. I've got a hair appointment in five. Bye for now!'

I stared at Guy for a moment. He looked stunned.

After the raft of emotions I'd experienced today, I wasn't sure what to believe or think any more. It was too much. An overwhelming feeling rose up inside me. I rushed to the toilet, locked the door behind me and threw up.

CHAPTER TWENTY-ONE

NATALIE

I've never fancied being a celebrity. This week I have had a small insight into exactly why. I'm not likely to grace the pages of *Hello!* and it is unlikely that my bottom will ever break the internet but for three solid days I have had to deal with phone and house-calls from journalists who claim that they 'just want to chat and hear my side of the story.' It was bad enough having to deal with my mother weeping down the phone because Daphne from the Bowls Club had shown her a picture on her iPad of me kissing Tim Chambers (curse those internet-savvy grannies). It was worse when Woody saw it and didn't speak to me for two days.

All of this neatly coincided with the run-up to the Choir Finals. We had a week of solid rehearsals planned and to say that the thought of these filled me with dread was a little bit like declaring George Clooney to be 'okay-looking'. I was plain terrified.

I also didn't have anyone to look after Woody. I couldn't ask Dan because we weren't speaking. He had tried to call, so I had sent him a text saying that I didn't want to talk at the moment. His reply – 'Of course, just call when you're ready. I only want to help.' – made me want to punch him in his ever-reasonable face. *Anger Management 0, Simmering Rage 1.*

I knew that I was getting everything wrong by blanking out what had happened with Tim, denying Woody his father's presence and generally being a crap mother and individual, but I didn't know what else to do. I felt as if I was just trying to exist, to get through the days really. I had tried to call Tim a couple of times but his phone had gone to voicemail and I decided that trying to visit in person would only add fuel to the fire of speculation. I had fielded calls from my editor (supportive, concerned), my agent (unhelpful, ranting) and Guy (sweet, worried). I hadn't heard from Caroline or any of the other choir members, but to be honest I had stopped answering the door and my phone after twenty-four hours.

I did have to pop to the shop for milk one day. I tried my best to channel my inner Grace Kelly by wearing gigantic dark sunglasses and a scarf wrapped up around my ears, just in case there was a photographer lurking. When I caught sight of myself in the shop window, I looked like less like a Hollywood star and more like a weirdo. I removed both before entering the shop. Doly's brother-in-law, Hasan, was behind the counter. He looked up and smiled when I entered but didn't seem to recognise me. I darted to the fridge, grabbed a four-pint bottle of milk and carried it over to the till. On impulse I grabbed a two-hundred-gram bar of Dairy Milk as well. On the survival-kit list of the broken-hearted, chocolate has to be the number-one choice. Along with wine. And ice cream. And possibly biscuits.

Hasan keyed in the prices. 'Two pounds forty please,' he smiled. 'Would you like a bag?'

'No thanks,' I replied, reaching hurriedly for my purse. I didn't want to run the risk of bumping into Doly.

'Natalie!' cried a voice. I turned to be confronted by the ample bosom of Pamela. Without further comment or warning she pressed me to her chest before holding me at arm's length. 'Oh, lovey, how are you?' she clucked, chucking me under the chin like a three-year-old.

'I'm fine,' I muttered, glancing furtively at Hasan, who gave me a polite nod, which confirmed that he recognised me now. 'Bit busy.'

'But you're coming to choir tonight aren't you? You're not going to let all this shenanigans stop you, are you?'

I stared down at my feet. 'Not sure. I haven't got a babysitter, so ...'

'Hasan!' came a voice from the door at the back. 'Do we need to re-stock the chewing gum?' It was Doly's voice and I wanted to be away but it was too late. She appeared from the back of the shop and stopped to stare at me.

She was embarrassed and I couldn't blame her. I was ashamed too.

'Doly!' called Pamela. 'Could your lovely husband watch Woody while Natalie's at choir this evening?'

'Oh no, it's fine, don't worry,' I said, starting to back towards the door. *Must get home before I start crying again.*

'Please, Natalie,' said Doly. 'Wait.'

I stood still as she approached me. She had such warmth and grace. I must have seemed so shabby in her eyes. She stopped before me and took my hands. 'You must not be embarrassed,' she said. She gestured towards Hasan. 'We are Muslims and we understand more than most that you should not believe or judge by the things you read in the news. It is the person that is most important and you are a good person. Of course Woody can come here this evening. Sadia would love to see him.'

I stared into her beautiful kind eyes and started to cry. I couldn't help it. Suddenly I felt Doly and Pamela wrap their arms around me and for the first time in so many weeks

I remembered that I had friends. I had been such an idiot, completely missing the point as usual. I had thought that I was alone, that no-one cared and yet, here they were, where they'd been all along. Right in front of me – my friends.

Before I left, Doly touched my cheek. 'All will be well,' she said. 'You will see.'

Doly's words consoled me and I decided that I had to try and talk to Woody after school. On the walk home, I told him that he was going round to Sadia's house for an hour or two while I was at choir. He took the news with a satisfied nod but didn't speak the rest of the way. Once at home, I made us both drinks and fetched the biscuit tin. We'd had a little ritual of sitting down and discussing our day ever since Woody had started school. It had lapsed lately but I decided that it was probably more important now than ever.

'Would you like a biscuit?' I called up the stairs.

'I've got homework,' he shouted down from his room.

'Please, Woody. I need to talk to you.'

Whether out of curiosity or a grudging sense of love, he sloped down the stairs and followed me into the dining room. Helping himself to a chocolate bar, he immediately set about devouring it, like a task that had to be completed. I could see that I would need to be quick.

'So I wanted to tell you firstly, that I'm sorry about those pictures you saw of me kissing that man.'

'Who was that man?' he asked.

I swallowed. 'His name is Tim Chambers.'

'Is he your boyfriend now?'

'No.'

'So why did you kiss him?'

Honest. Always be honest with your children. 'I don't really know.'

Woody frowned. 'That doesn't make any sense.'

'I know.'

He sighed. 'Grown-ups are weird.'

'That's very true.'

'And they make everything far too complicated.'

Quick, put this boy in charge of the world. 'Also true,' I smiled. 'I need to talk to you about your dad as well.'

'He's not coming back.'

'Yes.' I was surprised. 'How did you know?'

He shrugged. 'He was unhappy for a bit and now he doesn't seem so unhappy, so it kind of makes sense.'

I felt sick. 'How did you know he was unhappy?'

Woody shifted in his seat. 'I just noticed stuff.'

'What kind of stuff?' I demanded. *Nat, calm down, don't interrogate him. Let him tell you.* 'Sorry. I just want to know.'

He thought for a moment. 'Well, there was that day when we watched your wedding video.' I nodded. Family tradition. Every year on our anniversary. 'And Dad went out to get a beer but he didn't come back for a bit.'

He glanced up at me, unsure of whether to continue. 'It's okay. You can tell me, Woody.'

He took a deep breath. 'So I went to find him. I said I needed the loo and you stayed and watched.' I remembered. We had got to the funny bit where Auntie Vi was drunkenly showing everyone her verruca. Disgusting, but funny. 'So I went to the kitchen but Dad wasn't there and then I heard a noise.'

'What kind of a noise?'

'Crying.'

I stared at him. 'Well maybe he was sad because he saw Grandpa on the video.'

Woody shook his head. 'He wasn't, because I walked into the dining room and I saw him.'

'Did he see you?'

'Not at first. I watched him for a bit. His shoulders were shaking. I thought he wasn't going to stop. So I did one of those coughs, like grown-ups do when they want someone to see them. Like this.' He cleared his throat with great noise and drama. *My dear boy. My dear Woody.*

'And what happened?'

'He wiped his eyes really quickly and turned round with this massive smile on his face and said, 'Hey, Woody, I thought I saw that cat in the garden again. You know, the one that poos in between Mum's geraniums, so I was shooing him away.'

'Well, maybe that's true,' I said. *And maybe the moon is made of marshmallow.*

Woody fixed me with a look, like that of an adult instructing a child. 'He didn't want me to see. He didn't want me to know that he'd been crying.'

My mind filled with horror as I scanned memories of the last year and saw a pattern emerging.

Christmas Day. Dan disappeared while we were watching the post-lunch-slump film. I found him sitting on our bed staring out of the window, rubbing his eyes and claiming that he'd fallen asleep.

My birthday. We'd just had a family breakfast and Woody had given me his home-made card – a picture of the three of us on the beach in Brighton. I had remarked that Dan's expression looked a bit sad. We laughed it off and Dan had offered to fetch me another coffee. He had disappeared for a long time but returned empty-handed, his eyes red and puffy. 'Bloody hayfever,' he'd said before remembering the coffee.

I was filling in the blanks with blanks – big black holes where my husband should have been.

You utter, bloody fool, Nat. He was disappearing from your life right in front of your eyes and you didn't even notice.

I stared at Woody, unsure of what to say. He looked worried. 'Are you okay, Mum? Was it my fault?'

Oh, Woody. I saw the little boy with his father's eyes and guilt clutched at my heart, shoving the anger out of the way and filling it with pure love. Love for my boy. It had always been there, it had just become hidden behind my stupid rage.

I reached for him and he accepted my arms. 'No, my darling boy. It isn't your fault. None of this is your fault.' *It's mine. For letting it happen. For being blind. For not seeing what was going on right in front of me. For not seeing what was happening to Dan and not trying to stop it.* 'I'm sorry. I'm so unbelievably sorry. I wish I'd known.'

'You can't see everything all the time, Mum,' he told me.

I smiled down at him and stroked his beautifully earnest face. 'No, I suppose you can't.'

'Doesn't Dad love you any more then?'

I swallowed. *Man, this is hard.* 'It's quite complicated but your dad was very sad after his dad died and it affected how he was feeling. It changed the way he felt about me. He still loves me. He loves us both. He just doesn't want to be married to me any more.'

'So will you get a divorce?'

'I don't know how we can stay being married, so probably, yes.' He started to blink rapidly and I could tell that he was trying not to cry. 'Oh, Woody,' I said, cupping his face in my hands and kissing him.

Fat tears rolled down his cheeks. 'I miss him,' he cried. 'I miss my dad.'

I wrapped my arms around him, protective and fierce, kissing the top of his head. For once I didn't cry. I just held and comforted him. 'All will be well. You will see,' I soothed. At that moment, I knew what I had to do.

I had become too caught up in my own hurt to see Woody's bubbling below the surface. I had let my anger towards Dan get in the way of my love for Woody and I was ashamed of this, but I would sort it. I would sort everything.

In that second, sitting there with the warmth of Woody's body in my arms, I was strong again. Call it mother-love or just maternal instinct but it was bloody powerful. I would do anything for my boy and nothing would stand in my way. If Woody was okay then I would be okay.

I felt braver walking into the choir rehearsal with Doly later that evening. Everyone seemed as friendly and welcoming as usual – everyone apart from Caroline, that is. She was in discussions with Guy as I arrived. She looked over at me as if I were a freshly barfed pile of vomit. It was disdain mixed with disgust and just a sprinkling of scathing judgement.

I was distracted by Pamela giving me one of her more bosomy hugs and telling me that she'd made a batch of my favourite chocolate brownies.

'Okay, let's make a start,' said Guy from the front of the room. I took my place next to Doly as usual and turned to greet Caroline. It was almost impossible for her to blank me, she couldn't avoid my gaze but she managed it somehow.

'Good evening, Caroline,' I said loudly and with more than a little irritation. She couldn't ignore me now, surely. She was the queen of disparaging looks and she managed to issue me with a particularly withering one before floating her gaze directly over my head towards Guy. My blood was boiling but Guy had gestured for us to stand. I rose to my feet, staring straight ahead, shaking with anger.

'Okay, let's do a run-through of "Fix You", shall we?'

It sounded bloody awful. We were out of tune, the harmonics were discordant and the whole song dragged like a saggy-bottomed dog. Even Guy couldn't pretend. 'I don't want to worry you lovely people but this is our last rehearsal before the Final. We're going to have to do better than that,' he grimaced.

Doly and I exchanged worried glances. Something wasn't right. I certainly wasn't feeling the love tonight and evidently I wasn't the only one. I looked behind at Caroline but she was still staring past me, refusing to make eye contact. I felt my anger bubbling up again.

I thought she might be peeved by what had happened but I didn't expect a cold shoulder. We had been through a lot together, some of it fun, much of it maddeningly irritating, but I had considered her to be a friend and felt that it was about time that she climbed down from her extremely high horse and gave me a break. I turned back to the front, my eyes fixed on Guy, but I could feel my fury simmering below the surface. *How dare she?* I think I deserved sympathy for what I was going through with Dan. Surely that wouldn't kill her.

We struggled our way through another couple of runs before Guy held up his hands. 'Maybe some tea and cake will help,' he said.

'This isn't good,' murmured Doly. 'There's some bad karma floating around tonight.'

'Yes,' I said. 'And I know exactly where it's coming from.' Caroline was already heading towards the tea table. I made my way over and tapped her on the shoulder. She turned and gave me such a superior look of dislike that I almost took a step backwards.

That's enough. I made a mistake. I didn't kill your dog, you judgemental old bag.

'What is your problem?' I demanded.

She regarded me with flared nostrils. 'Seeing as you ask, my problem is that you have effectively ruined months of time and effort, all our time and effort,' she declared, spreading out her arms to bring in the rest of the room.

Clearly, she wanted to hold me up as the villain so that she could save face if we lost the hall. People carried on talking but their voices were hushed, listening but pretending not to. There was nothing better than a good drama, particularly if you had no part in it. I would have done the same.

In days gone by, I would have run a mile from conflict, said 'Whatevs' to a woman like Caroline and left her to stew in her own juices. But not any more. These days I lurched between wanting to cry and wanting to punch someone. Unfortunately for Caroline, the latter was taking precedence tonight.

'How dare you blame me?' I cried. 'How dare you stand in judgement on me? I made a mistake, pure and simple, and if you had given me half a chance or even taken a moment to ask how I was, I would have apologised to you as I have apologised to others. But you wouldn't do that, would you Caroline? That's not in your nature, is it?'

I probably should have stopped there. That would have been the sensible thing to do but everyone was watching now. The show must go on and there was stuff that needed to be said. I needed to say this stuff. She was staring at me, looking a little unsure. I decided to set her straight.

'You don't actually care about anyone, do you? About me. Or this choir. Or even this hall. Because you're only in this for yourself, aren't you? To make yourself look good and affirm your sad lonely stay-at-home mum's existence by spouting a load of crap you don't believe about communities and people.'

'Natalie …' began Guy.

'No, Guy, I'm sorry but sometimes these things need to be said.' I squared up to Caroline. 'You are a control freak and a bossy cow. You have zero empathy or self-awareness beyond the needs of your own ego.'

Caroline had gone pale and I feared I'd overstepped the mark but to her credit, she faced me head on. 'How dare you? How dare you question my motives and intentions? Just because I am organised and keep my emotions in check, it doesn't mean that I don't care. I have given my all to this campaign and for what? For some chaotic, emotional train-crash of a woman to wreck it all by sleeping with an MP!'

There was a gasp from Pamela. I stared at her open-mouthed. 'I did not sleep with him,' I said. 'It was one kiss and that was all.'

Caroline turned on me. 'Maybe, but it didn't help, did it? Your sordid moment of weakness will probably be the nail in the coffin of this campaign.'

'You don't know that,' I said. 'Nothing has been decided.'

She shrugged. 'Perhaps, but you haven't helped, and worse still, you've behaved like a sulky teenager throughout. I've had to hold your hand, listen to you weeping and wailing, and all for what?'

I glared at her. 'Whereas you've shown about as much compassion as a dustbin. Hold my hand? Keep an eye on me, more like. You're a glory-hunter, Caroline. You don't care about anyone but yourself.'

She regarded me with contempt, her body completely still, like a lion just before it pounces on its prey. Then she delivered the killer swipe. 'I'm not surprised your husband left you. You're a mess. He'd probably had enough of picking up the pieces.'

I was only aware of my hand moving through the air as it made contact with Caroline's face in a stinging slap. She clutched her cheek and glared at me in fury, looking as if she might be about to retaliate.

'That's enough!' shouted Guy, pulling us apart with help from Pamela and Doly. 'Both of you. You're angry and you need to stop.'

'Oh, piss off, Guy!' said Caroline. We gaped in surprise because Caroline rarely swore. 'You're just feeling guilty because you've found out that we share a father. You don't have to do the protective-brother routine on my account.'

'What?' I asked, stunned.

'Oh yes,' said Caroline. 'Seeing as we're having a cards-on-the-table moment. I've found out that my father was leading a double life and Guy here was the result.'

Everyone stared from Caroline to Guy. 'Wow,' breathed Pamela.

'Yes, wow indeed. Well if you'll excuse me, I have to get back home now. My dementia-ridden mother needs me and my husband has decided to give up the chance to earn a decent living in the city by becoming a baker, so it really is all go. Apologies to any of you if I have been overbearing or a bossy cow, as Natalie so charmingly called me. I have obviously failed somewhere, when all I was trying to do was help. Goodnight.' She swept from the room, leaving us staring at one another in awkward silence.

'I don't think there's much point in carrying on tonight,' sighed Guy. 'Let's clear the chairs away. We meet here on the morning of the Final, okay?'

I approached Guy. 'Are you all right?' I asked.

He nodded. 'You?'

I looked sheepish. 'Infuriating as she is, I shouldn't have slapped her.'

'You were both out of order but for the record, I'd want you on my side in a fight,' he smiled, putting a hand on my shoulder. 'You know where I am if you ever need to talk, okay?'

'Thanks.'

I walked home with Doly, desperately wanting to know what she thought. I trusted and valued her opinion. 'You must think I'm a nightmare,' I said after a while.

She caught my eye and smiled. 'You are just having a difficult time at the moment. I think Caroline is too.'

I hugged her. 'You are wise and kind. I'm glad you're my friend.'

'I'm glad you're mine too,' she said, patting my hand. 'I meant what I said earlier. All will be well. For you and Caroline.'

I smiled. I hoped she was right.

After I'd picked up Woody, we returned home to find Dan sitting outside the house in his car. 'Dad!' cried Woody, rushing towards him. Dan caught him in a tight embrace and spun him round. 'Are you coming in?' he asked, staring up at his father.

Dan glanced over at me and I nodded. 'Let's have a cuppa. Woody, go and put on your pyjamas and Dad can tuck you in.'

As Woody scooted up the stairs, Dan turned to me in the hall. 'Thank you. I've missed him,' he admitted.

'He's missed you too,' I said.

Dan stared at me. 'Are you okay?'

I raked my fingers through my hair. 'Yes, no, maybe. Does that answer your question?'

He smiled. 'Sort of.'

I filled the kettle and turned to face him. 'Our priority has to be Woody. Whatever else is said or done, he comes first.'

Dan nodded. 'Absolutely.'

'We need to find a way for you to do this, to be here to see him after school or at bedtime.'

'I really want that, Nat. It's been torture not seeing him. I'll do whatever I can to make it right for Woody,' he said. 'And for you,' he added, reaching out to touch me on the arm.

I pulled away gently. I had to learn to stand on my own. 'I know you will,' I replied. 'Why don't you go upstairs and chivvy him along? You know what he's like about cleaning his teeth. He'll be up there all night if you let him.'

'Some things never change, eh?' he smiled before disappearing upstairs.

Some things never change and some things change forever. All you can do is look to the future, to keep going towards it, keep reaching. I stared out into the dark garden and despite everything or maybe because of everything that had happened over the past few months, I felt a hint of something new inside me. It was hope. It was only tiny but it was there all the same and that was enough for now. As long as I had Woody and that grain of hope, I would survive.

CHAPTER TWENTY-TWO

CAROLINE

I ended the call, placing my phone on the kitchen counter. I poured myself another coffee and carried it into the living room. Matilda and my mother were watching cartoons. Actually, to be more specific, Matilda was watching and my mother was staring. I sat down next to her. She raised her head slightly as if acknowledging my presence. It felt warm and comfortable. Oliver appeared in the living-room doorway.

'Shouldn't you be getting dressed?' he asked. 'We're due to meet the others at the hall in half an hour.'

'I'm not going,' I said, taking a sip of my coffee and staring at the screen. A blue cartoon cat was dancing with what looked like a goldfish wearing green socks. It was rather amusing. 'What is this?' I asked.

'*The Amazing Adventures of Gumball*,' laughed Matilda as the sock-wearing fish broke into song. 'It's really funny.'

'Caroline, are you okay?' asked Oliver, frowning at me.

'Never better,' I declared, crossing my legs and curling my hands around my mug. 'It's a relief not to have to go to the Choir Finals, to be honest. I think we would have embarrassed ourselves.'

'O-kay,' said Oliver, not sounding very sure. 'And you are giving up be-cause …?'

'Because,' I said with a breezy smile, 'I have just had a call from John Hawley at the council. They've already met and decided to sell the hall to the property developers.'

He moved towards me and knelt beside the sofa, placing a hand on my shoulder. 'I'm so sorry, darling. You've worked so hard. I know things have been stressful lately, what with finding out about your dad and your worries over my job. You must be disappointed.'

Don't be nice to me. Please don't be nice to me.

'It's fine. It's absolutely fine.' My voice was starting to crack and I had an urge to run away, to escape the kind words and compassion. I sensed my mother turn to me and felt her frail hand rest on one of mine.

'Caroline,' she said.

I turned to face her, looking beyond the woman I thought I'd known, to the mother I knew now. I saw the weight of the past in her eyes but also a softness, a longing to help.

'Oh, Mum,' I sobbed. 'I'm sorry. You must have been so lonely and sad. I wish I could make it better. I wish I'd known.' I felt her place a bony arm around my shoulder and I rested against her, fearful that I might crush her but comforted by the embrace.

'Caroline,' she repeated, pressing me to her with surprising strength. 'My Caroline.'

Oliver reached down to kiss the top of my head and suddenly Matilda noticed what was happening. 'Ooh, group hug,' she proclaimed, wrapping her tiny arms around us all. We sat like this for a while, in an awkward family embrace, but it felt wonderful too – spontaneous and wonderful.

The doorbell rang. 'I'll get it,' said Oliver, heading down the hall.

Moments later, he reappeared with Natalie and Guy at his side, the former looking a little sheepish and the latter frowning with concern. My mother started to get agitated as soon as she saw Guy.

'It's all right, Mum,' I said, squeezing her skeletal shoulder. 'You don't need to worry about that any more.'

My mother frowned but seemed reassured.

'We were worried that you weren't going to come,' said Natalie, staring at my pyjamas. 'And it seems as if we were right.'

'Mummy says there's no point in going because the council are giving the hall to those other people,' explained Matilda.

'I thought you were watching the television?' I said in surprise.

She gave me a sage look. 'I can multi-task,' she explained. 'I'm a girl.'

'Like mother, like daughter,' laughed Oliver. 'Now why don't we go into the kitchen?' he added, giving me a meaningful look. 'Natalie, Guy, can I get you a coffee?'

They both stared at me for a moment, like children waiting for their mother to allow them a treat. I rolled my eyes and stood up. 'Come on then,' I said, walking out of the living room, gesturing for them to follow me to the kitchen.

I sat down at the kitchen table. Guy and Natalie exchanged glances before taking their places opposite me. Natalie regarded me for a second before speaking. 'I am sorry for slapping you the other night and for the things I said. I was angry but that's not an excuse. It was wrong of me.'

I wasn't used to people apologising unprompted and it caught me off guard. I could see that she wanted my forgiveness and I realised that I needed hers too. I took a deep breath. 'I'm sorry for saying what I did about your husband. It was cruel and also not true.'

She smiled with relief. 'Well, I'm glad we got that out of the way. And for the record, I am truly sorry about what happened with Tim and the impact it had on the campaign.'

I sighed. 'In truth, I think the council had made their decision a long time ago so it probably didn't make the slightest bit of difference.'

She nodded, taking a sip of the coffee Oliver had just placed in front of her. I noticed Guy watching me. We hadn't spoken properly since our meeting at the coffee shop but I had done a lot of thinking. I liked Guy. He was a good man and if you had to choose a half-brother, you could do a lot worse. Matilda wandered into the kitchen.

'Tilly, the grown-ups are talking,' warned Oliver.

'I know,' she grinned. 'It's always so interesting when grown-ups do that.'

Everyone laughed. 'Tilly, why don't you go back in with Nanny?' said Oliver.

'No, it's all right, Oliver,' I said. 'Matilda, I have something to tell you.'

'Oh yes,' she said, approaching the table. 'Is it exciting?'

I eyed Oliver, who smiled at me. 'Yes, it is, actually. It's a bit complicated to explain but I've found out that your Grandpa had another son, and that son was Guy.' Matilda stared at Guy in amazement. 'Which means that he is officially your uncle.'

Matilda punched the air in delight. 'Yesss! This is so cool. I've always wanted an uncle. I mean, I've got an aunt but I really wanted one of each, and you're my music teacher, which makes it extra cool and everyone at school is going to be *so* jealous. Thank you so much, Mummy, Uncle Guy,' she cried, rushing from me to Guy and back again, giving us tight hugs of glee.

'First thing you have to realise about Tilly,' observed Oliver, 'is that she has a LOT of words.'

Guy laughed, wiping away an escaped tear. Matilda stared up at him. 'It's very emosh, isn't it, Uncle Guy?' she said, hugging him again.

He looked over at me. 'Thank you,' he said. 'Really.'

I nodded, feeling a little teary myself. I glanced at Natalie, who was weeping uncontrollably. 'I'm sorry!' she cried. 'But this is just so lovely!' I shook my head and laughed.

So this is what a perfect moment actually feels like – emotional, noisy and incredibly wonderful.

'What about today then?' asked Guy, looking serious.

I looked down at my pyjamas. 'Is there any point?'

Guy and Natalie exchanged glances. Natalie stood up. 'Today it's my turn to be the bossy cow,' she said with arms folded.

I stared up at her. 'What do you mean?'

'I mean, Caroline Taylor, that one thing you have taught me during this whole messy, fantastic experience is that we never give up. Ever.'

'I know, but—'

'Uh-uh-uh,' she interrupted, holding up a hand to shush me. 'There are no buts today. We may not be able to save the hall but we can bloody well go down singing. So you're going to get up those stairs, get dressed, brush that perfect hair and come with us to the Albert Hall. Okay?' Her mouth twitched into a smile. 'Sorry, I find it difficult to be serious.'

'I've noticed,' I grinned.

She gave me a look of feigned outrage. 'Get up those stairs and get dressed, young lady! We're not leaving without you!'

Matilda giggled. 'Yeah, Mummy, get up those stairs!'

I laughed. 'Okay, okay, I'm going.'

'Yay!' chorused Matilda and Natalie, high-fiving each other. Guy gave me a beaming thumbs-up. Oliver put an arm around my shoulder and kissed my cheek.

'I'm glad you changed your mind,' grinned Natalie. 'I couldn't face Danielle on my own.'

'That's what I thought,' I smiled, before disappearing upstairs to change.

I never fail to be awe-struck by the Royal Albert Hall. Everything from its perfect dome shape, its terracotta façade and mosaic frieze to its location in the heart of London with Hyde Park on the opposite side of the road, makes it a thing of true beauty. I had goose-bumps as we made our way through the glass doors into the plush red-and-gold interior. This was the epitome of elegance and class. Kings, queens, world leaders, rock stars and classical musicians had all walked through these doors, and now it was our turn to perform here. During the train journey I had broken the news about the council's decision to the rest of the choir. No-one seemed that surprised. Pamela had patted my hand to reassure me.

'Never mind, ducks. It was a long shot and we did our best. Now let's just enjoy today, shall we?'

I replied with a grateful smile. She was right of course. Today was all about our choir and the singing.

As we made our way through the entrance, I noticed Pamela grab Doly's hand with an excited yelp and Natalie gave me a grin that said, 'We've arrived.' Guy and I made our way over to the organisers. We were told that we would be singing last and they directed us to the choir seats behind the stage.

'That's good,' said Guy. 'The last slot is the best one.'

As we made our way back down the stairs to the others, I heard a familiar voice. 'Caroline! Darling! You made it.'

'Hello, Danielle,' I said, turning to face her but moving away before she could air-kiss me.

'How *are* you?' she said with emphasis. I noticed that her group had gone to town today. They were wearing matching red, white and blue trouser suits with white roses in their button-holes. She noticed me looking. 'Do you like it?' she said, taking a step back. 'We're tapping into the "Land of Hope and Glory" theme,' she grinned with smug satisfaction.

'Very patriotic,' I observed.

'Danielle!' barked one of her fellow singers. 'Small problem with the running order,' she said, handing over a piece of paper. Her face was pinched and mean.

Danielle pursed her lips in annoyance before giving me a practised smile which didn't reach her eyes. 'Excusez-moi, Caroline. I just need to speak to the organisers.'

I turned back to the group. 'Right, shall we take our places?' I said.

'How was the witch?' asked Natalie as we made our way up the stairs.

'Witchy,' I smiled.

'Good luck, Mum,' cried Woody from the entrance hall.

'Yes, break a leg!' giggled Matilda, who was standing next to him.

Dan, Oliver and my mother were with them. Oliver had suggested that we bring her. I'd had my reservations but he had waved them away. 'I'll put the wheelchair in the back of the car and make sure she's okay. I promise.' She seemed impossibly small propped up in her chair but she was beaming from ear to ear as Woody and Matilda took turns to help push her.

We waved and smiled at them before making our way up the stairs. 'How are things?' I asked Natalie as we reached the door to the concert hall.

She gave a considered nod. 'Better. As long as Woody's okay, I'm okay. Let's just say I've readjusted my focus in life.'

'I'm glad,' I smiled.

'It's lovely that your mum was able to come,' she observed.

I nodded. 'Yes, yes, it is.'

'Excuse me, Mrs Taylor?' said a voice beside me.

'Yes?' I replied, turning to face a woman in her fifties, whom I recognised as one of the organisers of the event.

'There's been a mistake in the running order,' she smiled. 'You'll now be the penultimate act, rather than singing last.'

Oh, really? How suspicious. 'This wouldn't have anything to do with the Dulwich Darlings, would it?' I asked with narrowed eyes.

'I couldn't possibly comment,' she said with a firm smile. 'All acts will be treated the same, regardless of their place in the running order.'

I shrugged. 'Well, we never thought we'd get this far so I don't think we've got anything to lose.'

'Good luck,' she said before turning away.

If the outside of the building made me tingle with excitement, the inside of the concert hall made my heart leap with joy. It was jaw-droppingly huge, beautiful and inspiring.

'Bloody hell,' declared Jim as we reached our seats. 'This is something else.'

'Ooh, I hope my vertigo doesn't kick in,' cried Pamela, closing her eyes.

'You will be fine,' assured Doly in a soothing voice. 'We are not too high.' Pamela took hold of her hand and nodded.

'Could I just have everyone's attention please,' said Guy. We all looked up at him. 'I just wanted to wish you all the best of luck. You are a truly amazing bunch of people and it has been my absolute pleasure to work with you all.

We may not have been able to save the hall but whatever happens, we have done a remarkable thing and I, for one, do not want this to end.'

'Hear, hear!' cheered Jim.

'So,' smiled Guy. 'Sing, be proud and, most importantly, enjoy.'

We all clapped and cheered as he sat down. The concert hall was starting to fill now. I spotted Matilda and my mother sitting with Oliver and the others in one of the lower rows reserved for wheelchairs. Oliver gave me a cheerful thumbs-up and Matilda waved with enthusiasm, doing her best to point me out to my mother. I wasn't sure if she could see me but for a second, I felt as if we locked eyes and she smiled. I felt a wave of pure love for them all, wishing that I could wrap them in my arms and keep them safe forever.

After a short while, the lights were dimmed and a hush descended. From one side of the stage, Andrew Munday appeared, his arms outstretched to the audience. A frisson of excitement coursed through the hall at the sight of such a familiar and well-loved celebrity.

'Hello and welcome to the Final of the first ever National Community Choir Championships!' he cried. The crowd cheered. 'As you know, singing and choirs are very close to my heart, so I was honoured to be asked to host this fantastic event. The choirs have been selected from every region of the UK and today we are going to hear from sixteen of the very best. I have heard recordings of all the choirs and I have to tell you that you are in for a huge treat. Our judging panel are all industry professionals and they have the incredibly tricky task of choosing a winner for this prestigious award.' He gestured to a trophy made of crystal etched with a treble clef. The audience oohed their appreciation and Andrew laughed.

'So, without further ado, we're going to hear from one of the finalists from the Scotland and North-east round. Please go wild for, Good Tooning!'

The audience applauded as the first group made their way onto the stage. Theirs was a moving rendition of 'Perfect Day' by Lou Reed and I noticed one or two people wipe away a surreptitious tear. Guy looked over at me, nodding with approval. The competition was off to an impressive start. Overall the standard was high. There were some good performances and some not-so-good performances. A Welsh male singing group did an ill-advised version of 'Bang Bang' including dance moves. The audience laughed along but it was a relief when they finished. I started to feel a little nervous after the interval, partly because of what we were about to do and partly because I was beginning to believe that we were in with a chance. The quality was high but I felt that we were matching it. Self-confidence is a wonderful thing. It can make you achieve all kinds of previously unimaginable feats.

As Andrew announced that it was our turn and I took my place alongside Natalie on the stage, I felt completely still and calm. My nerves seemed to disappear as I looked up towards my family and smiled. It was as if there was nothing else to worry about any more. Guy stood in front of us smiling. He gave the briefest of nods, raised his hands and we began.

Moments of pure happiness are rare in life. We experience most of them as children and even then, they are tempered by the constraints set by our parents. As adults, we have complete freedom of choice and yet often, happiness eludes us because there's always something that needs to be done. In lots of ways, I feel as if I've spent my entire adult life 'just completing one last task', before I can get on with the job of being happy.

It's ridiculous when you come to think of it. The world is full of heartbreak, of children dying, of people killing one another. You have to grab that dose of happiness whenever it presents itself.

Today, standing in the Albert Hall, singing with a group of people who I realised had become my friends, in the presence of those I loved most in the world, I was grasping that happiness with both hands.

For singing made me happy in a carefree way. When I was singing I didn't worry. My mind and soul were calmed, my body felt still but it also felt powerful. I felt that I could face anything without fear – the truth, the lies, the joy and sadness could all be captured by music and shared with the world.

As we performed 'Fix You' the words of the song, the sentiment of those lines seemed so salient to me, to our choir, to my mother and to Guy. It felt like our anthem, as if this song had been written for us, for me.

That was the power of music, the power of this choir. It held you in its arms, it let you cry and it comforted you. Shivers of melancholy ran through my body. I felt tears prick my eyes but I didn't mind. We all felt it – this group of singers who had started out as strangers and who were now friends; family, even.

I caught Natalie's eye and we smiled at one another – sharing that understanding, that moment of pure joy. I could tell she was suppressing the tears too. I reached out my hand, took hers and squeezed it.

I understand. I feel the same. It's all right.

When it was over, I looked to the front and could see that several of the audience were wiping away tears and that Oliver, Dan, Matilda and Woody were on their feet, whooping and cheering with delight. Our choir turned to one another, grinning and we embraced in a moment of sheer elation and pride.

'Ladies and gentlemen, the fabulous Hope Street Community Choir!' cried Andrew, striding onto the stage.

We made our way back to our seats, beaming with joy. I barely remember the Dulwich Darlings' performance. I know it was 'Land of Hope and Glory' and I know they persuaded some of the front row to get up and wave flags but I didn't care. Nothing could take away what we had just done and how good it had made us feel.

I was wholly unsurprised and not even that disappointed when The Dulwich Darlings were crowned champions.

'The moral victory was ours,' declared Natalie as we left the concert hall. Danielle's victory crow was inevitable but this time I was ready for her.

'Darling Caroline. Commiserations,' she cooed. 'But you did sooo well for beginners. I was impressed. Really impressed.'

'Thank you,' I said with a saintly smile. 'And congratulations on your victory. It was well deserved.'

She stared at me as if trying to work out if I was being genuine. I kept the smile fixed to my face. 'Thank you,' she frowned. 'I have to say you're taking it very well, considering you lost this and your little community hall.'

I continued to smile as I looked directly into her eyes. 'What you fail to understand, Danielle, is that life is about so much more than being a bitch and taking pleasure in other people's discomfort.' She looked shocked and started to open her mouth in protest. I held up a hand to silence her. 'My choir,' I said, gesturing to Natalie and the others, 'has taught me what true friendship is. This has been about far more than a choir competition. It's been about understanding what's important and standing up to fight for it, even if you fail. But I wouldn't expect you to understand that. Your choir may have won the award but we've won far more than that. I'm proud of us and I know that with or without the hall, the friendships and music will endure. I really hope the award makes you happy. But I seriously doubt that it will. Goodbye, Danielle.' I walked away before she could respond. I felt Natalie link her arm through mine.

'Nice speech,' she grinned.

I smiled as we walked out into the sunshine and the open arms of our families. 'I meant every blessed word.'

CHAPTER TWENTY-THREE

NATALIE

I was on time for once and felt really rather proud. Even Woody seemed surprised as he found me waiting for him at the bottom of the stairs that morning.

'But, Mum, we're actually early. Are you all right?' he asked with a wry grin.

'Cheeky boy,' I laughed, ruffling his hair. 'I wanted to make sure we'll be there when the demolition team arrive. I promised Caroline and the rest of the choir.'

He nodded. 'Are you sad that they're knocking down the hall?' he asked.

'A bit, but I know we did everything we could. Sometimes that's all you can do.' My phone buzzed with a call. Woody rolled his eyes. 'It's okay,' I told him. 'It's a mobile phone, see? I can talk as we walk. Hello?' I answered as we left the house and I locked up. Doly, Dev and their three girls were just passing by our house. I gave them a wave as Woody ran off to join Sadia.

'Natalie? This is Anita Vangani from the BBC.'

'Oh, hi.' I was surprised to hear from her.

'Listen, I heard about your hall. I'm really sorry and I'm also sorry that you got dragged through the media mill with the Tim Chambers story.'

I sighed. 'Well, it seems to be forgotten now.'

'I just wanted to give you some information about Mr Chambers because I have a feeling he may be in touch again.'

'Oh yes?'

'I've heard from a reliable source that he has designs on standing in the London Mayoral elections.'

'Really?'

'Really, and that actually he was keen to up his profile within the media so he tipped off a photographer to snap you two on your doorstep.'

'You're kidding. That's outrageous!'

'Trust me, it's a twisted world out there.'

'But how will that make people want to vote for him?'

Anita sighed. 'People have short memories and it wasn't a cardinal sin. Plus everyone loves a bad boy as long as no-one gets hurt. It was just to get media attention. I'm sorry.'

'Bloody bastard.'

'Well, exactly. I just wanted to warn you in case he makes a sudden and contrite reappearance in your life.'

'Thank you. Really. I appreciate it.'

'You're welcome. And obviously, keep your source confidential. I have a reputation as a hard-hearted bitch of a journalist to maintain.'

I laughed. 'Bye, Anita.'

'Bye, Natalie, and good luck.'

I had reached the hall and could see a crowd including Pamela, Caroline, Jim and Guy gathering. John Hawley, who had been our staunchest supporter from the council, was there too. I made my way over. There was a collection of men in hard hats and hi-vis jackets standing by the door. One of them, who I took to be the foreman, was giving out instructions.

'So this is it,' I said sadly as I joined the group.

'This is it,' admitted Caroline.

'I'm sorry I couldn't influence the decision in the end,' said John, looking as if he had the weight of the world on his shoulders. 'If someone offers the council a wad of cash these days, they grab it faster than you can say, "austerity measures".'

Pamela nodded, tears forming in her eyes. 'I know you did all you could, John. You're a good man and a good friend to our community.'

'Stories don't always have happy endings,' I murmured.

Everyone nodded. There was an atmosphere of sadness but there was also an air of something positive within the group, a strength that comes from a shared, hard-fought fight, even if that fight has ended in defeat.

'I thought about lying in front of the bulldozers,' admitted Jim. 'But these fellas are just doing their job. It's not their fault.'

A woman and a man with a camera appeared. 'We're from the local newspaper,' explained the woman.

'Could we get a picture of you all standing in front of the hall before it's demolished please?' the photographer asked. We duly obliged.

'So, can you tell me how you're feeling today?' she asked. 'It must be a huge disappointment after all your hard work.'

'It's a tragedy for the community,' said Caroline gravely.

'It's a bloody crime against humanity!' cried Pamela, adding a note of drama to the proceedings.

The journalist nodded before turning to me. 'You're Natalie Garfield, aren't you? Didn't you have an involvement with one of the politicians influencing the decision – Tim Chambers?'

I opened my mouth to protest.

'That doesn't have anything to do with what's happened,' said Guy, appearing next to me. He looked really quite cross.

'And you are …?' asked the journalist.

'Guy Henderson. The choirmaster.'

The journalist flicked through some notes on her iPhone. 'Ah, yes, Mr Henderson. You were the one who found out that you were related to Mrs Taylor. Isn't that correct?'

Guy gave the woman a venomous look. 'I fail to see what that has to do with this story,' he snapped.

The journalist gave the briefest of smiles. 'It's human interest, Mr Henderson. It's good to have all the facts. And what with Mrs Garfield's dalliance with Mr Chambers and your father's double life, there's a lot which will interest our readers. I just want to get my facts straight.' Guy glared at her.

'Well, here's a few facts for you, young lady,' said Caroline, joining the conversation. 'I know your editor personally and if you decide to make a soap opera out of our lives in your newspaper, I shall personally make sure that you are demoted to editing lonely hearts ads for the remainder of your time there.'

The journalist held Caroline's gaze for a moment before giving a flick of her hair. 'Come on, Dave,' she said, turning away. 'I think we've got all we need.'

'What a bitch,' I declared as we watched them go. 'Thank you, Caroline,' I added, touched by her intervention.

'I won't have my family or friends dragged through the mud,' she declared.

'Right, sorry folks, but I'm going to have to ask you to move back to the other side of the road, please,' said the foreman with a sympathetic smile. 'We need to cordon off the area before we start to pull it all down.'

We traipsed over to the other side of the road and stood side by side, watching as the workmen prepared the area, making a passage for the vehicles to travel down. We heard an engine roar into life and looked towards the end of the road to see a large yellow monster of a bulldozer chugging towards us.

'This is it!' cried Pamela, squeezing my hand on one side and John's on the other, closing her eyes, unable to watch.

'Come on, everyone, let's sing something to mark the moment,' said Guy. '"Thank You for the Music"?'

'You can always rely on Abba in times of need,' I remarked.

We began to sing the chorus, smiling at one another and holding hands. We realised that even if we didn't have the hall, we still had the choir. At least that was something. Some of the workmen looked over and grinned.

John's phone started to ring and he fished it from his pocket. 'Sorry all. I need to take this,' he said, sticking a finger in one ear so that he could hear the caller. His face transformed into a smile as he listened. 'You're kidding me. Are you sure? What does that actually mean?' He grinned as he heard the reply and then, hugging his phone to his chest, he rushed across the road to the foreman.

'Stop!' he shouted, waving his arms like a man on a life-saving mission. 'Stop the machines!'

The foreman looked irritated as he made his way over to John but the bulldozer was stopped in its tracks. John was explaining something to the man, who looked surprised and then shrugged, turning to his men. 'It's off, boys,' he said.

John turned back towards us and practically skipped across the road, his face a picture of delight. 'It's off!' he cried. 'The property developers have lost their backing. The deal has fallen through!'

We stared at one another in utter amazement. 'But what does that mean, John?' asked Caroline. 'Won't they just sell it to someone else?'

He shook his head. 'They have insurance for things like this and they'll let you have it as a political gesture of goodwill. It will bring them at least a year's supply of good press,' he said cheerfully.

'I don't understand politics,' admitted Jim, shaking his head.

'Lucky man,' smiled John. 'Congratulations,' he added. 'You did it.'

There was a moment's silence before the cheering began. 'We did it! We did it!' We jumped up and down, hugging one another. I turned and found myself bumping straight into Guy, who aimed a kiss on my cheek which ended up on my lips.

'Whoops, sorry,' he laughed. 'Actually, I'm not really, but you know, you have to say these things.'

I giggled and gave him a tight hug. 'It's okay,' I said. 'I can cope with being kissed by a handsome man.'

He grinned. 'I noticed you on the phone as you arrived earlier,' he said. 'You looked annoyed.'

I sighed. 'I was. I'd found out that I was a political pawn in Tim Chambers' popularity campaign.'

'Ouch.'

'I know. But it's over now.'

He wrapped an arm around my shoulder and we all closed in to a tight group hug. I felt my throat tighten as I looked into the faces of the people with whom I'd become so close – Doly, Pamela, Jim, Caroline and Guy. It felt like the end of something special and hopefully the beginning of something even better. Woody, Sadia, Matilda and the other children were there too, right in the middle of the hug, right where they should be.

'I think this calls for a celebration,' said Pamela. 'I'll phone my Barry and tell him to bring some fizz down here. Let's reclaim our hall, shall we?'

'Good idea,' declared Caroline, turning to Oliver. 'Could you nip home and get a couple of bottles for us and just fetch Mum, please, darling?'

He kissed her hand. 'With pleasure,' he smiled.

As we made our way into the hall, I heard a car horn and turned to see a sleek black car. My heart sank as I saw Tim

Chambers climb out of the driver's seat, closely followed by a camera crew.

'Natalie!' he cried, jogging along the street towards me. 'I came as soon as I heard. What wonderful news!' He leant forwards to kiss my cheek but I moved backwards, causing him to stumble slightly. He looked towards the camera with an embarrassed chuckle. 'So this is Natalie Garfield, a very special friend of mine and a famous children's writer. We became close when she asked for my help with her campaign to save this fabulous community hall. I'm absolutely delighted to say that we have been able to save it for her choir and for future generations.'

I stared at him in disbelief, utter loathing rising up inside me like a tidal wave. Suddenly, Guy appeared from nowhere and landed a light but effective punch on Tim's jaw, sending him reeling and clutching his face.

'What the fuck?' he cried, staring at Guy in anger.

'Er, Tim? We can't use this if you swear,' said the twenty-something director.

Guy addressed the camera. 'That man is a disingenuous low-life, who has used Natalie for his own political ends. He shouldn't be allowed on the streets, let alone be allowed to represent constituents. Voters be warned!' He turned to me and offered his arm. I accepted it, feeling like a woman in receipt of true chivalry.

'Natalie, I can explain!' cried Tim, trying to follow me.

'I very much doubt that,' I said, turning on him. 'Now why don't you crawl back into whichever swamp-hole you came from.'

'Erm, Tim, I'm not sure if you're going to want to use much of this,' frowned the director, nudging the man behind the camera.

'Oh, for Christ's sake, Gavin, will you stop filming!' shouted Tim.

'Thank you,' I said to Guy as we walked into the hall, where a definite party atmosphere was beginning to take hold. Pamela was pouring Prosecco into some plastic cups she'd found. She handed one to John Hawley before planting a lipsticky kiss on his cheek. He grinned at her.

Guy turned to face me. 'I care about you, Natalie,' he said, fixing me with a look that made my heart dance. 'I know you can handle yourself but sometimes it's nice to know that someone's got your back.'

Never a truer word. 'Yes,' I smiled. 'Yes, it really is.' *Look out, Natalie, you're in danger of actually feeling happy today and you haven't thought about Dan since breakfast.*

This unnerved me slightly but then I caught sight of Woody, laughing and messing about with Sadia and Matilda. I felt reassured.

Woody's happy. I'm happy.

It wasn't a straightforward sort of happy – the all-singing, whooping like a loony kind of happy but I had come to realise that this didn't really exist. That was the stuff of adverts for cars or phones with actors having the time of their lives in neat twelve-second segments. Mine was more a 'settling down to watch crap Saturday-night television with my boy and a huge cheese pizza' or a 'singing with the choir in the pub' or a 'sitting down with a book and a glass of wine' kind of happy. I couldn't complain at that. That was more than a lot of people had.

'Cheers, Natalie,' said Caroline, knocking her plastic cup against mine. 'We did it.'

I grinned. 'Cheers. Here's to never giving up.'

'But to realising when your best is good enough,' she added with a wry smile.

'I'll drink to that.' I laughed, taking a sip of my drink before going off to find Woody and embarrass him with a gigantic hug of pure love and pride.

CHAPTER TWENTY-FOUR

CAROLINE

'I think that banner needs to go up to the left a bit, Oliver,' I said.

'Yep, definitely, lovey,' agreed Pamela, unfurling another roll of bunting and handing it to her husband, Barry. 'These need to go all along the side walls and then I've got more for outside,' she told him sternly. 'You make a start and I'll come and check you're doing it right.'

'Yes, my little Obergruppenführer,' grinned Barry, giving a sharp salute.

'Oh, get away with you,' chuckled Pamela. 'And be careful on that step-ladder. You're not as sprightly as you were, Barry Trott.'

'You feed me too well, my sweet,' observed Barry, patting his not-insubstantial belly.

'Anything I can do to help, Caroline?' asked Jim, his giant form creating a large shadow in the doorway. 'It's looking grand in here, by the way.'

'Yes, it's amazing what you can achieve with a clean-up and a lick of paint. I mean, it really needs to be completely renovated, but all in good time,' I said, standing back to take in my surroundings. 'Did Pamela tell you that we should get the National Lottery funding? Together with the money we raised, this place will go on for years.'

Jim grinned. 'And they say community spirit is dead.'

'Not in this street it isn't,' I smiled.

Since we won the hall just over three months ago, we had worked like dervishes to spruce it up. We had advertised the clean-up in all the local online forums and been amazed when a veritable army of helpers turned up to lend a hand. My ex-cleaner Rosie had given her time for free and organised the volunteers so that the whole job became less of a chore and rather enjoyable in some ways, as if we were all pulling together to do something worthwhile. Today was the day of the grand re-opening with the choir due to sing too.

'Well there's lots to do. Why don't you help Mr Trott with the bunting?' I suggested.

'Please call me Barry,' smiled Barry from his step-ladder. 'Actually, Jim, my lad, how about we make use of your height and I pass the bunting up to you? I am basically five-foot-four in all directions, so it makes more sense,' he chuckled.

'That'll be Mrs T's cakes,' teased Jim. 'I've put on about a stone since I started singing with the choir.'

'Oh, you boys,' clucked Pamela, dismissing the pair of them with a wave of her hand. 'I just know the way to a man's heart.'

'What have you made today then, Mrs T?' asked Jim.

Pamela gave him an enigmatic smile. 'That would be telling but it is rather special.'

'Took all week to make. And I haven't been allowed a single piece,' observed Barry ruefully.

'I let you lick the bowl,' said Pamela. 'Now hurry up with that bunting. Doly and Nat will be here with the food soon.'

'How's that now?' asked Oliver, having adjusted the banner and climbed down from the ladder.

We stood side by side to admire it. 'Perfect,' I said, even though I probably would have moved it down slightly.

He planted a kiss on my cheek. 'I'm so proud of you,' he said.

I gazed up at him. *My darling Oliver.* 'Well, ditto,' I said.

He raised his eyebrows. 'This is new.'

I gave him a playful push in the chest. 'All right. I know I don't say it enough but for the record, I think we're a good team and I'm looking forward to the future.'

'To Taylor-made Bakeries?'

'Are we definitely going with that name?' I grimaced.

'The focus group liked it,' he grinned.

'The focus group containing you, Natalie, Woody and Matilda.'

'That's a pretty broad demographic,' he replied sagely.

'We'll see,' I smiled, putting my arms around him. 'But I think it's going to be great working together.'

'And you can cope without your Ocado shop?'

'Natalie has promised to take me to Aldi every week.'

'And Rosie?'

I shrugged. 'I can clean my own house, Oliver. First World problems.'

He wrapped me in his arms and kissed me again. 'See? I told you I was proud of you. You've been through a lot these past few months. I know it's been hard but I just wanted to tell you how beautiful you look today.'

I stared down at my outfit. It was one I only wore for painting or gardening. 'Really?'

'Really,' he said, kissing me again. 'There's something about you these days that's different. You seem transformed and you're even more beautiful than before. You coped so well with your Mum too. I know it knocked you sideways.' He pulled me into a hug.

I felt my throat tighten at the memory. Mum had died at the end of August after a short illness. It had hit me very hard. There was the inevitable sadness at the death of a parent but at the same time, I felt cheated. I had only just got my mum back, only just started to get to know her properly, to understand what she had been through. It felt too brief and too soon.

Oliver had tried to tell me that it wasn't my fault, that there was nothing I could have done. That it was pointless punishing myself. And yet, I had spent days crying, wracked with guilt and regret. I would sit in her room with her things around me, feeling the weight of sadness on my shoulders as tears streamed down my face.

One day I had found the Ella Fitzgerald CD we had danced to and tortured myself by listening to the whole thing whilst sobbing at the kitchen table. In the end Oliver had come running from upstairs because he thought I'd hurt myself, which was actually partly true because my heart did hurt. It ached with longing and loss.

In the end, it had been Matilda who pulled me to my senses.

'Nanny wouldn't want you to be sad,' she said one day as we sat at the breakfast table, my eyes red and sore from weeping.

'How do you know?' I asked with the naivety of a child.

She looked at me as if the answer was obvious. 'She loved you best of all. I could tell. When you love someone that much, you definitely don't want them to be sad.' She approached me and put an arm around my shoulder. 'I don't want you to be sad, Mummy,' she added. I pulled her petite form to my body and hugged her tight, not wanting to ever let go. 'It will be okay,' she said. 'You're sad because she's gone but she's watching you from up in heaven and making sure we're all okay.'

I nodded. 'Thank you,' I whispered. 'Thank you, Tilly.'

She looked at me with surprise. 'I like it when you call me that,' she said.

'Then I'll call you that all the time,' I smiled.

She nodded with satisfaction before reaching for my hand. 'Come on, let's go and do our nails to cheer ourselves up. I'll let you use the purple glittery one if you like.'

'Coming through!' cried Natalie, bursting into the hall with a tray of food, grinning at Oliver and me. 'Where do you want these?' she asked. 'Doly and Dev have made enough food to feed the whole street!'

'Wonderful. Let's put them over here for now,' I smiled, gesturing towards the decorating tables that we had covered with crisp white tablecloths, courtesy of Pamela.

Doly and Dev appeared moments later, carrying more trays. 'I will bring the hot-plates, curries and rice later on,' said Doly.

'Ooh, what have we got here?' asked Barry, appearing at the food table and smiling up at Dev and Doly.

'Shingaras, pakoras and samosas,' smiled Doly proudly.

'Delicious!' said Barry. 'I love Indian food.'

'Bangladeshi!' cried Pamela, bustling over. 'Pardon my ignorant husband,' she added with an embarrassed smile.

Doly and Dev laughed, waving away their concerns. 'It's all right,' said Dev. 'Most Indian restaurant owners are from Bangladesh, so we're used to it.'

'You should definitely be running your own restaurant,' said Barry in admiration.

'Please,' smiled Doly. 'Try one.'

'Well, if you're sure,' said Barry, helping himself to a pakora. 'Mmm, that's the stuff. You'll have to give Pamela the recipe!'

Doly blushed with pride. 'Right, well, I need to get back to the kitchen. I cannot trust Hasan for long. He will either eat it all or let it burn. Natalie, are you coming back with us or shall I just bring Woody along with Tilly and my girls later?'

'No, I'll come with you. We need to get changed before the reception. Unless you need me here, Caroline?'

I shook my head. 'I think we're pretty much under control, thanks,' I said, just as the sign at the far end of the hall came crashing down.

'I've got it,' said Jim. 'Don't worry.'

'I'll give you a hand,' said Oliver, following him.

'Controlled chaos?' asked Natalie.

'You've taught me well,' I grinned.

Natalie laughed. 'Cheeky mare. See you later,' she smiled, waving over her shoulder as she followed Doly and Dev out of the hall.

CHAPTER TWENTY-FIVE

NATALIE

I had invited Dan. I wasn't sure if he'd come but I hoped he would. I wanted us all to be there. It felt like a defining moment in some ways. I hadn't realised it at the time but the choir, the hall campaign and even Caroline, in her bossy, control-freakish way, had been my saviours – the normality in an increasingly upside-down world.

I would like to say that I was okay with everything now, that I had reconciled myself to the fact that my marriage was over, but life isn't about neat conclusions. I knew it was still going to be hard, that I would have days of despair and moments when I questioned everything I knew, but I'm pretty certain everyone has these days. I'm fairly sure that even the well-adjusted, happy and settled people have days when they wake up and think, 'What is the bloody point?'

So when I have this thought, I'll remember that I'm not alone, that there is a point and that there are people out there who care about me; people who will be there if I need them. And the best thing is that most of them live right on my street.

After I left the hall, I fetched Woody and we went home to change. I had the usual wrangling with him about what to wear. He favoured jogging bottoms and a Real Madrid football top. I was less keen. We compromised on a Minion T-shirt and ripped jeans that Ed had bought him. After the truth had emerged about Dan, things had been tricky for a time with Ed. I wanted to sort everything out with him but something prevented me. One night, just before the Choir Final, he had appeared, carrying a bottle of expensive vodka and a large bag of Doritos.

'I thought it was about time we got drunk together and sorted this out,' he said, his eyes pleading forgiveness.

I stared at him for a moment before rolling my eyes and taking a step back. 'You better come in.'

Within an hour, we were telling each other how much we loved and had missed the other. He begged my forgiveness, I told him there was nothing to forgive and we were all square. If only I'd been married to Ed. Still, I was glad to have him back in my life. Husbands aren't compulsory but I'm pretty sure that best friends are.

Whilst Woody got changed, I began my inevitable hunt for a decent outfit. Predictably, my son was ready in a matter of minutes. 'I hope you're not going out like that,' he said, staring at my jeans and shabby T-shirt combo.

'I'm just trying to decide what to wear,' I said, pulling outfits from the wardrobe like a woman possessed.

'You should wear that one,' said Woody, pointing at a fancy green 1950s dress with a ribbon sash.

'Really?' I asked. I had only worn it once, to a wedding. 'It feels a bit dressy for today,' I observed.

'Dresses are meant to be dressy,' remarked Woody with an earnestness that made my heart ache with love. 'You look nice in a dress.'

As most mothers will tell you, it's nigh on impossible to refuse your child when they give you a compliment. I put on the dress and stood in front of the mirror to appraise my appearance. Actually, it didn't look too bad. I had found a pair of respectable-ish flats and applied some make-up and a dab of perfume by the time someone knocked at the door.

'I'll get it,' shouted Woody, bolting down the stairs.

'Only if you know them. Check at the window first.'

'It's Dad,' Woody confirmed, before opening the door.

I felt my stomach churn with nerves as I checked my appearance in the mirror one last time. 'You look good,' I told myself. 'You're going to be all right.' And for once, I believed it.

I walked down the stairs as Woody and Dan smiled up at me. 'Doesn't your mum look beautiful?' asked Dan, his eyes showing the love of a friend but not the longing of a lover.

'Yeah, you look great, Mum,' grinned Woody.

I put my arm around him before reaching over to kiss Dan on the cheek. 'Thanks for coming,' I said.

'My pleasure,' he replied.

As we walked along the road, Woody ran ahead, his bobbing form reminding me that he was still just a little boy, a little boy full of hope and happiness. I slipped my arm through Dan's. 'I wanted to tell you something,' I said. 'I've made a decision.'

'Oh yes?' he replied, smiling at me.

'I think we should apply for divorce.'

He blinked at me. 'Are you sure?'

I nodded. 'I think it would help all of us.'

He paused in the street before reaching down to kiss me on the cheek. I caught the scent of him and felt a pang for something loved and lost but I also realised that it didn't hurt as much as it had. 'I will always love you,' he told me.

'I know,' I said, pulling away and smoothing my hair. 'Me too.'

'We can make this work,' he said. 'If anyone can, we can.'

'I know,' I repeated.

'Will you tell Woody?' he asked.

'Let's do it together,' I replied. 'After the party. I don't think he'll be surprised.'

'Okay,' he said. 'Whatever you think best.'

We reached the hall and Dan held the door open for me. He gave me a smile filled with love and regret. I touched him on the arm. 'It's going to be okay,' I said, because I knew now that this was true. I had fallen apart for a while but the people in this hall, these wonderful, inspiring people, had helped me piece everything back together. They wouldn't let me fall apart again.

As we walked into the hall, the delicious aroma of Doly's food filled my nostrils. 'Glass of bubbles?' smiled Barry, handing me a plastic wine glass without waiting for a response. The room was filled with the buzz of happy chatter, children laughing and our choir songs playing from an iPod that Guy had set up with speakers in the corner of the room.

'Isn't this fantastic?' cried Pamela, hurrying over and wrapping me in a tight hug. 'And you must be Dan. So lovely to meet you,' she gushed. Dan smiled.

'Mrs Trott, your cake is amazing,' declared Woody, wide-eyed and impressed.

'Aww, thank you, ducks,' she grinned.

'Dad, come and see,' said Woody, pulling his father by the sleeve.

Dan gave me a wink as he was dragged away with Pamela in tow.

I spotted Guy by the food table and made my way over. 'I'm told that the pakoras are very good,' I said with a smile.

He grinned. 'I know. I've had three already. How are you?'

'I'm very fine,' I replied.

'And so you are,' he agreed, standing back to look at me. 'You look lovely in that dress, by the way.'

'Thank you,' I said, feeling my neck grow warm. I never could take a compliment. 'Is Caroline going to make a speech?' I asked, changing the subject.

He shook his head. 'She says there's no need. That she's going to keep her mouth shut today.'

'She said that?' I grinned.

He gave a smiling nod. 'I'll announce us in a moment and then we'll say it with music.'

My heart started to beat a little faster as I panicked that he was about to disappear. 'Guy?'

'Mhmm?' he replied, looking at me with those lovely blue eyes.

I swallowed. 'I was just wondering if you might fancy going for that drink some time?'

'What drink?' He frowned with confusion and I started to feel sick. His face dissolved into laughter. 'I'm kidding,' he cried.

'You bugger!' I said, punching him on the arm, feeling braver. 'Well. How about it?'

He fixed me with a look. 'I'd love to. One condition though.'

'What's that?'

He glanced over to where Dan was talking to Jim and Barry. 'We take it one date at a time.'

'It's like you read my mind,' I declared.

'Well, I do have that particular skill with the ladies,' he teased, holding my gaze for a second longer. 'And now, I think it's time for some music.' He clapped his hands together. A hush descended over the room.

'Ladies and gentlemen, boys and girls, my dear friends. I don't think I need to make a grand speech. You all know why we're here. But I would just like to say how proud I am of the Hope Street Community Choir for saving this hall and for changing all our lives for the better.' His eyes flicked towards Caroline and I felt genuine fondness as I saw that he was acknowledging his new sister. Then he glanced in my direction for a second before turning back to the audience. I felt that grain of hope inside me grow a little bigger. Doly caught my eye and smiled.

Guy continued. 'Our wonderful Pamela has produced this baking triumph.' Everyone oohed with appreciation as he stood aside to reveal a huge cake topped with a group of little singing people.

'It's us!' I cried.

'It's awesome!' declared Woody. Pamela blushed as everyone applauded.

Guy said, 'We'll share it out after this performance. So if the choir could assemble at the front please? We're going to do a short set and if you know the words, please join in.'

I followed the others to the front and took my place next to Caroline. 'This is rather wonderful, isn't it?' she remarked.

'Very wonderful,' I agreed. 'You've done a great thing. Really.'

She smiled at me. 'Thanks, Nat. I think we all have.'

I grinned. 'You just called me Nat!'

'Did I?' she laughed in surprise. 'Do you mind?'

I gave her a nudge. 'Course not. All my friends call me Nat.'

We smiled at each other for a moment before Guy clapped his hands. 'Okay, everybody. How about we start with "God Only Knows"?'

We turned to face our audience. Guy raised his hands, we took a deep breath and began to sing.

Life isn't filled with perfect harmony. The world is littered with bum notes, off-key moments and tuneless episodes. The trick is to find your own music, to ignore the discord and sing your own tune. That's what I was learning to do and as I looked at the faces of my fellow choir members, I realised that I wasn't alone. We were all learning to sing our own song, loud and proud and happy; facing the music and loving every wonderful second.

Loved *The Choir on Hope Street?*
Then read on for an extract from
LIFE OR SOMETHING LIKE IT

CHAPTER ONE

Cat Nightingale strode confidently through the bar and took a seat on an elegant tan leather sofa by the window. She placed her Kelly bag next to her and took out her iPhone. Ava was always late and Cat was always early. Cat liked things this way. It gave her time to check e-mails, Twitter and anything else that required her attention. She swiped a neatly manicured finger over the screen and flicked her way through her correspondence. Cat had a relationship with her iPhone that was more serious than any she had ever experienced with a man. It was always by her side, faithful and reliable, except when its battery ran down.

As Deputy MD at Hemingway Media, keeping in touch and up to date was vital but she also knew that it was something of an addiction – a good addiction. She had to get that digital hit throughout the day. She had to be on top of everything. Their portfolio of celebrity clients was impressive and her relationship with each and every one of them had to be maintained with a delicate mix of discretion, professionalism and a smattering of the friendly banter that she was known for.

Cat was good at her job and she knew it. Her boss, Jesse, worshipped the ground beneath her feet. She had helped him set up the company three years after they graduated from university and the combination of his easy charm and her sharp intellect had meant that they quickly attracted a host of high-profile clients through word of mouth alone.

You need to launch your new range of perfume? Call Cat. You're flying to New York and need a go-to for the best clubs and restaurants in town plus reservations to boot? Call Cat. You've been caught in a compromising position with your wife's sister? Call Cat.

Her phone buzzed with a call. She glanced at the ID and swiped to answer immediately.

'Will. How are you?'

'I'm hoping I'll be a lot better after this call.' Will Bateman didn't do niceties. He was the most powerful football agent in the country and time really was money in his world. Hemingway Media was organising the launch of a new coffee for the Daily Grind coffee shop chain and Will's biggest football star, Alvarro Diaz, was going to front it.

'I'll do my best.'

'Can you assure me that there will be no cock-ups on Thursday? I'm taking a big punt using Hemingway and if it goes pear-shaped, it will be my arse on the line too.'

Cat took a deep breath. 'Everything is in place. Daily Grind love working with Alvarro and we're already getting a huge response on social media to the *From Bean to Cup* promo film.'

'I'm more concerned about Alvarro behaving himself,' admitted Will.

Cat shared these concerns. Alvarro was the latest in a long line of footballing bad boys. He was young, had too much money and since moving from his native Costa Rica, was making the most of his freedom by hitting the London nightlife hard. He was a journalist's dream and a publicist's nightmare. 'I've organised a dinner with some journalists for the night before the launch and we'll make sure there are no detours on the way back to the hotel afterwards.'

'Okay. Let's hope you can keep him in line,' said Will. And with that he was gone.

'Bye then,' said Cat to the silent phone.

'Who you gotta screw to get a cocktail round here?' cried Ava sweeping through the bar towards Cat. People turned to stare and Ava smiled and waved like the Queen. Cat grinned and stood up in readiness for their air-kiss greeting. Ava Jackson liked to make an entrance; she loved the attention almost as much as the celebrities she featured in her magazine. She was a pint-sized New Yorker with a fearsome reputation and immaculate hair. She had landed in the UK twenty years ago, forging an impressive career as a red-topped paper journalist before founding her own celebrity gossip magazine called *Mwah!*.

A handsome, slick-haired waiter appeared by their side. Ava gave him an approving smile as they ordered their drinks. 'So,' she said, fixing her gaze on Cat, 'tell me everything.'

Cat smiled. She was used to Ava's ways. She was an important contact in the world of celebrity gossip magazines and probably the closest thing Cat had to a best friend, but she didn't trust her. Not really. Ava would sell her grandmother and probably Cat's too for a good story. They had playfully named these informal monthly get-togethers as 'The Tuesday Night Mojito Club', but Cat was careful to be measured in both her drinking and divulging. Still, they enjoyed each other's company and for the most part the relationship was mutually advantageous. Cat gave Ava the stories that would help her sell magazines and Ava gave Cat the publicity her clients required. It was beautifully simple. Most of the time.

'Saffy Bridges's agent has asked me to find the right home for her engagement pictures,' said Cat, casually. The waiter delivered their cocktails and Cat nodded her thanks.

Ava sat up in her seat. 'I'm listening.'

Cat smiled. Saffron Bridges was the pop sensation of the moment and she had recently announced her engagement to the floppy-fringed songwriting star, Sam Taylor. As soon as it had been announced, #SaffSam had trended worldwide and the Tiffany's engagement ring that Saffy had posted on Instagram shortly afterwards now had a six-month waiting list. Cat had overseen the entire thing. 'The problem is, there are obviously a number of other channels interested,' said Cat, studying her fingernails.

Ava didn't blink. 'What do you need?'

'Positive coverage for the Paradise Rivers perfume launch.'

'Done.'

'No bitchy comments about her being a limelight-grabbing drama queen?'

Ava put her hand on her heart. 'By the time we've finished with her, she'll be more popular than Kate Middleton.'

Cat raised an eyebrow. Paradise Rivers was a former reality TV and now wannabe pop star. She was headline-hogging and about as far from paradise as a person could be but her agent had a number of other top celebrity clients so Cat had to ensure that she got the best coverage possible. 'Just a few hours trending on Twitter for all the right reasons will be fine.'

'You got it,' said Ava, taking a sip of her drink. Cat sat back in her chair feeling satisfied. 'So, how are you doing?'

Cat smiled. 'I'm good. Busy but that's how I like it.'

Ava fixed her with a look. 'Too busy if I know you.'

'What's that supposed to mean?'

'I mean, sweet-cheeks, that you gotta look after number one. Listen to your Auntie Ava. Trust me, I know this. All work and no play will burn you out in the end.'

Cat shrugged. 'I signed up to this job. It's just the way it is. And besides, I enjoy it. It makes me happy. But I appreciate you looking out for me, Mum,' she joked.

Ava blew a raspberry. 'I'm serious. I worry about you.'

Cat shook her head and laughed. 'Why would you worry about me?'

Ava counted on her fingers: 'One: you work too hard; two: you're never off that phone; three: when was the last time you had sex?'

Cat nearly choked on her mojito. 'What's sex got to do with anything?'

Ava fixed her with a knowing look. 'Sex has got everything to do with everything.'

'I have sex,' insisted Cat.

'When?'

'Last month. With that comedian.'

'The one with the awful hair and sweat-patches? Euw!'

'He was very funny.'

'A funny comedian? There's a thing.'

Cat stuck out her tongue. 'Well what about you and all the sex you're having?'

'I do pretty well and anyway I've got Sergio.'

'Oh yeah, your "friend with benefits",' laughed Cat, making speech marks in the air. 'You're so old-school, Ava.'

Ava shrugged. 'You may mock but it works. You should get one instead of rejecting every male because he's not Jesse Hemingway.'

Cat folded her arms. She cursed the day she had told Ava about Jesse. They hadn't known each other long; it had been after the launch party for *Mwah!*. Cat remembered that tequila and Ava's nose for an excellent story had been to blame.

'So he's the man of your dreams and yet you've never slept with him?' Ava had slurred, reaching over to top up their shot glasses with expensive golden tequila.

'We had a moment,' Cat had said wistfully.

'A moment? Oh, well, that's almost as legally binding as a marriage.'

Cat wished she'd never mentioned it but Ava had the memory of an elephant and was fond of bringing up the subject whenever their talk turned to affairs of the heart. Fortunately this didn't happen very often; the celebrity world kept them more than occupied and Cat had no desire to air her innermost feelings to herself, let alone the editor of the country's favourite gossip magazine.

Still, Ava was right in that there was no-one who ever came close to Jesse and, as the years went by, this never changed. Cat enjoyed the odd flirtation and night of passion but nothing ever lasted and it suited her fine. Jesse was now married to an ex-model but it was still Cat who got to spend the majority of time with him. He even called her his 'PR wife'. This suited her fine as well.

'I am not rejecting anyone. I'm just not looking because I'm happy as I am.'

'Really?' said Ava with narrowed disbelieving eyes.

'Really,' declared Cat. 'This single life works for me. I think I might be the one.'

Ava gave a hollow laugh. 'If you say so, honey. And for the record, it works for me too. I don't know what I'd do if you got hitched and popped out a couple of kids.'

Cat shook her head. 'You know me. That's never going to happen. Let other people repopulate the world. Between you and me, I've got a woman working for me who was the best in the business but since she's had a baby, I've had no end of trouble.'

Ava nodded. 'Tell me about it. The kid's sick and suddenly it's your problem. Am I right?'

'Pretty much. I mean it's the twenty-first century so women should be able to go out to work but you've got to be responsible for your own life and get organised, for heaven's sake. The number of times I've had to let Nancy have time off because of childcare issues. It's not on.

You've got to take control and if you can't, then find another job.'

'I'll drink to that,' said Ava draining her glass. 'Want another?'

Cat nodded. 'Please.' Her phone buzzed with a call and she glanced down to see her brother's number. 'I need to take this,' she said, excusing herself from the table and making her way out into the lobby away from Ava's gaze.

'Andrew? Are you okay?'

'Hey, Cat. That's not like you to answer your phone to me first time.'

'Ha ha. What's up?'

'Just calling to catch up with my favourite sister. I expect you're somewhere posh and up itself.'

She smiled. 'Always. How are Melissa and the kids?'

'Well actually Mel's got to go to Australia. Her dad's not well.'

'Oh, shit. Is it serious?'

'Cancer. They're giving him weeks to live.'

'Oh, God, I'm so sorry. Poor Melissa.'

'I know. She's leaving first thing tomorrow so we're just trying to sort out the childcare.'

'Let me know if there's anything I can do to help.'

'Ah, thanks, Nanny McPhee. Could my children come and stay with you?'

'Well, er—'

'Cat? I'm kidding. You're so easy to wind up. Much as I relish the thought of you dragging my six- and ten-year-old to the Ivy and the management looking on in horror as Ellie and Charlie ask for ketchup with their caviar, we should be fine.'

'They don't have caviar at the Ivy, so, ha! Anyway, I would help you out if you needed me to. You know that.'

'Thank you but luckily, Mel's sorting it so you're off the hook. I'll call you at the weekend, okay?'

Cat gave a shiver of relief as she ended the call. It wasn't that she didn't like her nephew and niece; it was more that she'd hardly spent any time with children. She recalled how Andrew had recently guilt-tripped her into attending Ellie's sixth birthday party. Cat had turned up with the biggest teddy bear she could carry ready to play at being the world's best auntie. She rang the doorbell and could hear small feet stampeding down the hall before the door was flung open and a small voice squeaked, 'Eeeee!'

Cat peered around the bear into the chocolate-smeared face of her niece. Ellie was wearing a white and blue princess dress. She was flanked by two girls in similar outfits with a small boy dressed as a slightly lopsided snowman trailing behind. Cat was good at dealing with most situations but being faced with these sugar-crazed miniature humans immediately caught her off guard. She was relieved when she heard her brother's voice.

'Ellie, what have I told you about opening the door to strangers? Oh, Cat, you made it! Come in.' Andrew smiled. Cat's heart surged with love and gratitude.

'Is that for me?' demanded Ellie, gesturing at the bear.

'Ellie! Don't be rude. Say hello to your Auntie Cat.'

'You told me not to talk to strangers,' said the six-year-old, baldly. 'Who is Auntie Cat?'

Andrew looked embarrassed but Cat dismissed his concerns with a small shake of her head. 'You're very clever to be careful and I'm sorry I haven't seen you for a while but Daddy is right, I'm your auntie and this,' she said, handing over the bear, 'is for you. Happy birthday.'

Ellie took the bear, which was much bigger than her. 'What do you say, Ellie?' coaxed Andrew.

'Thank yoo,' said the small girl, looking up at her aunt suspiciously.

'Andy!' shouted a voice from upstairs, which Cat recognised as Melissa's. Andrew glanced up at the frowning face peering over the banisters. 'Oh, hey, Cat,' said Melissa as she spotted her sister-in-law. Cat could tell that she was surprised and a little irritated by her presence.

'Hey,' said Cat. 'I just popped in with a present for Ellie but I can see you're busy.'

'Oh no, you don't,' said Andrew, grabbing her arm and pulling her over the threshold. 'Are you okay, Mel?'

'I need you to come and talk to your son,' said Melissa with meaning. Cat could hear her ten-year-old nephew rampaging like a wild animal upstairs.

A shadow of embarrassment passed over Andrew's face as he glanced at his sister. 'I'll be back in a sec. Ellie, take your aunt through to the other room and don't let her leave, okay?' He disappeared up the stairs leaving Cat standing in the hall with her four minders.

She smiled down at them cheerfully. *Use your PR charm, Catherine*, she told herself. 'Which princesses are you?' she asked the three girls. 'I always used to like Sleeping Beauty.'

Ellie rolled her eyes. 'Duh. I'm Elsa and they are Anna,' she declared, gesturing at her friends. A look of confusion passed over Cat's face. 'From *Frozen*?' continued Ellie as if she were addressing an idiot. 'You know – Let it go, *Let it go-ooo*,' she sang tunelessly, dancing the gigantic bear round and round. Her two friends joined in and they were soon spinning down the corridor with giggling glee. Cat and the snowman were left staring at one another. She recoiled in horror as a thick slug of snot seeped from his carrot-covered nose.

'I'm Olaf,' he declared before pushing his tongue up his lip and licking experimentally at the snot. Cat did her best not to gag and looked desperately up the stairs, praying that her brother would come back soon and rescue her. However, Ellie had not forgotten her father's request. She plonked the huge bear on the floor and spun back down the hallway towards her aunt. Grabbing Cat with one hand and dragging the bear with the other, she pulled her towards the dining room. 'Come on. You have to meet Finn,' she said.

Cat followed reluctantly, expecting to be introduced to another grubby little boy with limited hygiene. She was surprised to find a man, sitting on the floor of the dining room, strumming experimentally on a guitar. The chairs had been cleared to the sides of the room and the table was pushed against one wall. It was covered with pieces of half-chewed pizza, curling sandwiches and what looked like strawberry jelly, all of which made Cat's stomach flip. She was used to politely nibbled canapés and bento boxes containing neat parcels of sushi. This was cuisine carnage.

Ellie plonked herself very close to the man, whilst one little girl sat the other side of him and the other stood behind him, wrapping her arms around his neck. He obviously had some sort of magnetism for children. To be honest, Cat couldn't quite see the attraction. He was heavily bearded with messy hair, a scruffy T-shirt bearing the words 'I like Biscuits', and an even scruffier pair of jeans paired with some ancient Converse trainers. He looked so at home on the floor with these pint-sized princesses, almost as if he were one of them. They clearly adored him.

Ellie put an arm round his neck and looked up at her aunt. 'This is Finn,' she said proudly as if she were introducing the Dalai Lama. Finn nodded up at Cat but didn't seem to see her. He was intent on the chords he was playing, lost in a musical moment. Cat found this quite rude. 'Come and sit down and we can sing,' ordered Ellie. Cat looked around her. The floor was worse than the table.

It was covered with crushed cheese puffs, squashed fondant fancies and pools of sticky juice. Cat glanced down at her Stella McCartney jeans and picked up what she hoped was a clean paper napkin. She placed it on the floor and sat down next to Ellie.

She glanced up to see Finn watching her with obvious amusement. For some reason this irritated Cat. How dare he laugh at her? She held out a manicured hand. She wouldn't stoop to his ill-mannered level. 'Good to meet you, Finn. I'm Andrew's sister – Cat.'

Finn leant over his guitar and took her hand. She noticed how cool his touch was. 'I didn't know Andy had a sister. Pleased to meet you.'

'It's because she doesn't come over very often,' said Ellie, rolling her eyes conspiratorially at Finn.

Finn glanced over at Cat, suppressing a smile. 'Is that because you're a right royal pain in the bum, Ellie?' he laughed.

Ellie glared up at him and then started to laugh. 'Finn, you are so funny. I am lovely,' she squeaked. 'No, it's because she doesn't like children. That's what Mummy says.'

Finn raised his eyebrows at Cat. 'How does the guilty party plead?' he asked.

Cat was incensed by his interrogation. 'I really don't think this is appropriate,' she said, trying to keep her cool.

Finn regarded her for a moment. This man infuriated Cat. *Who was he to judge her?* She stared straight back at him with cool indifference. His face broke into a knowing grin as he turned back to the children. 'And now, would Mr Bear like to sing a song?' he added, gesturing at Ellie's newest friend.

'He would,' said Ellie, handing him over.

Finn reached his arms around the gigantic toy and started to play the guitar, giving a rendition of 'The Bear

Necessities' in a gruff, teddy bear type voice. The children giggled, hugging themselves with delight.

Cat was done. This man was a judgemental show-off and she was ready to leave. She had delivered Ellie's present, put in an appearance. What more did she need to do? She didn't have children, didn't want children and going on today's performance, this would never change. She was about to get up and leave when she felt someone standing next to her. She turned to see Olaf the snowman grinning at her, the plug of snot still very much in place on his top lip. Before she could move, he placed a hand on her knee and nestled down next to her. It was impossible to leave because he was now leaning on her lap and she watched in horror as he rested his head on her leg, leaving a slimy trail of mucous on her pristine jeans.

She could see that Finn had spotted what was happening, a wide grin of satisfaction spreading over his face. However, he didn't realise that Cat was an expert at getting the best out of bad situations. She leant forward and whispered into the boy's ear, 'Why don't you see if Ellie and the girls fancy a dance?' she whispered. At these words, the little boy leapt up and started to bounce up and down with delight. He looked over at Cat who nodded with smiling encouragement. Before long the others had joined in and Cat found her moment to make an escape. She glanced at Finn imperiously but he merely smiled and nodded. She left the room feeling irritated and annoyed that she had allowed a stranger to wind her up so easily. She met her brother in the hall.

'Sorry, Cat, that took a bit longer than expected. Charlie's been a tad challenging of late. Are you going?'

Cat looked pained. 'I have to. I've got somewhere I need to be but I'll call you in the week, okay?'

Andrew did his best to mask his disappointment. 'Okay. Thanks for coming.'

She had smiled and waved as she walked swiftly back to her car, before driving back to her real life without a backward glance.

Cat felt a similar sense of relief now after ending the call with Andrew. She did worry about her little brother and was sorry for Melissa. She resolved to get some flowers delivered to Melissa and her mum, send the kids an extravagant present and take Andrew out for lunch next week.

Family taken care of, Cat made her way back through the bar to Ava and another round of mojitos. She smiled and waved at the various people she knew. She felt at home here. It was full of like-minded individuals – vibrant and creative people, getting on with the important business of life. Cat loved this world and, despite Ava's reservations, she was as happy as it was possible to be. Work hard. Have fun. No drama. That was Cat Nightingale's mantra and she followed it to the letter.

Has *The Choir on Hope Street* left you singing from the rafters? Follow along with this exclusive playlist!

'Truly Madly Deeply'	Savage Garden
'I Gotta Feeling'	The Black Eyed Peas
'California Dreamin''	The Mamas & The Papas
'Something Inside So Strong'	Labbi Siffre
'Rumour Has It'	Adele
'Weather With You'	Crowded House
'Everybody's Changing'	Keane
'Chasing Cars'	Snow Patrol
'Halo'	Texas
'Boogie On Reggae Woman'	Stevie Wonder
'Miss Otis Regrets'	Ella Fitzgerald
'True Colors'	Cyndi Lauper
'Good Vibrations'	The Beach Boys
'Let's Face The Music & Dance'	Ella Fitzgerald
'Fix You'	Coldplay
'Thank You For The Music'	Abba
'God Only Knows'	The Beach Boys

ACKNOWLEDGEMENTS

To my brilliant editor, Victoria Oundjian for the incredible support and time she has given in helping me bring Hope Street to life – I can't thank you enough.

Thank you to Jennifer Krebs for her amazing marketing ideas and work on this campaign – you are a marvel.

Huge thanks to the rest of Team HQ for your passion, enthusiasm and endless support. Special thanks to Lydia Mason for her fantastic revision notes.

Extra-large thanks to my fellow writers, who offer advice and show an incredible generosity of spirit – particularly the super-talented HQ authors past and present and all the friendly, brilliant people I've met through the RNA – you have helped me in ways you probably don't even realise.

To the wonderful bloggers, who read, review and enthuse all for the love of books – your comments and support mean the world to me.

Thank you to my best book buddies – Sarah Livingston, Helen Abbott and Chris Goodman – for advice, wisdom and kindness.

Thanks to Jane Bobbin for letting me use her lovely boy's name for the super-hero character in Natalie's books.

Extra special singing-from-the-heart thanks to Kari Olsen-Porthouse for starting the choir, which inspired this book, and for reading and checking the musical details for me. Perfect harmony-type thanks to the Churchfields Community Choir for all their support and cake because everyone knows that a good choir needs cake.

Finally, thanks and love to Lily, Alfie and Rich for everything else.

One of the characters in this book suffers from dementia, which I know affects a lot of families, mine included. If you or people you know are affected by this debilitating illness or if you would like more information about how to support people who suffer from it, please visit www.dementiauk.org/

HQ Young Adult
One Place. Many Stories

The home of fun, contemporary
and meaningful Young Adult fiction.

Follow us online

 @HQYoungAdult

 @HQYoungAdult

 HQYoungAdult

 HQMusic

Discover the perfect New York love story...

Meet Molly

New York's most famous agony aunt, she considers
herself an expert at relationships... as long as
they're other people's. The only love of her life
is her Dalmatian, Valentine.

Meet Daniel

A cynical divorce lawyer, he's hardwired to think
relationships are a bad idea. But then he finds himself
borrowing a dog to meet the gorgeous woman
he sees running in Central Park every morning...

Molly and Daniel think they know everything
there is to know about relationships...
until they meet each other that is...

One Place. Many Stories

Amber Green is back!

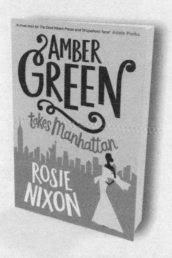

Join Amber as she takes on the glittering
celebrity world of Manhattan, one fashion
disaster and wardrobe malfunction at a time.

Will Amber's new styling company be able
to handle the big apple, or will the big
apple send her packing?

One Place. Many Stories

The eagerly awaited debut novel from the much-loved winner of *The Great British Bake Off*

The four Amir sisters are the only young Muslims in the quaint English village of Wyvernage.

On the outside, despite not quite fitting in with their neighbours, the Amirs are happy. But on the inside, each sister is secretly struggling.

Yet when family tragedy strikes, it brings the Amir sisters closer together and forces them to learn more about life, love, faith and each other than they ever thought possible.

One Place. Many Stories